Keepers *of*
POWER

JOSHUA UNDEM

Copyright © 2022 Joshua Undem
All rights reserved
First Edition

PAGE PUBLISHING
Conneaut Lake, PA

First originally published by Page Publishing 2022

ISBN 978-1-6624-5142-3 (pbk)
ISBN 978-1-6624-5143-0 (digital)

Printed in the United States of America

Acknowledgments

I would like to thank God for all the blessings in my life. My wife, Anne, for all her love and support. Also, thanks to my parents, Tim and Laura Undem, for helping fund this work. I want to thank all those who have ever defended this great country and to the families of those who gave their lives to protect this country.

Lucky Harvest

The Lucky Harvest shipping company specializes in the shipment of rare and expensive foods. John founded the company when he created his special shipping pods to simulate the atmospheric conditions of the food. This new style of cargo ship allowed him to transport these unique foods across the Nebulan Cluster. Coltin is where the Lucky Harvest started and grew exponentially, with its prosperous location centered in the heart of the cluster. Coltin is a lush planet; most of the planet maintains a good climate for farming most of the year. There are five other planets within the cluster. Abrax is the main hub within the cluster, housing the Nebulan Council. The council manages interplanetary disputes and issues involving the entire cluster. There is also Crypto, a mostly frozen world; Ferit, mineral rich; Marina, mostly aquatic; Ebra, part dessert, part rain forest; and Eon, a massive gas giant with an asteroid belt just beyond its orbit.

John had worked in the shipping business, transporting massive quantities of food to other planets within the cluster, and that was when he found the massive list of clients desiring the rare vegetation requiring very specific environments to maintain the items' freshness. He had to seek out approval from the council to be able to gain the permits to provide this service to the cluster. After a few years, he petitioned to transport out to the nearby clusters, Heribo and Multian. Within a decade, he established a solid reputation within these clusters.

On a delivery to Marina, his customer, a local historian and healer, requested him to transport a rare creature from Crypto. At first, John refused, stating that "he was just in the business of shipping rare foods." He continued his deliveries, but every time he would come to Marina, the healer would inquire about getting that creature. During one delivery, John was waiting on repairs to the slipstream drive on his cargo ship, known as Lucky Harvest. Lucky Harvest is a five-hundred-meter-long cargo ship with six independent pods with individual climate controls. Each pod is built to hold three thousand kilograms. Lucky Harvest is designed to be run by one person, in extreme cases, but is optimally controlled by two with room for two additional crew.

While repairs are underway, John waits in the cantina. In a corner booth, he runs the numbers on how this delay would impact not only current inventory but also future shipments. He is enjoying his steak when the local historian known as the Healing Hermit sits across the table. Now John did not have any issues talking with the hermit, but he was not in the mood to discuss the shipment of the creature. He tries to look busy reading his shipping orders, but the hermit sees right through his act.

"John, I thought you would be halfway home by now."

"I was, but a slipstream drive mount snapped," he replies, irritated.

"How long will you be grounded?" the hermit asks as he signals the serving droid for a drink.

"The tech said about three hours, but I never trust what they say." He takes a bite of his steak then a drink of java. "I just hope the backup power cell on pod 2 holds out. It didn't get a full charge before I shut down." He tosses the tablet on the table then rubs his temples.

"Is there something special in that one?" asks the hermit.

"Not really, just some Ebrarian brandy. But if the power fails, it will get really hot in there."

The hermit nods but appears more interested in the music. "So…" the hermit starts.

John interjects, "Don't even start about that stupid chillard again!"

"Come on, John, just give me a moment to explain," he starts then takes a drink. "See, I have a contact on Crypto's third orbital city that has a small one that they want to get rid of, and I would like to have it as a companion. This chillard would be nice to have around my house, I think."

"Look," John says, pointing at the hermit. "I have already told you, I don't do animal transports. Plus, I don't have the papers to transport animals."

The hermit, nods holding up his hands. "Yes, I know, I know, but my contact says they will be able to get the chillard through security with no problems."

John picks up the tablet and starts scrolling through it without looking up. "I won't do it! So why do you keep asking?" John asks, annoyed.

"Well, my contact really wants to get rid of this chillard. They can't get anyone to buy it due to how small it is," the hermit says. Rolling his eyes, John stands, heading toward the bar for some milk. He stops midstride when the hermit says quietly, "They will pay double your fee to get it."

John sits back down, trying to act like it wasn't the money bringing him back, and looks at his tablet again. "Double my fee, you say?"

"Yes," the hermit replies.

"Twenty thousand credits? When would I get paid for this slight change in cargo?" John inquires with piqued interest.

"I have five thousand now, and if you can get to Crypto before tomorrow, my contact will pay twenty thousand when you arrive."

"Okay, so I am interested," John says. "But why me? I just ship exotic foods."

The hermit smiles widely. "We need you because you are the only person I trust."

"Fine, I will do it," John agrees.

The hermit slides the five thousand credits across the table as he stands. "Here is the transceiver frequency needed to reach my contact when you arrive." The hermit continues over his shoulder as he leaves, "Also, if you can keep the pod moist and just about freezing with some ice for the little chillard."

Just then, John's transceiver chimes from the tech. "Thanks for the talk and credits. I will have your pet for you soon."

John heads toward the spaceport to check his cargo and plan his course for the special cargo. As he nears south berth 18 where the Lucky Harvest was docked, he spots additional security. He starts to regret agreeing to this special request. He meets the tech and settles the bill, but when he turns to board his ship, a security team stops him.

"We saw you discussing what appeared to be a shipping request with the hermit," said the captain.

"I am a legitimate businessman trying to make a living in the galaxy," John snaps. *Every time I talk with that crazy hermit, I get stopped by security*, he thinks. "What's the issue if I talk with him or anyone else?"

The captain replies, "He is under surveillance, and we saw him give you credits. What did he want?"

John rolls his eyes and heads to the Lucky Harvest. "He was paying off a debit from a previous shipment. Is that against the law?"

Uneasily, the captain replies, "Okay. Have a nice day. Move out, squad."

He quickly boards his ship and starts the checklist. As the engines warm up, he checks on pod 2's Ebrarian brandy supply. As he pulls up the status, he notices that it is at 3 percent power, and the temperature is ten degrees above optimal levels. Cursing the security team, he transfers the charging power from pod 4 to help cool pod 2. He returns to the pilot's chair and ponders if picking up this chillard is a good idea. He looks at the tablet and runs numbers for the last year. He knows that if he doesn't do this job, he will lose his ship. A corporate shipping company has been buying out the small shippers, and he is the last one in the entire cluster. Reluctantly, he looks up a local dealer to get four hundred kilograms of ice for the chillard. Once the ice is loaded in pod 5 and climate controls set, he sets course for Crypto.

Lucky Harvest smoothly rises and begins its ascent from the spaceport when his transceiver chimes. "Great. Who is it now?" He slaps the transceiver. "Who is it!"

"Calm down, John. It's me," the hermit says, panicked.

"What do you want now? I am already getting your pet!" John says, annoyed.

The hermit replies, "I apologize for the security snag today, but the new political group doesn't like the way I work."

"I know." John snorts.

"I don't have much time before they hack our transceiver," the hermit says quickly. "Your contact's name is Lilian, and she is the real package."

"Wait! What about the chillard?" John says, confused.

"John, please don't interrupt. We don't have the time. The Cryptics, a local crime ring, have placed a price on her head, and if she does not get off Crypto, she is dead," the hermit says frantically. "Please hurry. Let me know when you are back. Bye."

The hermit ends the transmission without giving John a chance to respond. Leaning back in the captain's chair, John runs his fingers through his hair and asks, "How can this get any worse?" So he leans forward, enters coordinates for Crypto, and engages the slipstream drive.

Relieved, John watches as the pinpricks of stars stretch into lines as he enters slip space. He stretches, stands, and heads to the refresher. Returning to his chair, he props his feet on the console and drifts off to sleep.

Ice Breaker

He is rudely awakened when the alarm chimes for the return to normal space. He stretches and straps in to complete his trip. He looks at the countdown to exit slip pace. Three, two, one, zero, and he kills power to the slipstream drive. The lines snap back to dots.

As soon as he enters normal space, he notices that there is an unusually large amount of ships rushing to leave the system. John is used to seeing lots of traffic here, but never has he seen so much outbound traffic at one time. Leaning forward, he keys the link for the spaceport. "Crypto Spaceport, this is Lucky Harvest requesting permission to dock." He gets a little concerned when he receives no reply and tries again. Again, with no response, he keys up the special code to contact Lilian. He waits for a response, and after fifteen seconds, he reaches to disconnect the channel when a female voice comes across the channel.

"Did the hermit send you?" she asks quickly.

"Yes. Where can we meet?" John asks. "What is going on?"

She responds, frustrated, "Look, there's no time to explain. I am on the planet, in the northern sector's warehouse district. I will have this channel act as a signal beacon. Once you get within a kilometer, I will give you a more accurate location."

"All right, but why is the whole planet running?" John asks insistently.

She agitatedly replies, "There is a huge fleet entering the system, and fighters are on the way."

John thinks, *I'll get that hermit if I make it out of this.* He shoves the throttle to the overload stops, and Lucky Harvest quickly accelerates toward the pickup zone.

He keeps the Lucky Harvest out of the atmosphere until the last moment, knowing it is significantly slower in atmosphere. Just when he reaches the point to start his not so safe descent, the general spaceport channel opens.

"This is the Shadow fleet Vorex's Might. Any and all ships attempting to flee will be fired upon."

"Great!" John slams his right fist on the arm of his chair and yells, "Anything else care to go wrong?"

Alarms start blaring as he keeps the throttle wide open, trying to gain some time to get out again. Suddenly, Lilian comes across the transceiver. "Where are you!"

John snaps, "I'm about three kilometers out and coming in much hotter than I like."

"Fine. Just land on the sixth warehouse in the southwest corner of the warehouse district!" Lilian shouts over the noise and chaos caused by the Void-raiders fleet. "It will be marked with a pulse beacon. Set your scanner to sweep for a thirty-five-nanometer pulse."

John replies, shocked, "How can I land on the warehouse?"

Lilian replies with a laugh, "Do you think in a time like this I want you to land? Just get close and lower your boarding ramp." She shuts off the channel, and John sets the scanners to locate the pulse beacon.

Lilian is running through the streets with the chillard right behind her. "Come on, Chi-Chi. We can't let the Cryptics find us." She maneuvers through the streets as fast as she can while trying to keep watch for anyone following her. "That's it, Chi-Chi!" Lilian says, out of breath, as she hits the control pad for the warehouse door, but the door does not open. Cursing, she drops her bag and grabs her security slicer. Quickly, she plugs it to the panel and presses a few buttons. With a quiet hiss, the door slides away. Right when she returns the security slicer to her bag, a pulse beam sizzles five centimeters past her head. Quickly, she kicks her bag inside and grabs Chi-Chi's front leg and jumps inside the warehouse. Slapping the door control, she reaches for the transceiver. "John, where are you?" she asks shakily.

John replies, "I am four hundred meters and closing fast. I don't see anyone on the roof."

"I know. I'm sorry," Lilian says softly. "I don't want anyone getting hurt."

John can sense something is wrong. "Lilian, where are you?"

She replies with a defeated tone, "Just forget about me and leave."

Annoyed, John snaps, "Look, lady, I have never missed a delivery, and I refuse to start now. I am over the warehouse on the northeast corner. Where are you?"

Lilian says, "We are by the front entrance on the opposite corner of the building, but there are some Cryptics outside trying to get in."

"Just stay put!" he yells.

His fingers dance over the console as he hits the hover control and activates the two auto defense turrets and the boarding ramp controls. Hitting the safety release on the crash harness, he runs to the equipment locker at the back of the cabin. He quickly dons his cold weather coat and belt and deftly sheaths two feritium daggers and a rappel kit. He loads his repeating crossbow and grabs an extra magazine.

He leaps from the ramp, and his lungs burn from the frigid air. John sprints across the roof, hooking the rappel clip onto his belt. As he approaches the opposite corner of the warehouse, he hears fighters off in the distance, strafing the city.

"Great!" yells John, nearing the edge. He fires the rappel anchor into the roof three meters from the edge and slides to get a look before he jumps. Peering over the edge, he spies the group below. *Four. This will be interesting*, he thinks as he checks his gear. *Too bad I left the concussion grenades. Oh well, I guess it's the hard way.*

Below, he sees a man in green armor, a blue crytan with half his left thermine gone, a young human with a heavy repeating pulsar rifle across his back, and an ebrat crouched at the control panel, trying to slice in.

"Hurry up, Crete!" he shouts. "You said you are the best slicer."

"I am, boss," he snaps. "She is inside countering my slicing."

Without notice, the bounty hunter quickly draws his pulsar pistol and blasts Crete in the back. "Lefty, blow the door!"

The crytan grabs his pack and heads to the door. John grabs his transceiver. "Lilian, run for the roof. They are gonna blow the door."

Lilian almost laughs as she easily subdues the pathetic slicing attempt from the other side. She hears someone from the other side say something about the best slicing and has to stop from laughing. Just then, her transceiver chimes, and she hears him say something about running for the roof. Without trying to respond, she rips her slicer out, grabs her pack, and runs toward the stairs on the other side of the building with Chi-Chi in tow.

John hopes she heard as he stows the transceiver and switches the safety off his crossbow and gets ready to jump. John stands 1.88 meters tall and weighs one hundred ten kilograms. He is proud of how he has been able to maintain his build even though he is just a simple cargo hauler. Coltin holds an annual competition, and he enjoys being able to make it home for these events. His father always wanted him to compete every year, as it has been tradition for six generations. John enjoys competing in the knife duels and shooting challenges, but he has had to miss the last three due to work. He has won the knife duel title the last four years and shooting title twice and second twice. John is thrilled at the chance to put his skills to the test.

He hears Lefty shout, "Three, two, one…" And he hears the door blast away.

Grabbing the rope, he jumps over the edge with his crossbow in his right hand. He rapidly descends the fifty-meter drop, watching as the three enter the building. He slaps the break three meters above the ground and releases the clip from his belt. Crouching by the door, he peers around to see the three searching the warehouse. He is thankful it is full of containers and speeders. *Lots of cover*, John thinks. He watches quietly for a few seconds to see what the bounty hunters do. He sees Lefty follow the long wall. The bounty hunter heads along the short wall behind a row of large speeders. John is surprised that the human is just standing ten meters in the door, scanning the warehouse for movement. John looks around and spots a palm-sized ice chunk. Quickly, he removes the magazine and scope and attaches the special cradle. John's father raised him not to kill unless it's to eat, and so he aims the ice at the human just behind his right ear. As soon as he fires, he drops the crossbow and sprints to catch the man before he hits the floor. He removes the magazine from the repeating blaster and grabs the unconscious man's extra ammunition. John moves the man from view so as to try and avoid detection.

John considers who to head after and decides on Lefty. He quietly heads down the long wall, hiding behind speeders and containers. The entire building is shrouded in darkness with very little light coming from the windows. Almost at the other end of the five-hundred-meter-long warehouse, he sees his opponent looking around a group of stacked containers. He notices that the crytan is wielding two half-meter-long ferioblades. Always being a fair sport, he stashes his crossbow and draws his two daggers. John slowly sneaks up on Lefty, staying in the shadows. Five meters from the crytan, he hears a large explosion to the left. Lefty turns to look out the window to see what happened and spots John.

"Hey, what are you doing here?"

John innocently responds as he spins his blades, "Nothing. Just thought tonight is a good night for a duel. Want to go a few rounds?"

Lefty smiles, seeing that his blades have a good ten-centimeter advantage on his opponent's little knives. "Sure, I'll play." Lefty smiles smugly.

John slowly approaches Lefty, and they begin to circle each other at a two-meter distance. Lefty has both blades' standard grip arms bent for quick reaction and smiles. John quick flips his left blade to a reverse grip since he has the disadvantage for reach. John slowly moves to his right around Lefty to get a good view of the area and sees that it is relatively clear.

Lefty shouts, "Let's go, human! I have a bounty to collect." With that said, Lefty comes in with a quick right jab, and John blocks with his left blade.

John is surprised at how powerful the crytan is and has to retreat quickly. John, while trying to recover from the first strike, almost loses his head from the right ducking then rolls right to gain some space.

Lefty laughs. "If that's your best, then you're dead."

John proceeds to play this to his advantage. He backs up after each hit to lure him to the edge of the shadows. Lefty attacks with his left blade at John's right shoulder then kicks John in the stomach, sending him sliding across the floor. John quickly rolls, stopping in a three-point stance. John rises just in time to stop a double-bladed strike from above. He quickly spins clockwise, sweeping Lefty's feet from under him, making him stagger back. John takes advantage of the stumble to get back on his feet.

John takes the momentary pause to come up with a plan to get to Lilian, knowing they must be closing on her. Lefty recovers and again comes at John with another round of powerful attacks. John blocks a left jab with his right blade and quickly steps inside Lefty's guard. Taking advantage of the opening, he deftly lands two quick punches on his opponent's ribs and then to the chin. Enraged, Lefty brings the hilt of his left blade around, slamming it on the side of John's head. Instantly, John hits the floor, seeing stars. And by reflex alone, he is able to roll away just as Lefty stabs right where he was. Slowly, he gets back to his feet, cursing himself for his carelessness. Suddenly, the windows in the warehouse shatter from a nearby explosion. John acts like he is having trouble recovering from the blow, and Lefty charges in to finish him off. He takes three quick steps and swings both blades at John's neck to end things quickly. Still having trouble seeing from the blow to his head, John senses the incoming attack. He shifts the grip of the blade in his left hand to standard and blocks both blades. Once he feels the impact of Lefty's attack, he slashes his right blade across both of his opponent's forearms, and Lefty yells as the strike catches him by surprise. Lefty howls in pain and drops both blades. With one quick move, he strikes Lefty's chin with his left hilt. The sudden impact on his chin knocks him cold, and John catches him as he crumples to the floor.

John checks on his fallen enemy and is satisfied that he will be out long enough to escape. He quickly retrieves his crossbow. He surveys the area, trying to find the bounty hunter and Lilian. He sees a figure running across the warehouse on the top catwalk heading toward the roof access. Looking toward the stairs, he spots the bounty hunter heading up the stairs two at a time to catch his payday. Quickly, he brings his crossbow up and fires an arrow just ahead of the leader to stop him. Just as he reaches the top of the stairs, the arrow flies within centimeters of his helmet.

"What the? Who's there?" he shouts, surprised. He spins to find his attacker and only then notices that the human and crytan are unconscious. He sees John a hundred meters away with his crossbow still aimed in his direction. "Where did you come from!" he yelled.

John casually shrugs and starts walking to the stairs. He stops at the bottom of the stairs and looks at the bounty hunter, saying, "Look, leave her alone and go before you get hurt."

"Not a chance." The bounty hunter laughs. "I don't fail on a bounty. Go home or die. Your choice," he snaps.

John takes a moment to try to anticipate what his new enemy will do. Quickly snapping up his crossbow, he fires three arrows, but the bounty hunter steps left. Two miss completely, and the third bounces harmlessly off his helmet.

"Fine, have it your way, slime." He levels his pulsar pistol and fires.

John did not expect to miss his quick counterattack, but he manages to move almost out of the way. An instant later, he feels searing pain as his left arm goes numb, and the scent of charred flesh assaults his senses. John almost drops the crossbow as he screams in pain. Jumping on the rail, the bounty hunter slides down to finish off his attacker. John staggers back behind a container to try and gain control of his arm. Looking at his left arm, he sees just below his shoulder a five-centimeter wound. He tries to close his hand to no avail. John quickly looks around for something to help win this fight. To his right is a case of propane gas cylinders, and to his left he sees an ice sled. He runs to it, hoping the sled works. He hits the ignition. John curses as it does not start, but he tries once more and is rewarded with the roar of the sled's engine. He looks to the cylinders just as the bounty hunter rounds the container.

"Hey, I got to run, but feel free to use the sled," John says, slapping the accelerator.

The ice sled crosses the fifty meters in a second, but in that split second, the bounty hunter dives to the side. An instant later, the sled slams the cylinders with a thunderous explosion. John does not check to see if his opponent is alive. He turns, sprinting to the entrance and the rappel line. He slings the crossbow as he reaches the front of the warehouse. Grabbing the rappel line, he hooks it into the ascender and makes the roof in four seconds. Across the roof, he spots Lilian waiting near his ship, and he sprints to meet her. Racing up the ramp, he hits the controls, tossing his gear at the equipment locker as Lilian and the chillard follow.

Climbing in the pilot's chair, John says, "Put the chillard in pod 5 and grab the controls for the turret." He releases the hover controls, and as he looks at the sensors, he activates the turret.

She straps into the copilot's chair and grabs the turret controls and snaps, "Chi-Chi will not go in a pod!"

John glares at her. "What? Fine. We have three fighters inbound. Try and keep them off us as we head for space."

A voice comes over the speaker. "Cargo ship Lucky Harvest, turn and head to the spaceport or we will open fire. You have five seconds to comply."

John shoves the throttle to the overload stops then slaps the transceiver off. "Let's get out of here," John says to no one specific. The first shots streak across the bow.

"I guess they mean it," Lilian says as she starts tracking the fighters with the turret. Rapidly, the fighters gain on the cumbersome craft, and soon the rear shield starts taking hits.

John shouts, "Do you know how to use the turrets?"

Lilian retorts, "Of course. Just waiting for a closer shot."

"They won't line themselves up like target practice." John scowls. "Just shoot!"

Suddenly, the small defense turret on the top of the cargo ship starts peppering the fighters' noses. The fighters quickly spread out, performing strafing runs. Shield alarms start sounding, and John shuts them off.

"Hold on. We are almost in space, then we will get away," John says as another alarm sounds. Lilian shouts as the whole ship bucks from yet another hit on the rear shields. Suddenly, a large boom ripples through the ship. John glances at the readout. "Good thing the chillard is up here. Pod 5 just got blasted. Can you please shoot them now?" John says.

Lilian growls as she watches the panel. Very intently, she watches the paths of the fighters, thumbs the firing studs, and is rewarded with a ball of debris. "One down!" she squeals excitedly.

John starts punching in calculations into the navigation computer for slip space. The transceiver crackles. "Lucky Harvest, power down and prepare to be boarded."

John rolls his eyes. *Not a chance*, he thinks.

"This is Captain Kato of the cruiser Vorex's Might. Last chance. Power down or die."

Lilian softly says, "We have to get out of here."

John nods and engages the slipstream drive. In an instant, they are safely in the light-streaked confines of slip space.

Relieved, John leans back, taking a deep breath. He gets up and heads to stow his gear. He checks his blades, wipes them down, and stows them away. Then he inspects the rappel kit, winds the cable, and replaces the broken anchor. As the adrenaline ebbs from his body, he screams and grabs his left arm. He forgot about the wound he received.

Lilian rushes over and sees the ragged wound. "Don't move. I'll get the med salve."

John wordlessly points to the refresher. She looks through the locker and finds the med kit. John sits against the locker and scolds himself for recklessly taking on the bounty hunter. Lilian kneels down and starts cleaning the wound. "Okay, now just sit there and don't move," she says. "So where are we heading?" she inquires, tending to the wound.

John snaps, "Marina, then home to fix my ship!"

As she finishes bandaging the wound, she whispers, "Oh. Thank you for saving me and Chi-Chi."

John looks up at her then smiles.

Lucky Harvest drops from slip space and starts descending to Marina. John opens a channel to spaceport control. "Control, this is Lucky Harvest requesting docking coordinates."

"Lucky Harvest, this is Control. Permission granted to south docks bay 16."

John calmly replies, "Control, understood, bay 16. Also, can you have a tech meet me? I have repairs…again."

"Understood," control responds.

"So what's the deal with the chillard?" John asks as they move toward the south docks.

Lilian laughs. "Chi-Chi is just a pet for him, but not what he wants."

Confused, John says, "Then what does that crazy hermit want?"

Carefully, she pulls a cloth-wrapped object from her pack and slowly unwraps it. Inside lays an obsidian-colored stone with what appears to be violet and silver symbols inscribed on all sides. John, mesmerized by the object, inquires, "What…is this?"

"I am not really certain," she replies. "I found it on Detritus Prime."

"What were you doing out there?" John says, shocked.

She laughs. "I research all sorts of artifacts across the galaxy." She rewraps the object and stores it back in the pack.

John finishes the power down sequence and opens a channel to his tech. "Red, it's John. Can you come to south dock bay 16 and look at Lucky for me?"

"Sure thing," replies the tech.

Lilian waits by the ramp as John grabs his belt with two ferio-blades and a hold out pulsar. "Where should we meet the hermit?" John asks.

"Let's head to his library," she says over her shoulder as she walks off at a rapid pace.

"How do you know where that is? He would only meet me at the cantina!" John replies, shocked.

"It's simple," she says jokingly. "He doesn't like you."

John is too awestruck by her humor and bold personality to get mad. They head to the northern edge of the spaceport when she takes a quick right and continues along the wall to the east. After fifteen hundred meters, they turn north through the plaza. John smiles, enjoying the presence of a companion. After an hour of moving past the different vendors and more than a dozen different turns, John wonders if she is lost. Suddenly, she stops and points. "Right there. That's his place."

John looks around, expecting to find a rundown shack, but much to his amazement, it's a pristine house. Lilian steps to the door and rings the buzzer. A moment later, the door parts, revealing a grand hall. The hall is fifteen meters tall with pure white marble floors and intricately carved lavender and turquoise columns. Extravagant chandeliers hang every ten meters with sapphires and amethysts of every shape and size, and lining both sides of the wall are statues of historical figures and mythical creatures. They are led down the hall by a security accounting maintenance droid, SAM, to the library at the other end. John is shocked by the grandeur of the house but not surprised at the size of the library. The hermit sits in the back corner, surrounded by stacks of data pads and ancient scrolls.

"Excuse me, sir," says the droid in its monotone voice.

Without looking up from his reading, the hermit dismissively states, "I'm busy."

The droid starts to turn, and Lilian pipes up, "So that's how you treat a friend who brings you interesting artifacts?"

The hermit jumps, knocking a stack of data pads over. "Lilian, John, you made it back safe. After reports of the assault on Crypto, I feared the worst."

Lilian moves forward to greet the hermit. "This is the chillard I told you about," she says, gesturing to the creature beside her. "This is Chi-Chi."

The hermit looks to her left and leans down to look at the chillard. "Chi-Chi looks great and will be a great companion."

John says, "So can I get my credits now? I have to fix my ship!"

The hermit says to the droid, "SAM, can you please get the credits for John?"

"Of course, sir," it replies as it turns, shuffling out of the room.

Lilian pulls out the cloth-wrapped artifact out, saying, "This is what I told you about."

Excitedly, the hermit grabs the artifact and rushes to an examining table. He carefully unwraps it then pulls out three different scanners and asks, "Lilian, can you find the tablet on ancient symbols and civilizations, please?"

"Are they along the back wall still?" she asks, heading into the library.

The hermit nods absentmindedly. Chi-Chi moves and sits beside the hermit, watching intently as he scans the artifact. John follows Lilian into the shelves, not quite sure why he was.

John tries to help her find the tablet and asks, "What will you do now?"

Lilian jumps, not knowing he followed her. "I am not sure," she says quietly.

"Well, Lilian, if you would like me to give you a ride somewhere, I will take you there." Nervously, he takes a breath and continues, "I want to thank you for your assistance in our escape."

Lilian nods, grabs the tablet, and heads back. The hermit tenderly rolls the diamond between his fingers, looking at the symbols. Lilian places the tablet down. "Any idea what this is?"

"Not quite sure," the hermit says quizzically. "I have deciphered some symbols. This one, I believe, is a key or gate, and that one..." He grabs the tablet, quickly scanning its contents. "Yes, yes, this one is sanguis, but it is...different slightly. I am not sure why." The hermit continues to look entranced by the item. "I will keep trying to find out what this is."

"Please, let me know when you have it figured out," Lilian says. "Chi-Chi, please watch out for the hermit." She scratches behind its ear.

John and Lilian leave the hermit and head down the main hall. They are met by SAM. "Here are your credits, sir."

John accepts the credits. "Thanks." John bashfully asks Lilian, "Would you like to go for dinner?"

She looks at him for a long moment and softly replies, "I would like that."

Surprised, John says. "Well, why don't you pick a place? You clearly know this place better than me." She laughs and leads the way.

The Family Business

Thirty-five years have passed since the obsidian diamond was given to the hermit. In that time, the Lucky Harvest shipping company has grown to be the largest rare food shipper in the Nebulan Cluster and started expanding into Heribo and Multian clusters. There are now fifteen more cargo ships like Lucky Harvest in service to keep up with demand. John and Lilian had a son and named him Kalob. Kalob took over flying Lucky Harvest when he was twenty, allowing John to enjoy trips with Lilian. Kalob met Julianne on a trip to Palatia and now has a three-year-old son named Tobius.

Kalob and Julianne are bringing Lucky Harvest into orbit around Coltin following a six-month haul across the Multian Cluster. The transceiver crackles to life. "Kalob, about time you make it back," John says.

"What do you mean? It was only six months." Kalob laughs.

Julianne jokes, "If he wasn't stopping at every cantina, we would have been here a month ago." Kalob flashes a silly grin at his wife. Julianne asks, "How is my little man doing?"

"Mummy, is that you?" a little voice says.

"Yes, sweetie. We will be home shortly."

"Yippee!" Tobius yelps and runs off.

John laughs. "He wants to come with you guys next time. He says he is ready to help Daddy fly."

Julianne wipes a tear of joy from her cheek. "I will meet you at the office landing pad in fifteen minutes."

John says quickly, "I'm glad you're back."

As they land, they spot John and Lilian, with Tobius sitting on John's shoulders. Quickly, they power down and head for the ramp. Before the ramp is down, Julianne jumps down and runs to her son, grabbing him from his grandpa's shoulders. She gives him a big hug. Kalob comes up behind them, hugging them both.

"Guess what we found you, Tobius?"

Tobius jumps up and down excitedly. "What, Daddy? What, what, what?"

Kalob laughs and brings a box out from his pack. Tobius grabs the box, rips off the lid, and squeals with glee. Inside is a plushy mur-rat, a creature native to Chaparo's plains.

"Daddy, Mummy, thank you!" Tobius says, rushing to John and Lilian. "Pa-pap, Mi-mi, it's a ma-mu."

Lilian laughs as she picks him up. "It's lovely."

Tobius looks back at his parents. "Can we have nuggets please?"

They laugh joyfully. "Of course, son," Kalob says.

They are all laughing around the dinner table, enjoying meals of varying styles of meat. There are nuggets for Tobius, and John and Kalob have medium well steaks with Coltin whiskey. Lilian chooses a fresh Coltin salad with a fruit vinaigrette dressing. Julianne, not caring for steak, chooses a filet of local sea crab fish. Both ladies enjoy a glass of Palatian wine. And of course, Tobius enjoys his strawberry milk shake. They laugh and enjoy the evening together as a family. Once dinner is finished, they play with Tobius and get him ready for bed. Once Julianne put Tobius to bed, she rejoins everyone in the study.

John waits by the door. "I am glad you are home, sweetie." He gives Julianne a hug. They enter the study, and John closes the door.

"Kalob, Julianne, we have some items to discuss," Lilian says, sitting by John.

"All right," John begins as C5T2, SAM droid, opens the door.

"Sir," it says. "Pardon the interruption, but there is an urgent subnet call from Marina."

Lilian jumps from her seat. "Who is it?"

"He refused to say, but it is urgent," C5 says.

Lilian looks at John, confused. "I will take it, honey."

C5 responds, "They insist on you both being present."

"Okay, C5," John says, standing. "Let's go, you two." He looks at Kalob and Julianne.

Their house is not fancy but has enough room for everyone, but John has a house being built for the whole family. The main floor has the dining room, study, family room, and transceiver communication room. The flooring is that of native wood of maroon color. John decided when he bought this house to have most of the lighting by use of candles. They both enjoy the relaxing glow of natural light. The only room that differs from the nature decor is the communication room. This room has a subnet station, transceiver monitoring station, and a constantly updating station tracking all shipping requests, cargo ships' locations, and inventory.

Lilian looks at the subnet and smiles. "It has been a long time, Hermit and Chi-Chi."

Excitedly, the chillard jumps around, and the hermit waves. "Hello, Lilian, John." Startled, the hermit says, "Is that Kalob?"

"It is," John says proudly. "And this is his wife, Julianne."

Hermit nods politely. "It's a pleasure. You should come visit me." Julianne nods.

Lilian asks impatiently, "So why the urgent call?"

"Do you remember that object you brought me?" Hermit asks.

"You will have to specify. I have only brought you thirty or so." She chuckled.

"The obsidian diamond from thirty years ago?"

John rubs the scar on his left arm. "Sure do."

"Well, I was able to find some vague references to someone called Sanguis, but it is done as though it was a curse." Hermit continued, "It's hard to be sure, but I found some possible locations for answers."

"Where could they be?" Lilian asks.

"Deep in the south jungle of Draken and a reference on Vorex," he answers hesitantly.

Lilian says, "We will be there soon. John, let's go."

"Hold on, Lil," John says, putting both his hands up.

"Please, honey." Lilian flashes her husband a seductive smile and bats her eyes in her "you can't tell me no" glance.

John shakes his head. "Okay, my love, let's go. But everyone is coming."

Julianne goes to pack stuff for Tobius. Kalob glances at the shipping charts. "Dad, we have an order for Marina. Do you want to take it?"

"Sure," John says as he heads to the study. Kalob tells C5 to let headquarters know about the order they will handle, and it whirs away.

Two hours later, John and Kalob are preparing Lucky Harvest for departure. "Control, Lucky Harvest ready to depart," John says.

"Depart when ready, Lucky Harvest," Control replies.

As they are leaving Coltin's atmosphere, a private subnet channel opens. Lilian opens the channel. "Lilian, are you there?" asks the hermit frantically.

"What's wrong?" she asks.

"Do not come here. It is not safe."

John spins. "Hermit, talk to me. Are you in trouble?"

"Yes. Do you recall when you picked up Lilian off Crypto?"

John calmly states, "Yes. Why?"

"The bounty was on Lilian, not for what she did but what she had. John, just stay away from here. It is not safe for any of you." The hermit cuts the transmission before he can respond.

Lilian turns to John. "What should we do?"

John looks at her. "If we are not safe, then we should find out all we can about that artifact." Kalob, Julianne, and Lilian all agree. So they set course for Marina and jump to slipstream space.

As they near Marina, they take extra precautions by powering up shields and defensive turrets. They exit slip space on the outer edge of Marina. The spectacle they see unfolding before them is eerily familiar.

Lilian gasps. "What is happening?"

Kalob looks at the scanners. Stunned, he stammers, "There is…a huge fleet on the other side of the system."

Lilian looks at John, terrified. He smiles back. "Don't worry. We will get in, grab the hermit and chillard, and skip out." They all nod, and Julianne goes to secure Tobius in bed.

Lilian opens a channel to the hermit. "Hermit, we are here to get you."

"What?" he exclaimed. "I told you to stay away."

"Just tell us where you are!" Lilian snaps.

"I am well south of the spaceport. When you get over the spaceport, let me know." He kills the link.

"You know where to go, honey," she says. John nods and accelerates, aiming right for the spaceport.

John keeps Lucky Harvest at top speed until the last moment so it won't burn up on entry. Kalob looks at the scanners. "Five cruisers inbound releasing lots of fighters. Dad, can we make it?"

John nods but does not look up. Lilian says, "John, do you remember when we met?"

"Yes, of course. Why?"

"Well, what was the name of the lead cruiser?" she asks shakily.

John turns his head. "Something Might, I think."

"Vorex's Might," she softly says. "What are the odds of the same attack fleet being in the same system the second time you have to save someone?"

"I don't like it," he states flatly. John looks to Kalob. "You better get ready for a fight." Kalob nods firmly.

* * *

Admiral Kato watches calmly from the command deck as the assault commences. He turns to the man standing to his right. "Last time, Craven, you failed to deliver what I asked. Do not fail me again!"

He stiffly nods and dons his green helmet. Kato brings up a subnet of the system on the right arm of the command chair. Surprised, he selects the icon of the lone ship hurtling toward the planet.

"Navigation."

"Yes, Admiral."

"Where did this ship come from?" He knows it is familiar somehow.

"Sir, the ship is Lucky Harvest from Coltin," the officer says.

"Captain Rumick, do you recall that ship?"

Captain Rumick runs the name through the databases. "Admiral Kato, we encountered that ship thirty-five years ago at Crypto. They destroyed three fighters and got away from Craven."

"I want that ship. *Now*!" he shouts as he stands to his full height of two meters. "Rumick, advise Craven to get that relic. And, Captain, if that ship escapes, you will pay."

* * *

Everyone in the cabin jumps when a voice comes over the transceiver channel. "Lucky Harvest, land at the spaceport and await your escort. Failure to comply will result in lethal force."

Kalob looks at his father. "Dad, that sounds personal."

"Yeah, they are probably still upset about your mom and me destroying three fighters when we met last. Son, we will make it. Let's just drop in, grab that crazy hermit, and scram out."

Kalob nods as he looks at his wife and hugs her tight. Lilian leans forward, softly kissing her husband, saying, "I love you, John. Thanks for giving me the ride of a lifetime."

Lucky Harvest streaks through the atmosphere toward the spaceport. Suddenly, John yells, "Hang on!" He yanks the yoke to the left. They shoot over the south end of the city.

Kalob shouts, "A squad of fighters inbound on an intercept course."

"Lucky Harvest, come about and land or be destroyed."

Julianne slaps the channel closed. "Let's go, Dad."

Lilian grabs her transceiver, enters the encryption key, and waits for the handshake to complete. The hermit says, "Hurry. Five point two kilometers straight ahead."

Julianne says, "The fighters are closing fast. Weapons are powered up."

John says, "Transfer power from the bow shield to the rear. We won't need them right now." Quickly, she does so, and Kalob starts firing even though they are out of range.

John looks to Lilian. "Get ready." She nods assuredly. Kalob looks at John, confused. "Don't worry, son. Just some modification from the last encounter," he says with a smile. Kalob shrugs and keeps firing.

Julianne says, "The fighters are about six hundred meters behind us and closing."

John smiles. "It is time to give them their present."

Lilian laughs an agreement. Suddenly, there were two thumps from the back of the ship. Julianne squeals in shock. Pod 5 and 6 are ejected from the ship and start accelerating toward the group of fighters. Lilian smiles as she guides the pods into the fighters.

Pod 5 shoots to the group on the port side while pod 6 screams to the starboard. The two pods cover the six hundred meters in a fraction of a second, slamming into the fighters. The sudden unexpected release of the pods stun the pilots. This tactic causes the obliteration of five fighters and damages two more.

* * *

Admiral Kato watches the main projector with disinterest as the assault continues. However, on his chair arm, a small projection of the Wraith Hound squadron chases after the Lucky Harvest. Seeing that they refuse to yield to the fighters, he commands, "Navigation, intercept that ship now!"

Obeying his command, the officer jumps to comply. "Sir, we will be in weapons range in twenty-four seconds."

Kato nods. He smiles to himself. "I have you now." He keeps watching the chase unfold when suddenly, he freezes. The target ship breaks into three parts. The smaller two accelerate toward the squadron, eradicating five fighters. "Are we in weapons range?" the admiral yells.

The ensign shakily responds, "Almost. Just five more seconds."

Enraged, Kato extends his left hand. Runic icons glow on his glove as a crimson thread of energy leaps from his hand, wrapping around the ensign's neck. Kato snaps his hand back, sending the ensign slamming into wall at the bridge exit with a wet crunch. "I want that ship destroyed now!" he bellows. "Captain, tell Craven to find the artifact at all cost, and do not return until he does. And Rumick, if you fail to destroy that ship, you will join the ensign." The admiral stands and strides out past the dead ensign.

The fighters relentlessly attack the cargo ship as it continues its course. Julianne silences the alarms and says, "Rear shields are at twenty-five percent and failing fast."

Lilian says, "Seven hundred meters ahead is where the hermit should be." Suddenly, the starboard sky flashes scarlet, and the ship rocks from the near miss. "The cruiser!" shouts Lilian.

John banks port to try and throw off the next shot. Alarms scream as the ship takes a direct hit. Pod 4 explodes, causing the ship to spin on its horizontal axis. Just after the pod explodes, the fighters hit directly on the top of the hull. Just as John starts to control the spin, another scarlet lance penetrates the ship and ruptures the slipstream drive. Alarms sounds long enough for John to realize what will happen.

Hope from the Ashes

In a brilliant flash, Lucky Harvest is reduced to a cloud of fire and debris. The hermit hears a loud explosion. He looks up just in time to see his friends vanish in flames. He falls to his knees in shock. Frozen from fear, all he can do is watch in horror as the cloud dissipates as the flaming debris crashes to the swamp land. Several heartbeats pass when something small catches his eye. He cautiously scans the horizon, ensuring the fighters are not returning, before heading in the direction of the object. With stealth abandoned, he sprints across the swampland, clearing the 150 meters of clearing in twenty seconds. Rolling into the brush, he checks to see if he is spotted. After several more seconds to catch his breath and steady his nerves, he moves to the object.

    The hermit knows the object did not fall far from him, but it feels like forever as the replay of his friends' demise circles in his mind. He arrives at the location near the object and finds the swamp smoldering and mangled hull everywhere. Looking across the wreckage, he sends up a prayer for his fallen friends. His eyes pass over a small cylindrical object that is out of place. Heading to the right edge of the debris field, he freezes when he is three meters from the object. Nervously, he approaches the cylinder, which appears undamaged. As the hermit reaches toward the object, he sees something move. Jumping back, he waits to see if it crawls out. He nervously watches for several heartbeats and realizes he is holding his breath. Slowly exhaling, he moves forward once more. He gives the object a wide berth and comes to the other side. The hermit stands there and stares, awestruck by the sight.

What lies in front of the pelagian is none other than the three-year-old grandson of John and Lilian. He is unable to comprehend how this little boy survived such a destructive force. It is beyond him. He knows the only way to honor his friends is to ensure their legacy lives on through this boy. He kneels and softly cradles the child and vows to keep him safe. He is unsure what to call this young human since they never met. He looks down and sees the name, Tobius, on the corner of the child's blanket.

"Tobius," the hermit quietly speaks. "I will teach you all I can about your family." He carries Tobius and his stuffed murrat back to his hut with Chi-Chi following behind, curious of their new friend. Three hours later, after extensive precautions to ensure no one can follow, they reach a secluded hut. To the species unfamiliar with the swampland, it would appear like a pile of fallen foliage. The hermit prefers his swamp retreat over his extravagant house near the spaceport. He always enjoys the solitude that this location allows, and it provides an excellent escape from the city rush. It took over five years to complete. It has two levels. The top level is a ten-meter-diameter room with a two-and-a-half-meter domed ceiling. There is a single half-meter pane of crysteel encompassing the room half a meter from the room's apex. The lower level has six rooms honeycombed around the ten-meter hall directly below the top level. North of the hall sits the dining room. To the left is the kitchen, refresher, and medical station, then two sleeping quarters with individual subnet stations and desk. And last is the smaller yet still impressive study. The outer rooms are slightly larger than the hall with a diameter of thirteen meters. There are some intuitive parts of his hideaway he is glad he added. The access to this building is through the lakes to the west through a fifty-meter tunnel to the bottom of the hut. The pride of his hideaway is the three buoyancy tanks under the building. Each tank is twenty meters long, five meters wide, and a meter and a half tall. When the tanks are at full buoyancy, the hut only extends out of the swamp one meter.

He kneels down and places the child softly next to him as he reaches down, collecting several leaves from the swamp lilies and long swamp reeds. Intricately, he uses the reeds as thread and makes a four-meter square patch. Gingerly, he places Tobius in the middle, removes a spare rebreather, and fits it to the young human's face. Chi-Chi watches with fascination as the hermit weaves the patch around the sleeping child. Once Tobius is completely encased in the lily reed container, the hermit weaves another reed through the overlapping leaves to ensure he is secured. Scanning the local area, he spots two three-meter swamp vines. Carefully, he weaves them around the child.

"Let's go home, Chi-Chi," the hermit says, nodding toward the lake. The chillard, without hesitation, takes three quick strides and dives into the lake. He laughs at the pure joy and innocence of his companion. He wades into the lake and shivers from the cool water. Pausing, he secures the young boy to his belt and dives below the surface. The hermit enjoys this area. The lake water stays around twelve degrees Celsius most of the time. During daylight, the lake is a warm aquamarine, but at night or cloud cover, it is pale lavender. When flying over, the lake looks much like the surrounding swamp due to the algae that live in the first two meters. But after penetrating that layer, the water below is crystal clear. Under the algae, the hermit can see the bottom anywhere on the lake. The light comes through the algae like a kaleidoscope seen through a stained-glass window. Any other day, he would enjoy a leisurely swim around the lake, but he must hurry to help the grandson of his late friends.

He approaches the hatch for his home. He slips his hand in a recessed slot and presses it against a scanner. Hearing the latch release, he backs away as the hatch opens down and away. Quickly, he climbs the ladder on the other side of the hatch and whistles for Chi-Chi. As the chillard climbs out of the hatch, the hermit hits the controls and scurries to the refresher station. Quickly and cautiously, he unweaves the leaf and reed patch covering the child. Softly, he places the young human on the table near the EMA (emergency medical assistance) droid. Removing the rebreather, he sees that the youngling's chest rises and falls at a steady rate. Relieved, he activates the med station and heads to the kitchen for some java. The hermit starts the java and gets Chi-Chi some ice water and raw fish. Once the java is done, he pours a cup and heads back to the med station.

Grabbing a stool from under the table, he sits, sipping on his java, watching the droid examine the human child. One hour and three cups of java pass with the droid still examining the boy. As the hermit goes to top off his java and grab a snack, the med station chimes, "The young human suffered trauma to the right front of his cranium. He will survive but is currently in a coma." He sits back down, relieved that he will survive. "It is uncertain how long the coma will last due to the uncertain cause for the trauma."

The hermit sets the droid to alert him if anything changes on its patient. He heads to his sleeping quarters and tries to get a few hours of sleep. But no matter how much he tries, the horrifying events of the day replay in his mind. He is sitting in the brush watching his friends frantically try and reach him. He recalls cheering as he sees the ingenious plan by John to use the pods as makeshift missiles and remove almost half of the enemy ships. With terrifying detail, he relives the sight of the bloodred shaft of light pierce Lucky Harvest's hull an instant before it erupted in flames. When he is not having a nightmare about his friends, he recalls the discovery of the young boy among the wreckage. Still utterly perplexed, he sees himself stare at the young child asleep in the debris field.

The days slowly pass as the hermit develops a routine. He makes breakfast for the chillard and himself. Then they both enjoy as they watch the med station check on the young patient. Next they both go for a swim around the lake for an hour or so. Upon their return, they go to the study and try and research more about the obsidian diamond that he has or find out why his friends had perished. After the midday meal, they check on Tobius once again. The hermit then checks the subnet for any information on attacks similar to what happened here or Crypto, but to no avail. He could not figure out how a fleet with such firepower can just disappear for decades. As days roll into weeks and weeks to months, the hermit ventures back to his house in the city some days to get any news.

* * *

Since the assault, Craven has spent his time trying to track down the artifact that the ungrateful Kato desires at any cost. At first, he would search and threaten local vendors and shipping companies to try and figure out where it may be. He then started looking for the eccentric and wealthy collectors on Marina. He had visited and bribed everyone from cargo shipping supervisors to wealthy executives to try and find what his boss demands. But after several weeks, he settles into just spending time at the cantinas, waiting for the drunks to pass on information.

Six months pass with no luck for the hermit or bounty hunter to get the information they seek. Craven is sitting in the corner of the cantina when he hears a drunk patron at the bar rambling about a strange collector nearby. He moves to an open seat near him, letting him talk more about this collector. Listening intently, he graciously buys the informant several drinks to ensure that he willingly answers every question.

"Everyone calls him," the man slurs, "healing hermit."

Craven smiles inside his helmet, thinking, *Finally, a name.* "What does he collect?" the bounty hunter says aloud.

"Anything he wants. Last I heard, he has a chillard."

Seeing his drink is almost gone, Craven signals the bartender to bring a new drink. "So where can I find this hermit?" Craven watches as the crytan empties his old drink. Waiting for a reply, he watches intently.

"Well…" the informant begins, and suddenly, he falls off the barstool and hits the floor with a thud. Craven stands, hand reflexively grabbing his pulsar pistol at the sudden collapse, and he hears the fallen drunk snoring. He looks at the crytan with disgust and rage and kicks him in the side for his trouble, cracking a rib. Settling the tab, he is even more enraged, not realizing the crytan was drinking one of the most expensive spirits here. Fifteen hundred credits later, he curses the crytan for being the most expensive waste of time.

* * *

It has been nine months since he rescued Tobius from the wreckage, and still the young human remains comatose. The hermit makes the trek back to his house in the city early one morning. He jogs three kilometers east of his hut to a camouflaged shed where he stores his speeder. He starts his speeder and shoots off north toward town. It takes forty-five minutes most days to cover the twelve-kilometer stretch to the city. Two kilometers away, he starts heading northwest so he can approach from the west. He enters the western edge of town and stores his speeder in the executive speeder parking.

He walks through the market, looking for anything of interest. And after wandering for over an hour, he heads home.

"Welcome home, sir," the droid says, whirring into the hall. "May I get you some java?"

The hermit nods, heading to the study. A few moments later, the droid delivers the java, and he dismisses it with a wave of his hand. Instead of looking through news feeds to try and figure out more about the mysterious fleet, he looks at the obsidian relic sitting on the table. He stares at the object for a long moment. He suddenly jumps with a thought. He turns, spilling dozens of data pads across the floor. Running through the study's vast array of ancient scrolls, he selects three different ones. He returns to the table and sets them down gently. He opens the top desk drawer and dons special gloves to help keep the scrolls in good shape.

Two scrolls are from an ancient library from Detritus Prime, and he is uncertain of the origin of the third. With extreme care, he unbinds the scroll, attaches the edge under a scroll mount, and unrolls it. Since he is working with ancient writing, he shuts off any artificial lights and brings over two candelabras. Unrolling the first scroll, he looks at the manuscript and looks at the ancient runic language, scanning for the symbols like on the obsidian diamond. He sees one rune that looks somehow familiar—a circle flattened on the right with a diamond inside the left edge. Grabbing the artifact, he sees a resemblance to the key or gate symbol. He pulls out his tablet, scanning that section of the scroll. Rolling it back up, he looks at the scanned section. He moves to his tablets and scans through several different pads about ancient translations. He finds several similar runes with translations. He sees that the meaning is dependent on the runes following it.

He quickly and carefully opens the second scroll, looking through its contents and finding no new information. After securing the second scroll, he takes a break and summons SAM. He waits for the droid to arrive and considers the last symbol on the artifact.

"How may I assist you?" the droid inquires.

"I would like some java and pastries."

"Of course, sir," SAM says, and he shuffles off.

He returns to the table and starts securing the third scroll, opening and scanning its content. This scroll is half the size of the previous two, and the hermit doubts it will contain much. Nearing the end of the scroll, he realizes that the runic writing has changed slightly. Suddenly, the scroll stops unrolling but appears to have not ended. He dons a set of magnifiers to help him examine the scroll in more detail, and he finds a small depression on the inside of the scroll spine just below the parchment's edge. Digging through his desk, he tries to find something to insert into the depression. Finding a wooden dowel, he carefully presses the notch on the scroll. The dowel inserts half a centimeter, and he hears an audible click. Startled, he waits to see if something will happen. When nothing does, he examines the scroll again.

Carefully, he tries to unroll the manuscript more, but it refuses to move. Looking over the spine, the hermit tries to see if there is another depression. On the edge of the top of the spine, he sees what appears to be a crack. Grabbing a measuring stick from the desk drawer, he sets a tablet to record the scroll. He measures the gap to be only three millimeters but sees that is it symmetrical on the scroll axis. Relieved that it is not a fracture, he carefully inserts the edge of the measure stick into the gap. First, he tries to slide the stick through the gap, but it stops after only a few millimeters. He moves the measuring stick to the right side of the slit and grabs another dowel to use as leverage to try and separate the objects. Slowly, the gap widens on the end of the spine, and without notice, a large cloud erupts from the scroll, rapidly filling the room. The cloud is so dark that it extinguishes the candles and blocks all artificial light. He is confused with the sudden reaction. Sitting in the darkness, the hermit waits a few heartbeats, and from the midst of the darkness, a lavender figure appears to float from the mist.

The shadowy figure strides around the hermit, gazing with intense crimson eyes as if looking for something. As it nears the other exam table, the obsidian diamond starts to pulse a cold purple. The shadowy figure turns and looks the hermit in the eyes. With a booming voice, the apparition says a single word: "Feridus."

Suddenly, the darkness implodes soundlessly. The hermit stares at where the phantom was for several seconds, thinking, *Was that real?* The hermit jumps as SAM enters with the java and pastries. He watches the droid place the items on a small table near where he usually reads through data pads.

"Is that all, sir?" the droid asks, and he dismisses it with a nod.

He turns and looks at the scroll once again. Everything is just how it was before, except the candles have been extinguished. Grabbing the data pad, he rewinds the video to just before he tries to remove the object from the end of the spine. The only thing that the tablet recorded was the candles going out, but it still has the light from the dimmed glow panels. He watches with extreme interest and hears what the apparition said: "Feridus." The only thing he notices is that after the word was spoken there was a flash of light at the end of the scroll. The hermit is now determined to have the object inside the spine at any cost. Grabbing the center of the scroll, he pries the object out, and much to his amazement, it is a smaller scroll. He unrolls it quickly, staring at what is hidden. Stunned, he is looking at a single rune, and it is none other than the last symbol on the top of obsidian diamond. In bloodred ink is written *Sanguis*, and only now does he realize that it is not a word but a name.

Suddenly, the connection hits him like a pulsar bolt. "This is what they wanted," he says, picking up the artifact. He curses the diamond. This caused his friends' demise. Looking at the relic, he recalls something Lilian told him when they arrived from Crypto.

"The bounty hunter was not after me but this," she told him as she revealed it. She never knew who was after it, but the hermit feels there must be a connection to the fleet.

"SAM, please come here!" the hermit yells as he grabs a pack, loads up several data pads, and looks through the scrolls.

"How may I assist you?" the droid asks, whirring into the study.

"I shall be returning to my retreat. Please send weekly rations to the designated location. I am not sure how long I will be gone." He finds the scrolls and puts them in the pack. He tells the droid as he is heading out of the house, "If anyone asks for me, tell them I have gone on business and uncertain of my return."

SAM responds, "Yes, of course." It shuffles behind him.

He reaches the door. "Inform me of anyone who inquires of my whereabouts." He realizes with astonishment that he forgot the relic. "Hold this," he tells SAM, sprinting back to the study. He returns to the droid, stores the relic, and prepares to leave.

* * *

Craven now has an idea of where to possibly find his target. "Where can I find the healing hermit?" he asks a local vendor.

The vendor seems disinterested with the question and keeps tending to his wares. Annoyed, he leaves fifty credits in front of him. With greedy interest, the vendor asks, "Who are you looking for again?"

"The healing hermit," Craven says again.

"Ah, yes, I have heard that name, but I do not know where," the vendor says with a slight grin.

"That's too bad," Craven says, flashing another fifty credits. He turns to walk away, and the vendor knocks over a small stack of items, grabbing his arm.

"Now hang on. Give me a moment to think." The vendor acts as though he has to recall. "He lives near the warehouse district at the edge of the plaza." He holds his hand out, half acting like he wanted to shake hands, but more so to get the credits. Craven shakes his informant's hand.

Taking a little more than half an hour and a few hundred credits to expedite his search, he finds the road he needs. He sees a pelagian leave a house with a pack heading away in a hurry. He walks down the street and arrives at the house the unknown person left. He hits the buzzer and waits a short while. He hits the buzzer again, and the door opens to reveal a SAM droid. "May I assist you?"

"I am looking for the healing hermit," he casually asks.

The droid replies, "I do apologize, but the master is away on business. Would you care to leave a message?"

"When will he return?"

Again, the droid says mechanically, "I am uncertain of his return."

Craven smiles. "Thank you. I will just come back another time." Turning, he heads the way the person went at a slight jog. "That had to be him," he says softly.

SAM shuts the door and shuffles to the transceiver station. It keys the emergency link for the hermit. An instant later, the hermit asks, "Yes, SAM?"

"I apologize for the interruption, but a human in body armor was just here asking for you."

"Thanks," he says, closing the channel. He looks back just in time to see someone matching SAM's description. He turns and runs to where he stored his speeder. *I have to lose him*, he thought. After several outrageous detours, he backtracks to the speeder. Stowing the pack, he starts up the speeder and accelerates. Just as the speeder shoots from storage area, Craven rounds the corner. Raising his left gauntlet, he fires a tracking beacon, and the gauntlet beeps a confirmation that the beacon is active.

Finding a speeder rental nearby, he rents the fastest speeder they have, not happy about the ridiculous price. He sets his visor to track the beacon. He hits the throttle to try and make up for the almost three-kilometer lead his target has. After a kilometer, he notices that his target is now heading southeast. He adjusts his course to intercept the only lead to acquire the relic. After thirty minutes, he sees that the beacon has stopped. He smiles to himself and chuckles. "I have you now."

He slows as he pulls within five hundred meters. He uses his visor to try and find the pelagian. The visor shows he is within fifty meters of the beacon, but he sees nothing but swamp and brush.

He shuts down the speeder and slowly walks around the area. As he approaches ten meters of the beacon, he starts sinking into the swamp. He fires his jet pack and jets fifteen meters up. He scans with his visor again but still sees nothing. Frustrated, he flies back to the speeder and returns to town.

The hermit watches from a nearby pool as his follower returns to the city. He waits another few minutes under the pool, ensuring that he is gone. He climbs out of the pool and checks the pack to ensure it was still dry. He slowly heads to the retreat and sends a message to SAM to bring another speeder to the drop off. He takes two hours to get back to the hut as he takes extreme caution to ensure that he is not followed. He makes it home just as night falls, and Chi-Chi is waiting by the hatch. He drops the pack in the hall and heads to the med droid.

"How is he?" he asks, looking at the human.

"He is showing a slight increase in brain activity," it replies. Nodding, he heads to make dinner.

A Quick Learner

Ten years pass. Tobius still lies in a coma under constant care by the medical droid. Craven still has no luck getting information about the hermit or his location for his business. The hermit still has not figured out the relic and has the med droid start subconscious education for the boy, who is now a thirteen-year-old. It has now been almost nine years since he left the city. He was able to find out a little about the person who followed him. Craven is a bounty hunter of relics more than people. Outside of that, he could find little else from his remote sanctuary. He was able to piece together some parts to the relic. It was a key, for what he was unsure, and did not know if it was on Draken or Feridus. Also, he develops a training curriculum for when Tobius would wake.

It is the eleventh anniversary of his friends' tragic death. He is out wandering the swamp, and after several hours, he finds himself in the debris field right where he found Tobius. He is shocked at where he finds himself. He looks around, slowly seeing that the swamp has nearly erased any sign of the ship. Looking to the other side of the clearing, he sees a shape that is abnormal for the swamp. He makes his way to the object.

"How did I miss this until now?" he asks himself aloud. He pulls the moss off and realizes that it is a locker. He pries the door and finds Tobius's grandfather's equipment locker. He puts the equipment back and runs to get a pack. After he gets the gear back to his house, he lays it out on the dining room table. He instantly sees the belt has decayed beyond repair. Next, he examines the repeating crossbow. He removes the magazine, draws back the crossbow, and pulls the trigger. It snaps forward but fails to reset. He grabs his tool kit from the study to repair the bow. After several hours, he sets the bow down and heads to the kitchen to make some fresh java and a sandwich. He returns the table after letting Chi-Chi out for a swim. He removes the four blades from their sheaths. One is damaged by the swamp and fell to pieces, but the other three are in reasonable condition. It takes a little more than two weeks for him to repair all the equipment since he did not have all needed tools and materials on hand.

One evening, as he relaxes in the top room watching the sun set across the swamp, his chillard lying on the bench beside him, the med droid calls, "Sir, come quick."

He swings from the top room and steps into the refresher. Shocked, he sees the young human sitting with his legs off the table, stretching his limbs. While Tobius was in the coma, the hermit ensured that the med droid stimulated the muscles daily to prevent atrophy. He is surprised at how well-built Tobius has become. He is standing nearly two meters tall and appears to weigh 105 kilograms. The hermit figures that it must have been the coma and precise balance of needed nutrients provided by the droid that caused the premature maturation of the boy.

"Whe...where am I?" asks Tobius, extremely confused.

"Tobius," the hermit replies carefully. "You are in my home, and you are safe."

"But who are you?" the human asks defensively.

"I am a friend of your family and saved you eleven years ago." He slowly explains what happened, and he spares no details. Tobius sorrowfully listens to every word the man says.

"May I see where they died?"

Shaking his head, the hermit says, "No, you are not ready to see it. We need to ensure you are strong enough."

Suddenly, Tobius stands and jabs a finger in his savior's face. "I want to see it now!"

The hermit explains how they will get there and gives Tobius the rebreather, uncertain if he can hold his breath for the fifty-meter swim. He ties a rope to Tobius's belt and then to himself. Opening the hatch, he climbs into the water and turns to watch the human.

Tobius feels angry, scared, confused, and senses immense power from inside himself. To the hermit's surprise, Tobius is easily able to keep up with him. Shocked at his physical strength, the hermit barely beats him to the lake's edge.

"It is a short jog to get there," he tells Tobius. He starts off slow to ensure that the human can keep up, but once again, Tobius has no issues keeping up. The hermit slowly accelerates to almost a full sprint, with Tobius matching him stride for stride. They reach the debris field in just under an hour. Tobius stops almost midstride, even before the hermit slows, collapsing to the ground and screaming in agony. Tobius's mind reels from sudden remembrance of what happened here.

He clearly sees his mother and father exiting a ship as he sits on his grandfather's shoulders. He feels the utter joy of dining with his family. The joy and happiness is ripped away as he remembers the fear in his mother's eyes as they leave the planet. Rolling on the ground, thrashing in the mud, Tobius yells in complete terror. He remembers hearing his family talking about something he could only feel as bad. He feels the ship shudder, hears a loud explosion, and feels sudden pain on his head.

The hermit squats, being able to do nothing more than watch as the human writhes in pain. After over an hour, the human finally passes out from the sudden expenditure of energy and emotion. Several hours pass before Tobius starts to wake from his episode as the first rays of the morning shine. Tobius slowly stretches his body and rises to his feet.

"Are you all right?" asks the hermit.

Tobius attempts to speak but cannot and simple nods. Taking a moment to stretch his back, he wanders toward the wreckage. Stopping on the edge of the crash site, he slowly takes in the entire scene. Tobius is transfixed on the entire scene. Slowly, he starts to wander into the field, as though he is drawn by something. Taking unsteady steps, he moves to different pieces as though searching for something. After several stops around the field, the young human stops by the locker. Kneeling in the muck, he looks inside. There is not much left inside, since the hermit grabbed the salvageable gear. On the back of the door, he sees an old-fashioned photo. Tobius pulls the picture from the door and slowly stands. The picture is from when he was maybe a year old. There he is, being held by his mother, sitting in a chair with his father to her left. His grandfather is standing behind the chair, and his grandmother is sitting on a stool next to his mother. He smiles through his tears and gently puts the picture in his belt pouch.

Tobius wipes his eyes and stands. He turns to head back to meet the hermit. He takes a step then stops. He looks left suddenly, as if he recalled something he left behind. He moves to a small object only half a meter tall. He asks the hermit, "What was this?"

"That is where I found you," the hermit says plainly. "I still have no idea how you survived the explosion."

"Maybe one day we will find out how." Tobius shrugs.

Nodding, the hermit inquires, "Are you ready to return home, Tobius?"

"Yes," the human states. "But what is your name?"

With a slight laugh, the hermit stands. "I am the healing hermit."

Tobius shakes his head. "Like I will say that every time." Slowly, they jog back to the lake. "What will we do now that I'm awake?"

The hermit replies, "Well, I will teach you here and get a training droid to help teach you how to protect yourself."

They return to the house and prepare dinner. Tobius sits at the dining table and pulls out the picture again. "Hey, Hermi," Tobius says. "Will you tell me about my family?"

Stunned, the pelagian looks from the kitchen. "What did you call me?"

Laughing, the human repeats, "Hermi. I said I wasn't gonna call you the healing hermit every time. So I will call you Hermi."

The hermit considers it then nods. "After dinner, I will show you around the house." The hermit brings dinner to the table, and they enjoy a quiet meal. For the remainder of the evening, Hermi shows Tobius around the home. "Here is your room, Tobius," the hermit, says pointing. "We will discuss things more tomorrow. Get some sleep, my friend." Tobius walks into the room and collapses on the bunk. He is fast asleep.

Tobius is roused to consciousness with the scent of breakfast wafting into his room. He staggers to the refresher then to the kitchen.

"Morning, Hermi," he says, leaning on the counter.

"Go have a seat, young man." He sits at the table as the hermit brings breakfast of oatmeal and fresh fruit. "So we will need to ensure you get a full education. Your family would kill me if I did not." Hermi continues to explain, "Once you do the dishes, I have a little test to see how much of the subconscious training you recall."

Tobius looks at him, confused. "What do you mean subconscious training?"

The hermit explains, "While you lay in a coma, I ensured to start your education with audio and subnet lessons." He pauses to drink some java and continues, "I also had the medical droid do muscular shock training and had additional growth hormones injected into your body. I know that you will never have a normal life, and for that I truly am sorry." Hermi looks at the human. "I promise to help you make the best of your life."

Tobius nods. "I will try and be the best student I can be."

"Your training droid will be delivered in a few days, so for now, we will start with your education."

After a few days, they work out a schedule they both agree on. First, breakfast is every morning at seven. After, Tobius washes dishes. Then they spend two hours in the study, working on math and science. Next, they swim around the lake for one hour with lunch afterward. The afternoons are spent learning how to read star charts, navigation, history, and language translations. Right before dinner, Tobius gets half an hour to do what he wishes. Dinner is served at nine.

Several months pass, and Tobius continues to excel on all aspects of the training that Hermi has for him. Even his physical training has excelled rapidly; the droid is programmed with forty-six different fighting styles. Fifteen are styles without a weapon, while the rest are with weapons from simple bow staff to single and double-bladed weapons. Tobius also learns how to use daggers, stun stakes, ebraxian whips, and his favorite, the Razik blades. The hermit updates the droid training to include ranged weapons. Tobius is able to catch on quickly but favors what his grandfather used—the repeating crossbow.

Tobius quickly learns all he can from Hermi, and instead of having set lessons, he can read whatever he likes in the study. First, he starts to learn as much as he can about his family. He learns about his grandfather and the special cargo ship he developed to help Lucky Harvest shipping company become a vast intersystem shipper. Lilian had her heart set on learning more about history and enjoyed the challenge of finding these relics. Kalob followed in his father's footsteps and helped the business. He met his wife on Palatia, and she followed him to the stars.

One day, when Hermi went to get supplies, Tobius wanders around the study, looking for something interesting to read. He grabs a tablet on historical civilizations and returns to the desk. Kicking back, he starts reading the data and drinks his milk. Most of the information in what he selected is the normal explanation for extinct societies. Tobius scrolls through, skimming the information, and is about to set it aside when something catches his eye.

"Keepers of Power," he reads. Curious, he reads with extreme interest. There is not much detail, but it explains a small group of all different species who would not allow outsiders in their villages. Only those who complete the Right of Power may gain entrance. Another intriguing fact is there is no information about where these villages were. The human knows that Hermi will not return for several more hours and chooses to head outside and duel the droid.

Tobius had studied the programing of the droid and increased the difficulty of the droid to max. He turns on the droid.

"Please select training module," a masculine voice says.

"Ultimate test," Tobius says.

"Weapon selection, please," says the droid again.

"I will use the Razik blades. Use what you want. Time limit, two hours," the young man says. He stretches and limbers up. Then he wields his blades in double reverse grip. The droid grabs a metal bow staff. "Begin," Tobius says as he starts to circle the droid. He waits for the imminent attack from the droid, but it never comes. He sees the droid take a defensive stance. He comes in quick with a right slash. The droid brings the left end of the staff up to block with ease. He quickly snaps a kick to the midsection of the droid to disengage for a moment. He jumps back at the droid, bringing both blades down in a double backhanded attack. The droid ducks down and brings the staff up to block the blades. Tobius lets the left blade's guard hit the staff a moment before the right and releases the right blade as it spins 180 degrees. He slides the blade down the staff and across the torso of the droid. Since it is a direct impact to the torso, the fight stops since Tobius dealt a fatal blow. The droid steps back and changes weapons to a ferioblade and ebraxian whip. Tobius nods, and they begin again. They battle for two hours with Tobius winning all but two rounds.

 Heading back to the house, he races Chi-Chi around the lake and loses. He decides to call it a day. He climbs through the hatch and steps into the refresher. Once done, he grabs some water and climbs to the top level to watch the sunset. After which, he decides to go prepare dinner. He shares it with Chi-Chi even though Hermi gets mad when he does. He cleans up then goes to the subnet to check local news. Nothing really interesting happened today, so he calls it a night.

 Hermi makes the trip back to town after breakfast. He does not have much time, so he just stores his speeder at the south gate. Quickly, he makes it back to his house and finds that the door has been kicked in. Slowly, he moves into the hall and instantly sees his droid has been cut in half. Seeing each door kicked in, he hurries down the hall to the study. Sliding to a stop in the doorway, he sees a figure in green armor sitting as his table.

"What do you want?" he asks.

"I have waited a long time to meet you, hermit," a voice says from the helmet.

"I was away on business," replies the Pelagian.

"Yes, yes, your droid said that, but I just cannot figure what business you have in the swamps."

"It is none of your concern," snaps the hermit.

"Now just tell me where you hid the key of passage, and I will leave."

The hermit retorts, "I do not know what you are asking for."

Standing, he shakes his head. "My employer wants this relic, and it will not escape me this time."

He tries to take an approach as an interested buyer. "Who is your employer? He sounds like he may have items of interest."

"He would not even consider getting rid of his items." Now they stand half a meter apart. "Where is it!"

"Of what are you referring to?" the hermit states.

"It is an obsidian diamond with different marks on it."

The hermit stifles a hint of surprise. "I think I recall that item, but I no longer have it." He invents a story. "Heron, a jeweler, really wanted it, so I let him have it. I had no interest in a jewel."

"What system?"

"He was headed into the Multian Cluster."

The man starts to leave then turns back and points at the hermit. "If you lied to me, I will kill you." After Craven leaves the hermit, he opens a channel to Rumick. "Captain, I have a lead on the item."

"You had better hurry. The admiral is not pleased with the slow progress."

The Start of a Journey

The hermit looks through the study and finds nothing missing. He waits for an hour to ensure that the bounty hunter is not waiting to follow him again. He contacts the spaceport to have his shuttle prepared for departure. He opens the secured transceiver channel to Tobius.

"You need to pack up your things and grab my pack from under my bunk. I will be there in twenty minutes." Grabbing a pack, he selects a few scrolls, a tool kit, and some small collectibles then heads to the executive landing pads. He nods to the guards as he scurries to the shuttle.

Craven had hoped his little visit to the hermit would cause him to panic. He had tried previously to bribe his way to the hermit's ship, but droids are impossible to convince with bribes. He concludes that his target stored his ship on the executive landing pads since his speeder is stored there too. He camps on a roof just outside the complex and watches the hermit move through the gate. He tags the ship with a tracking beacon. Rising, he leaps from the rooftop, using his jump jets at the last moment to slow his descent, and he makes his way to his ship with no real hurry.

Tobius is waiting with his and Hermi's gear at the designated location. Without landing the shuttle, he lowers the boarding ramp and puts the craft in station keeping as he helps load the gear. Before they lift off, he calls for his chillard, and Chi-Chi comes bounding up the ramp. The hermit never understood why this creature loved to travel, and he thinks that Lilian had something to do with it.

Smiling to himself about the cheerful memory of his friend, he waits for Tobius to buckle in then heads for orbit.

Tobius asks as they ascend, "What is this all about, Hermi?"

The hermit shifts uneasily. He never wanted to get the grandson of his friends involved, but reluctantly, he starts to explain, "Grab the pack that was under my bunk, please." As Tobius grabs the pack, he continues, "It was before your grandparents had even met. Lilian, your grandmother, loved searching for ancient relics all across the galaxy." Tobius gives him the bag. "She would always give me the first chance to purchase whatever she found."

"Why?" the young man asked with interest.

Laughing, the hermit replies, "She knew that I loved the history behind it all, and she enjoyed sharing the history." Digging through the pack, he continues, "I would study the items, and most of them I would return to the correct civilization so they can know their own history. There are some rare artifacts that I keep, some for personal reasons, and some for the safety of people. This"—he hands a wrapped object to Tobius—"is why your family was killed. They gave it to me, and I studied it for over thirty years. Just before they died, I found out what this could be. I was so scared at what my research was leading to that I needed their help." With extreme sorrow and regret, the hermit turns to the young human. "Tobius, I am so very sorry. It is my fault that you have no family."

Tobius, having yet to unwrap the object, looks at the pelagian with tearful eyes. "I know you are, and you should not blame yourself. Whoever is after this is to blame, and they will pay one day for the lives they ended!"

The hermit suddenly sees rage burning in the human's eyes, and it feels like the shuttle's air froze. "I found some possible locations to find out more on this relic, and I think we should start where this was found."

Relaxing, Tobius looks at him eagerly. "Where is that?"

"Detritus Prime," the hermit says as he engages the slipstream drive.

They arrive at Detritus Prime without any incident and land at the Bijou Morass spaceport. Thankfully, the hermit's reputation preceded him, and it helps streamline the processing. Once outside the space docks, they head to the local historical database. The hermit is trying to see if there are any local references to the obsidian diamond. He fills Tobius in on the basic information that he is trying to locate and has him search as well to maximize their efforts. However, even with both looking for eight and a half hours, they come up empty. Mutually, they decide to go back to the shuttle and get some sleep.

As they slept, Tobius kept tossing in his bunk, as though caught in a nightmare. He sees a dense jungle with a small foot trail leading south from the spaceport. The visions blur as he is rushed to another place. There is a small crevasse in the face of a cliff with a strange crest made of a purple and silver. He appears to travel into the crevasse but sees nothing but darkness. Suddenly, a pair of violet eyes shine from the darkness and stares at Tobius for what seems like hours. Below the eyes where the middle of the torso would be on most creatures burns a crimson hexagon, and without warning, everything vanishes, but a voice bellows, "Sanguis."

Tobius sits straight up in his bunk, feeling like he just ran ten kilometers. Swinging his legs over the edge, he places his head in his hands, panting. "Was that a dream?" he asks himself aloud. Unsure what exactly that was, he gets up to get some water. He rummages through his pack and brings out a data pad. Mindlessly, he scrolls through it, looking for anything that may help him make sense of the dream. The first one was no use, so he dumps his pack on the bunk to look at them all. He reads the summary so he does not waste time. He picks the third one up and reads the summary: psychology and dreams. At first, he dismisses it, but then he sets it aside to skim through. He finds the tablet he read back in the hut about the "Keepers of Power" and decides to reanalyze it. He rereads the part of the Keepers of Power and finds nothing to help with his dream. He tosses it back on the pile and grabs the psychology data pad. First, it has general information about types of psychology and psychosis treatments, but in the middle of the explanations for some medical treatment, it mentions something about possible visions. Intrigued, he reads on, finding that sometimes visions are the result of severe head trauma, and others can be caused by a close connection to someone or something involved. Tobius ponders on this new information for some time and is startled when Hermi walks up behind him with some java.

"Is something wrong, Tobius?" he asks, sitting across from him.

The young man shrugs. "Couldn't sleep."

The hermit laughs. "Really? I find that hard to believe. You never wanted to get up at seven. You would sleep all day if I let you."

The human looks at him as the hermit sits. "I think I had a vision, but I do not know what it means."

"What did you see?" Tobius takes his time to recall and explain everything he saw from the trail to the crease, even the crimson outline. He decides to keep the information about the Keepers of Power to himself for now at least.

The pelagian leans back and sips his java, pondering what it could mean. "I think you may have seen a way to find what this"—he pulls out the unwrapped obsidian diamond—"goes to."

Instantly, Tobius is drawn to the item. He stares at it with extreme hunger and longing. He sees the symbol on the top of the diamond. Pointing in shock, Tobius gasps. "What does that symbol mean?"

The hermit looks at it. "I believe it means power, but I also think it's a name. Sanguis."

The human freezes at the word. "Tha...that is exactly the word spoken in my dream."

Hermi looks at him, shocked. He stands and mixes a drink and gives it to Tobius. "Here. This will help you sleep until we can get back to the historical data."

He nods as he swallows the offered liquid and feels himself drifting fast asleep.

Tobius is tossed from his bunk as a powerful gale rocks the shuttle. He staggers to the main cabin and sees the hermit just sitting in his chair, watching the storm outside.

"Are storms always like this here?" he asks, joining the pelagian. He nods and sips on his java, captivated by the scene outside the vessel. "Will we wait for the storm to end before we head out?" the human asks. Again, he receives a wordless nod. Tobius decides to get something to eat and heads to the little kitchen at the back of the ship. Looking through the cabinet, he chooses some flash dried fruit and water. He always enjoyed the flash dried fruit; he would dip the fruit into the water and watch it soak up the water like a sponge. Plus, dipping the fruit in the water also made the water taste like fruit. Returning to his seat, he finds himself mesmerized by the storm raging just a meter in front of him.

Three hours later, the storm abates, and the two companions venture back to the archives. Tobius thinks to himself, trying to decide what to research this time and hopes for more luck. Arriving at their destination, the hermit stops to inquire the directory droid while the human moves on his own through the shelves of information. He sits down at a terminal at the far end of the hall and pulls up a map of the local area. Then he scans the map, trying to find a place like in his dream, but to no avail. He gets up and moves to the section about groups and tribes. He selects several different data cards then returns to the terminal. Tobius knows what he is looking for and searches each card for the Keepers of Power. The first selections were unfruitful. Then he returns them and grabs the rest. He starts to get very discouraged and enters the last chip. He does like he has with the others and searches for Keepers of Power, and like the others, he gets nothing. Frustrated, he gathers them up, returning them to the shelves.

As the human puts them back, a cloaked humanoid figure approaches him. "Why do you seek power?"

Tobius, surprised by the sudden question, jumps, dropping the remaining chips. "What do you mean?" Tobius asks hesitantly.

The figure responds with the same question, and Tobius considers it for a few brief moments.

He responds firmly, "I want power to get justice for my family."

Without a response, the figure reveals a data chip, offering it to the young man. Tobius pauses for a second then reaches for the chip. The figure turns to leave and says, "Only those worthy of power can find true justice."

Confused, Tobius returns to the terminal, inserting the data chip. On the screen he reads "please enter password." He thinks,

Great, he did not tell me a password. He takes a moment to recall what the figure said and decides to guess. First he tries *justice* and sees "Incorrect! Two more chances." Then he thinks longer about the short conversation. He enters *power*, and the screen flashes green.

"Head outside the city tonight at midnight, continue south, and you shall be met by the Guide." Ejecting the data chip, he hurries to find the hermit. He finds the pelagian surrounded by piles of data chips. Whispering, he says, "Hermi, I think I found what we are looking for."

"Really?" the hermit replies enthusiastically.

He thrusts the data chip forward. "This was given to me by a cloaked figure, and I think they are part of the Keepers of Power."

The hermit quizzically asks, "Who are the Keepers of Power?"

Tobius quickly explains what he found on one of the data pads in the hut. The hermit enters the chip into his reader. Nothing comes up on the screen. Confused, Tobius grabs the hermit's arm, dragging him back to the terminal he used, and still nothing comes up. Defensively, he explains what the figure said, along with the message from the chip.

Hermi sits in a nearby chair, pondering what this could be. After several long heartbeats, he nods. "Okay, Tobius, let's follow this lead, but we must proceed cautiously."

They spend the rest of the afternoon preparing for their midnight venture. Both load some rations in their pack along with survival kits. Hermi tucks two holdout blasters in the folds of his tunic while Tobius secures his grandfather's repeating crossbow and his Razik blades to the sides of his pack. They both get a few hours of sleep, and an hour before midnight, they venture out. The hermit closes and secures the shuttle behind them. They approach the gate and pass through with nothing more than a glance from the guards.

"Where do we go now?" the hermit asks Tobius.

"All it said was to head south and we will be met." Tobius is amazed at the look of Detritus outside the city. He looks intently at the vast change from the within the city to the pure savage-looking jungle just beyond the gate. The main path is illuminated by glow panels every ten meters. This helps keep travelers from accidentally wandering into the jungle or off cliffs. Tobius checks his chrono seventeen minutes before midnight and asks, "How far do you think we have gone?"

The hermit quietly responds, "Probably three kilometers."

The path up ahead narrows along a cliff edge, and just before they reach the cliff, they hear a voice behind them. "Why do you seek power?"

Tobius turns to the voice and replies, "To find true justice."

"Follow me and we shall see if you are worthy." The figure turns, heading down a small hidden footpath.

The human whispers to the hermit, "This looks familiar." They follow the guide for several hours and are now unable to tell where they are. The jungle is dense, and there are so many twists and turns that even if he wanted to leave, he was unsure if he could make it out.

Source of Power

As dawn breaks across the jungle canopy, they come to a small village. It appears to be inhabited by no more than one hundred people. The hermit asks their guide, "Where are we?"

The guide says nothing and passes several small huts. Stopping in front of one of the huts, the guide says, "Wait here until summoned."

Tobius and Hermi do as instructed and observe the people move about in silence. The only sound they could hear was the sounds of the jungle and a small creek trickling nearby. The sun is almost over head when they are called into the hut. The inside is just as plain as the rest of the village, but the chair a cloaked figure is sitting upon is completely out of place. The chair is encrusted in jewels and made from many different expensive metals. The back of the chair appears as though it is a fire trapped within the metal and gems. The arms are designed like two serpents emerging from the flames with a large gem in each mouth. The figure resting on the chair is clad in a dark lavender robe with the hood completely obscuring any features of the individual wearing it. For a long moment, silence rests on the chamber.

"You have come seeking power," the figure suddenly speaks in a deep bass voice. "I am known as the Gatekeeper, and you must prove to me if you are worthy to follow the path." He stands and steps toward the newcomers. "You may never leave unless you can claim the power." Waving his hand, he dismissively says, "Now go to the first hut and learn."

The guide enters and beckons them to follow. They proceed to the first hut and are ushered inside. This building has half a dozen tables with a subnet projector in the middle of each table with four stools by each table. The guide instructs them to sit and wait. They place their packs along the wall and sit at the table closest to the door. The projectors glow a light blue, which is the only light in the building. Tobius wonders if this is a test of patience, and if it is, he wonders how long they will wait. Both of the new arrivals wait quietly, and after a while, a few more people are brought in and told to sit. Several hours later, every stool is occupied. From the opposite side of the room from the entrance appears another figure clad in a long ruby red robe, but she had the hood off, letting her long silver hair flow down to her belt. Until now, they are unsure what species are here.

In a soft voice, she greets the room. "Hello. I am the Mistress of Knowledge, and I shall teach you of the power sought." She moves among the tables as she continues speaking. "You shall come here every day until you can explain the meaning of power and recite the creed of the Keepers of Power." With that said, she exits the hut, and the projectors start humming.

For the remainder of the day, they sit in the hut, learning the meanings of power. Without warning, the projectors shut off, and the guide appears.

"It is time for the evening meal, and then we will get you settled for the night."

Gathering their packs, they file out of the hut, and it is only then that Tobius realizes how long they were in the hut. It is completely dark except for the two fires burning in the village. They are led to the closest fire where everyone is given a plate with some meat and cooked local vegetation. Tobius sits at the table and eats without much concern for the taste. Once everyone is finished eating, the guide leads them to an area just outside the circle of huts to a small raised hill. The guide explains that until they prove they are worthy of being seekers of power, they will sleep here.

Tobius is roused from his slumber by the morning rays. Looking around, he sees that everyone is still sleeping. Standing, he decides to stretch his legs and begins to wander around the local jungle. He remembers the dream he had about a path within the wall and

KEEPERS OF POWER

decides to try and find it. But before he gets much time to search, he hears the guide waking the others. He jogs back to the group and sees the hermit's look of shock and follows his gaze. There, where one of the other people slept, now rests a charred corpse.

The guide explains, "Those who are unworthy of power shall perish. Now follow me for the morning meal."

The young human sees that they are serving the same food for breakfast. He eats the tasteless food with little satisfaction, and afterward, they are led back into the classroom, the two agreed to call it. The Mistress of Knowledge is standing among the desks as they shuffle in.

"As you are now aware, the price for those seeking power and are not worthy is death." She gestures to the desks. "Please sit where you did yesterday. These tables are now set to each of you at a specific seat, and your learning is specific for you."

Tobius sits on his stool and looks at the projector. He sees images but only hears sounds in his mind. A mysterious voice starts his lecture.

"Power. Most species refer to power as a form of energy needed to complete a task. Here, power is not an item for our use, but it is something we seek." Tobius sees a robed figure standing like a professor. "No matter what species we are, we all seek this power. It is a primal instinct. Some seek the power for knowledge, others for use of wealth, and a small few seek it for justice." Tobius listens with ravenous hunger. "For those who seek power in knowledge, they strive to learn everything the power offers and enjoy sharing this power. Using power for wealth can be noble but does have chance for failure. Power is not to be kept but shared. There must be a master of power to ensure the power is shared. If you seek the power for that of personal gain, you will be consumed." The instructor shows two symbols. "The one on my left is the glyph for the power of knowledge." The symbol is a pyramid with a circle within, intersected by two lines. The left line starts on the inside top of the circle and heads down and away until it meets the base of the triangle. The right line starts at the bottom of the circle and proceeds up and meets the right side of the triangle. "The glyph on my right is that for power of wealth." This symbol is an oval with three lines that never intersect. The first line is from the right middle to the left side near the bottom; the second is left middle to the right side, almost at the top with a vertical line between the first two.

The two symbols disappear and are replaced with a third glyph. The instructor continues, "This is the glyph for the power of justice. This is the most revered and feared power. Many in the past have sought the power of justice, but anyone searching for this power must respect it." Tobius stares at the glyph. The subnet explains this glyph in detail. "I sense this is the power you seek, and I shall explain the meaning of this. It starts with a hexagon. This represents the ability of justice to stand up to forces from any direction with ease. From all six corners emanates a line that curves clockwise until they meet in the center. This shows the unwavering balance that justice must maintain."

Tobius recalls that in his dream, he saw a crimson hexagon floating in air. He asks the instructor, "Why is this power so dangerous?"

"Unless you can maintain the balance needed to enforce true justice, your ideals become corrupt, and the power consumes you." The instructor continues, "Those who have failed to keep the balance not only have themselves destroyed but will destroy everyone the power affects."

Tobius thinks about what was just said. Sensing the student is considering what was just said, it waits. He leans forward to study the glyph. For some time, the human tries to comprehend how justice can be so difficult to balance. Just when he settles to continue the lesson, the guide comes in to escort them to the evening meal. The young human is again shocked with how long he was learning about the forms of power. He still ponders on what he learned today as he eats. Tobius enjoys what he is learning but does not like how there is no time to talk with the hermit or to practice his fighting skills. Once they finish, they are again escorted to the sleeping area. Tobius tries to talk with Hermi about what he found out today, but the pelagian is already fast asleep. Tobius, on the other hand, has trouble finding refuge in sleep. His mind is still racing about what he learned.

Tobius suffers through the night with phantoms and the recurring crimson hexagon burning into his mind. He is slow to rise when the guide arrives. This morning, everyone makes it through the night. As they finish breakfast, they are again escorted to the classroom. But as they approach, the Mistress is standing outside the hut.

"Everyone, please enter and take your seats and begin your lessons. Through the day, your lesson will pause, and it will ask you to come outside. Learn well."

Tobius quickly tosses his pack down and is ready to learn more about the power of justice. The projector hums to life once again, but to his dismay, it is not what he wanted. A female voice drifts into his mind.

"Today, you will learn the creed." Tobius knows he must learn it but is disinterested. "Keepers search for power. Power is for all and must be shared. Power kept to one's self will corrupt. Keepers strive to become masters of power." Tobius thinks, *I do not care about the creed. I just want to learn about the power of justice.*

The instructor scolds him. "If you do not learn the creed, you will not be worthy of any power."

He cringes from the intense pain that he feels from the reprimand. He puts what he wants aside and focuses on the creed.

The day moves on, and one by one, they are called from the hut for a few minutes then return. The hermit stands and heads out of the room. Tobius watches with interest but does not neglect his studies. A few minutes later, he walks back in, collects his pack, and follows the Mistress to the front of the room. Tobius wants to ask what is going on but knows he cannot, and all he can do is watch his friend disappear into the darkness. He hears the instructor say, "Please proceed outside."

Tobius stands, stretching his back, then heads outside. He expected to see a guide or even the Mistress of Knowledge, but who he sees shocks him beyond words.

Before him, over two meters tall, stands the Gatekeeper. In his deep bass voice, he states, "Follow me." Without waiting for a response, he turns and strides away from the village. Tobius has to jog to keep pace with the male's immense stride. Suddenly, the man turns and thrusts his hand out. If not for his quick reflexes, Tobius would have had the air knocked from his lungs and probably some cracked ribs.

He rolls into a backward somersault, springs to his feet, and shouts, "What is this about?"

The man stands. "You seek the power of justice. You are only the second person in over six decades to seek it. I must test you to ensure you will not fail." With that, he attacks Tobius with full force.

Unsure how to handle this, Tobius settles for a defensive stance. His opponent constantly assaults him with punches and kicks for several seconds, unable to land a successful hit. Tobius blocks a left jab with his right forearm then brings his arm down in a counter-clockwise sweep to block a right punch and spins behind his attacker.

The large man spins around, opening the space between them to four meters. He stands and lowers his arms. "Why did you not attack?" Tobius stands, not letting down his guard.

"I was not in any danger, but if you would have become a threat, I would have had no choice but to stop you." Relaxing slightly, he looks at the hooded man. "What was the real purpose for this?"

"Many people have come looking for justice, but it is nothing but a self-justified need for revenge." The Gatekeeper starts walking back to the village. "I tested them the same way I just tested you, and every single one attacked at the first sign of conflict." Nodding, the young human follows him back. Upon reaching the classroom, the Gatekeeper nods. "You have earned the right to continue learning of justice. May you become a master." He enters the room and sees the hermit once again sitting, studying at the terminal.

He returns to his stool and looks into the projector. To his pleasure, he sees the instructor from the other day. "I was informed that you received the right to learn more about justice." Tobius nods as the instructor begins. "Justice is the most powerful source of power. With it, we impact the lives of every being we come in contact with." The subnet takes a solemn stance. "Most people use the term *justice* for misguided revenge." Pacing, the instructor says, "Justice is the hardest power to control since it is easy to let personal feelings and views sway the true lines. In order to master the power of justice, you must be able to let go of how you feel or think things should be and look at the entire situation as it is."

Tobius considers what was said very carefully. And then he looks and asks, "What do you call this true justice?"

The instructor laughs. "There is no name for true justice, but the Keepers refer to it as Judicium."

The day continues with the subnet educating the newest seeker of justice with understanding of the gravity of the power he seeks.

That evening, they have the same dinner, but after that, there is a select few including, Tobius and Hermi, that are led to a hut and not the hill. The guide explains that since they now have a focus, they are now initiates and thus allowed to live within the village. Now that they have been allowed into the village, they will not return to the outsiders' classroom.

Tobius asks the guide, "So where will we go tomorrow?"

Looking at the human, he replies, "Tomorrow you will be given the initiates' robes."

The guide exits the hut. Looking at the pelagian, he asks, "What do you think they mean by that?"

The hermit shrugs but asks, "What focus are you, Tobius?"

"I am a seeker of justice," he says quietly. "What happened when you left with the Mistress?"

His companion just sits on his bunk for a while then replies, "The same thing that happened when you were with the Gatekeeper." Smiling, he looks at the grandson of his late friends. "I am a seeker of knowledge."

Tobius laughed. "Well, that's not a surprise. I am sure you are looking forward to it."

Nodding, the hermit replies, "Of course, I get to study with the Mistress herself."

That night, they sleep well, knowing they are one step closer to finding out why Tobius's family was killed, but Tobius still dreams of the crimson hexagon. Morning comes, and a different guide comes to gather the newest initiates, standing in the doorway. A female voice emanates from the hood.

"Good morning, initiates. Welcome to the first true day of being a seeker of power." She steps into the hut and lets her hood fall back. Tobius is stunned by the new guide. She stands just over a meter and a half. Her dark brown hair falls in curls just past the shoulders. Her dark hazel eyes are like none that Tobius has ever seen before. She moves to each person, shakes their hand, and asks their focus. There are eight initiates in the room, not including the human and pelagian. There is a pretty even split for the knowledge and wealth seekers. She steps to Tobius and freezes. For several intense heartbeats, her hazel eyes are locked with his dark blue gaze. After another second, Tobius bows a greeting to allow him to breathe.

"I am Tobius, a seeker of justice."

He hears a gasp escape the female standing before him. She bows in return and softly says, "Melissa, a seeker of knowledge." She moves on to the pelagian and greets him. Then she turns to the group. "I am a seeker of knowledge. Please follow me."

They are led by the female guide around the village. She identifies the other huts that they had not been allowed to enter. The three huts past the outsiders' classroom entering the village are the knowledge and wealth seekers' huts, along with what she calls the runic room. Then she points to the robe weaver's and physical training huts, which are just before the Gatekeeper's tent. Finally, she points out the kitchen hut.

"Every initiate will work in the robe weaver's hut and kitchen at some point," she says. She leads them to the robe hut.

A small robed figure emerges from the hut. "Please enter one at a time, and we will measure you for your robe." The day progresses slow as they take one person at a time.

Tobius is the last to enter the hut to get measured for his robe. Once he gets finished, he turns to leave but hears a deep bass voice. "Initiate, please wait."

Entering from the back of the hut is not only the Gatekeeper but the Mistress as well. Tobius turns and nods as a way of greeting. The Mistress steps close, looking him over. She returns to the Gatekeeper's side, and they whisper to each other for a few moments. The Gatekeeper summons the robe weaver and gestures to Tobius.

The robe weaver again measures the young human and returns to the pair. The weaver leaves when dismissed with a wave of the hand.

Tobius looks at them both and inquires, "What was that about, may I ask?"

The Mistress steps to the human and places both hands on his shoulders. "The robes are designed to represent the weight of the power we search for. Since we very rarely get seekers of justice, the weaver meets with us both to ensure that the robe is designed correctly for each initiate."

Tobius leaves the hut and finds no one waiting for him. He scans the village to see if he can find out where the other initiates were taken, but he does not find a single person. He decides to explore the local area, and he is amazed by the jungle trees, over five meters in diameter. Small creatures scurry around the brush as he wanders around and sits by the creek and just listens to the local sounds. The longer he sits near the creek, the more he feels like something is reaching out to him. At first, he shies away from the feeling, but he senses that it feels somehow familiar. He stands and allows his body follow the echo. He wanders through the creek and between trees, and he feels like he is seeing as though through a haze. With sudden realization, he sees where he is standing, and it is none other than the spot where the person was found charred. Shocked, he has no idea why he was drawn to this place. Kneeling down, he examines the area. Confused, he sees a small glassy spot on the ground in a shape like the glyph justice. He studies it for some time, trying to figure out why this is here. It appears as if this glyph is the reason the person died. Was it possible that he was just unlucky and had lain on this glyph, or was it because they were unworthy of power?

Tobius remains kneeling for some time and is startled from his pondering by a hand on his shoulder. Turning, he sees Melissa standing behind him.

"What are you doing here?" she asks quietly.

Tobius explains that when he emerged from the tent, he saw no one and decided to get familiar with the local area and wound up here. Tobius stands and points. "Do you see that?"

She looks down at the ground. "Look at what?"

He says, looking back down, "The glyph…it was just there."

She shakes her head and turns. "It is time for the evening meal, initiate."

* * *

Craven enters the bridge on Vorex's Might. Admiral Kato is looking out at the vast star field, absentmindedly scanning reports.

"Admiral, the hermit has stopped on Detritus Prime."

"What makes you think he has it?" asks the admiral pessimistically.

"Just a gut instinct," replies Craven.

"Captain Rumick, take my apprentice and accompany Craven." The captain bows and exits. The admiral rises, saying, "Craven." He starts walking to the front of the bridge. Turning, he continues, "You are the best bounty hunter I have ever worked with, but this is now twice you have failed to retrieve what I asked." He raises his left arm, gauntlet glowing crimson, lifting the bounty hunter a meter and a half off the deck. "If you fail me again, I will kill you." Kato opens his right hand, and a lance of violet lightning slams into Craven's chest. Craven flies across the bridge and lands with a crash.

He clutches his chest and snaps, "I understand." He stands and leaves the bridge, still twitching from the lightning.

He curses the admiral and walks down the hall to the lifts. "Like I really need to have his lackey and pet follow me to get this stupid relic," he says, speaking to no one. Exiting the lift, he strides to his ship, the Phantom's Blade. The Phantom's Blade is a modified armored support transport, Pacifier class, shuttle. He appreciates his ship that he has slowly been perfecting the performance of it over the years. The Pacifier typically comes with two antimatter missile launchers and three pulsar cannons. Craven prefers to catch his targets and swapped one launcher for an ion stasis missile bank. Also, he changed the top rear laser to a double-barreled manual or automated defense turret. The Phantom's Blade is a dark sage but has emitters along the vertical axis to provide additional camouflage. His enjoyment quickly turns to rage when he sees Captain Rumick and a robed zyback.

Nearing his ship, he keys the security code on his gauntlet, lowering the boarding ramp. The zyback nods as he approaches. "I am Apprentice De' Ron."

Craven nods as he ascends the ramp. "Let's go." Normally, he would remove his armor, but since he has two unwelcome visitors, he decides to stay in his gear. He quickly runs through the startup and lifts off. The bounty hunter takes some enjoyment hearing the captain scramble for his seat as he accelerates.

Curse of Justice

Once they receive their initiate robes, the newest members spend two weeks learning the Runic Rules. Every day after the morning meal, they are taught and tested to ensure they understand how to control the flow. Rule one, the power of the flow is borrowed. Rule two, you must be strong enough in mind and body to handle the flow. Rule three, you cannot stop the flow. Rule four, the flow responds to the will of the seeker. There are twenty runes within the runic language of the Keepers. These must be inscribed on inanimate items, and the optimal number of runes per item is three. These runes are basic ideas that are influenced by the one summoning the flow. Once an item is inscribed with a rune, it cannot be removed. One can summon the flow through the item if it is intact. Once the item is damaged, the abilities used through that item will cease. The flow will respond to the runes on the item as well as the thoughts of the summoner.

Three weeks since receiving his robe, Tobius still feels like an outsider within the Keepers. They react to him as if he were a mythical beast. After learning about the runes, he now spends his time learning from the Gatekeeper, Mistress, and time to learn on his own. He keeps trying to learn why everyone acts as though he will destroy them, but no matter who he asks, he gets nothing except that it happened before. Tobius is determined to get to the bottom of this and seeks out the Mistress.

Bowing, he asks, "Mistress, why am I looked at as though I am a source of evil?"

The Mistress enters the hut and announces, "Seekers and initiates of knowledge, please assist the kitchen and weaver." Quietly, everyone rises and exits the hut. She says, pouring an herbal tea, "Please sit down, initiate." She hands a goblet to Tobius as she sits down. "It was over one thousand years ago. There was another seeker of justice. The Gatekeeper tested him, like you were. And like you, he passed." She took a moment to take a sip of tea. "He was allowed to learn from the leaders of the village, and like you, he was inquisitive and eager. He became a seeker, and as such was allowed to travel outside the village." She took another sip of her tea, set it down, and took on a very sober expression. "He was gone for several months, and everyone thought he had perished in the jungle, but a rainy day, he returned. He, without warning, attacked the village. Killing almost everyone, he then fled, and rumor has it, he created a perversion of the Keepers."

Tobius, mesmerized by the tale, asks, "How could he kill most of the village? What did he use?"

She took several sips of tea before answering his questions. "He used the flow, but rumor was it was such a dark force that it has been referred to as the void. It was said that he was able to control the power without the use of the runes. We believe that it was a local cave where he found this power, and it corrupted his being." Before he could ask where the place was, she raises her hand, stalling any question. "We have sent dozens of initiates and seekers to try and locate this place, but it was never found, and not all returned. I believe there is a reason to this." She sets her tea aside. "Tobius." He was caught off guard by the use of his name. He almost misses what she said next. "You must be very careful. I think this place lies several kilometers along the base of the cliff."

The young human nods. "May I seek this place?"

The Mistress stands, grasping his shoulders. "Please do. But take an initiate of knowledge with you."

Tobius leaves the hut and hurries to find the hermit. He finds him in the kitchen, grabs him by the arm, and drags him from the hut. "Come on, Hermi. We have a mission," he says, pulling the pelagian behind him. "I have an idea about the vision I had before we got here."

The hermit shakes his arm free. "What do you mean, Tobius?"

Quickly, he reveals what the Mistress had told him. They both pack and get ready to set out on their mission.

After Tobius leaves, the Mistress steps outside the hut and summons a nearby initiate. "Please find my protégé and bring her to the Gatekeeper's hut." The initiate nods and runs off. She quickly heads to discuss this with the Gatekeeper. She enters his hut and gives a slight curtsy as way of greeting. "Greg," she says, rushed.

"Yes, Malinda," he replies, standing to meet her.

"I have informed the initiate of justice about the tragedy." The Gatekeeper nods as she continues. "I told him to take an initiate of knowledge, and I am certain he took the pelagian with him."

Pacing, he asks, "What will we do if the same thing happens?"

She grabs his hand to stop his pacing. "I have summoned my protégé, and I will ask her to follow them."

He nods, pulling her in for a kiss. "Very well, my love."

An instant later, the protégé enters. "You summoned me, Mistress?"

She nods. "Yes, Melissa." She hands her a bracelet and turns to stand by the Gatekeeper. "We have a mission we need you to complete."

The Gatekeeper steps forward. "Follow the initiate of justice and report back if he perishes or becomes corrupt."

Nodding, Melissa responds, "As you wish. And may you become masters of power." She exits the hut and rushes to gather her pack.

It is midafternoon as they leave the village. They did not have a guide, but Tobius has an idea of where he is heading. They head away from the village, taking the path they came in on. They follow a faint trail, but Tobius watches the cliff wall to their left. As the jungle thins, he looks around carefully and spots the main trail they took away from the city. Stopping ten meters before they reach the trail, he takes a moment to carefully survey the surroundings.

The hermit sees the young man looking and asks, "What are you looking for?"

Tobius looks a little more as if he did not hear the question and suddenly thrusts a finger out. "There. That's it." Confused, the hermit looks in the direction his friend pointed. For several heartbeats, he sees nothing, but then he realizes that there is a path. It looks as though the path is protected by a shield. Moving across from the path entrance, they take refuge behind a plant to ensure that no one can see them. They sprint across the road and into the hidden path.

Melissa had gathered her pack just in time to see the duo head away from the village. She looks at the bracelet she was given and sees the runes of deflection, vision, and conjure and is confused on why she was given it as she slips it on her left wrist. She knew why she was selected. Through her training, she had excelled at hiding her presence and remaining unseen when she wanted to. She had to use these instinctual skills from a young age.

Melissa never knew who her parents were because she was raised in a local orphanage. She was moving through the market one morning, looking for something to eat. Moving close to a fruit vendor, she waits for a moment to take some fruit. Watching, she sees a woman in a black robe move to the vendor. She slowly moves up behind the woman and reaches for the fruit, but right when she can almost reach it, the woman turns, grabbing her wrist.

"What are you doing, young one?"

Melissa looks up at the woman, terrified.

The woman purchases the fruit then looks at the young girl. "Come sit on the bench with me, and I will share the fruit." Sitting down, she offers the fruit to the child. Melissa hesitantly takes the fruit and sits on the farthest part of the bench. The woman watches her eat the fruit with a ravenous hunger then asks, "Where is your family?"

The child stops eating long enough to shake her head and shrugs.

The woman waits a few moments then asks, "Do you not have a home?"

Again, the child responds with a shake of her head.

"How would you like to come live with me?"

Melissa looks at the woman, shocked. Forgetting about the fruit, she timidly asks, "Really?" The woman nods with a smile, and from that day on, Melissa strived every day to repay that debt to the Mistress.

She keeps about a twenty-meter gap between her and the two initiates. Following them is easier than she thought. She watches them look around and wonders if they are unsure where to go. Without warning, they sprint across the road, and she loses sight of them after they pass about five meters on the opposite side. She, too, waits for a few seconds to see if anyone is around and follows. She moves to the area where she lost them and cautiously moves forward. She steps past the point where they vanished and could again see her queries. She dives behind a tree, not realizing that they stopped just a few meters behind the veil. On the tree, she finds two faintly glowing icons, one of protect and the other of vision.

"Why would someone put these on a tree?" she says quietly as she watches the duo.

Tobius and Hermi sprint the dozen meters or so from where they hid and pass through to the hidden trail. Tobius stops due to gut feeling. "What's wrong?" asks the hermit.

Quietly, the human says, "We are being followed."

They wait for several seconds. They hear something approaching quickly and suddenly move to the side behind a tree. "Let's keep moving for now."

Nodding, the pelagian follows close behind. The human moves slowly, following the overgrown trail, but he somehow knows that he is heading in the right direction. The trail keeps turning and bending through the jungle and down a slope. Several hours later, as twilight approaches, they come to a canyon bottom.

"Which way, Tobius?" the hermit asks.

"Now we find out who our tail is." Tobius nods. "I'll hide there, and you hide behind that rock."

Hermi nods and replies, "We better use these." He pulls out two leather bands. Tobius looks at him, confused, and he inscribes some runes on each of them. He hands one to the human and heads to his place. Tobius moves to his spot as he straps the leather band on his wrist and looks at the inscription. The only one he recognizes is protection, but the others he is unsure. Tobius feels the power flow through the band and is surprised at how small the energy is used by the band.

Melissa struggles to keep an eye on them through the dense jungle. As dusk nears, she starts to curse the jungle. From behind a tree, she sees the canyon bottom just ahead and starts to worry as she can no longer see the duo. Rushing, she jogs the remainder of the trail out on to the rock and sand ground. Quickly, she tries to find footprints, but it is too dark. Trusting her instincts, she heads left deeper into the canyon. She screams as suddenly, her foot catches something, causing her to fall. She curses and starts to get up and is tackled back to the ground. Now realizing that she is in danger, she starts fighting back. She elbows her assailant in the stomach with a thud, knocking the breath from him. Her attacker still manages to trap her left arm behind her back. She calls on the flow to throw him off, but somehow, he is able to redirect the flow and use it to pin her to the ground.

"Okay, I give up," she says angrily.

Feeling her attacker stand, she hears, "Melissa?"

She rolls onto her back and looks up. "How did you know it was me?"

The young man replies, "I knew you were following us since before we crossed the road. That is why I stopped just inside the veil." She stands and silently curses her lack of caution. Tobius helps her off the ground.

"Why are you following us?" the hermit asks, walking from behind the rock. She quickly explains what was asked of her. Tobius takes several moments to consider what they just heard.

"They think that I will do the same thing that happened hundreds of years ago?"

The pelagian interjects, "You can't blame them. Last time they had a seeker of justice, they were almost wiped out."

Shocked, Tobius looks at him. "How do you know about that?"

Laughing, the hermit says, "When you told me what your focus was, I did my own research."

The human looks around. "So now what?"

"What do you mean?" Melissa asks.

Shaking his head, the hermit says, "It's obvious. We continue on. We are on a mission to find this place, and she is here to observe." The other two nod. "But," the pelagian says, "let's camp here tonight."

They set up camp, eat some rations, and go to sleep.

Unbeknownst to the trio, as they sleep, a greater threat lands.

* * *

Craven brings the Phantom's Blade into land and completes the shutdown sequence. He looks at his two unwanted guests. "Captain, how do you want to handle this?" he says in a mocking tone.

Either ignoring or ignorant of the tone, Rumick eagerly assumes control. "First, let's speak with the security check-in station and see if they know where he may be." De' Ron nods his agreement.

Craven rolls his eyes behind his visor at the stupidity of their plan. "Yes, let's just walk up to security and ask them where someone we may have to kill is."

They move through the check-in station, thankful the guard does not give Rumick the time to ask.

Craven says, "Where do you think a collector would go?"

The apprentice shrugs as they leave the checkpoint. They head to the market, looking for the rare collectors, but most are closed for the night. Rumick says, "We won't find anyone out here right now. Let's go check the cantina." The others nod in agreement.

Craven, Rumick, and De' Ron spend several hours at the cantina trying to get any information about their target, but the only slight lead is an inebriated Ebrat. Craven's helmet translator helps him figure out that the hermit was noticed in the historical library about three months ago. Craven finds out where the library is and meets with the other two to call it a night. They bunk at the local inn because Craven refuses to sleep in the same room as them. The following morning, they head to the library to track down their query.

* * *

The trio rise with the first rays of sun. Quickly, they pack up and head deeper into the canyon. They move slowly, letting Tobius set the pace. In no time, they pass under the main road a half kilometer above. As if passing through a curtain, the air beyond feels thick and full of malice.

The pelagian places his hand on Tobius's shoulder. "Tobius, be very careful here."

Tobius nods as they move even more cautiously. The sun is almost directly overhead, but the farther they proceed into the canyon, the darker it gets. Violet lances of energy start randomly appearing as if tentacles from a bane creeper. They follow the flow of the canyon, and the walls are well over a kilometer tall with no end in sight.

They travel over five kilometers along the canyon floor when Tobius suddenly stops. He begins to look around as though he lost something.

"What is wrong?" Melissa asks softly.

Tobius replies distractedly, "We are almost there, and we have to hurry." The canyon is almost three quarters a kilometer wide, and he sprints to the right wall.

The hermit says as he follows him, "There is nothing there." The human ignores him and reaches the wall. He runs his hands over the stone wall as if looking for a switch. "What are you looking for, Tobius?"

Tobius frantically snaps, "I need a stone shaped like a hexagon to place here."

Melissa begins to look for one, and the pelagian wonders as he reaches into his pack. "Tobius, hang on." Frustrated, the human turns and looks at his friend.

Slowly, Hermi uncovers the relic that was given to him over thirty years ago.

"Tobius, this is what your grandmother found on this planet."

Tobius gingerly grabs the obsidian stone. He rolls it between his fingers until he finds a symbol. He points at it and asks, "Hermi, what is this symbol?"

The pelagian steps closer to look at the symbol his young friend is pointing to. With startling realization, he says, "That is Sanguis. Now it makes sense."

Tobius and Melissa look at him, confused. Tobius shows her the symbol too. She says, "It looks similar to the glyph of justice."

"What do you mean it makes sense now?" Tobius asks.

"The inscriptions on this say that 'those worthy to possess power, this is the key for the gate.'"

Tobius takes the stone and walks up to the wall, placing it against the wall. Tobius tries to force the stone in, but it does not move. He takes a deep breath, letting his instincts take over. He clears his mind.

Relaxing his mind, Tobius suddenly feels enormous power flowing through his body and into the stone. The obsidian diamond slowly slides into the wall, as if it is being absorbed. The young human just flows within the power. Suddenly, he finds himself standing in front of the figure from his dream. But instead of the crimson hexagon, he sees the glowing red-hot symbol of Sanguis.

A voice emanates from the figure. "You have proven yourself worthy of my power. I am Sanguis."

Tobius looks at the figure, confused, and asks, "Who are you?"

The figure's eyes flare. "I am the true power in the galaxy. I am the current of the flow, and I will destroy all who are unworthy of power."

The human considers what was just said. "Why does that symbol look like the glyph of justice?"

The violet eyes of the figure change to red, and its voice fills with rage. "How dare you compare me to those pathetic, unworthy creatures!"

Tobius takes a breath then asks, "How are they unworthy?"

The figure appears to calm slightly. "They say you can only search for one power and say that power must be shared." Tobius continues to listen. "When one seeks power, he seeks it all."

Tobius asks the figure, "How should it work then?"

The figure appears to grow larger. "A small number of masters and a select group of apprentices strive for the power." Pointing, the figure booms, "You have proven yourself worthy of my teachings. Leave these pathetic beings and head to Vorex."

Tobius bows slightly, and the figure vanishes. Tobius opens his eyes to see Hermi and Melissa standing over him.

"Are you okay?" they ask.

Melissa helps him up as the hermit explains, "You were holding the stone against the wall, and you suddenly collapsed. You have been laying there for over two hours."

Rubbing his head, he starts to explain what he saw as they head back through the canyon. "We have to go to Vorex."

* * *

Rumick inquires in the library about the hermit, and all he was able to get was that he was looking for something. De' Ron moves through the library, feeling for ripples in the void. He makes his way to a secluded terminal. As he looks around, he senses two distinct presences' echoes. He can sense that one is older, and one much younger and stronger. He heads back to the captain to explain what he had discovered. He sees them still up at the front of the library.

"Captain Rumick, Craven, I have a lead."

"What do you mean?" Rumick says, turning around.

"I felt ripples in the void and believe I found our target."

Craven snaps, "Where did he go?"

De' Ron replies quickly, "They left the city."

Rumick inquires, "They?"

"Yes," the apprentice replies. "One has lived here for many years, but the other only has an echo lasting a few months."

Rumick says commandingly, "All right, De' Ron, let's follow the path."

They head outside the city and follow the trail. As they are jogging along the trail, De' Ron says, "There are several powerful void walkers nearby along with the one you seek."

Rumick pulls out his pistol, checking its charge. "Get ready for a fight." They come to the hidden path, and the zyback heads left into the jungle. After several minutes, a village is in sight. Standing at the entrance to the village is a tall robed figure with a dozen others behind him.

"You are not welcome here!" he bellows.

The captain steps forward in response. "We are searching for a hermit from Marina."

The robed man responds, "There is no hermit here. We are the Keepers of Power."

Rumick raises his blaster and again asks, "Hand him over and no one gets hurt."

Without any response, the man simply raises his right-hand gauntlet, glowing dark blue, and summons the flow, and sends the captain flying back from an invisible blast. De' Ron sensed the gathering of energy and uses his own skills to soften the blow for the captain. And with this, the dozen behind the robed male storm forward. Craven smiles inside his helmet, raising his own pistol and joins the fight. He fires a pulse at the closest ensuing enemy but misses. Again, he fires, and still another misses. Lifting his left arm, Craven fires a stun bolt, but that also misses. Quickly holstering his blaster, he grabs his ferioblade from his back. The enemy armaments consisted of archaic swords, but they are still dangerous weapons.

De' Ron does not rush in like his counterparts. He watches as Craven's shots miss wide and senses why. The attackers are not the only ones here. For everyone attacking, there are at least two more waiting and protecting their friends. Rumick finally recovers and charges headlong at the leader of the group. He fires his weapon, enraged at the disrespect, but his shots strike nothing but air. Craven laughs when he sees Rumick run through by the large sword the leader wields. Effortlessly, he parries a thrust from the enemy on his left and uses his enemy's momentum to run him into his ally, sending both to the ground. Taking advantage of the slight distraction, he cuts down a young crytan and turns to survey the fray. De' Ron takes a step back, letting his cloak fall from his shoulder. He lets his rage fill him and brings his bloodlust to a boil. He summons his weapon to his hand and ignites both scarlet blades. The energy blades are eighty centimeters long, and the ends erupt into eight five-centimeter spikes perpendicular to the blade. He takes a moment to listen to the hum of his blades and hears their cries for blood. Leaping into the fray, he feeds off the shock as the enemy realizes their weapons cannot stop his blades. In a single sweep of his double blades, he slices two in half and severs the left arm at the shoulder of a third.

The Gatekeeper's Sacrifice

Tobius, Melissa, and the hermit come running across the path, and Tobius grabs his forehead. He staggers slightly. "Something is wrong. We have to hurry."

They double their pace to an all-out sprint, and as they approach the village, they hear screaming and clash of metal. The closer Tobius gets to the village, the more empowered he feels. Slowly, Tobius starts gaining ground from his friends as he feels his power growing. By the time he is close enough to see the village, he is a dozen meters ahead of his friends. He sees half a dozen Keepers dead and more severely wounded, and he also notices that there is one man in a uniform dead as well. He slides to a stop as he sees an almost two-meter-tall zyback wielding a double-bladed void blade, and he appears to cut down every opponent who crosses his path. Suddenly, the Gatekeeper confronts this seemingly invincible enemy. Tobius watches in fascination as the sword stops the void blade without even a spray of sparks. The enemy is shocked at the sudden stop of his blade and spins away to gain some space.

His enemy spins away and growls. "How did you stop my blades with that ancient weapon?"

The Gatekeeper laughs then snaps, "You come to my home and demand me to give up a friend. Then you start killing my family, and now you want to know what my weapon is?" He resecures his grip on his weapon—the glyphs of power, protect, and deflect glowing blue in the heart of the blade—and begins to circle his enemy. With almost lightning speed, he swings his blade in at the head of his enemy. His blade is blocked with ease, and he has to spin his blade down to his left to stop the counterthrust. Pushing the blade back, he follows with a sweeping kick, but his well-trained opponent deftly backflips over the kick. Hoping to catch him off guard, he completes his spin and follows through with a thrust, but he feels the blade hit the enemy's. Quickly, he thrusts his left hand out, knocking his opponent off-balance with aid of the flow. The Gatekeeper takes the moment to regain his composure. This time, it's his enemy that begins the assault, and never in his life had he been confronted with such a ferocious opponent.

The hermit and Melissa catch up with Tobius and are riveted by what they see. Tobius is a broiling pool of emotions.

"Tobius, what should we do?"

The young human just stands there, transfixed with the fight before him. With a voice full of conviction, he says, "Go help the others against that one." He points to the bounty hunter in the green armor.

Melissa steps close to Tobius. "What will you do?"

Without looking from the fight, he says, "I must see how that fight ends."

Softly, she says, "Okay, but please don't die."

Without waiting for a response, she heads with the hermit to the smaller fight. Tobius watches as they both would attack and counter-attack in a deadly dance. Slowly, he steps forward as he watches the fight. After about another five minutes, Tobius has a realization that the Gatekeeper will not survive this encounter.

The Gatekeeper disengages from his opponent once again. Taking a deep steadying breath, he looks around and is shocked to see none other than Tobius, the seeker of justice. He also sees Melissa and the hermit heading to help against the other enemy. He looks back to his target and suddenly senses Tobius's enormous power. He recalls what every Gatekeeper passed on to their predecessor.

"Seekers of justice will have enormous power, but the one that nearly destroyed us was full of palpable rage. A true Master of Justice will emanate power pure and light."

Closing his eyes, he takes a moment to let the flow rejuvenate him. He can see in his mind's eye the crimson and black cloud surrounding his enemy and can feel the pure light coming from his young ally. He looks at the zyback and smiles. "You will fall here." With that, he charges at him, knowing that he will not survive.

The young human sees the Gatekeeper smile and say something to his enemy and suddenly charge. Tobius can do nothing but watch. The man brings his blade in a quick downward slash. Anticipating his enemy's block, he kicks out into his opponent's chest. The zyback staggers two meters back from the unexpected blow.

Scowling, the zyback yells, "You will die here!"

Tobius sees the Gatekeeper smile and settle in for a final bout. The zyback steps forward, spinning his two-meter-long weapon between his hands. The two competitors fight even more intensely than they have before. They move almost quicker than Tobius can follow. The zyback and Gatekeeper trade slashes, blocks, thrusts, faints, and kicks. The Gatekeeper sees a small opening and takes his chance. He brings his blade around from his lower left up to meet the zyback midthigh, and as his enemy positions his blade to block his attack, he grabs the middle of the handle of the void blade with his right hand. The zyback yells in shock as his attacker brings his blade down next to his hand cleaving the weapon in two. Silently, the Gatekeeper curses as he realizes that he did not destroy the weapon. Sparks fly from the left end of the hilt as the blade shatters a crystal within. Enraged, the zyback blasts his enemy with violet forks of lightning and runs him through to the hilt in the center of the man's chest. The Gatekeeper convulses with the blast of electricity suddenly coursing through his body and feels a punch in his chest and smell of singed flesh and cloth.

Tobius watches in complete horror as the Gatekeeper is run through with the blade. Before he realizes, he is racing forward with the power of justice propelling him at insane speeds. He crashes into the person responsible for his friend's death, and they both sprawl into the brush. The zyback grunts in surprise at the force behind the hit. Tossing the young human off, he realizes that this boy is the stronger presence he sensed. As he is starting to rise, he is slammed in the back with a massive blast of energy. He even tries to slow his tumble with the void, but the only thing that stops him is when he crashes into the side of a hut. Hitting the wall with such force, he hears a few ribs snap. Grimacing, he stands and lets the pain fuel his hatred even more. He unleashes lightning at his young enemy, but the young human hurls a dead branch to intercept the violet energy. Tobius is unsure on how he manages to compete with his enemy but does not question it. The zyback summons his weapon to his hand and races the thirty meters to meet his opponent. Tobius summons his fallen friend's weapon to his outstretched hand and is shocked at the weight. He is barely able to raise the blade to block the over handed strike from his enemy, and the force of the blow drops him to one knee. Tobius rolls to his left to escape his enemy for a moment.

Craven is enjoying the fight as he uses the sheer number of enemies to his advantage. He keeps blocking attacks and tripping opponents to ensure that he is not overwhelmed. He has eight enemies in a semicircle in front of him and keeps them at bay. He manages to catch a glimpse, through the mass before him, as his ally runs the leader through with his blade. He relaxes slightly as he concludes that his ally will be over to assist him dispatch the rest. He raises his blade to send another robed figure crashing to the ground. Suddenly, his head is ringing as someone smashes a six-centimeter thick limb across the side of his helmet. Staggering left from the blow, he engages the jet pack to escape any ensuing attacks. He lands on a branch fifteen meters up. After several seconds, his vision clears, and he sees his attackers. A woman and the hermit both have branches, but only the hermit's is broken. He looks to his ally and is surprised to see a young human holding his own in a battle he would not even join.

Tobius brings the weapon in a sweeping arch at the shoulders of his enemy. The zyback effortlessly parries his attack, but he raises a six-centimeter stone with the flow slamming it into the zyback's open flank, smashing his right knee with a loud crunch. Tobius takes a moment to rest as his enemy hobbles back. De' Ron tries to put weight on his injured leg but can barely stand on it. Summoning the void, he fortifies his leg to try and finish the fight quickly.

"How do you have such power?" he snarls through clenched teeth.

The human does not respond for a few heartbeats. "You come here and kill these people without purpose, and you must be stopped. That is why I will beat you." Tobius charges at his injured enemy.

The zyback steadies himself for the impending attack. Tobius uses every ounce of energy he has and summons the flow to exponentially increase the strength of his attack. Swinging the blade in a slash from his right shoulder, the blades collide with a snap. The zyback tries to block the blade, but the impact causes his knee to buckle. As his leg collapses, he feels his blade spin from his grasp. Tobius screams in pain as the void blade burns across his thigh before it extinguishes itself. Tobius sees every millisecond that transpires as his blade parts his enemy's head from his shoulders with a wet thwack.

Craven watches with intense fascination as his other ally falls. Then he hits his jet pack, leaving the battle. Melissa watches him leave then turns to see the outcome of Tobius's fight. She turns just in time to see him drop the weapon, collapsing to the ground. She grabs the hermit's hand, dragging him to the human. Tobius is lying on the ground, unmoving. The hermit kneels, examining the young man, and lets out a long breath. "He is alive." Rising, he heads to check on the other friends involved. It takes several hours after dusk before the true damage of the fight is realized.

Of those that survived the fray, the only ones that are without injury are the hermit and Melissa. They lost nine seekers and the Gatekeeper. The Mistress holds the lifeless body of the Gatekeeper, crying. Tobius wakes to the sight of the aftermath. He grunts as he tries to stand, and Melissa hurries over to help him up. He nods his appreciation. They slowly make it to the Mistress.

He touches her on the shoulder. "I am very sorry, Mistress." He receives only a small smile in response. He asks Melissa, "Please, is there any food?"

She squeezes his shoulder. "Of course." She helps him to the kitchen to get some food. After they eat, everyone solemnly tries to get some sleep.

As a fresh morning dawns, a somber mood still hangs over the village. Tobius stiffly gets off the bunk but is still drained from his fight. Hermi enters the hut. "How do you feel, my boy?" He grunts as he tries to step. "You are lucky. The blade missed anything vital, but it will take several days for the salve to help heal it." Handing the young man a cane, he asks again, "How do you feel, Tobius?"

The human takes a moment to consider the question. "I am sad but at peace."

The hermit nods. "How did you manage to beat him?"

Tobius replies, "I am not really sure. I had no runes to help me with the flow, but I knew if I did nothing, then everyone would perish."

The site of the village is nothing like it normally would be. No one is studying or trying to learn more about the power. The village is unnaturally silent, and Tobius sees that all of the village is just past the edge of the huts. They head toward the group, and the group makes way for him as though he is different. Just beyond the group are ten stacks of wood with the Mistress in the middle.

She looks at Tobius and waves him to her side. He slowly makes his way to her, ensuring to give a respectful berth to the pyres. As he reaches her side, she begins, "Yesterday was a very sad day for us all. We lost several friends." She gestures to the pyres around her. "And we lost loved ones. Yes, Greg and I were lovers, and I apologize for the deception." The Mistress takes a moment to regain her composure then continues, "We do not know why the men attacked us yesterday, but I do know that without this brave man"—she gestures to Tobius—"we all would have died." Tobius blushes at the comment, and she continues, "A millennium ago, we had a seeker of justice come here and almost destroyed our village, and yesterday it was a seeker of justice that saved us." The Mistress steps forward. "We now say goodbye as our friends become one with the flow, and we shall not forget their sacrifice."

She grabs the torch from the stand next to her. She hands it to Tobius.

Tobius shies away from it as she says, "As the savior of our village, it is your duty to help honor the fallen."

He nods, accepts the torch, and proceeds to light one pyre after the other until all but one is lit. He whispers to the Mistress, "You should light his." She shakes her head, trying not to cry. "It will help you grieve, and he would want you to."

She takes the torch shakily and ignites her lover's pyre. Tobius stands next to the kneeling woman with a hand on her shoulder.

* * *

Craven still does not understand how that little kid was able to defeat De' Ron. He heads back to the Phantom's Blade and leaves Detritus Prime. He heads back to the fleet to report what transpired. He meets up with fleet and opens a channel to Vorex's Might.

"Admiral Kato, this is Craven."

Kato responds, "Yes."

"I have bad news, Admiral."

"Craven, land in the dorsal bay and report to the bridge."

He slaps the transceiver, cutting the transmission and bringing his ship into dock. Completing the shutdown process, he dons his armor just in case Kato loses his temper again.

As soon as he steps onto the bridge, Kato snaps, "How did my apprentice die?" Craven quickly explains how Rumick and De' Ron both met their demise. "You say a young human overwhelmed my apprentice?"

Craven nods. "I still have the tracking beacon on their ship."

The admiral stands and moves to view port. "Craven, you must bring me this human."

Craven bows slightly. "Yes, of course." He leaves the bridge and heads back to his ship to find out where the human would be and is pleased to find that the ship has left Detritus Prime.

* * *

That night, they host a feast in memory of their lost friends. Tobius understands the purpose of the feast but does not feel like participating. He sits on the outside edge of the feast, thinking about the last two days. He recalls the conversation he had with the figure calling himself Sanguis, and with painstaking clarity, he recalls the moment when the Gatekeeper fell. He can remember every moment when he killed the zyback and the searing pain from the void blade. He is startled from his recollection as Melissa sits down next to him.

"Will you stay here?" she softly asks.

He shakes his head. "I must go to Vorex, but I will stay until the village has recovered."

She nods, taking his hand. "Thank you for saving us."

Shocked, he looks at her and smiles. The feast continues well into the night.

Over the next few weeks, the village slowly recovers. Two months after the tragic day, Tobius and Hermi pack up and prepare to head to Vorex. They head to the Mistress's hut to say their farewells. They enter the hut and give a slight bow.

The Mistress stands and walks to them. "Follow me please." When she exits the hut, she calls for the village to assemble. After several moments, the village has gathered. "Today we say goodbye to some of our friends as they continue their pursuit of power." She looks at the human. "Tobius, will you come here?" He steps forward, and she continues, "This young man has saved our village. He is the youngest person to ever achieve the title of Master. Tobius, we would like you to become the first Master of Justice in over a thousand years." She reaches into her robe and presents him a gift. "This is a small token of appreciation and also the weapon of the man you saved us from."

Tobius looks to see a medallion with the justice glyph on it and the hilt of the void blade. The young man bows. "Thank you, Mistress."

She now calls the hermit forward and awards him the title of Master of Knowledge. She also gives him a medallion with the crest of knowledge and a data pad. Tobius and the hermit begin to turn when she asks them to wait. The Mistress smiles. "One more person we will say goodbye to."

Tobius freezes as he sees none other than Melissa. He can't take his eyes from her. She has her hair pulled back in a ponytail, and instead of the normal robe, she is wearing a formfitting flight suit.

Tobius is amazed at how beautiful she is. The hermit playfully elbows him in the ribs to break his stare.

The Mistress turns to her. "Melissa, I have known you since you were just a child, and I am very proud of you. I humbly bestow the title of Mistress of Knowledge." Melissa is shocked at what was just said. "You have proved worthy of this title, and I shall miss having you here. I know that you want to travel with our new friends, and you may do so with our blessing."

Melissa's face shines with respect and joy. She hugs the Mistress and, without another word, heads to join her friends.

Tobius, Melissa, and Hermi all wave farewell as they depart from the village. They head back to the city at a steady pace.

"Melissa," Tobius says. "Why are you coming with us?"

She looks away from Tobius for a moment to hide her blushing cheeks. "I want to help you find out more about this Sanguis." She smiles. "Plus, Hermi already informed me of everything that has happened since he found out about the relic."

The hermit adds, "She also has the most knowledge on the Keepers of Power and will be very helpful in finding any other Keepers."

Tobius nods his agreement. When they arrive at the city, the hermit gives Tobius and Melissa some credits and tells them to go get some additional supplies and robes for the environment on Vorex. They head to the market, and he heads to settle the docking fees. Boarding his shuttle, he checks the subnet to see if there is any news about that mysterious fleet, but no luck. After half an hour, the other two enter the shuttle and prep for departure.

The Academy

The hermit looks at Tobius. "Are you sure that we need to go to Vorex?"

He nods. "Yes, Hermi, I am certain, but I do not know where to go once we get there."

The pelagian turns to Melissa. "Do you know where the Keepers of Power are on Vorex?"

She pulls a tablet out of her pack and looks at it for a few moments. "From the information that I have, it will be somewhere outside Dreshdae."

Tobius asks, "So how can we find them? It's not like we can just stroll up to a kiosk and ask about them."

Melissa chuckles. "No, but we can look in the archives, and I am sure that someone will find us."

They all agree that would be the best option and descend to the spaceport. Before exiting the shuttle, they all don the robes to help reduce the chance of being seen as outsiders. The hermit is extremely glad to have a robe for two reasons. First, he does not see very many nonhuman species. Second, the robe gives him extra protection for the dry weather. As they head down the boarding ramp, he says, "Tobius, Melissa, you guys should lead here."

They nod and step off the ramp. They start heading into the city when a security patrol stops them. "Stop!" says the captain through their helmet. "What is your business here?"

Melissa steps forward. "It is none of your business. We are acolytes, and we may go where we wish."

The captain steps forward, pointing at her. "You are lying. Show me you are what you say you are."

Without hesitation, Tobius draws and ignites the void blade. The guard steps back as the tip of the blade ends a centimeter away from his visor. Tobius hides his surprise as the blade no longer has the spikes but flares out into four triangular blades that form a spear tip. "Very well." With a wave of his hand, the security team moves on. Not wanting to look foolish, Melissa immediately starts walking again.

They make their way into the city, inquiring about where the archives are at. They continue to maintain the persona of being acolytes, and as such, Tobius decides to hang the void blade from his belt. This helps speed up the process for getting to the archive. Once there, they split up to expedite the search. The hermit and Melissa immediately head off in different directions, but Tobius takes a moment to calm himself. Taking a deep breath, he clears his mind as he starts his search. He wanders through the rows of data pads, just letting his mind guide him. He walks past Melissa and pauses for a moment to admire her. And as he walks by, he gently places a hand on her shoulder. He feels a shudder ripple through the flow when he makes contact with her. Wanting to stop, he opens his mouth, but no words escaped. With nothing being said, he moves on and up an ancient spiral staircase to a balcony. There he finds three terminals. The first one is being used by an older man. Tobius moves to the third one and sits down. He quickly enters *Sanguis* and waits for the response but finds no result. He quickly tries to run through all possible key words that would help him find out where to go. With no luck, he looks up to see the captain standing at the entrance with two dozen guards with stun batons and energy pikes.

The captain looks around then up to the balcony and points. "There he is. Capture him and his companions."

Quickly, the human stands and tries to find an exit, but then he realizes that even if he could escape, Hermi and Melissa would not. Making his way downstairs, he gives up and calls for his friends.

The guards escort the captives outside the city into a secluded location at the base of a mountain. They are escorted into a vast chamber with barely enough light to illuminate the room. They are led to the other end of the chamber to a stone dais with an obsidian throne. Sitting on the chair is a middle-aged woman. The captain stops at the base of the dais and kneels.

"Master Kyron, we have captured these three acting like one of your acolytes." He raises his hand. "The man had this on him."

She quickly calls it to her hand to examine it. Standing, she dismisses the guards with a gesture. She turns the weapon around in her hands and steps down the stairs. "How did you get this?"

The trio stand there with stun cuffs clasped to their wrists, but no one responds. She steps in front of Tobius. With a wave of her hand, she removes the hoods from all three.

"I know you did not build this weapon." She waves the hilt in front of him. "This belonged to Master Kato's apprentice, De' Ron. So how do you have it, young man?" Tobius looks at her but says nothing. "I know that it had to have been you who managed to defeat him because your two friends are weaker than you are."

Defiantly, he snaps, "What's your point?"

Her laugh sends chills down the young man's spine. "Apprentice De' Ron was one of the most skilled fighters we had, and his skills with his"—she wiggles the hilt—"void blade were rivaled only by our weapons masters."

She moves around behind the trio. Without warning, the snap hiss of a void blade echoes through the chamber. The hermit looks down to see a red blade protruding from his chest, but with no spikes or blades on the tip. Tobius looks over to see his friend impaled by the blade.

"No!" he bellows in rage at the sight of his doomed friend. He uses the flow to shatter the stun cuffs and reaches out at Master Kyron. He tries to shove her into the wall, but nothing happens to her. Instead of her hitting the wall, he feels himself lifted eight meters by his throat.

Kyron looks at Melissa. "Now, young lady, if you would like him"—she nods at Tobius—"to survive, tell me how he acquired this." Fearing the death of both her friends, she quickly explains what happened to the apprentice.

She extinguishes the blade and lowers Tobius to three meters and lets him drop to the floor, gasping. Before Tobius could regain his breath, the hermit had already passed. He looks from his dead friend to glare at his murderer.

"How dare you murder him!" he growls through clenched teeth.

She lets a sinister chuckle escape her throat. "He was weak, and we do not accept weakness here." Master Kyron returns to her chair and sits, saying, "You two now have a choice. Either you can stay and earn the title acolyte, or you join your friend."

He glances at Melissa, and she nods. He glares up at her. "Fine we will join you."

Smiling, she calls the security captain back in. "Please remove her cuffs and escort them to instructor Phylox and inform him that these are two potential acolytes."

They are led from the left side of the chamber through a series of interchanges and stairwells. Several floors below the chamber, they enter a training room with dozens of people. They are working on fighting and meditation, and even a select few appear to be performing a duel. Tobius watches in fascination as the duel begins. A human and a red crytan both have void blades ignited and stand ready to fight. The human starts the fight with a quick low slash, but the crytan deftly jumps over and behind his enemy. He drops low, sweeping the legs out from the human to send him sprawling across the floor. Then he kicks him ten meters across the room. The human slams his head on a pillar, knocking him out. Tobius is amazed with the ease that the crytan dispatched his opponent.

The crytan steps away from the ring toward the captain. "Welcome, I am Master Phylox, and I am one of the instructors here." He turns away as he says, "Follow me, adepts."

The two young humans quickly follow, having to jog to catch up. Phylox stands over two meters tall without a single ounce of fat weighing ninety kilograms. Tobius can understand why he was instructing in the dueling ring. He leads them through the door on the opposite side of the room and down some stairs into what appears to be a dorm chamber. The room is five meters tall, twenty meters across, and nearly one hundred meters long. Along both walls are rows of single bunks every four meters, and each bunk has a security footlocker and a half-meter-wide, two-meter-tall wall locker. They are led most of the way down the right side of the room to a set of empty bunks.

Phylox turns around. "This is where you will stay as long as you are adepts."

Melissa looks around. "Where are the refreshers and changing rooms?"

The crytan laughs. "Adepts are nothing, so they get nothing. The pillars in the center of the room are showers, and you will learn to change in front of both sexes and many species." Tobius looks at Melissa and sees that she is blushing. Phylox says as he strides away, "Be back in the training hall in fifteen minutes. The robes are on your bunk."

Tobius takes a step toward Melissa. "Are you okay, Melissa?"

She hugs herself, nodding slightly. "I can't believe they killed Hermi."

Tobius pulls her into an embrace and relishes the feeling of her against him and her scent. After a moment, he gently lifts her chin. "We will make it. We just have to play their game until we figure out where to go next."

She nods, regaining her resolve. She playfully pushes him. "Now no peeking while we change."

He laughs and turns to don his new robes. He places his pack in the footlocker and begins to undress. He hears Melissa doing the same thing just meters away. He picks up the robe and dreads having to put the rough fabric on. The pants and tunic are a red brown color, and the boots and robe are dark black. Tobius glances at Melissa and sees her standing at the foot of her bunk and finds himself transfixed at the sight. Melissa is standing there, looking at the robes with a dreaded look. Tobius admires her toned feminine figure and tan skin.

Just then, Melissa glances over her shoulder. "Tobius," she says jokingly. "You said you wouldn't look." She winks and starts to put on the clothes. Tobius could do nothing but sheepishly turn away and laugh.

They make their way back up to the training hall and are met by Phylox. Without as much as a greeting, he says, "Take that hallway." He points to their right. "Within you will find Master Gamite, and he will instruct you on becoming Void-raiders."

They bow slightly and head as directed. Beyond the door lies an octagonal chamber with five rows of descending benches leading inward to a half-meter dais with a subnet projector. Standing beside the projector is an old man with a long white beard extending to mid torso and a bald head. Without turning around, he speaks with his gravelly voice. "Welcome, adepts. Please have a seat." He turns, looking at the two newcomers. "What do you know of the Void-raiders?" As they sit down, they both shake their heads unknowingly. The old man chuckles. "We are Void-raiders." He strides to them. "Void-raiders rule everyone in the galaxy. We are the masterminds to everything. We are strong, and we rule the weak." Slamming his hands on the bench, he bellows, "This, adepts, is the Void-raider's code. Follow this and you may become acolytes." He dims the lights and turns on the projector. "Power is for the strong."

A robed figure appears and continues, "The strong command the void. The void devours the weak. Embrace the void, and all shall be yours."

For the remainder of the day, they learn about the Void-raiders. They learn about the code, to old Void-raiders, and several places of great Void-raiders' historical importance. Tobius is unsure of how long they were in that room but was relieved when they were escorted from the room to the dining hall. They enjoy a meal consisting of food they did not know. After that, they return to the bunk hall, and they are amazed to see that almost every bunk is occupied. Tobius and Melissa make their way to their bunks.

Tobius whispers to Melissa once they arrive at their bunks, "I will be right here if something happens." They both lay down and try to get some sleep.

Tobius feels like he had just fallen asleep when he hears an alarm blare through the bunk hall. He jolts up and looks around the dimly lit hall and sees all the other adepts getting dressed for the day. He steps over to Melissa and gently shakes her awake and is surprised that she slept through that alarm. He dons his rough clothes and follows the other adepts with Melissa close behind. They move up to the dining hall for breakfast. Tobius prefers his flash dried fruit instead.

The Tests

As they are all eating, Master Kyron enters the hall. Without any device, her voice echoes through the vast chamber. "Adepts, we have two new people to introduce." She gestures to Tobius and Melissa. Hesitantly, they both stand and head to her. "This is Adept Melissa." She gestures to Tobius. "This young man is Tobius, who defeated apprentice De' Ron, and he brought his fallen enemy's weapon as proof." She raises the damaged weapon. "Please." She smiles sinisterly. "Ensure that they are welcomed."

With that being said, she spins then leaves. Tobius and Melissa head back to their seats, and she whispers, "I think she just made you a target."

When they get three meters from their seat, a trio step in front of them. All three of them are human, two males and one female. They all are about Tobius's height, but their skin is so white as if they have not seen daylight in years.

"I am Morrin," the middle one says. "I knew De' Ron, and there is no way you killed him." Tobius just looks at him. "If you are smart, you would join up with my group. We are the strongest adepts and are in the trials for acolyte." Tobius dismisses what he says with a shrug and shoulders past them with Melissa close behind.

After breakfast, all the adepts are lined up in the training hall. Phylox is standing there with Gamite and a younger human female both to Phylox's right. "I am sure you are all familiar with our new adepts." Stepping forward, he continues, "Today begins our assessment. For those who do not know what that is. We"—he gestures to the other two—"will be testing you on three things. Your knowledge of the Void-raiders' code, your combat skills, and your ability to command the void." He paces in front of them. "If you do well, you will remain here. But if we find you weak, you will be cast out to the desert. Embrace the void, and all shall be yours," he concludes, quoting the code. Without a word, he raises his arms, and the group is split into three groups.

Tobius tries to see Melissa but cannot, so he reaches into the flow and senses her in group 1. The female is in front of group 1, Phylox selects group 2, and Gamite takes group 3.

Each group has thirty adepts in them, and the training hall has enough room for each group to spread out. Tobius glances through his group and sees Morrin and his entourage standing a few meters away. Tobius growls at the fact that he may have to put up with their stupidity all day. He hears Phylox say that the assessment will take a week and to remain with their group through the day. "Trainers, please begin the assessment." With that, Gamite escorts his group into the octagon room, and the female leads her group out the opposite end from Gamite. Tobius feels a spike of fear from Melissa, and he tries to calm her with a mental touch. Tobius is curious about how he can feel her so well but does not mind. It appears that Phylox will be testing the combat skills of everyone. Tobius figures that each leader will have a group for two days, but that would be six days. Trying not to figure out their thinking, he plays along.

Phylox gestures to his group, and they huddle around him in a large circle. "Today you will all duel with me, one by one, and shall be ranked on a scale of one through five." He points to the wall. "All the weapons there you can choose from. The duels will go for twenty minutes, or until you cannot continue, whichever comes first." He walks to the wall and selects a bow staff. "Anyone care to volunteer?" he asks, deftly spinning the staff around his body like a blur. For a few silent moments, no one answers the challenge. Phylox stops spinning the staff and moves to the center of the circle. Morrin steps to the wall and selects a practice void blade.

Phylox turns to see his opponent and nods. "Begin." The two combatants slowly circle each other. Phylox holds the staff in a ready position with it angled upper right to lower left, and Morrin holds the blade in a double-handed grip, with the tip at eye level. Before completing a full rotation, Morrin charges in at Phylox. He brings the blade in a quick jab from his right. The staff is spun, knocking the blade out of position, and he receives a kick in the chest for his ambitions. Morrin sprawls on the floor and slowly climbs to his feet. He again recklessly charges in at Phylox, but even before he can start his attack, he is hit in the shoulder with the staff sending him to one knee.

Phylox steps back, asking, "Can you continue?"

Enraged, Morrin jumps at his opponent and tries to push him with aid of the void, but Phylox blocks the attack and rewards the man with a blow on the side of his head. Morrin collapses to the floor unconscious. His voice is filled with rage, and his eyes burn. "There is to be no void use in these duels."

Tobius watches as the next few hours proceed. Phylox manages to dispatch his opponents one by one with less than three strikes per duel. A bell chimes through the hall, and Phylox stops. "Good. Adepts, it is time for lunch. Head to the dining hall. And after you finish, return to the bunk hall for one hour of meditation."

Tobius is pleased to see that Melissa is smiling when she joins him in the dining hall. She proceeds to explain that her trainer is Master Rochelle, and she tests the ability to control the void.

Tobius inquires, "How did you do?"

Melissa smiles. "I went first, and I was able to complete all the requested tasks."

Tobius laughs. "That does not surprise me." Through lunch, they continue to talk about the morning.

They head down to the bunk chamber after lunch for the meditation. Tobius never really had to do anything like this and looks around. Most of the adepts are sitting in various places and just appear to be relaxing. So he looks at his bunk and considers where to sit. He decides to sit cross-legged on his footlocker, looking toward his bunk. He rests his hands on his thighs and closes his eyes. He focuses on relaxing. He inhales for four counts, he holds for two then exhales for four. He does this while he keeps his back straight, allowing for deep relaxing breaths. Slowly, he is able to hear everything going on in the hall with extreme clarity. There is one who is taking this time for a nap three bunks down. Across the hall, a group of adepts are just talking quietly. After several minutes of this, he lets his mind roam and follows a flow. His mind's eye steps from where he is and looks around the room. He can see every person in the room. He looks at Melissa and sees a pure turquoise glow. He sees every person has a slightly different color. He begins to learn that the lighter colors are associated with peace and tranquility and dark colors for anger or rage. He moves around the room, looking at everyone. He nears Morrin and is not surprised when he sees a raging storm of crimson and black. Tobius pulls back from him and his friends. He starts to make his way back to himself. When he opens his eyes again, he finds himself shivering from the frigid contact with Morrin. He stands up, stretching his muscles.

He steps over by Melissa and rests a hand on her shoulder. He can feel the steady rise and fall in her breathing but feels her pulse quicken slightly. She slowly opens her eyes, looks up, and smiles. Tobius thinks he sees a flash of something different in her smile for a second. He is about to ask how she is holding up, but the bell chimes, advising them to return to the training hall. He simply gives her shoulder a reassuring squeeze.

Phylox is standing in the same place as this morning, and the group assembles around him. "So will anyone of you adepts be able to cause me to break a sweat?" He laughs.

Tobius bides his time to watch how he reacts to the pointless assaults of his group. He watches another half dozen people try and challenge Phylox. After another pitiful attempt by a female zyback, Tobius steps to the wall and selects two half-meter-long Razik blades. He steps into the circle, standing five meters from his opponent. He readies his two blades, left reverse grip and normal for right. Phylox spins the staff and keeps it just in his left hand behind his back. Tobius nods to his duelist, and they begin to circle. As they circle, Tobius slowly closes the gap between them. Once he gets within three meters, he begins his attack. He quickly strides at his opponent and brings his right blade in a quick thrust which he knows will be blocked. But to his surprise, his competitor does not block but simply ducks under his attack while bringing his staff to crack into Tobius's unprotected side. He gets lifted off his feet from the blow and staggers back. He reprimands himself for the careless tactic. Recovering, he starts in again. This time, he brings his left blade in a sweeping upward slash. Phylox sees the incoming attack and deftly spins his staff, deflecting the blow. He was rewarded with the right blade of his opponent slapping his left thigh. Tobius spins around and prepares for a possible counterattack. After the two quick exchanges, they begin in earnest.

This time, Phylox begins the exchange. He spins his staff quickly and has Tobius on the defensive, barely able to defend himself from the relentless barrage. After countless moves, Tobius has more than a few bruises. Tobius takes the brief pause in the attack to return the favor. He quickly swaps the grips in both hands. Stepping in, he slashes low with his right hand as Phylox spins his staff to intercept the blade. Tobius uses the reverse gripped blade to knock the staff out of position and uses the left to spin the staff, landing a solid hit on his ribs. He quickly sweeps at the legs and catches his opponent's left leg. Phylox stumbles back and uses the bow staff to help steady himself from the attack. Right when he settles to start again, the timer sounds. Phylox stands a meter from Tobius, breathing a little labored and with sweat on his brow. He gives the young human a slight nod, and Tobius returns his weapons to the rack.

Phylox looks at the group. "There is someone who knows how to handle himself in combat, and that is why De' Ron fell at his hand."

Several people in the group cheer at Tobius's display, but Morrin and his crew glare at him. For the next hour, Phylox finishes testing the rest of the group. Once the tests are complete, the groups form up in the hall once again.

Phylox steps forward and addresses the group. "Your scores from today will be posted on this wall." He gestures to the wall next to the entrance of the bunk hall.

After the group is dismissed, there is a free hour before dinner. Tobius takes the time to refresh from the duel he had. He returns to his bunk and gets ready to shower, removing his cloak, tunic, and boots. Melissa walks up to him and stops a meter short. Tobius turns and sees her there. "Hey, Melissa."

"Tobius, Master Phylox would like to see you." She nervously rubs her hands together. He quickly puts on a fresh set of clothes and returns to the training hall.

Tobius enters the hall to see Master Phylox and Gamite conversing in a corner. He walks up and stops a few meters from the two. Patiently, he waits until he is summoned over. "You requested to see me?"

Phylox nods, stepping to him. "I would like to know how you managed to defeat De' Ron."

Tobius bows slightly then explains everything he saw from the battle between the Gatekeeper and De' Ron to the final blow.

Gamite steps to him. "Who is this Gatekeeper you refer to?"

The human knows he must be careful not to expose his friends, but he answers carefully. "He was the elder of the village I was at on Detritus Prime."

The older male places a hand on his shoulder and guides him to the octagonal room. Touching a few controls on the projector, he nods at Phylox. They look at him. "What is your focus?"

Confusion flashes across Tobius's face, but he quickly hides it. "What do you mean?"

Phylox laughs. "We are grateful for protecting our fellow Keepers. I am a Master of Knowledge, and Gamite is a Master of Wealth." Tobius shows pure shock on his face. He could not believe what he just heard.

The young human sits on the bench, still stunned by what he just heard. "You both are Keepers?" They both laugh. "How can you be Keepers and be Void-raiders?"

Phylox looks at him. "It is very simple for us. We keep the Keepers safe by being a part of the group that would want us destroyed."

He looks at them both. "How did you know I was one?"

Gamite steps forward. "We both noticed when you entered the first day, but Phylox was clear when he fought you."

Tobius stands and rubs his forehead. "If you knew I was a Keeper, why did you just summon me?"

Both Phylox and Gamite look perplexed by the question. "What do you mean?" replies Gamite.

"There is another Keeper here with me."

"Who are they?" the old man questions.

"You couldn't tell?" Tobius smiles.

"Melissa, the young woman I arrived with."

Phylox looks at the older man. "How did we miss it?"

Gamite takes a few moments to ponder the question. "Either she is good at hiding her presence or your power is so strong we could not feel hers." The two men stand and look at Tobius. The bell chimes through the hall, signifying dinner.

"Tobius," Phylox says, heading out. "Tomorrow, please bring Melissa with you."

Tobius meets up with Melissa, heading to the dining hall. "What did they want?" Melissa inquires softly.

He shook his head, replying, "I will tell you later."

As they head into the dining hall, Morrin steps in front of Tobius. "What do you think you are doing?"

Tobius stops, glaring at him. "What do you mean? I am going to become an acolyte."

Morrin shoves his finger into his chest. "Listen here. I have been here longest, and I will become an acolyte before you do."

Tobius slaps his hand away, stepping closer. "If you want to settle something, let's do it now."

Laughing, Morrin turns. "We will later."

Tobius and Melissa watch him leave, as she asks, "What is his problem?"

Tobius continues to glare at him. "He is just jealous because I did better today than he did." They move through the line. They get dinner, and they find a table in the corner. "Tomorrow they want you to come with me."

She looks at him in shock. "Why?"

He reaches across the table and touches her hand. "They are one of us."

She is barely able to control the surprise. "Really! How did they know? Why are they here?"

Tobius smiles. "I will let them explain it. They want to meet tomorrow." They both enjoy the remainder of the evening in peace.

The following day, Tobius's group goes with Gamite, and Melissa is with Phylox. The group enters the octagonal room and take their seats.

"I am Master Gamite," the old man says, entering the room. "I will be testing your understanding of the Void-raiders' code." He quickly recites the code. "I will summon each of you up in pairs, and you will stand on opposite sides of the projector. Each of you will be given a scenario, and you must figure it out as Void-raiders. Just like yesterday, your scores will be posted from one to five." Gamite brings up a data pad. "Tobius and Morrin, please come forward." They both stand and move to opposite sides of the projector. "Morrin, you are in a high stakes poker tournament at the last table. The stake is fifty million credits. And despite all odds, you are facing the son of the establishment owner. You have determined that he rigged the deck in his favor. How do you handle it?" He turns to Tobius. "You are working with a crew on an archaeological site for a very rare Void-raiders artifact. The foreman realizes that he can get triple the price you are paying to unearth the find. You find out that he has hired a mercenary to take you out so he can increase his return. What do you do?" Gamite turns around and addresses the group. "They have five minutes to consider this question, and they will input their response on the projector pads. We will then see how it will play out with what they entered."

The five minutes pass, and a bell chimes from the projector. Master Gamite turns around. "We will see how they respond, but you will not see their scores."

He turns and presses a button. The projector hums and shows two people sitting at a poker table with a droid standing next to it. It shows Morrin laying his five cards down, showing a high straight. His opponent grins and quickly shuffles the cards in his hand and lays down a high straight flush. Morrin stares at the cards in disbelief and tells the droid to deal a new hand. The droid deals both players a new hand, and Morrin grabs the cards dealt to the other man. The cards are blank. He flips his own cards over then looks at the other cards to see they changed to be the better hand. The droid begins to announce the outcome when Morrin pulls out a ferioblade and cuts through the droid and kills the opponent. The projection dissolves, and Gamite nods.

The old man steps forward to start Tobius's scenario. A thick jungle appears from the projector. There are dozens of crates, some of tools and some of artifacts. Tobius walks from the tent to the foreman. The foreman is joined by his crew and a bounty hunter. They demand the rare artifact. Tobius heads to the tent and enters the security code to release the case. He hands the case to them. Cheering, the group heads from the tent, boarding the bounty hunter's vessel. Thirty seconds after liftoff, the entire ship explodes. Tobius smiles, returns to his desk, and retrieves the artifact from the desk. The projection fades as Tobius returns to his seat.

Master Gamite addresses the room again. "Very well." For the remainder of the morning, he calls them up in twos. The situations vary from housing disputes to fraudulent banking and even estate disputes.

The bell chimes for lunch, and they head out of the room to the training hall. Tobius exits the octagonal room to see Melissa dueling with Phylox. From what he sees, the match has just started. She is using a whip and dagger against Phylox's staff. He watches her attempt to catch him off guard from the odd weapons combination, but with no luck. Forty-five seconds later, she is sent tumbling across the floor and gets tangled in her own whip. He sees Phylox step to her, kneel, and help her out of the whip. Tobius thinks he whispered something to her but is not quite sure. She heads to the weapons rack as the rest of her group moves to the dining hall.

Tobius walks up to her, commenting, "Interesting choice of weapons."

Defensively, she snaps, "I thought it would catch him off guard, but all it did was get me tied up."

Tobius touches her arm, and she spins around, clearly upset about how easily she was bested. He takes a small step back.

"I am sorry," she softly says. "It's not your fault."

He playfully nudges her shoulder. "You did better than Morrin, and he is sure to be an acolyte." That makes Melissa laugh. They head toward the dining hall, and he asks, "What did he whisper to you as he helped you up?"

After several steps, she replies, "He said that I am so uncertain of myself that I cannot gain control."

Tobius looks at her quizzically. "What did he mean by that?"

She shakes her head. "It cannot be explained, but I am sure that you will have to face this problem someday." Tobius nods.

After lunch, they have their meditation time. Tobius again sits cross-legged on his footlocker, looking toward his bed. He is able to let his mind wander much easier this time and just lets it go where it feels. He leaves his own body and again lingers on Melissa's turquoise presence for just a moment. He then quickly takes a look around the hall. His mind then moves to the training hall. He can hear the silence of the vast room. His mind moves through the halls of the academy, and he comes to the main hall, lingering where his friend was murdered. He can still feel the raging anger and deep sorrow for his friend. Right when he is about to move on, he feels a slight tug on his mind. He follows it to the opposite side of the hall behind the throne. Looking at the base, he sees a crimson hexagon. He lets his mind move forward, and he passes through the floor under the throne.

There is a passage half a meter wide and barely two meters tall that continues down the slime-covered corroded steps. He seems to follow the stairs more than three hundred meters down, but it is hard to say because every eight steps, there is a small landing, and it turns ninety degrees left then continues. He makes it to the bottom of the staircase, but before he can look more, he hears the chime. He quickly returns to his body. The rest of the afternoon is spent in the octagonal room, listening to and watching scenarios play out. Tobius is only partially paying attention. He cannot get his mind off the mysterious staircase under Master Kyron's throne. He isn't sure if he should ask Phylox and Gamite or not. He decides to tell Melissa about it first and see what she thinks.

The bell chimes, and the adepts start leaving the room, but Tobius waits for the last to leave and walks up to Master Gamite. Without turning to look, the old man asks, "Is there something on your mind, adept?"

Tobius notices the formality and follows suit. "Master Gamite, how does this"—he gestures to the projector—"show understanding of the Void-raiders code?" In reality, he could care less, but he doesn't want to ask about the Keepers without ensuring it is safe to.

Turning around, Gamite recites, "The strong command the void. What does that mean?"

Tobius considers the question for a moment. "Peace is a goal the weak strive for, but the strong control the views of the weak. Everyone has their own passions that tells them what goal is theirs."

Nodding, the old man replies, "The void devours the weak."

Tobius crosses his arms, thinking about the implied question. "Those without the will to act become pawns for my own goals."

The old man strokes his beard approvingly. "Embrace the void, and all shall be yours."

Tobius considers this for a good minute. "By using the drive from my passion, I earn the power to reach my goals."

The old man sits down on one of the benches. "Tobius, the Void-raiders and Keepers are not too dissimilar. We both seek power, but Keepers share and help." Tobius joins him on the bench. "These scenarios demonstrate the code by how you solve the problem. You did very well with the code. You used your passion for the relic to distract the foreman and in turn gave them what they wanted. You achieve victory by removing those that opposed you." Tobius nods understandingly. "Morrin, however, was pure hatred. He was just after the immediate result. His actions did nothing to achieve power."

Phylox enters the room and heads down the steps to join the two men. Tobius nods a greeting and is slightly caught off guard when Melissa steps from behind him. She laughs softly as he jumps. Phylox sits next to Gamite, and Melissa settles next to Tobius.

"So," Phylox starts, "why are you two here?"

Tobius looks at Melissa, and she nods. "We are looking for a place, but we are not sure where exactly it is."

Phylox and Gamite both look at them, dumbstruck. "What is this place for?"

Tobius quickly explains what he saw in the canyon on Detritus Prime. Phylox stands and paces while Tobius regales them about the feel of the air, the symbol, and the apparition's revulsion about being called a Keeper. Tobius stops for a second and says, "He calls himself Sanguis, and that name does not seem to exist in any database."

Gamite stands. "We will research this information. Do not meet with us again until we summon you."

Tobius and Melissa stand, bow, then retreat from the room. Once they exit the room, Phylox turns to Gamite. "This could get very tricky for us. If we get careless, the Void-raiders could discover who we truly are." The old man nods his agreement, and they leave the room.

The following day, group 2 is taken into the room opposite from the octagonal room. This room is cylindrical, thirty meters across and fifteen meters tall. This room seems misplaced in the academy. This room has a bright interior with a subnet-projected sky. There are also sixty-meter-wide cushions in three rings. Levitating cross-legged ten meters in the air is a middle-aged female. She is wearing black boots, pants, tunic, and robe. Her hair is as black as her outfit, but her skin is pale white. She gracefully lowers herself to the floor.

"Welcome, adepts." She sets her feet back on the floor and continues, "I am Master Krystelle, and I will be testing your ability to command the void." She takes three steps forward and gestures. "Take a seat on a cushion. I will call you forward one at a time and give you some tasks to complete with the void. You will be rated from one to five like the other two tests."

Everyone takes their seats, and she begins to call people forward. She gives them a series of tasks, each more complex, and they try to complete each task. The first task they fail to complete will end the test. Tobius watches one after another come forward and do things from simple levitation to extremely intricate tasks. He starts to worry about this test.

I have no idea how to do any of this, he thinks. The morning slowly passes as the young human dreads his turn. Just as Master

Krystelle summons Tobius forward, the bell chimes for lunch. He lets out a small sigh of relief. He quickly leaves the room and searches for Melissa. He grabs her arm and pulls her aside. "I don't know how to use the flow to move things."

Shocked, she looks at him. "Really?" He nods shamefully. "How have you managed to do all you can so far?"

He shrugs. "When things got tough, I just relied on my gut."

She laughed. "You just have to do the same thing for the tests. Just picture what you need to do and focus. The rest you will have to figure out yourself. But remember, the flow reacts to your emotions. This will help focus the flow." She hands him a small wristband with a trapezoid with a diamond in the middle, and Tobius smiles slightly.

"I'll try." They make their way to lunch. Tobius quickly eats and heads to his bunk for meditation.

Quickly, he sits like he normally does and puts the wristband on his left hand. He takes some deep relaxing breaths. Instead of letting his mind wander, he tries to lift the few items he set on his bunk. First, he reaches out to find the data pad. He feels the device and senses the electricity within. He pictures the pad rising to three centimeters and starts to feel the energy drain. He opens one eye and sees the pad just above the bunk. Melissa taps his shoulder, and Tobius jumps, falling from the footlocker.

"Just trying to practice?" She laughs.

He nods, sitting back on the locker. "Melissa, yesterday, I had a vision. Under Master Kyron's throne I think is a hidden stairwell, but I am not sure."

Shocked, she looks around and sits next to him. "What do you mean?"

Tobius rubs the back of his neck, replying, "Like what I saw on Detritus Prime. There was a crimson hexagon at the base and a long staircase under it, but I have no idea where it leads."

She ponders what he saw. "Did you ask the guys?"

He shook his head. "I don't completely trust them yet."

She nods. The bell chimes for them to return to the training hall. She squeezes his hand. "Don't worry. You will do fine." Tobius smiles.

They enter the cylindrical room and take their seats. Master Krystelle enters the room and calls Tobius to the center. He stands, waiting on his task. She steps to him. "So you are the one that killed De' Ron?"

Tobius can sense extreme venom in her voice. Defiantly, he stands tall and replies, "Yes, I did."

She slowly circles him as if she was a hound circling its prey. She flashes a snarling grin. "These tasks should be no problem then. Shall we begin?" Tobius nods, dissuaded. She takes three quick strides from him and points. "Lift the stack of blocks."

He focuses his mind on the six blocks of different size and weight. He raises his left hand, and the blocks slowly begin to lift. After thirty seconds, he opens his eyes, and to his surprise, the blocks are almost at the ceiling. She nods, and he lowers them to the floor with a slight relief.

"Now do not let these orbs"—she pulls out of her robe a dozen silver orbs—"hit the floor." She begins to toss the orbs in different directions.

Tobius's eyes widen, but he quickly focuses on the orbs. He forces his mind to encompass the room to ensure he does not miss one. The first orb is tossed to his right, and he catches it at shoulder height. Just as he catches the first, he senses the second tossed to the left wall. As he is catching that one, the third is already tossed toward the door. Krystelle senses as he reaches to the next orb, and she decreases the time between tosses. Four…five…six…seven. As Tobius stops the seventh one, he feels sweat rolling down his face. Eight…nine. His legs are starting to shake from the massive expense of energy to keep them from all falling. Ten…eleven. Tobius feels Krystelle toss the eleventh to the far wall and nudge it with the flow to make it harder for him to stop it. He catches the orb a mere half meter from the far wall. As soon as the eleventh orb stops moving, Krystelle's eyes burn red with rage and simply drops the final orb from her waist.

Tobius is completely drained of energy. His body can barely stay upright, but he refuses to let himself fail. He summons every ounce of strength left and reaches out to the last orb. He can feel the orb nearing the floor millimeter by millimeter, and every fraction of a second takes an eternity. Tobius is relieved when he manages to stop the orb five centimeters from the floor. He begins to smile when a clang rings through the room. He looks and sees the twelfth orb rolling on the floor. Tobius collapses to the floor in a heap. *I swore I stopped it*, he thinks. As his vision fades, he sees Krystelle staring at him with a smug satisfaction.

He crawls his way to a cushion and settles in. He is so drained that he doesn't even watch the remainder of the adepts. He just tries to rest. He slips into a meditative state, and his mind begins to wander. His mind is instantly assaulted by dark broiling hot rage. He hears a voice slither into his mind.

"How dare you kill De' Ron! I will ensure you will die for it."

He quickly retreats to the safety of his own mind and looks at the trainer. She is giving this female crytan with light skin simple tasks to complete, like cushion levitation and stacking blocks. The bell chimes, and Tobius shakily rises to his feet. He waits several heartbeats to ensure he won't collapse. Now everyone has left the room, and he staggers his way to the door. After a dozen agonizing steps, he can no longer summon the energy to move and collapses at the doorway. The last thing he remembers is hearing Melissa yell for him as his head hits the floor.

Three days later, Tobius wakes up in the infirmary. He slowly looks around and sees three medical droids. He tries to move, but his body is sore. He looks at the closest droid and opens his mouth, but only a squeak escapes his lips. The droid's head turns and registers he is awake. One of its many armatures extends, hitting the transceiver on the wall.

"Yes," a male's voice said.

"Sir, you wished to be notified when the adept regains consciousness."

"Thank you."

Tobius lets his head relax, falling back asleep.

He is gently roused from his slumber with a slight shake. He looks to see Master Phylox and Gamite standing beside the bed. They help him sit up. Rising, he sees Melissa quietly sitting at the foot of the bunk with a mix of anger and relief on her face. Tobius settles into a comfortable seated position. "What happened?" he says hoarsely.

The old man hands him a goblet of water and a bowl of fruit. "Drink. You have been screaming off and on these last three days."

Tobius ravenously drinks the water and feels instant relief on his raw throat. Melissa timidly steps forward. "You kept screaming, 'She will kill me' and 'You failed.'"

Phylox steps forward. "I think we should move to my study." Melissa and Gamite help steady Tobius as they move to Phylox's study. Once they enter, Phylox turns and punches a series of controls. A soft beep comes from the panel.

They all take seats in the cushioned lounge chairs. They help Tobius settle into his chair, and Gamite hands him the bowl of fruit. Melissa drags her seat closer to him. Phylox takes a moment to head to his cabinet and pulls out a crystalline flask of an amber colored liquor. "Hey, old man, you want a drink?"

Gamite chuckles. "Yeah, and it better be the good stuff."

He fills two matching tankards three quarters full and joins the others.

"Tobius," Gamite starts. "Please tell us what happened in the room with Krystelle."

Tobius takes a bite of fruit and chews for a few moments. "She first threatened me for killing De' Ron. Then she asked me to lift six blocks in a group." Gamite nods as he takes a large drink. "She then pulls a dozen orbs from her robe and says to catch them before they hit the floor." Phylox sets his half-full drink on a table and folds his hands together. "She starts by simply tossing the first by my right shoulder, and then she escalates, quickly throwing them all over the room at various heights and speeds. I was able to keep up somewhat. The eleventh she threw fast at the far wall opposite the door, and I was barely able to stop it. I thought she was done." Tobius takes a moment to eat some more fruit. "I was completely exhausted and barely able to stand when she simply drops the last orb. I used every last ounce of energy to try and stop it. I could have sworn I stopped it about five centimeters above the ground, but suddenly, I heard it hit the floor." Tobius takes another bite of fruit.

Gamite leans forward and asks, "How sure are you that you stopped it?"

The young man considers the question as he enjoys the fruit. "I saw it in my mind's eye stop just above the floor, and as I start to collapse from exhaustion, it hits the floor."

Melissa looks concerned. "But who will try and kill you?"

Tobius sets the bowl of fruit down and leans forward. "Krystelle. After I collapsed, I made my way to a cushion and sat. I was too spent to watch the remaining adepts. I just sat and let my mind roam." He starts rubbing his temples. "Suddenly, a female voice invaded my mind and screeches something about paying for killing De' Ron."

Phylox stands and refills his glass. "I was afraid this would happen."

The young man looks at him, confused. "What would happen?"

Returning to his seat, he explains, "De' Ron was a much-respected apprentice and was in line for Master, but Krystelle was obsessed with him."

Gamite interjects, "It was even suspected that they were lovers, but nothing ever came to light."

Tobius leans back, trying to stretch his back that is still stiff from everything. "Well, that explains the death glare she was giving me during the test."

The old man drains the remains of his drink. "So we need to ensure that he spends the least amount of time with her."

Phylox nods. "Well, enough debriefing. We have some good news." Tobius looks at him. "You and Melissa are both acolytes now. Your combat and Void-raiders code scores are fives, but the affinity aspect was a three."

Gamite goes to refresh his glass. "You will be studying under Master Phylox, and Melissa will be my charge."

Phylox stands and heads to the door and enters a code. "Now, Acolyte Melissa, please help Acolyte Tobius back to his room."

Melissa helps Tobius to his feet and nods. "As you wish, Master Phylox."

Tobius is still hurting from the ordeal, but he is able to move easier. They leave the study, and Tobius is expecting to return to the bunk hall. Instead of heading back to the training hall, Melissa guides him right through the main hall to the opposing doors. Through the doorway, the hall splits into five different paths. Melissa stops for a moment and identifies the different paths. From their left to right, bunk rooms are to the left, next are the archives, the middle leads outside where the training grounds are, then the meditation chamber, and to the right is a meeting room shared by all. Tobius nods, understanding.

"So you said bunk rooms?" Tobius asks, confused.

She chuckles, helping him down the hall. "Now that we are acolytes, we each have our own room." Tobius looks at her, shocked. "It is like the bunk hall before, but each bunk is divided with stone walls. Each room has a control panel, and you can secure it." She gets to Tobius's room and hits the control to open the door. It slides sideways into the wall.

Tobius steps into the room. "Where is your room?"

She laughs softly. "I am right next door." With that, she turns and heads to her room.

New Blades

The days pass by with constant training on different fighting styles, both armed and unarmed, and learning more about meditation and void uses. During this time, Tobius spends his extra time working on his flow skills, while Melissa all but lives in the archives. Both of them spend time with Master Phylox and Gamite, and to Tobius's relief, none with Krystelle.

Two months have passed, and they develop a nice routine. Tobius and Melissa get up an hour before breakfast and complete a three-kilometer run. After breakfast, they split and spend the morning learning from their respective teachers. Tobius spends the first part of the morning with combat training, and the second is testing his flow skill. Melissa spends more time on the power and history. In the afternoons, Tobius spends time in the archives, but he mostly learns from Phylox.

This morning, however, is different. Tobius and Melissa are just finishing their run when they hear, "All acolytes, please report to the combat yard."

Tobius glances at her. "I bet I can beat you there."

She laughs and elbows him. "Like you stand a chance."

They enter the courtyard just as the other acolytes file into the courtyard. They look at each other confused, seeing them assemble into three groups behind each Master. They gather in the back of their respective groups. Tobius looks to his left and sees Morrin in Krystelle's group. Each group has twenty-five to thirty acolytes. A horn sounds across the yard, and Master Kyron proceeds to the front of the group and onto a raised platform.

"Welcome, acolytes. Today we are here to see who will be selected for apprenticeship." A loud roar comes from the groups. Kyron lets the roar subside. "Each Master will select one acolyte to face the trials for apprenticeship." Outrage beckons from the crowd. She raises her hands to settle them. "I know that we usually select five from each group, but we are going to have the trials every three months instead of every year." A slight cheer rises from the assembly. "Master Krystelle, if you please."

She steps to the platform and takes a moment before she says, "My selection for the trials is Acolyte Morrin." Cheers erupt from her group.

"Master Gamite," Kyron says.

The old man makes his way to make his announcement. "Acolyte Melissa, please come forward."

Shocked, she makes her way to stand beside him.

"And last, Master Phylox."

He steps forward. "My acolyte will be Acolyte Tobius."

Tobius makes his way through the crowd and joins the others on the platform. Master Kyron dismisses the rest assembled.

Master Kyron turns around to the six people behind her. "Congratulations on being selected for the trials. Now you will be taught about the trials and the design and creation of your weapon." With that being said, she turns and leaves the six. Each Master leads their acolyte back to their respective studies.

Master Phylox motions Tobius to enter his study. Once they are inside, Phylox leads Tobius to a workbench. "Here are the basic components inside every void blade." Tobius looks at the workbench. "First, you have the casing, then the blade emitter. Here is the power cell, and then there is the crystal."

Tobius looks at Phylox. "Am I to create my own weapon?"

Phylox steps away from the bench. "There is a cave south of the courtyard. In this cave are crystals suitable for your blade." Tobius nods, understanding. "Please go prepare for this task, and I warn you that in past trials, acolytes have been found dead or just disappear. Remember that justice dances on a razor's edge." Tobius nods, leaving the study. Tobius reasons that Melissa is receiving a similar speech. He jogs back to his room to pack.

He grabs his pack and dumps it so he can ensure that it contains what he needs. Tobius is caught off guard from what he sees laying on his bunk. It's his picture of his family, Hermi's personal data pad, and the obsidian diamond. Tobius sinks to his bunk with the sudden weight of emotions. Melissa comes to Tobius's room right as he starts crying from the sudden realization of all he has lost. She steps in, shutting the door, and kneels by him. Tobius looks at her with tears streaming down his face and intense sorrow in his eyes. She embraces him and tries to console him. After a long moment, Tobius pulls away. "Thank you, Melissa."

She simply smiles and nods. "Are you okay?" she says, looking at him.

"Yes." He nods. "I just miss everyone."

Melissa stands, pulling him to his feet. "True, but now you must use that to gain strength to find out how to cherish them." Tobius looks at her. "Let's get ready for our trials." With that, she turns and prepares herself.

Tobius packs some glow rods, his survivor's kit, and a data pad. He dons his belt and secures a stun baton and two Razik blades. He leaves the room and sees Morrin coming down the hall. Tobius just watches him pass. Melissa exits her room just after Morrin exits the hallway. She looks at him then at Tobius.

"This will be very interesting," Tobius says as they head to the combat yard.

Phylox, Gamite, and Krystelle stand by the gate. Master Phylox steps forward. "Acolytes, your first trial is to find a suitable crystal for your weapon." He steps aside and waves them on.

The three step through the gate and begin the trial. Morrin quickly sprints off in the direction of the cave Tobius was told about. Tobius pulls the hood on his robe up to cover from the sun. They walk at a steady pace for well over an hour. Tobius looks around and does not see much difference in the landscape. "I wonder how far this cave is."

Melissa looks around really quick. "I think we are almost there."

Tobius looks at her. "How do you know?"

"I took a long time learning as much as I could about this area."

Tobius nods and keeps looking around. The sun has begun dropping toward the horizon.

Melissa points to the left. "I think it's right there." They head the way she pointed. Once they get seventy meters from the cave, Melissa turns around. "I think this is it."

Tobius raises his left hand and whispers, "Melissa, stop."

She stops and looks over her shoulder. Behind her stands a young brim gargoyle. Melissa shrieks, running from the beast. Tobius draws his blades, stepping forward. This specific gargoyle is just under three meters tall. The fangs and claws glisten in the fading daylight, and its albino skin shows red in the dusk. Tobius glances over his left shoulder and sees Melissa wielding a ferioblade. Melissa whispers, "Do you think we can get around it?"

Tobius shrugs, not wanting to lose sight of the animal. He nods to his right and gives the gargoyle a wide berth, but as they move, it follows.

Tobius and Melissa look around, trying to figure out what to do, but no matter where they move to, the animal moves, keeping a dozen meters from the cave's mouth.

"Now what?" Melissa asks.

Tobius looks around. "I know we can't take it head on, but do you think we could use the sand and try to shield us from it?"

Melissa looks around then shrugs. "I will try. Just give me some time."

Tobius nods. He steps forward to give enough space for Melissa, and she lays a small mat down with some of the runic language within the intricate design. The gargoyle roars and starts rumbling toward Tobius. He sets himself in a pure defensive stance while ensuring Melissa's safety.

As she clears her mind and focuses, she can feel herself, Tobius, and the gargoyle's presence through the flow. Reaching all around, she gathers as much sand she can handle. Suddenly, she senses another presence. She takes a few moments to focus on the person. Melissa feels that the gargoyle is being controlled by the other presence. With a sudden realization, she stands up. "Tobius, Morrin is controlling this creature."

Tobius rolls under a slash from the animal and looks at her. "Are you sure?"

Melissa draws her blade, joining the fray. She jumps, driving her blade down into the right shoulder of the gargoyle, and it howls in pain. As the creature is recovering from the surprise attack, she shouts at Tobius, "We either have to knock it out or kill it!"

Tobius nods and charges the beast. As the creature swings its left arm down, he dives under the attack. The claws dig into the sand where he was a moment before. Jumping to his feet, he brings both blades around and slices through the forearm of the gargoyle. He aims carefully to disable the left arm while avoiding any major arteries.

As Tobius is still by the animal's legs, he hears a bone-crunching thunk. Tobius quickly jumps from under the gargoyle and looks at Melissa. "What happened?"

Melissa is in mid-shrug when she drops her blade and starts grabbing at her throat. Tobius looks toward the cave and sees Morrin emerging with his right hand stretched in Melissa's direction. Rage flares in Tobius. "Release her, now!"

Morrin lets a maniacal laugh escape him. "Why would I release her? I killed the gargoyle for not killing you." With a flick of his hand, Melissa flies into a wall of sandstone, and she crumples to the ground. Tobius quickly reaches out to her and finds, with relief, that she is just knocked out. Morrin draws his own ferioblade and starts moving toward Tobius.

Morrin and Tobius slowly circle each other at a two-meter distance. "You should join me." Tobius gives no response, preparing himself for a fight. Tobius grips both blades in standard grips. Morrin charges in, holding the blade in both hands.

Tobius raises his left blade to block the double-handed overhead strike. He looks at his opponent. "Why are you doing this?"

Morrin smiles. "Master Krystelle will reward me with apprenticeship if I kill you."

Tobius glares at him. "Fine. Have it your way."

With that, Tobius aggressively starts at him. Tobius swings his right blade at Morrin's left knee, but he steps back a moment before. Spinning, he hits Tobius in the chest with the hilt of his blade. Tobius sprawls back from the hit, feeling a rib crack. Taking the momentum, Tobius rolls back onto his feet and charges at his enemy. He brings his left blade in a sweeping arc from the ground. He tries to knock him off-balance. Morrin absorbs the impact and kicks Tobius, catching him in the stomach. He gets lifted half a meter off the ground from the impact.

Morrin sneers. "How is it that you kept up with Master Phylox but can barely keep up with me?"

Tobius gets to his feet. He flips the left blade to a reverse grip as he had in his duels on Marina and charges Morrin. He brings his right blade across his chest and locks it with Morrin's blade. Tobius slams the hilt of the left blade into the back of his opponent's right hand with an audible wet snap. Morrin screams in pain and hurls Tobius away with the void. After flying fifteen meters, he hits a pile of stone. Tobius gets to his feet just in time to bring his right blade up to stop his head from leaving his body. He starts to swing his left arm but realizes he has no blade. Improvising, he punches Morrin in the stomach. As his enemy staggers from the sucker punch, he grabs Morrin's blade, wrenching it from his hand. Tobius drives the tip of the ferioblade into Morrin's right foot then jumps, delivering a roundhouse kick to the side of his enemy's head.

Tobius checks Morrin to ensure his is still alive then collects his weapons. He hurries over to Melissa, giving the gargoyle corpse a wide berth. He gets to Melissa's side right as she begins to stir. He helps her sit up.

She asks, "What happened?"

Tobius quickly explains, "Krystelle sent Morrin to kill me, and he is currently knocked out. We should hurry."

She nods as she slowly rises. They make their way into the cave. Tobius pulls the glow rod out.

The cave is dark and cold. They move slowly to ensure they do not spook any creatures in the cave. There is no way to tell how far or long they have been in the cave. The air seems to cloud their senses. They come upon an open cavern wherein lies thousands of luminescent crystals, like a starlit night with every color of the spectrum. Tobius lets loose a whistle at the spectacular sight. Moving to the closest wall, he examines the crystals and sees that these are all just shards smaller than two centimeters. Tobius finds a small passage and follows it to the right.

"Tobius," he hears echoing from somewhere ahead. "Will you help us?" he hears again.

Keeping his hands on the wall for support, he moves through the meter-diameter tunnel. Making his way by all sorts of cave stones, he finally emerges into a small opening. He steps out of the tunnel and stretches after making the almost seventy meters crouched. It looks like an explosion happened in the area while ferocrete was drying. No more than a half square meter at any point is smooth. Tobius carefully makes his way into the middle of the opening. He looks at the eight cubic meters or so of space around him.

Suddenly, a violet figure emerges from the void. "I see you made it."

Tobius looks around. "Sanguis," he simply responds.

The figure nods. "Glad to see you escaped the confines of the Keepers."

Tobius nods. "What is this place?"

"This is a fount of power," the figure states, floating around him. "There are unique crystals here that allow for unique weapons."

Tobius closes his eyes and lets his mind explore the area around him. He feels a crystal to his right slightly behind him and three and half meters into the wall. Outstretching his hand, he focuses the flow to extract this crystal. At first, the crystal refuses to move, but Tobius takes a moment to seek out fractures near the crystal. Finding a small crease, he wills the flow to loosen the crystal. After several minutes, a crack emanates from the wall, and the crystal floats from the wall to his hand. Tobius opens his eyes and looks at the sage crystal resting in his palm. Just when he begins to leave, he senses something else. He steps to his left deeper into the area. Kneeling, he looks into a small crater, and there is a crystal, half the size of the sage crystal, the color of amber. Placing the crystals in a belt pouch, Tobius crawls his way out of the tunnel. Melissa is still looking around the cavern.

Tobius asks, "Have you found any yet?" She nods as she heads to him. She opens her hand and shows a lavender crystal.

As they exit the cave, dawn is breaking across the horizon. They look around the area and see the gargoyle corpse, but Morrin is nowhere to be seen. "Come on," Tobius says, jogging back to the academy. They enter the courtyard as Master Phylox's acolytes are entering the courtyard for training.

Melissa squeezes Tobius's hand. "I will go find Master Gamite."

Tobius jogs over to Phylox. "Master Phylox, I have returned."

He turns from the two acolytes dueling. "Welcome back, Acolyte Tobius." He looks back to the duel. "Hey, if you have chance to disarm your opponent, you take it." Master Phylox takes Tobius by the shoulder and leads him to a corner of the courtyard. "What happened out there?" Tobius quickly explains what happened. "So Acolyte Morrin used the void to get that albino gargoyle to attack you, and Master Krystelle will grant him apprenticeship if he ends you?" Tobius nods. "So show me the crystal you found." Tobius pulls the two crystals from his belt pouch.

Phylox examines the two crystals. The sage crystal is just over four centimeters long with a pentagonal cross section just under three centimeters across. The amber crystal has a circumference of only three centimeters but is a dodecahedral.

"May I?" he asks the young man, gesturing to the crystals. Tobius nods, and he picks up the crystals. First, he looks at the sage one and holds it to the morning light. He cannot believe the clarity of this crystal. The light shining through it shows almost no flaw within, and the way it allows the light through is just like a prism. Holding the amber crystal to the light, he is just as amazed. This crystal welcomes the light, and depending on how you position the crystal, it amplifies or refracts the light. "Either one of these crystals will make you an outstanding blade. Go get some breakfast and come to my study after."

Tobius nods, collects his crystals, and heads to the dining hall.

After a filling breakfast, he checks the courtyard and still sees Master Phylox out there and heads to his room to change. Tobius sees Melissa coming out of her room. "What did Master Gamite think of your crystal?"

"He is very pleased by it. I am heading to his study to work on making my void blade."

Tobius nods and shows her the crystals he found. "I am heading to Master Phylox's study after I change."

"Those are amazing, Tobius," she says, mesmerized. "I better go. I don't want to be late."

"Good luck, Melissa."

She smiles. "You too." And with that, she jogs down the hall to the study.

After watching her leave, he then turns to his room. Quickly, he dons a fresh set of clothes and heads to Phylox's study. He arrives and hits the chime on the door control. Right as he reaches to open the door, he hears a voice behind him. "Did you enjoy your breakfast?"

Tobius spins to see Master Phylox approaching. "I did," he replies with a slight bow.

Phylox uses the flow to depress the door control so he would not break stride. "Come in, please." Tobius obediently follows. Phylox heads to his cabinet and pours himself a glass of the amber liquid. He gestures Tobius to the workbench. "Now the other two will be given the pieces needed to complete their blade, but you will do like I had to."

Tobius looks at him quizzically. "What do you mean?"

Laughing, Phylox sits on a stool. "I was not given anything but a reliable power source. I had to go the refuge outside the city and find what I needed."

Tobius sits down, pondering this. Then he asks, "Why?"

He looks at his young acolyte. "Both Morrin and Melissa will be getting similar parts. By them being given these parts, their blades will be just like every other acolyte who faces the trials." He stops to enjoy his beverage and to give Tobius time to complete the puzzle.

After a few moments, Tobius looks at him. "I will be able to create my own blade the way I feel it should be."

Phylox grins and nods. "I have a speeder stored just outside the courtyard gate. Head east from there for about five kilometers, and you will find the refuge."

Tobius stands and bows again. "Thank you, Master Phylox."

Tobius exits the study, sprinting to his bunk to grab his gear and cloak. He swings by the dining hall to grab a quick bite then heads to the courtyard. Once outside the courtyard, he sees the speeder. He removes the cover and climbs on, hitting the accelerator. Tobius is thrilled about having a chance to get away from the academy and pushes the speeder to maximum speed of sixty kilometers per hour. In just a few minutes, he sees the refuge ahead and slows down. Tobius stores the speeder just outside the refuge, placing the cover on it. Entering the refuge, he starts searching for what he needs. Spending most of the day rummaging around, he finds two phase pulse laser emitters, a set of speeder throttle control handles, two wrist gauntlet shield emitters, two kill switch cylinders, and a meter-long steel power conduit.

He returns to the speeder and secures his pack. He starts the speeder and makes his way back to the academy. When he is about halfway back, he sees a sandstorm heading his way. He quickly jams the accelerator to max and hopes he can make it back. More than half a kilometer from the courtyard, Tobius slams on the brakes as he runs headlong into the sandstorm. He jumps off the speeder and quickly secures the cover. Keeping the antigrav pods engaged, he starts pushing the speeder. It takes well over ninety minutes for him to move the speeder into the storage slot. He is completely covered in sand, but the speeder is okay.

After a quick shower, he grabs his pack and jogs to Master Phylox's study. Even though it is two hours after dusk, Phylox is sitting in his study. The door is open, but he still hits the chime. Master Phylox looks up and beckons him in with a wave of his hand. "How was your search?"

Tobius bows slightly, replying, "It was okay, but I did encounter a sandstorm on my way back."

Phylox stands and meets him at the workbench. "Let's see what you found." Tobius quickly lays out what he found. "Why did you get so much?"

Tobius looks at him and replies, "I will make two."

Nodding, Phylox hands him another power supply then steps back. "Very well. If you need any other items, just ask."

Tobius sits on the stool and starts assembling his blades. First, he cuts the steel conduit into four sections—two ten-centimeter and two thirty-centimeter sections. Then he removes the throttle handles. He cuts the thirty-centimeter sections in half on its length and in one half cuts a hole for the throttle handles. He bores a small slot on both handles where his palm will rest and sets the emergency kill switch and a lock lever by his thumb. He then fits the power cell into the conduit and the emitter on end of the conduit. On the other half of the conduit, he secures the gauntlet shield emitter and fine-tunes them to emit a centimeter off the half of the conduit. He covers the entire thirty-centimeter length. Once he completes the formatting for the weapons, he gathers all the items.

Phylox steps forward. "Tobius, use this," he says, handing him a rolled-up rug.

Tobius unrolls the rug and notices that it has every rune the Keepers know. Confused, he looks at Phylox. "I thought only three runes could be used on one item?"

Laughing, Phylox says, "Look closer."

Upon closer inspection, each rune is on its own patch, and then they are all connected with the rune of power in the center of the others. Tobius arranges the items on the floor then sits cross-legged in the center of the rug.

Tobius had been constructing his weapons for three hours before he started the final process. Master Phylox has been silently monitoring his process, and he is quite pleased with the progress. When he created his blade over twenty years ago, he was not allowed to stop from the initial creation until it was complete. He also has not allowed any of his acolytes to stop, and any that were unable to complete the task were expelled from the academy. Phylox is amazed because never in his history has an acolyte attempted to complete a double-bladed void blade, and he has never heard of any acolyte try and complete two blades with completely different crystals. It takes extreme concentration to ensure that the crystal is aligned correctly to ensure that the blade forms and that the crystal will not fracture from the stress and heat. He refreshes his glass, grabs a pastry, and returns to his seat to watch.

Tobius spends the next fifteen minutes focusing on the upcoming task. Master Phylox advises him, "It is the flow that completes the weapon, and it reacts to your emotions."

Tobius nods and checks everything one last time. Taking in one more deep breath, he reaches out to his weapons. He feels the power of the flow rushing around and through him. The power is so pure that a chill races down his spine. He senses a presence older and wiser than any he has ever met. Remembering what Phylox says, he focuses on why he is here. He thinks about his lost family, the hermit, and the fallen Keepers. A tear rolls down his left cheek, but he continues to focus. A memory of Sanguis surfaces, but he just lets the anger wash away in the flow. Tobius finally sees the parts of his weapons through the flow and begins to assemble them. He sees thousands of colored threads weave from him into the weapon itself. The threads cover the crystals, and as each thread contacts the crystal, a rune appears then fades. He is transfixed by the flow. Tobius can just watch as the threads reach from the crystal to the other items, stitching them together. He sets the sage crystal where the energy flows through the length of the crystal evenly and forms the conduit around the crystal to secure it. Then he switches his focus to the amber crystal. With the multiple facets, he takes time to use the power to find the best position for it. He finally finds the angle he wants and secures it to the handle. Now he starts at the back of each weapon individually and molds the back into a rounded end.

Phylox walks around Tobius, watching as he simultaneously assembles both blades. Moving a stool from the workbench, he takes a seat just in front of Tobius. In this time, the emitters have fused to the conduit. He is now fusing the second halves of the conduit together. He watches as the two halves are stitched together with an almost unnoticeable seam. He watches as the young man fuses the gauntlet shield to the back of each blade and feeds the power wires through the conduit to the power cell and the ignition cable to the activation switch.

After nearly three hours of constant concentration, he begins check the connections within the weapons. Once he ensures the connections are complete, he tests every switch to ensure the power flows through each blade as it should.

Tobius slowly lowers both hilts to the ground and opens his eyes. He is shocked to see Master Phylox sitting not more than a meter away, watching intently. The young man leans forward and collects his blades. Exhausted, he carefully examines both hilts. Both hilts look like metal tonfas, and Tobius grabs both handles. He spins both hilts around the handle and is pleased to find that the weight is evenly balanced across the weapon.

Master Phylox leans forward. "May I examine them?" Tobius nods, handing them over. He spins, twists, and tosses the hilts to get a good feel of the design and nods his approval. "Very well, Acolyte Tobius." Returning the hilts, he asks, "Shall we test them?"

Tobius smiles, excited. "Yes, Master Phylox." Heading from the study, they jog down to the courtyard. Tobius is surprised to see dawn breaking as they enter the courtyard. "I was working on it all night?"

Phylox laughs and nods. "Now let's see if your work was successful."

Hesitantly, Tobius caresses the handles in both hands, and after a few heartbeats, he switches hands. Tobius takes a deep relaxing breath then sets his feet. He thumbs the activation studs on both blades, and with a crisp sizzle, both blades spring to life.

Tobius slowly spins both blades as he looks at his new weapons. He is surprised to see that the shield on each hilt reflects the color of the crystal within. He takes time to spin each blade and get used to its feel, and he is pleased that each weapon is perfectly balanced. The hilt is thirty centimeters from emitter to end, with each blade extending to a point at eighty centimeters. He begins slow patterns, weaving the weapons in figure eights on both sides with little more than flicks of his wrists. Tobius starts working steps, ducks, and spins into his movement. Within ten minutes, the young man is surrounded by a sage and amber shield of seeming impregnable energy. Slowing his blades to a stop, he beams with pride, but he looks at Master Phylox in shock.

Seven meters away, Phylox watches his acolyte familiarize himself with his weapons. As his acolyte slows his blades, he quietly unclips his own and removes his cloak. His weapon's hilt is twenty centimeters, and the blade is 115 centimeters in length. *It will be very interesting to see how he can fair against my blade, and I against his*, Phylox thinks, igniting his maroon blade. He laughs at the face of his student. "Shall we see how they handle with a quick duel?"

Tobius nods, setting his stance. He spins his blades quickly and bends into a crouch, stopping the amber blade in his left hand just a hair's breadth from his forearm and the sage blade slightly behind him with the tip sizzling just a centimeter off the ground. "Let's dance." The young man smiles, eager to try his hand. Phylox grins and settles into his stance, feet shoulder width apart and double-handed grip in a low ready position.

The sun crests over the horizon as the two prepare to duel. Tobius waits for several heartbeats to see if Phylox will start, and when nothing happens, he starts to advance, spinning the sage blade beside him. At two meters, Phylox quickly releases his right hand and swings the blade in an overhanded strike. Tobius stops the blade on the amber weapon. He pushes the blade up and rotates left, bringing the sage blade in a low sweeping arc, scorching the ground with the tip. Phylox takes the momentum from the push, backflips over the sage blade, and twists to sweep his blade at Tobius's left shoulder. The young man ducks, letting the amber blade deflect the maroon weapon three centimeters over his left shoulder. Tobius slams the shield of the sage blade into Master Phylox's right thigh and rolls past.

Cursing himself for not seeing the simple shot, Phylox stomps his leg to remove the pain. "Nicely done, Tobius." Quickly, Phylox starts his counterattack. Using his familiarity and skill with his weapon, he turns it into a storm of lightning-fast maroon strikes.

Tobius remembers that those who wield two blade weapons often settle into defensive stances with little positions, but against this barrage, he would fail if he does that. Tobius lets the first few strikes hit both blades, and after a half dozen or so, since they came to fast to count, he shifts his left blade to accept a blow on the outer third of the amber blade. This impact allows him to get his blade spinning. Tobius withstands another dozen blows and now has both blades spinning around him. He begins to block and counterattack in the same fluid motion, letting a block reverse the blade it hits, causing a slight stagger from the fluidity of Master Phylox's attacks. He spins the amber weapon counterclockwise up to stop a thrust and spins to his right, bringing his sage blade around, extended away from his hand. Phylox steps back, having to adjust for the odd attack angle. He kicks at Tobius and is surprised to see his left heel bounce off the shield of the amber weapon. Phylox staggers back two meters and charges back in with a double-handed overhead strike. Tobius senses the attack and smacks his hilts together horizontally in a defensive reflex. When the two hilts collide, a wave of power erupts from the weapons, and the concussive force sends Phylox rolling backward in the dirt.

Phylox rolls to his feet, extinguishes his blade, and glares at the young human. "What was that?" he snaps.

Tobius is stunned by the edge in his mentor's voice. "I have no idea. I was just reacting to your attack."

Phylox rubs his chin as he walks toward the young man. "Very good, Tobius," he says between breaths. "I would like to duel with you every other morning at dawn. This way, you can better learn your weapon, and I can learn from you as well."

Tobius shuts off both blades and staggers slightly from exhaustion. "Sounds good to me. Shall we go to breakfast?"

Phylox claps him on the shoulder and leads the way. "Keep the hilts hidden for now." They make their way from the courtyard as most of the other acolytes are heading out for the morning combat training. They sit down and enjoy a nice quiet breakfast.

The Ryft

After Phylox finishes his food, he starts, "Now that you have your blades, you will now progress to the next trial." Tobius takes a bite of fruit and a drink of his milk. "You will now be required to venture into one of the old tombs in the Ryft and retrieve an artifact."

Tobius looks at Phylox, confused, and asks, "What is the Ryft?"

Phylox leans forward, interlocking his fingers with his elbows on the table. "The Ryft was a fount of power here, and several millennia ago, some void raiders tried to channel all the power from the fount. We do not know who or what they did, but we do know that it backfired. The resulting explosion formed a three-kilometer wide, one-kilometer-deep crater." Tobius looks at him, shocked. "Ever since then, it has been a tainted place, and only the most powerful void masters get buried there." Before Tobius can ask any further questions, Phylox waves his left hand and continues. "Once you return, you will then duel in front of every Master that will be looking for an apprentice."

Tobius swallows his bite then asks, "Who would I fight?"

Master Phylox takes a drink of his java. "Every time, it changes, but almost every time, someone does not survive."

Tobius takes several moments to ponder this and replies, "Do you think I can find something about Sanguis?"

Phylox considers that for a few moments. "I am not sure, but there are a lot of areas in most tombs that are yet to be discovered." Tobius nods as he finishes his breakfast.

Once they both finish, Tobius heads back to his room, showers, and gets some sleep. Tobius is restless in his bunk. He can see the Ryft and a cloaked figure. He sees him move from tomb to tomb until he enters the Tomb of Shadows. He pauses by the doorway, carving his symbol into the stone. The figure enters the tomb, and the vision blurs. Tobius jolts upright. Quickly donning his cloak, he heads to find Master Phylox.

As he makes his way to the study, Master Kyron's voice echoes in the hall. "How are your trials progressing?"

Tobius spins around and is surprised to not only see Kyron but also Krystelle. Bowing slightly, he replies, "It is going well." The young man is wary of the two Masters.

"Master Kyron, Master Krystelle, to what do we owe this pleasure?" Glancing over his shoulder, he sees Phylox, followed by Gamite and Melissa. "Acolyte Tobius's trials are progressing well, and we are about to send him into the Ryft."

Kyron gives the young man a menacing glance and looks to his teacher. "Master Phylox, I am pleased to hear it." She nods a greeting to Master Gamite. "I would like to speak with all of you about the third trial." Tobius finally sees that Morrin is standing subserviently to Krystelle's right. "So it is safe to assume that all your acolytes have completed their void blades?" Both Gamite and Phylox nod.

Kyron continues past them to Master Krystelle's study. Unlike Master Phylox's study, Krystelle's is based mainly for comfort and not study. As they enter, Kyron and Krystelle sit on two lush lounge chairs while Phylox and Gamite sit in the other armchairs. Morrin stands just behind Krystelle while Melissa and Tobius stand beside their respective masters.

"In one month's time, we will have all the masters present, and if you would like, all three of you have the right to pick an apprentice. We will allow all apprentices who have lost their masters engage in a tournament for a new master." The three instructors nod. "Now the acolytes will head toward the Ryft for the second trial, and they will depart in the morning." Master Kyron stands and leaves the room. Master Krystelle remains seated as she exits, but the others stand and give a slight bow. Phylox motions Tobius and Melissa to the exit.

Once they are well away from Krystelle's study, Gamite speaks. "Please come to my study to discuss this impending challenge."

They make their way to his study, and Tobius is shocked at what lies within. He expected to find an old-looking archive, but Master Gamite's study is a cross between a fancy lounge and a science lab. He can tell that credits were no concern when this was put together, but what else would you expect from a Master of Wealth? When the door closes, a small service droid whirrs from its corner. "Welcome back, Master. May I get you something?"

Gamite replies, "Just some pastries for me and my guests."

"This is amazing," Tobius says, awestruck.

The old man chuckles. "Yes, my lounge to relax in and the lab to explore things." They all sit on three luxurious couches surrounding a dark blue crystalline table.

"Now," Phylox says, leaning back, "where will you look in the Ryft?"

The droid brings the pastries, sets the gem-encrusted serving tray on the table, and retreats. Tobius eyes the tray of pastries as he says matter-of-factually, "I will go to the Tomb of Shadows."

A shocked silence fills the room as they let what was said sink in. Master Phylox leans forward. "Why will you go there?"

Tobius looks at him. "I had a vision of the figure from Draken entering that tomb."

The old man pipes in, "Did you ever find anything about Sanguis, Phylox?"

Phylox shakes his head. "Whoever this guy is, he did an excellent job making sure not just anyone could find him."

Tobius stands quickly. "Now it makes sense. The Keepers are a secret group that only allows select people know they exist, and Sanguis was the one that all but destroyed them. So it makes sense that the Keepers did everything possible to hide him so they were not discovered."

Excitedly, Melissa says, "That's why we could not find much in the Keepers' archives."

Master Phylox stands and nods to Gamite. "Now I must discuss things with Tobius in private."

Tobius is led out by his instructor, and he touches Melissa on the shoulder as he goes. They move to Phylox's study to continue the conversation.

"Tobius, most people facing the trials go to simple tombs, but the one you seek will not be very easy. I have yet to see an acolyte return from there."

Tobius nods understandingly. "This may be true, but I must."

"Very well. Tomorrow morning, you will be given a speeder to head to the valley. Each one going is advised to just worry about completing their own task, but we have had acolytes killed by one another."

Tobius considers this for a moment. "So you are saying that Master Krystelle may have Morrin follow me and try and steal whatever I find?" Phylox nods. Tobius bows to him. "Thank you for the warning." With that, he leaves the study to prepare for his trip and get some sleep.

He gets back to his bunk and begins to pack. After getting his gear stowed, he hears a light knock on his door. Curious, he opens the door to see Melissa standing there. She appears sad. "What's wrong?" Tobius guides her in with his right hand and shuts the door. As soon as the door closes, she spins around and embraces him, sobbing into his shoulder.

After several heartbeats, she steps back. "Tobius, what will you do? You know that Morrin will try and kill you tomorrow, and the Tomb of Shadows is the most dangerous in the Ryft."

Tobius takes her hands. "I know, but I have to go there. Though I do not know what I am looking for, but it is there."

Melissa looks at him, tears streaming down her face. "Please promise me you will be safe."

Tobius smiles at her. "I will, Melissa." He asks her, "What can I do to help settle your mind?"

She looks deep into his blue eyes. "Can I stay with you?"

Tobius is caught off guard from this request, but something in her hazel eyes keeps him from saying no. The young man blushes slightly and replies, "Yes, you can, Melissa."

Tobius holds on to her as she sleeps. Throughout the night, he gets images of the tomb, but nothing is clear. He sees Sanguis moving through different halls and rooms, and just before he wakes, he sees him standing in front of a wall with a crimson hexagon in the middle. A bell chimes through the acolyte bunk hall, and they both get ready to leave. Before leaving, Tobius grabs the obsidian diamond and stows it in a belt pouch. He also slips his hilts into the loops where the Razik blades used to go and dons his cloak.

"Are you ready, Melissa?"

She turns to him, looking just like she did when they first met—strong, determined, and full of pride. "Yes, let's go."

They head out to the courtyard. As they leave the hallway, they see the masters on a platform, and they move to them. Tobius receives nods of greeting from Phylox and Gamite but glares of hatred from Kyron, Krystelle, and Morrin.

Kyron addresses the acolytes. "You will now head to the Ryft and retrieve something from the tombs. Once you have done so, you return here."

The three head toward the speeders. It takes just over an hour to get the Ryft, and of course, Morrin is nowhere to be seen. As they near the Ryft, the air becomes heavy, and even though it is midday, it looks more like dusk. Even though he knew a little about what had happened to form the Ryft, he was not expecting what they see. The Ryft is well more than a kilometer in radius. The sand is almost black with streaks of silver within. The stone walls absorb both light and sound, making the Ryft seem even more lifeless. In the center stands the Tomb of Shadows. This pitch-black structure, two hundred meters wide, has five pillars on top, which is believed to be where the people who caused the formation of the Ryft stood. Tobius stops about half a kilometer from the tomb and looks at Melissa.

"Which tomb will you go to?" Tobius asks Melissa. She smiles and shrugs. "Okay, have it your way," he says jokingly. Tobius glances over his shoulder and sees Melissa heading to the cliff wall on the right. He jogs to the entrance of his target tomb. Arriving at the tomb, he finds the entrance blocked by a mound of sand. At first, Tobius considers using the flow but decides to clear the sand manually. It takes him over thirty minutes to dig out the entrance, but he enjoys the manual labor to help relieve tension. Once the door is clear, he looks around until he finds the symbol he is looking for.

Reassured that he is in the right place, he starts trying to open the door. First, he tries to push the door with no success, and then he looks for a control panel. Again, no luck. He tries to use the flow to move the door, but the door refuses to open. Tobius sits down, trying to figure it out. He lets his mind reach toward the door, and behind the door he feels a switch. He applies pressure to the switch, and it moves with ease. A deep groan emanates from the wall as the door slowly lifts. Tobius is amazed that the door is over a meter thick. He carefully heads inside the tomb and examines the interior. He heard stories that this tomb was protected not only by skreapers but also droids and traps.

The main hall has five support pillars with a dozen attached rooms and pathways. Tobius figures that most of the first rooms have been raided from previous acolytes. He slowly moves to his left, checking each room or passage. Some of the rooms are filled with rubble while others have been ransacked. Looking into the third doorway, he sees three skreapers sleeping within. He moves quietly so as not to stir the slumbering creatures. He moves farther along the wall. After checking eight more doorways and three short passages, he locates a set of stairs partially blocked with debris. Examining the stones blocking the path, he sees a way through the rubble.

Tobius starts climbing through the debris and hears something behind him. Fearing that he somehow woke the skreapers, he stops and glances over his shoulder. All he sees is the empty path he came from. Waiting for several heartbeats, he holds completely still, and when nothing happens, he continues forward. It takes nearly thirty minutes to pass through the debris. Several times, he feels the pile shift and waits for it to settle. Once he clears the rubble, he pulls a glow rod from a belt pouch and starts forward. The stairs double back toward the main chamber. There are some cracks in the ceiling, letting small shafts of light in, but it does little to dispel the darkness. The young man must take more time to examine each doorway, but there are seventeen paths from what he can tell. After circumventing the room twice, he has no idea where to go.

Getting frustrated by the lack of logical paths, he sits down to figure out where Sanguis went. He sits in one of the shafts of light and starts meditating. It takes him a lot longer to focus with how thick the atmosphere is. Finally, he relaxes and tries to force his mind's eye to where he wants it. But the more he tries to force it, the more anger builds within him. He looks over his right shoulder, back to the path he came from, and finally catches an echo of Sanguis at the wall at his eight-o'clock position to how he is sitting. Finally with a direction, he opens his eyes and jumps back in shock. Standing not even half a meter from him is a massive skreaper. This animal is over five meters long including the tail, and at its shoulder, almost two meters tall.

Tobius curses himself for not sensing its approach. The crimson bloodred eye burns red-hot with animalistic rage. He rolls back, grabs his weapons as he rises to his feet three meters away. He recalls the gargoyle and how Morrin controlled it. Reaching out with his mind, he tries to persuade its mind, but that only enrages the creature.

He steps back and tries to figure a way out of this mess. There is no obvious escape path, and there is no way he can make it back to the stairs. The creature starts forward with a massive roar. Tobius is unsure on how to handle this, so he just keeps distance between them. The skreaper charges at him in a flash. Tobius ignites both blades just in time to use the shield to intercept the poison barb on the tail. The young man manages to keep the creature's tail and claws from finding their mark. He realizes that he has no choice but to try and incapacitate the creature. He brings his left blade up to deflect another tail strike. He reaches out, trying to shove the creature into the wall, but the skreaper digs its massive claws into the floor, weathering the blast. Cursing, he steadies himself for a fight to the death with this beast.

Finally setting his resolve, he begins to attack the skreaper. Waiting for a strike from the tail, he uses the shield to redirect the tail into a column to his right. The tail strikes deep into a small crack in the column. Rolling to his left, he rises to his feet just in time to have the skreaper's right hind foot connect with his upper back. He feels the razor-sharp claws slice deep into his back and right deltoid. Instantly, he feels the arm go limp, and the hilt drops from his hand. Through the intense pain, he focuses, summoning the flow. He keeps the sage blade active and hurls it at the skreaper, embedding it to the hilt behind its right foreleg. Tobius looks to see the tip of the blade emerging just behind the skull, and with a crash, the animal falls to the floor. He breathes a sigh of relief, but then he feels the poison from the claws burning though his body. Quickly, Tobius removes an emergency med kit and finds the poison kit. This kit has four vials within and one autoinjector. He looks and doubts the three standard antitoxins are strong enough for the skreaper's venom. He selects the fourth vial and uneasily makes his way to the fallen beast. He scrapes some of the venom dripping from the claws, and once he has half a vial, he inserts it into the top half of the poison kit. He slumps down against the column where the tail is still embedded. He can feel the venom ripping his body apart from within and wills the poison kit to work faster.

Two agonizing minutes slowly tick by as the kit works an antidote. He can feel his pulse quicken, trying to fight off the toxin, but he knows without the antitoxin, he will not survive. A small green light illuminates, indicating the antidote is complete. He struggles to remove the vial as the venom slowly immobilizes his limbs. Struggling, he manages to remove the vial and insert it into the autoinjector. He has to inject it into his thigh, but as he moves to turn the injector, his hands go slack, and it falls into a crack in the floor not quite half a meter away to his left. His vision blurs as his time is running out. He reaches for the injector, but his hand cannot close around it. Sensing time is short, he summons his last bit of strength and rolls to the injector, bringing his right thigh down hard on the injector.

Phantoms of the Tomb

As Tobius and Melissa part ways, she watches him head to the structure in the valley. She turns to her right, moving toward the cliff wall. She takes her time to decide which tomb to enter. Reaching into the flow, she ensures she is not anywhere close to Morrin. She now comes to the fourth tomb and sees the door has been damaged. She cautiously makes her way into the tomb. She is unable to tell whose tomb this is to begin with. Carefully, the woman makes her way into the tomb, moving slowly, glow rod in one hand and her hilt in the other. She can sense intense dark energy flowing through the empty paths. Moving along the paths, she sees that several paths are dead ends, or the bridges across caverns have collapsed.

She makes her way deep into the tomb, finding a single bridge less than a meter wide spanning more than forty meters over a seemingly bottomless cavern. She takes a moment to rub her temples. The deeper she progresses into the tomb, the greater difficulty she has focusing. She cautiously makes her way over the chasm below. As soon as she steps from the bridge, she collapses to her knees, holding her head. After a few minutes of intense pain, she looks and sees the Mistress of Knowledge glaring at her with rage.

"I save your life and teach you how to become strong. Now you fail me by giving up what it means to be a Master of Knowledge."

Before she can reply, the fallen Gatekeeper steps before her with a hole in his chest. His deep voice echoes all around her. "You were supposed to protect us from the seeker of justice, but you can't even find other Keepers."

She shakes her head in shame, and the hermit steps forward. "You let me die, and now you will give the Void-raiders what they want. You are no Keeper of Power."

Image after image flows in front of her, constantly saying she has failed. She is in tears, on her hands and knees, unable to keep back her fear and regret. She thinks about the friends she lost and softly says, "I have not failed." This simple statement bolsters her resolve, and she again says, "I have not failed." She slowly makes her way to her feet as the figures bombard her with failure. She sets her feet, takes a deep breath, and yells, "I have not nor shall I fail!" With that profound statement, all the figures vanish.

Melissa stands motionless for several moments then picks up the glow rod and looks around. The light reflects off something small against the right wall. She makes her way to the object and finds a small chest. It is a mere half meter wide, fifteen centimeters tall, and twenty-three centimeters deep. She slips the chest into her pack and heads back the way she came. After fifteen minutes, she reaches the mouth of the tomb.

Dusk is settling on the valley as she exits the tomb. She sees Morrin heading back to the academy and hears his laughter as he speeds off. Jogging to the speeders, she finds both speeders irreparably damaged by Morrin's blade. She shoots a hateful glare in Morrin's direction and decides to wait for Tobius. She stores the chest and settles in between the two speeders. As she settles in, she activates some emergency glow rods and tosses them around to illuminate the surrounding area. Of course, she does not try and sleep since she has no idea what may be lurking in the Ryft.

* * *

Tobius slowly opens his eyes. "Well, that was fun," he says to no one. Slowly, he rolls onto his back and feels like he was run over by a star cruiser. He stretches his arms and sits up. Rolling onto his side, he carefully rises to his feet. He takes a moment to try and feel the wound from the skreaper. He glances at his chrono. It has been over eleven hours since they arrived in the valley. "Talk about a knockout blow." He removes a med kit and pulls out some med salves, but he realizes that he can barely raise his right arm. Tobius kicks the dead skreaper in frustration. Summoning the flow, he secures the salves along his back and shoulder. He also grabs a health stim and adrenaline stim shot from the med kit and injects them in his right shoulder. Then he grabs another vial and gathers a sample of the venom. "Who knows if this would come in handy, but if not, Melissa and Phylox would probably like to study it."

Even though almost twelve hours have passed, he still has no idea where to go. He quickly takes a moment to try and follow Sanguis's echo, but he cannot pick anything up. He slowly makes his way around the room, checking briefly down the possible paths. He goes full circle around the main chamber, but there are no discernible leads. Tobius keeps moving along the wall, knowing it must be here somewhere. When Tobius is almost above the main entrance, he gets a tingle in his spine. Moving to the wall, he ignites the amber blade to illuminate the area. He examines every square centimeter within a three-meter area of him. At knee level, Tobius finds what appears to be a three-line crossing in the middle, forming a star pattern. Dropping to one knee, he wipes the dirt off the walls and sees that the center of the lines cave inward as he brushes over it. Grabbing a nearby piece of debris, he pushes the middle of the lines and sees them hinge into a hexagon.

Tobius looks at the hexagonal recession and ponders. "I wonder," he says to himself. He quickly removes the wrapped artifact from his belt pouch. He inserts the diamond, and an audible click echoes through the room. Tobius tries to push the key in more, but it does not move. Next, he tries to remove the diamond, but again no response. Thinking about the possible ways Sanguis thinks, he reaches for the power of the flow. Focusing on the crystal, he pulses some energy to it. The pulse exponentially increases through the diamond and flows along what feels like a crystalline wire. With the minuscule amount of energy, it powers up a mechanism, and a small door pops open.

The young human looks a meter to his left at the new door. It's only two meters tall and half meter wide. He waits to see if anything will come out, and after several heartbeats, he starts moving inward. Using his amber blade both for lighting and defense if needed, he enters the hidden room. Tobius moves slowly through the passage, stopping every few steps to make sure he does not trigger any traps. After several dozen meters, the passage seems to be widening. Tobius takes a few moments to look around. The passage widens to about three meters wide and almost looks like it was just a natural crevice. Looking at the small area, he starts to turn around when a lavender cloud races into the passage. Reflexively, he raises his amber blade in a cross bodyguard. His shield and blade react to the cloud, but no attacks fall.

A deep bass voice sounds behind him. "Why are you here?"

The young man turns around, looking at the figure. "I seek power."

The apparition seems to grow larger with that statement. "What makes you think you're worthy of the power I possess?" Tobius gets no chance to respond as the cloud surrounds him. "Prove to me if you are strong."

The young man can see nothing, but he feels Sanguis. In a moment, he finds himself in a cell with only a bunk and lamp. He stands, and he can tell it is an illusion. Sanguis is just outside the cell. "Why do you conform to the Void-raiders? First it was the Keepers, and now Void-raiders." He paces around as he continues, "You seek justice, but it cannot be attained through conformance." Tobius looks around the cell. The ceiling and floor are stone, but all walls are energy fields. "Tobius, you either escape this cell or die."

Looking shocked, he inquires, "What do you mean?"

A menacing laugh erupts from the figure. "The door to this passage is on a timer. You have twenty minutes or the door shuts."

Tobius glances around the room, and there is nothing but the bunk and lamp in the cell with him. He reaches out his right hand and touches the field. The instant his finger makes contact with the field, his entire right arm goes numb.

He curses himself as he shakes feeling back into his arm. He looks at the lamp. Grabbing the lamp, he moves to the corner. He puts the lamp into the corner of the field and waits for the anticipated shock. Looking at the end of the lamp, Tobius sees the field crackling around the lamp. He removes the lamp from the field and looks at the bunk. Setting the lamp down, he pushes the bunk close to the field. He sets himself then shoves the bunk into the field and is rewarded with a jaw-clenching blast of electricity. After a few heartbeats, Tobius picks himself off the ground. He looks at the bunk and ponders about what just happened and hears Sanguis laughing from everywhere. Tobius stands and looks at the bunk and lamp. He lays the lamp on the bunk with its tip just ahead of the end of the bunk. He moves the bunk slowly to the field, and as the lamp touches the field, the field starts destabilizing. Another centimeter and the bunk makes contact with the field. But instead of a massive shock, the field disperses. He looks around the bunk and sees a gap between the legs of the bunk. Quickly, he crawls under the bunk, and once he leaves the cell, the vision evaporates.

"You are one step closer to the power you seek." Tobius looks and sees a small crystal on a pedestal. "Give this crystal to appease the Void-raiders, but behind the throne, use the obsidian diamond to find out where you must go."

He grabs the crystal from the pedestal. Tobius turns, hurrying down the passage. He sees the door shutting. He picks up the pace and dives from the passage. Tobius lands on his right shoulder with a thud. He yells from the impact, rolling onto his back. He examines his shoulder to ensure that it is not further injured and is relieved to feel that nothing is broken. He takes a moment to eat some of his emergency rations and pops the last stim from his med kit.

After the quick snack, he packs up, pulls the diamond from the wall, and starts heading back toward the entrance. He makes his way back to the passage leading to the main floor. Cautiously, he works his way through the rubble, and once he gets a few meters from the edge of the rubble, he hears scraping. The young man scowls at the persistence of the creatures. Since Tobius crawled through the rubble, they have been trying to crawl, scrape, or push their way through to get their prey. Knowing he will not be able to face them with only one arm, he tries to think of a solution.

As Tobius lays in the pile of stones, he feels a presence touch his conscience, and he instinctively recoils. Thinking it's a trick by Sanguis, he looks for the lavender cloud, but nothing is there. A moment later, the presence reaches to him again, but he hears Master Phylox's voice. "Where are you?"

Tobius is caught off guard from this and responds, "I am still in the Ryft. Why?" Tobius feels a sense of reassurance from his master.

"Morrin is telling everyone that you and Melissa are dead."

Tobius reels in anger, smacking his head on a stone. "That no-good jerk," Tobius curses. "With his statement, you both have until midday to make it back, or we continue to the final trial without you." Sensing his acolyte's confusion, he says, "It is almost dawn."

"Do not worry, Master Phylox. I will be there."

Quickly, he refocuses his mind on the task at hand. First, he opens his mind into the depths of the flow to examine the rubble for a piece he can use to either scare or pin the animals beyond, but he is unable to find a piece big enough to do the job and keep the rubble stable. He recalls something the old hermit would always tell him: "Every puzzle has a solution, but you must find the right angle to see it."

A tear rolls down his check at the thought of his lost friend, and he smiles. "Even from death, you are still teaching me, Hermi." He settles and expands his awareness in all directions. With beads of sweat now forming on his brow from the effort, he is about to stop when, to his right, he senses a slight shift of sand. With renewed focus, he aims all his awareness to the area of sand. He starts by just moving the sand and finds a crack that leads outside. He can smell the fresh air from just beyond the wall. The wall is over three meters thick, but he knows he has to get out fast. He crawls to the wall and scribes the push glyph onto the wall to help focus his efforts. "Here goes nothing," he says aloud as he starts to direct the flow into the glyph to push the wall apart. One minute passes, then two, then three goes by with nothing. He stops for a moment to gathers himself, and he hears laughter from everywhere.

"You say you are a seeker of justice, but you cannot even use the power."

Tobius scowls and then considers what was said. He thinks of his family killed years ago, his friend and mentor murdered by Master Kyron, and all the Keepers killed for the diamond. Power surges within him, begging for release, but it is not flaming anger or hate. Tobius has clear purpose and pure energy to deliver justice. The young man places his hand on the wall, and says, "Move."

Melissa is startled at the sound of a massive explosion. Jumping to her feet, she looks to the Tomb of Shadows. Breathing a sigh of relief at the sight of the tomb still standing, she heads toward the sound. Hilt in hand, she cautiously crosses the valley. She sees no sign of damage at the front of the tomb and proceeds around in a clockwise manner.

Tobius blinks his eyes to help clear his view from the dust cloud. Over four square meters of the wall is gone. Quickly, he climbs through the hole into the morning air. Squinting in the morning light, he is relieved to be outside again but is also shocked at how long he was inside. Tobius looks at the tomb and takes a moment to ensure nothing follows him through.

Melisa sees a dust cloud next to the wall several dozen meters ahead. She ignites her blade and cautiously moves to it. She sees a figure crawl from the wall and waits to see what they do. For several heartbeats, the figure stands and then turns back toward the hole. In that instant, she realizes that it is Tobius. She shuts off her blade and runs to him.

Tobius looks at the wall and laughs. He revels in the achievement of finding what he needed. He senses a warm flow of passion and smiles when he sees Melissa heading toward him. He stows his blade just in time to get tackled by the relieved young woman. He grunts in pain as he lands on his back.

She winces at the sound of his grunt. "What happened?"

Chuckling, he slowly sits up. "Just had some fun with the local critters."

She shakes her head and laughs. "Let me look at it." She carefully removes the med salves and gasps. The wound is deep enough that she can see part of his shoulder blade. She opens her med kit and sprays antimicrobial foam on the wound. Tobius winces at the application but says nothing. She prepares three new med salves to cover the wound. The foam is absorbed in seconds, then she fills the wound with a med gel to help increase the healing. Then she applies the salves.

Tobius rolls his shoulder as he stands. "Thanks." She nods and packs the med kit. "Let's get the bikes and head back."

Melissa angrily replies, "Morrin sabotaged them. We will have to walk."

Tobius feels the anger well inside him. "We are going to have to run." Before she can retort, he continues, "If we are not back by midday, they will continue without us."

She nods. "Let's grab the emergency kits and go." Smiling, he nods, and they jog to the bikes.

* * *

Meanwhile, Morrin has just finished a lavish breakfast of meat, fruit, and milk in Master Krystelle's study. "What will happen in the next part of the trials?"

Krystelle laughs as she steps from the refresher. "What, you think I will just tell you how to beat the trials?" Morrin nods as she crosses the study, securing her robe. "Just because I have given you several private lessons does not mean I will give you everything."

Morrin laughs. "Sure you won't, Krys."

She sits on his lap and smiles. "I do not know much about the final trial since it is never the same, but I have heard it will be the most entertaining one in years." Morrin raises an eyebrow at her disbelievingly. She gives him her best innocent smile. "Honestly, that is all I know, except that it will involve several fights, and just make sure you take the advantage when it comes." They both laugh.

* * *

Twelve kilometers from the academy, Tobius and Melissa get set for the quickest run they can muster. "We have just about an hour to make it back."

Melissa nods and says, "Well, I guess we should set personal bests then."

With that, they start heading back. In the morning, they both would run to help keep in shape, but this is completely different. If you are having a slow run, you can try better tomorrow, but today they both know that they do not have that luxury. They both do well for the first kilometer, but after that, there is about six kilometers of sand dunes. Knowing that the sand will be the hardest part, they pace themselves.

The first dune stands before them, and it only took about five minutes to get there. Taking a quick moment to drink before facing the sand, Tobius says, "Let's try and use the flow to help steady the sand so we can avoid sliding."

Melissa nods and charges up the first dune. Tobius follows close behind. Slowly, they crest dune after dune, heading back to the academy. After twenty minutes in the dunes, Tobius's footing falters, and he tumbles down the dune.

Melissa summons the flow to slow his fall. She jogs down to him as he gets to his feet. "Are you all right?"

Tobius wipes the sand off his face and nods. "Yeah, just slipped." He opens his canteen and takes a drink. "I think we are almost out of the dunes."

Melissa finishes her canteen and secures it back in place. "Good. I bet I can beat you back from here."

Tobius laughs. "Right. The heat must be messing with your head."

She flashes him an evil grin. "Last one back gets lunch for the other."

Tobius smiles. "I would like—" Tobius is cut off by Melissa as she pushes him back into the dune. Tobius scrambles to recover and sees her already up the dune. Quickly, he accelerates up the dune after her.

* * *

Master Phylox and Gamite are standing in the main hall, waiting for their acolytes to return. Phylox glances at his chrono. Seventeen minutes and they will miss the final trial. He glances at Gamite, who is focusing at nothing.

"Melissa, can you hear me?"

A few moments pass. "Yes."

He sighs in relief. "They moved the meeting to the main hall. Where are you?"

He can sense that she is tiring, but she replies, "We are about twenty minutes from the academy." He looks at Phylox and mouths, "How long?"

Phylox responds, "Seventeen."

Gamite quickly passes on the information. "Hurry. Use the power of the flow to help you."

* * *

They have been making good time, and she looks at him. "We have seventeen minutes to make it to the main hall."

A shocked look flashes across Tobius's face. "We still have over three kilometers."

Tobius and Melissa stop and use chalk to scribe the glyph of speed on their boots. They stand, take deep breaths, and focus. They tap into the flow and begin again. Tobius is surprised at the speed they are moving.

"Thirteen minutes," Melissa hears Master Gamite advise her through the flow. Both of their legs burn from the constant sprinting. "Ten minutes," she hears as they hit the final stretch to the academy, still two kilometers to go.

Victory or Death

Master Kyron is sitting on her throne in the main hall, looking out over the assembly. She sees several other masters not normally at the academy, several local officials, and aides. She keeps an eye on the chrono built into the arm of her chair and glances to her right. There stands Krystelle and Morrin, but more interesting is that Phylox and Gamite stand without their acolytes. An evil grin slips onto her face.

Finally, those two fools will fail, and I can be rid of them. She has never cared for the two. Phylox, she thinks, is stupid for not using his power to gain more control, and Gamite is an old fool with no place in her academy.

She is startled from her thoughts as a commotion rises from the back of the hall. Standing, she looks to see who enters, and it is Admiral Kato. That is not the surprise, but it is the fact that he is dressed to fight. Also following just to his left is a bounty hunter armed as if to storm a blockade singlehandedly. She can sense his use of the void to move anyone in front of him, not in a forceful way but just so that anyone who does not know him will fear him. She smiles as he nears the base of the throne, but it quickly changes to rage as Kato continues up the steps to stand in front of her. Kyron knew that he was one of the masters you did not mess with. Not only was there few who could challenge him in a fight, but he also commands the entire Void-raiders fleet.

She begins to bow as way of greeting when the unmistakable sound of a blade echoes through the halls. Kato's blade has a triangular cross section. Each side is five centimeters at hilt and tapers into a point. Her eyes flare with rage as she glares at him. "Tell me, Kyron, how long have you known my apprentice's killer was here?"

She looks at him. "Why do you care?"

With a deft move, the tip of his black blade starts searing into her right forearm, right above the wrist. "I want to meet him. Is that so much to ask?"

Master Kyron summons the void to keep herself still. She looks at her arm and sees the skin charred around the tip of the blade. "I did not think you would want to know unless he was able to pass the trials."

His eyes flare with rage at the response. "He was able to defeat De' Ron with a basic sword." Without warning, he flicks his wrist, severing her right hand.

* * *

Tobius and Melissa can see the practice yard and breathe a sigh of relief. Wordlessly, they nod and summon more of the flow to increase their speed as they enter the academy. As they pass the acolyte main hall, they hear a scream echo from the main hall. They both ready their hilts as they finish the last stretch. They are slowing as they enter the hall and see Master Kyron clutching her right arm, glaring at a man in black armor. They move toward their masters as they watch with fascinated confusion.

The man is looking at Kyron. "The council placed me in charge of the final trial."

She hisses, "You have no right to do this!"

The tall man turns to look at Tobius and Melissa. He gestures with his blade. "Is he the one?"

Kyron does not answer but ignites her scarlet blade. She screams, but before she can start to attack, a bolt slams into her chest, throwing her from the platform. Kato shoots a punitive glance at Craven then nods approvingly.

He turns to the assembly, finding reactions from fear, to rage, and even some approval. Void blade still in hand, he gestures towards Kyron. "She was weak. She tried to keep someone from me. If you want to keep a secret, first make sure those you are keeping it from are not stronger than you." He shifts his gaze to the three acolytes. "The final trial shall continue." He starts down the steps. "Let us go to the training yard to finish the trials." With a thunderous roar, the mass moves outside.

Morrin and Krystelle follow behind Kato, but Tobius, Melissa, Gamite, and Phylox let the gathering proceed. Phylox looks at Tobius. "Things just got difficult."

They all look at each other as the people move past. Tobius recalls the vision he had about the throne. He grabs Melissa's hand and heads behind the throne. Before they have a chance to ask what he is doing, Tobius grabs the obsidian diamond and kneels, looking for the slot.

Phylox grabs Tobius's right shoulder. "Tobius, what are you doing?"

Tobius collapses in pain, and Melissa quickly explains what happened in the Ryft. Phylox looks past the throne and sees that the mass has almost left the room. Tobius crawls toward the base of the throne, looking for something even through the pain.

"Tobius, we have to—"

"I found it," Tobius says excitedly.

Before he can insert the diamond, he is pulled from the floor as they quickly move to the training field. Tobius looks annoyed but knows that they have to go. They enter the yard and see that the assembly has been spilt into the four corners. Tobius is surprised at how quick they set up the platform on the right edge of the training field. Making their way to the platform, they join Krystelle, Morrin, and the others competing for a new master. Tobius is still surprised at how everyone has accepted the new leadership without question.

Admiral Kato approaches the front of the platform, raising his right hand, hilt still gripped. "We are here to complete the trials for these acolytes and to see who will earn the right to become an apprentice." A roar erupts from the crowd. He turns toward those on the platform. "Acolytes, you have a chance to claim the title of a Void-raiders apprentice." He looks at all three in turn. He then looks to his left. "Apprentices, you have lost your masters from the continued struggle for Void-raiders dominance, and now you have the chance to prove your worth as apprentices." The four apprentices bow respectfully. There are two human males, one female, and one blue crytan. He turns back to address the crowd. "There are seven competing today, but there are only two masters looking for an apprentice."

Master Phylox steps up to the front of the platform. "With respect, Admiral." Kato turns to him, rage burning in his eyes. "I am looking to select my first apprentice." Phylox stands his ground as he is stared down by Kato. After several long moments, Kato nods his approval.

Kato turns back to the crowd, saying, "This trial will be one by fire. Each acolyte must face an apprentice in combat. The fight ends when the opponent is unable to continue." He waits for several long moments. As the cheers die off, he continues, "Since we have an odd number, we will have an apprentice face a surprise opponent." Murmurs echo around the crowd. "Apprentice Mikel, you are first."

The smaller of the two human males steps forward, removing his robe. Standing barely a meter and a half tall, he flips from the platform, landing in a three-point stance, slate-colored blade ignited and held high behind him in his left hand. This blade is just over meter in length and three centimeters thick in a crescent shape from hilt to tip. An enthusiastic cheer erupts from the display.

Kato nods. "His opponent shall be Craven." Kato's companion steps to the front of the platform. Shouts of outrage come from all corners of the training yard. Kato raises a hand to silence the crowd. "Yes, this is unorthodox, but this is a test for the apprentice and Craven. He has failed me and now must prove his worth."

Craven glares at him from inside his helmet. He knew that he would have to fight today, but he did not expect him to explain why. *Did I really expect anything else?* he thinks. He steps down from the platform and draws his custom-made blade. It looks just like a standard sword, but he did some research after his encounter on Detritus Prime. It cost him almost a million credits to get a weapon that can stand up to a void blade.

Admiral Kato moves to his seat and nods. "Begin." With that said, the crowd cheers as the two combatants start to circle. They start at an eight-meter distance, and after a rotation, they reduce distance to four. Mikel looks at his opponent to try and find a weakness to exploit. Craven watches patiently, knowing that he is at a disadvantage against the apprentice. He keeps his blade in the ready position in his right hand. Mikel is the first one to strike, lunging forward. With the power of the void, he covers the gap in a heartbeat. Craven follows his gut feeling and steps to his right. Mikel's blade slices clean through nothing. Craven hits Mikel on the back with his left hand sending him tumbling. Craven gets knocked from his feet before he can take a step. They both roll and rise to their feet. Craven takes a step and tries to catch him off guard. He charges right at him, bringing his blade around in a horizontal sweep, but Mikel deftly brings his blade up to block. Mikel is shocked when the blade stops against his rather than splitting in two. Craven takes this moment of surprise to grab his left hand and locking his gauntlet, shattering his wrist. Mikel screams in pain, but before he has a chance to respond, he is run through by Craven's blade.

The crowd is stunned with the sudden ending of the duel. Kato stands, nodding to Craven. "Well done." He steps to the front of the platform. "Now we have six contestants. Next will be Acolyte Morrin and Apprentice Bryce."

Morrin looks to Krystelle and removes his robe and leaves the platform. His opponent stands over two meters tall and is ninety-five kilograms of pure muscle. Bryce shrugs off his robe and spins the sixty-centimeter-long hilt in his right hand.

Before they can start the duel, a sandstorm blows into the training yard. Kato announces, "We shall resume the trials the morning after the sandstorm ends."

With that said, everyone quickly heads into the academy. Sandstorms can last anywhere from a few hours to a couple of days. Gamite, Phylox, Melissa, and Tobius join the flow of everyone taking refuge from the storm. They make their way to Gamite's study. Gamite opens the door to his study and heads to prep the med station within. Tobius lays facedown on the examination table, and Gamite injects him with a sedative. The young man falls fast asleep within seconds. The medical droid cuts the tunic off and begins to sterilize and bandage the ragged wound.

Phylox places a hand on Melissa's shoulder. "You should rest. Tomorrow will be a busy day for all of us." She nods and heads to her room to get some sleep.

The sandstorm lasted for three days, and the morning after it ended, everyone gathered in the training yard to complete the trials. Tobius remained sedated for two of the three days to help maximize the healing process.

Kato steps to the podium and announces, "Now, Morrin and Bryce, step forward and prove who is worthy of becoming an apprentice." With that said, the crowd cheers, and the two combatants prepare to fight.

Morrin ignites his maroon blade, standing straight and looking at Bryce. Morrin's blade is eighty-five centimeters long, three centimeters thick, with three one-centimeter-tall spines helixing around the blade's length. Bryce has yet to ignite his blades, staring back at Morrin. Morrin looks at Kato, then Krystelle, then back to Bryce. Bryce ignites his meter-long navy blade, holding it with both hands.

Tobius watches with interest at the ignition of just one blade. Morrin and Bryce nod at each other and begin to move in slowly. Morrin has now mimicked his opponent's grip. Both spend several moments about two meters apart. Morrin starts to take a step in to attack but is quickly hurled a dozen meters. Tobius is amazed as he looks at the hilt and sees parts of two glyphs glowing under Bryce's hands. Being caught off guard from the sudden hit, he lands flat on his back, expelling the air from his lungs. He quickly uses the rage and shock from his foolish mistake to empower him. Morrin surges to his feet and charges his enemy. Morrin no longer views this fight as a challenge but a personal insult and must destroy him. The two collide in a fierce strike, and the crowd erupts. They both exchange blows at an incredible pace. For several moments, the crowd can only see blurs surrounding the two combatants.

Morrin sweeps his blade around him in a quick strike at the legs of his opponent, and the navy blade streaks around blocking his blade. Planting his right foot, Morrin tries to land a solid hit on the left side of his opponent's ribs, but Bryce drops his left arm to absorb the hit. Quickly spinning his blade over his head, Morrin backflips, kicking Bryce under the jaw. He hears his jaw snap shut, and Bryce staggers back. Morrin readies himself for the expected counter, but nothing comes.

Bryce rubs his jaw, glaring at his enemy. "You are pretty good, but let's shake things up." He extends his left hand, and a navy plasma blast flies at his opponent. He smiles as he watches his enemy raise his blade to absorb the attack. He quickly slides a hidden release in the middle of his hilt. The last fifteen centimeters of the hilt pop free. He depresses the thumb switch, and a long wire spools from the shaft. Two meters of carbon steel cable now extend from the other handle. He slowly flicks his left hand to start the cable moving, and every motion causes a crackle of electricity. Smiling, he moves forward, snapping the electro-whip back and forth.

Looking at his enemy trying to recover, Morrin almost does not sense the plasma attack. He barely gets his blade up to intercept the projectile. He is again caught off guard, seeing his opponent's hilt now in two. In his right hand is the navy blade, but his left is holding a crackling electro-whip. Fear ripples down his spine at the now unique challenge in front of him. He has faced opponents wielding one, two, or even double-bladed weapons, but he never considered a weapon combination like this. He finds himself unprepared to face this unique style.

Tobius watches this duel with extreme interest. He remembers facing the training droid on Marina. It was not easy learning to anticipate the angles of whiplike weapons. He had numerous welts and bruises from that droid. He suddenly feels a pang of sorrow of his lost friend and the heat of rage. He keeps watching, pushing the emotions away.

Morrin finds himself retreating after each attack, trying to figure out how to counter. The navy blade swings in toward his left shoulder, and he instinctively moves his blade to block. Suddenly, his right leg is numbed by the whip. Stepping back again, he almost stumbles from the numb limb. His rage spikes again at how his enemy is making him look like a fool, and he uses his anger to fuel his power. He steps in as Bryce swings his blade toward his waist. Morrin blocks the blade with little effort and summons the void to stop the whip just before hitting his open flank. Flicking his left hand, he redirects the whip around the arm, holding it. Bryce howls in rage at the unexpected tactic. Morrin grins and begins his assault. Whipping his blade around, he swings at his enemy's left arm. His blade is blocked just before making contact.

Taking advantage of his opponent's flawed defense, Morrin presses the attack at the left arm, swinging his blade high and low at the left side. Jabbing low and sweeping high, he continues the assault and forces him back step by step. With the unrelenting assault, Bryce has no time to get the electro-whip from his arm. Morrin now has complete control of the fight, but he still is unable to break his enemy's defenses. He now attacks without reserve, striking at the right shoulder, spin kick to the knee, followed by a jab at the chest. He can sense his enemy is wearing down. Blocks are arriving microseconds before finding its mark, and his breathing is labored. Granted, he has the upper hand, but the fight has now gone for more the twenty minutes, and even Morrin is tiring out.

Giving up on the flashy moves, Morrin just tries to break through his opponent's defense. He summons the void to shove Bryce back and charges. He covers the ten-meter distance just as Bryce rolls to his feet. Morrin brings his blade down in a double-handed strike to finish him off. Shock flashes across his face as his attack strikes the navy blade and the electro-whip arcs toward his legs. Cursing himself at his lack of foresight, he uses his momentum to flip over Bryce. Landing, he turns just to see Bryce snap his wrist, sending the whip straight at his neck. Morrin stands and extends his left hand, but instead of trying to redirect the whip, he lets the weapon wrap around his hand. Letting the pain fuel him, he yanks on the whip, pulling his enemy toward him. He brings his blade down at the hand holding the whip.

Morrin was hoping to take off the hand holding the whip, but his blade just cleaved the handle in two. Just as the blade clears the wreaked weapon, the navy blade pierces his right thigh. Pure rage ruptures from his mouth. He plunges his blade down, pinning Bryce to the ground through his right forearm. He staggers back, grimacing in anger and pain. The two combatants glare at each other. Morrin reaches down, thumbs off the navy blade with his left hand. Turning the blade back on, he takes a step toward his enemy. Just as he places weight on his injured leg, he crumples. Kneeling, he looks at Bryce and sees him reaching to try and remove the blade. Morrin lunges forward, letting the anger fill him. With a single strike, he finishes off his opponent.

The training yard cheers at the amazing fight that just finished. Exhausted, Morrin summons the last of his strength and rises to his knees, looking around then at the platform.

Admiral Kato stands and steps forward. "Well done, Acolyte Morrin." Gesturing to his left, Kato says, "Master Krystelle, please assist your acolyte. He needs medical attention." She bows then hurries to assist him. Tobius watches as the two head into the academy.

The cheering increases as Morrin is escorted from the training yard. Kato smiles as the crowd continues its enthusiastic approval of the trials. A few more moments pass, then he raises his hands to silence the crowd. As the cheers subside, Kato takes a moment to let the anticipation build and looks around the crowd.

"We have had two entertaining trials so far, but we are just getting started." The crowd is feeding off the fights, and Kato revels in the sense of control. "Now will Acolyte Melissa"—he gestures to her as she rises and steps from the platform—"and Apprentice Vernice please step forward."

Vernice barely stands a meter and a half tall and could not weigh more than fifty-five kilograms. Tobius knows that just because someone is small, they can be more dangerous than large enemies, and he reaches out to Melissa's mind. *Be cautious. She is powerful.*

He gets nothing back but the sense of indestructible determination and a slight nod. Melissa removes her cloak, tossing it toward the edge of the platform. Both combatants remove their hilts and nod toward each other. Suddenly, they both sprint at each other as they start the fight. An instant before their hilts pass each other, both blades erupt to life. The crowd goes wild at the amazing display. For a moment, the lavender and orange blades stay locked, but just as quick, the two women retreat to a ten-meter distance again. Melissa's lavender blade has a diamond cross section five centimeters tall and three centimeters wide with a flat end seventy-five centimeters from the emitter. Vernice's orange blade is eighty centimeters in length, with a half-centimeter gap splitting the blade from hilt to tip.

Tobius watches the first strike with amazing fixation. As he watches them fight with intense emotion, he feels an eddy in the flow. He closes his eyes and focuses first on himself, then he slowly looks out. He can sense everyone in the training yard and even their power. Tobius is surprised that most in the crowd are not very strong, but he can sense at least a dozen who are very powerful. He is stunned as he sees Melissa through the flow as a solid pillar of peace and resolve, but the other is a raging inferno of red and black emotions of rage and despair. He watches the battle for what seems like ages when he again feels a subtle pull. He allows his mind to follow the call through the academy. Whatever is calling to him is like a beacon just pulsing every few moments to direct him in the general direction. He follows the call to the main hall behind the throne, where he was trying to enter the hidden passage. He sees a young male kneel behind the throne and insert the crystal in the floor like he did himself. The man looks at the crystal just like he did when it locked into place, but nothing happens. The man sends a blast of electricity into the crystal, but still nothing happens. Tobius watches as the man paces back and forth, enraged at the lack of response. The young man again kneels, placing his palm on the top of the crystal and closing his eyes.

He is jarred from his trance by Phylox. Tobius glares at him for a moment, but Phylox nods to the fight. Melissa is struggling to keep Vernice's vicious strikes at bay, but Tobius does not see at first that now she has two orange blades. Tobius realizes that Vernice's hilt was designed to look like a single weapon but could be easily separated. Melissa is doing everything she can to just keep the blades from striking her. The scent of burnt fabric and singed hair floats on the breeze, surrounding the chaos in the yard. Tobius can sense that she is getting frustrated, but her resolve is unwavering. He cautiously reaches to her. *Melissa, use what you are good at.* He does not even wait for a response and breaks contact.

Melissa is breathing heavy and staggers again with another ferocious blow from Vernice's relentless assault. Bringing her lavender blade to stop the right blade, she has to duck back to avoid the left blade which again slices through some of her hair. Rolling back, Melissa tries to get some space and recover. Suddenly, she feels a touch on her mind and is relieved to hear Tobius reassure her. She realizes that she was being very stubborn to try and beat her opponent in the way they want. She takes a moment to compose herself before the next attack. Taking a deep breath, she uses a technique the Mistress of Knowledge taught her to revitalize herself. Quickly, she feels the power rejuvenating her limbs, and her breathing slows. She stands with eyes closed, hilt griped in both hands. She can see the red and black storm of her opponent but is unafraid. The orange blade swings in at her legs. She does not move, but the blade stops a mere centimeter from her right knee.

Vernice stops her right arm mid-attack at the sudden change in her enemy's tactics. She tries to pull her left blade back but is unable to move it. She glares at Melissa and releases the hilt, taking a step back. Right as she steps back, the blade vanishes as the hilt falls. Rage flares inside her as she looks at the hilt then the woman who stands defiantly, eyes closed. She summons the hilt back to her hand and steps forward to attack again, but right where her left foot lands, a ten-centimeter-deep hole formed. Vernice stumbles from the sudden imbalance.

Melissa lets the flow surround and infuse every part of her being. Continuing to use the power to keep her opponent off-balance, she rolls some stones underfoot or pushes on Vernice's foot or knee. She can hear the other woman grunt and yell in frustration, surprise, and anger. She continues to use her skill of the flow to wear her down. She begins to channel the power again, but Vernice has gotten too comfortable with the little tricks. A scream of pain explodes from her lips as orange forks of lightning dance across her back. Melissa releases her blade, eyes wide with shock and agony, as she falls to the ground.

Vernice finally figures out what her enemy is doing to keep her off-balance and studies her for a few moments. An instant before her foot would hit the ground, the void would surge around her. She waits a few more moments to see if she can time it. Step…step…step…hole…step…step…step stones moved under foot…step…step…step… "Now!" she yells to herself and hurls the strongest blast of energy she can manage at her enemies back. Rolling to avoid the childish tactics, she gets back to her feet. She sees Melissa lying face-down in the dirt, writhing in pain as the energy courses through her body. She is enjoying the torture she is inflicting on her enemy. She approaches the fallen woman as she continues to pulse energy into her. Stopping a meter and a half from the woman, she says, "You are not worthy to be an apprentice. Using childish tricks will get you killed." She drops her left hand and grabs her hilt. "Void-raiders never give their enemy mercy nor a chance to find a weakness in their attack." Igniting her blade, she moves counterclockwise, keeping the distance of a meter and a half, and is unrelenting with the barrage. "My master told me to never give an enemy the chance to find a weakness. Beat them with all your strength, and never allow them to recover."

Melissa feels her body thrashing from the immense energy forced onto her. The smell of singed fabric, hair, and ozone fill her nostrils. Despair starts to gain a foothold in her mind. *You are a failure.* She recalls the tomb and sets her resolve again. *I am a Master of Knowledge, and I will not fail.* Using the flow to clear her mind, she starts looking for a way to get free. Melissa hears Vernice rambling on about something about her former master and not giving an enemy a chance to recover. She draws the protection glyph in the dirt under her right hand to redirect the energy from her back to the ground. Unsure of what Vernice will do, she bides her time, waiting for the right moment. She sees her opponent's foot from the corner of her left eye.

Vernice stops even with her enemy's neck. Grinning, she raises her blades to deliver the final blow. "Now you die!" she yells, bringing her blades down. The crowd begins to cheer as the blades streak toward its target, but they are stunned into silence. Instead of seeing her enemy's head separated from her body, she sees a scorched line in the dirt. Five meters away, her enemy is rising to her feet with her back still smoking from her attack. "How were you able to?" she yells in rage.

Melissa smiles slightly, breathing heavily. She responds, "What do you mean?" She stretches her back to relieve the pain from the attack. "You had the element of surprise, but you wasted your time." She sees the rage flare in Vernice's eyes. Securing her grip on the hilts, Vernice slowly steps forward. The two women stare at each other as they circle at a five-meter distance. An instant later, the two women cross blades in a final effort to claim victory. The lavender and orange blades continuously collide in a barrage almost faster than the eye can track. The pop and sizzle of the blades echo around the training yard like fireworks. Both women, exhausted from the struggle, have given up on fancy moves and revert to basic strikes and counterstrikes.

Melissa feels her strength waning, and even the techniques to keep her fatigue away have little effect. She can sense the same from the woman in front of her. *I have one final chance to beat her*, she thinks. She waits for Vernice to attack at her left side. The orange blade arcs in toward her shoulder. She absorbs the impacts in the middle of her lavender blade, but instead of trying to stop it, she rolls with it. Using the motion of the blow, she rolls to the right while bringing her lavender blade across Vernice's knees, severing both limbs. Continuing the rolls, she gets to her feet and extinguishes her blade. Turning, she sees the other woman fall to the ground in complete shock.

Melissa takes no chance and quickly summons the fallen warrior's hilts to her hand. Turning toward the platform, she bows as the crowd erupts into enthusiastic approval of the fight. Admiral Kato steps to the front of the platform, raising his hands to quiet the crowd. "Well done, Acolyte Melissa. What a great display of combat skill and your ability to command the void." He steps from the platform to stand a meter from Melissa. "May I see that, Acolyte?" he says, gesturing to Vernice's hilt. Melissa gives a slight nod and hands it to the admiral. He turns toward the injured woman. "You knew coming into this the cost of failure." Fear emanates from the woman as she tries to defend herself. Kato quickly ignites the blade and runs the woman through without any remorse.

Melissa watches in horror as he kills the defenseless woman. She feels sick to her stomach, and her body trembles with uncertainty.

Admiral Kato turns with the weapon still on. "You may keep this as proof of your position." With one swift motion, he turns off the weapon and tosses it back to her. Still shocked with what just transpired, she barely catches it then simply bows.

Heading back to the platform, Kato uses the void to amplify his voice. "We are down to the final match, and it should be very interesting." He places a hand on each side of the podium. "We have Apprentice Braulie." He gestures to his right, and the over two-meter-tall blue-skinned crytan steps forward. He removes his cloak and thrusts his hilt in the air with a roar. Tobius sees the massive male and feels a tingle of fear at the base of his spine.

Master Phylox senses the tension in his acolyte. "Relax, Tobius. He is a decent fighter but has never encountered a style like yours. Try and use yours like a regular blade until you need to gain the upper hand."

Tobius nods understandingly and takes a deep breath.

Admiral Kato continues, "And Acolyte Tobius, who defeated my very own apprentice De' Ron." The crowd's attitude shifts from enjoyment to disbelief. Kato holds the damaged blade up for the crowd to see. "This is what remains of my apprentice's weapon." The crowd starts to whisper at first then cheers with renewed vigor about the imminent fight.

Tobius stands, readying himself as the crowd cheers. Stepping from the platform, Tobius moves to stand twelve meters in front of Braulie. Looking at the massive opponent, he still feels the chill of fear at the base of his spine but shakes his head to clear his mind. Admiral Kato nods. "Begin!"

Braulie does not hesitate to ignite his weapon and charges. Tobius is shocked at the size of his blade. The crimson blade is eight centimeters wide and almost two meters in length. He holds one hilt in both hands, trying to hide the handle, and ignites his sage blade.

The crowd murmurs at the sight of the strange blade color, but this is quickly forgotten as the two combatants collide.

Tobius assumes that the crytan is powerful but is still unprepared. The crimson blade comes down from a doublehanded strike and drives Tobius down to one knee from the force. Braulie sneers at Tobius. Struggling to keep the blade from slicing him in two, Tobius shoves up and quickly rolls to his left. He rises to his feet and has little time to recover as the crimson blade comes arcing in toward his right shoulder. Barely getting the sage blade in place to absorb the blow, he lets the force of the blow push him into a backward summersault. Tobius lets the flow carry him to a six-meter gap between them. He quickly sets himself to continue the fight. He can sense that his opponent is enraged that his first two blows did not finish the fight.

He thinks, *It is really difficult to keep my fighting style hidden.* Braulie again closes the gap, but Tobius adjusts his defense to not stop the blows but simply redirect them. A strike comes in at knee level. He swings the sage blade down to deflect the attacking blade into the ground just by his right foot. Another strike comes in at chest level. Using his blade, he redirects the attack over his head and plants a roundhouse kick in the crytan's unprotected left side. Tobius figures that his attack will at least cause him to pause for a second, but he is barely able to get the blade up to stop the backhanded strike aimed at his neck. Without having time to get his blade into position to completely block the attack, the impact numbs his left hand. Braulie kicks Tobius flat footed in the chest, sending him sprawling five meters away. Tobius goes to roll and realizes that his sage hilt is missing.

"I guess the surprise is gone now," he says, summoning the weapon to his hand again. The hilt hits his right palm with the long part pointing straight at Braulie. The crytan looks puzzled at the unique grip of the weapon. Tobius knows that he will be vulnerable if he only uses one. Reaching behind his back, he releases the clasp and withdraws the other hilt. Holding the second hilt reverse of its twin, he thumbs the activation studs of both simultaneously. The crowd erupts with cheers of excitement. Never before has this academy ever witnessed this type of technique.

Phylox watches the whole fight unfold and is not surprised at how quickly Tobius reveals his blades. He could tell that if Tobius had a standard blade, he would have lost in no time to this massive warrior. Tobius holds his ground, waiting to see how the crytan will respond to the sudden change. Braulie takes a moment to look at the new weapons and does not come charging in.

The two begin to circle at the five-meter distance, neither one willing to make the first move. Tobius has yet to move either weapon, not wanting to give away any idea of his technique, and Braulie waits to see if his enemy will give any hints of his tactics. Several seconds pass as the two combatants make a complete rotation. The crytan jumps forward, covering the distance in two quick strides, swinging his weapon around at Tobius's left side. He deftly steps into the attack and blocks the attack with the shield covering the left hilt. Braulie is surprised to see that his blade is hovering just off the hilt. He scowls at the trickery. Tobius does his best to keep the blades from spinning so he has that if things go bad. The crytan constantly attacks with thrusts and slashes but is unable to even weaken Tobius's defense. Tobius blocks a thrust with his right blade and spins left, and then he swings the left blade around at his opponent's knees. Braulie performs a one-handed back spring to avoid the attack and jumps back at the human.

Braulie brings his blade down in a doublehanded strike. As soon as his blade connects with the amber bar, he spins clockwise, throwing his enemy's arm out of position to maintain his defense. He continues his rotation and steps to his left. The human's momentum has carried him past where he stood. Snarling, he kicks the human square in the back of his ribs.

Admiral Kato has been watching this fight with extreme interest. "I will see the man who killed my apprentice fall," he whispers to himself. He knows that Braulie is nothing more than a pawn for his grand scheme of revenge, but he does not care. He still has no idea how that human was able to not only beat his apprentice but best him with little effort from what he heard. "If this human could defeat my apprentice with little effort, he is a threat to the Void-raiders." Kato's mind begins to wander as the fight continues with an elegant display of skill on both sides. He keeps thinking of what he will do now that he is in control of the academy and how Master Kyron was inadequate to ensure proper Void-raider training. Kato is jolted back from his wanderings as he hears a scream of pain from the human and looks up.

Tobius was not expecting such an agile tactic from the crytan, as the massive creature elegantly spins around behind him. Before he even has a chance to counter, his back erupts in pain from the force of the blow. Stars flash in his vision, and his involuntary bellow of pain expels the remainder of his breath. Tobius slams face first into the ground two meters away, and he rolls onto his side, gasping for air.

His entire world now revolves around the pain in his back and need to breathe. Tobius fights frantically to regain control of his body when he hears a familiar laugh echo through his mind. Closing his mind off from the laughter, he refuses to let that phantom interfere. Every heartbeat, he struggles to shut out the pain. The stars are clearing from his vision, and he sees the crytan striding toward him. Again, the laughter of Sanguis rings through his thoughts. He is about to implode from the pain, but he senses fear from Melissa. Like an electrical shock to his body, the pain vanishes.

Looking up, he sees Braulie thrusting his blade at his chest. Tobius summons the flow to move himself out of the way. This tactic catches the crytan by surprise as the weapon pierces the ground. Tobius rises to his feet and summons his weapons to his hands.

Setting his feet, Tobius says, "Let's finish this."

An evil grin slides onto the crytan's face. He twists his right wrist until his weapon is parallel with the ground palm up. He places his left hand just below his right. He twists the lower half of the hilt a quarter turn counterclockwise, sliding the upper half thirty centimeters. The crowd is immediately silenced, and the crimson blade morphs to a meter and a half in length but now has a twenty-centimeter-wide, forty-centimeter-tall ax blade. Braulie locks his hilt, stands to his full height, and bellows, "Now you fall!"

The crowd enthusiastically jumps to its feet as the fight has escalated to a whole new level. Tobius suppresses the shock of the hidden tactic of his opponent. He decides to settle into a defensive stance to let his opponent tire himself out. For the next ten minutes, Tobius keeps the ax from finding its intended target, even though several times his forearms went numb from the impact of the blows.

Braulie is attacking without reprieve, but everyone can see exhaustion is creeping in. The blue crytan brings his blade in an arc, intending to cut the human in half across his waist. Tobius instinctively swings his left blade around and intercepts the blade, but he does not pay attention as the impact starts the rotation of his weapon. Phylox sees the blade start to rotate and stands. The young man feels the blades start to spin and is too exhausted to try and stop it. In a heartbeat, both blades are spinning to form a virtual shield. The crytan, either from exhaustion or utter surprise, is caught off guard from the sudden change that he is unable to get his right arm out of the way. The sage blade scores a two-centimeter-deep gash across the forearm and the crytan drops his weapon.

Tobius steps back to see if the crytan will give up. Braulie reaches with his left hand and ignites his blade again and charges in with reckless abandon. The crimson blade comes in rapid strikes, and even though he fights with one hand, the strikes are no less ferocious. Tobius simply uses his fighting style to deflect and wear down his opponent. He knows that he can finish the fight, but there is no justice in killing him. After another five minutes, Braulie is at the point of collapse. The huge male stagers as Tobius deflects another attack. Taking three steps back, Tobius stops his blades, waiting to see what his opponent will do. Pure rage emanates from the crytan standing three meters away. The tip of the ax blade is resting on the ground sizzling as Braulie stands unsteadily. A full minute passes with utter silence filling the training yard. Suddenly, Braulie grabs his hilt with both arms, lifts it overhead, and charges forward with a primal howl of rage. Tobius reacts by instinct, raising his arms using the hilt shields to block the blow. Tobius senses immense power coursing through him to his shields. The instant the ax contacts the shields, a massive blast erupts. Braulie is lifted three meters in the air as his hilt shatters. The crytan lands fifteen meters away on his back, unconscious.

Admiral Kato jumps from his seat, enraged. "Get him!" he bellows. Suddenly, six cloaked figures ignite void blades throughout the crowd. The crowd is now screaming and running in fear.

Craven steps forward to Kato and asks, "Should I attack?" The admiral simply shakes his head in response. Phylox, Gamite, and Melissa are all shocked at the turn of events.

Tobius's smile turns to a face of confusion at the sudden proclamation and surveys the chaos. Six red blades slowly make their way toward him. He is already exhausted but shakily stands his ground. Uncertain of what to do, he just looks around as the six new opponents close the distance. When they are three meters away, Tobius flicks his wrists and settles in to defend. As the group closes to within two meters, Tobius has both blades spinning at top speed, humming their defiant tune. Not wanting to provoke any of them, he stands his ground but hears three other blades ignite from the platform.

Could this get any worse? he thinks and is surprised when he hears the clash of blades to his right. Taking a quick glance, he sees Phylox, Gamite, and Melissa all engaged with an attacker. With that distraction, he quickly takes the fight to the closest attacker. Even though they watched the fight between Tobius and Braulie, they did not really see him attack, and the first attacker falls in three quick strikes. The attacker to his left loses confidence as his companion falls, but Tobius gives him no chance to run. In a quick stride, he brings his sage blade in a low sweeping arc at their knees. The attacker takes a step back, avoiding the strike, and positions his blade to block the shoulder-high strike. The third attacker finally covers the distance, joining the fray.

Tobius senses the attack at his back and flicks his amber blade around to deflect the blow. He now stands using his sage blade against the attacker on his right and the amber for his left. He has never tried to take on two opponents at once, but he is doing his best not to give. The second attacker strikes his amber blade and causes the motion to slow. This throws Tobius off-balance, and he staggers. He tries to break free from the other one but is unable to. He sees the second attacker swing his blade in at his shoulder. Clumsily, he tries to intercept the incoming blade. He deflects the blade, but it still sears the back of his shoulder. Grunting in pain, he kicks the one who wounded him. Using the sage blade, he batters down the defenses in three successive overhand blows. And with the amber blade, he runs his enemy through his chest. A shocked expression flashes on his attacker's face as he falls back off the blade.

Tobius turns to face his final attacker, but they are running from the training yard. He looks and sees that his friends have finished off their enemy and are heading in his direction.

Melissa asks, "Tobius, are you okay?"

He nods as he extinguishes his blades, returning them to his belt. He cringes in pain from the wound on his left shoulder. Melissa grabs the med kit from the platform and grabs a med patch, placing it on the wound. Tobius grimaces from the sudden contact of the cool patch.

"Can anyone explain what this was about?" Tobius asks, looking at Phylox and Gamite.

A few heartbeats pass, and finally Phylox answers, "I think Admiral Kato was seeking vengeance for you killing his apprentice, but that only seems like part of it. I do not understand why he would have had six warriors hidden." Tobius looks at the platform and is surprised to see Kato and his companion are nowhere to be seen.

They head back into the academy slowly to make sure they do not walk into an ambush. Tobius is still confused about what just happened and why. They cautiously make their way through the academy and see nobody.

Tobius, speaking to no one in particular, says "Now what?"

Melissa considers for a moment and replies, "What about taking Hermi's shuttle?"

Gamite shakes his head. "We could not. They sold that ship since it was left unattended and the owner was killed."

Tobius fights back the wave of rage and sorrow that surges from the news. Clenching his fists, he takes a deep breath to control himself. The group passes the acolyte dining hall. Passing the hall, Tobius remembers that he is exhausted and hungry. Eagerly, he says, "Let's get some food first. It has been a busy day." Happily, they all agree and head to get some food. For a moment, they forget the chaos that just transpired.

The Cavern

They enjoy their brief refuge, enjoy their meals, and laugh about anything to forget the chaos. Tobius keeps recalling the vision he had in the throne room. He closes his eyes, focuses, and pushes his presence toward the area behind the throne. He sees the figure again, just as if he had paused a subnet vid. The figure has his hand on the obsidian diamond. He looks as he slides the whole tile forward about ten centimeters, and the secret door slowly swings inward.

Just as he sees the figure start to open the door, he gets nudged back to reality by Melissa. He looks at her and then looks at the others. They all have this really confused look on their faces.

"What?" he asks defensively.

Phylox laughs as he replies, "You suddenly said, 'That's it.'"

Tobius laughs and clarifies, "I know how to open the secret passage." With that, they all quickly finish their meals then head to gather items from their rooms. Ten minutes later, they meet up in the dining hall, each wearing a pack.

Moving cautiously, they proceed to the main hall. Since the fights in the training yard, there is no telling what could happen. They scan the hall and see four guards now at the main entrance. One by one, they quickly move behind the throne. Thankfully, it has a four-meter-wide base. Tobius again withdraws the obsidian diamond and inserts it into the slot. Placing his palm on the stone, he tries to move it forward, but nothing happens. He tries once more, but still nothing. Tobius starts getting annoyed and takes a moment to recall what the figure did. He tries again, but nothing happens.

Phylox senses his aggravation and leans down to whisper, "Clear your mind and focus."

Taking a deep breath, the young man relaxes, letting the tension flow from his body. Again, he places his palm and starts to focus, and Tobius feels power start to charge the crystal. Several heartbeats pass with no movement. He thinks, *Sanguis is obsessed with power, but not just from the flow.* He pours all his will to move the crystal forward and is rewarded when the tile starts to move forward. Ten centimeters…fifteen centimeters…Tobius is starting to feel fatigue in the back of his mind from the exertion but is undeterred. He cannot believe how much effort he has to use to open this door. Sweat is rolling down his face with the effort. Now he has moved the tile almost twenty centimeters, but the door has opened only five centimeters. Tobius is about to rest when the tile slides forward fifteen centimeters with a click, and the door slams open with a thud. All four jump at the sudden commotion.

Gamite looks from behind the throne and can see that the sudden noise caught the guards' attention. "Hurry," he quietly urges. No one challenges him. Tobius reaches to remove the diamond, but there is nothing there. Panicked, he looks at where the crystal was, but there is nothing. Melissa steps around Tobius into the passage followed, by Gamite. Phylox grabs Tobius's shoulder and tries to urge him down the stairway. Tobius refuses to move, staring at where the stone was.

Phylox quickly glances to where his young friend is looking. "Tobius we have to go." Tobius keeps looking down, perplexed. Again, the older male urges him into the passage. Tobius still is unwilling to move. "It's a trap door with a chute."

Unsure if his mentor is correct, he reluctantly moves into the passage. Once they clear the door, they turn to close it, but to their surprise, it silently seals itself. Both wait for several heartbeats to see if the guards saw where they went, but they feel no one attempting to follow them and head down the passage.

Tobius did not expect to see such an elegant passage. In his vision when he was an adept, it looked like a rundown, hand-dug tunnel, but that is nothing like what he saw. The walls seem to be made of a mirrorlike crystal, and every meter there, inlaid within the mirror, are heptagonal crystals. These crystals, almost ten centimeters thick, are self-illuminating. The crystals do not glow all the time but appear motion activated. As they all move slowly down the stairs, Tobius begins to notice that the crystals change as they passed by.

Tobius quietly says, "Wait." The others stop and look at him. "Look at the crystals," he says, pointing.

Gamite looks then chuckles. "Yes, it is a very fancy trick."

Shaking his head, he points again. "Melissa, touch the crystal in front of Gamite." The crystal glows a vibrant gold color, but as soon as Melissa touches it, the color changes to lighter amber color. Intrigued, Phylox reaches out and touches the same crystal, and it instantly changes to a pale blue color. All three look at Tobius, waiting for him to touch the same crystal. He leans forward and touches the crystal. The color first ripples purple, then black, then crimson, and finally silver light fills the passage.

"Fascinating," says Phylox, looking at the crystals. "They must somehow react to our eddies in the flow."

They continue down the passage, and Melissa looks at everything with utter amazement. "I wish we knew who made this place."

Tobius keeps quite as they move through the passage. After what seemed like hours, they arrive at the bottom of the passage, which opens into a massive cavern. They all look around at the vast darkness. Phylox moves to the wall but finds nothing like the passage walls. "This must be a natural cave," he says back to the others. "I cannot find anything over here." Tobius hears Gamite say the same thing from his right.

Reaching into his survival pack, he removes an emergency glow rod. He hits the base of it against his leg to activate it. He tosses it into the vast space beyond. Fifteen meters ahead, he sees the rod hit the ground and roll about another meter. He glances at the others then begins to step forward and stops. He can no longer see the glow rod.

"Did anyone see something take the glow rod?" he asks. He receives three quick and quiet nos. The tension in the cavern is palpable. Removing another rod, he activates it then hands it to Melissa.

"Hold this." He removes his survival cable, securing it to the glow rod. He throws the glow rod in the same area as the last one. It hits and bounces past the first rod. They all watch to see if the glow rod will go out. After a few seconds, the light fades away.

He pulls back the glow rod and jumps when he tries to pick it up. "What's wrong?" Melissa asks.

Tobius shakes his hand as he responds, "It's frozen." He lifts it by the cable, and everyone sees a thick layer of ice encasing the entire device, but it is not on the cable.

Phylox steps forward, examining the glow rod. "It appears that the ice is forming because of the power." They all look at him like he is a madman. "Watch," he says, quickly drawing his hilt and tossing it to the same place as the glow rod. He waits for five seconds then summons it back to his hand. An instant before it hits his palm, it stops. Melissa is holding her hand out, using the flow to stop it from slamming into his palm. Not only is there ice on the hilt, but there are icicles jutting from every side. At first, Phylox glares at her then looks at his hand. A thumb-sized icicle rests mere millimeters from the center of his palm. He nods his apology and thanks the young woman.

"It was only out there for a few moments," Tobius says, looking at it. "Can you ignite your blade?"

Phylox looks at his hilt. "Drop it, Melissa."

Confused, she nods, letting it fall. The cavern echoes as the ice shatters from the hilt. Phylox grabs the hilt and is shocked with how cold it is and summons the flow to warm the weapon. Once he can hold it without feeling pain, he thumbs the activation stud. For several heartbeats, nothing happens. He hits the activation stud again and holds it with both hands to try and warm it up. He hits the stud again, and the hilt pops and hisses. The blade jumps forth and flickers for several moments. A shower of sparks erupts from the emitter, and the blade stands true.

"Now what?" Melissa asks. They all quietly contemplate the situation at hand. Without a word, Tobius draws, ignites, and hurls his sage blade into the darkness. The blade spirals through the air. Ten meters...fifteen meters...twenty meters...the blade does not waver.

The blade has traveled over thirty meters in a straight path with no visible issues. Tobius is just about to summon the blade back when, without warning, the blade disappears.

A rumble rolls through the vast cavern as massive overhead flood lamps illuminate the entire area. They are all shocked with the enormous room. The ceiling is over forty meters high, and the walls are well over one hundred meters left to right. The room is so long that only part of the room is lit with the lights overhead. Tobius guesses that this must have been a secret bunker or training ground. At the point where the blade vanished, a ten-meter-tall, fifteen-meter-wide metal container stands.

The group looks at each other and starts toward the container with their hilts in hand. Tobius hates that he only has one of his weapons. He feels completely off-balance, like a shuttle with one wing. They all cautiously move to the front of the container.

"What is it?" Melissa asks to no one. She reaches forward to touch the side.

Phylox lunges forward to try and stop her. "No, wait."

Melissa looks at him, surprised, but her hand rests on the container.

A voice that seems to emanate from everywhere booms, "Only those worthy of power shall gain entrance."

Tobius looks around to see if there is anyone else in the cavern, but no one else is there that he could see. He looks back to the huge container to see that Melissa is completely encased in ice. Gamite looks at Melissa to see if there is a way to release her from her frozen tomb.

Phylox looks around the side of the container. "Tobius, come here."

Tobius moves around the left side of the container to where Phylox stands. This side of the container is thirty meters long with a three-meter recession in the middle. Tobius looks into the area and sees the obsidian diamond. Eagerly, he steps forward, but Phylox grabs his shoulder shaking his head. "Remember what happened to Melissa." The older man nods to the front. "Go get Gamite."

Nodding, he jogs to the edge and almost runs into him. Gamite has a morbid expression as he passes Tobius. Looking back, he sees that the ice is getting thicker around Melissa. Tobius's rage flares, and he jogs back to Phylox.

"Tobius, can you sense your blade?"

Tobius closes his eyes and expands his awareness. "It's just below the diamond."

Gamite ignites his blade and slices through the gate to the recess. The gate falls to the ground, cut clean on both sides. Before the metal has a chance to cool, two turrets spring up from the top of the container, one on each side of the opening. Gamite instinctively raises his blade, anticipating an attack, but he is frozen in place by a stasis field.

"I'm sick of this." Tobius scowls and tries to summon his blade. The blade rattles, but nothing more.

Phylox steps forward. "The blade is locked down." The recess tapers to a meter wide and extends five meters into the center, where it opens wider. He steps next to his young friend. "Do you still have a glow rod?" Tobius nods and removes his last one from his pack. "There looks to be a release about ten centimeters below your hilt. Can you hit it from here?"

Tobius rolls his shoulders as he replies, "Well, we are about to find out, aren't we?"

Tobius turns on the glow rod and hurls it at the target. It takes only a second for the rod to travel the distance, but it feels like hours to Tobius. The rod is spinning end over end as it nears its target. Tobius is so transfixed on the glow rod that he does not see the turret on the wall near the diamond pop up. Phylox, on the other hand, was anticipating something like this. Thrusting his hand forward, he summons the flow to shoves the glow rod into the release. Tobius is so caught off guard by the reaction of Phylox that he almost misses the rod hitting the release. He quickly recovers and summons the hilt to his hand and thumbs the activation stud. The sage blade erupts to life with a resounding thrum.

Tobius smiles and nods at Phylox, but the joyful expression fades. "You have chosen the means of the trial." Suddenly, the stasis field lifts Gamite, moving him into the opening within. Tobius sprints to the edge of the container, and the same thing happens with Melissa. Returning to Phylox's side, he inquires, "So now what?" The older man simply shrugs and readies himself for anything.

From within the container, the sounds of gears and hydraulics echo through the cavern. Tobius and Phylox look at each other then take a few steps back from the container, stopping ten meters from each other. In unison, four hatches slide open. Tobius looks to his right and sees similar hatches opening on the side. Tobius is about to jog to the side to see how many hatches have opened when suddenly, a set of crimson eyes open from within each hatch. Uncertain of what to do, he just spins his hilts and looks at Phylox. The older man calmly waves his right hand in a "just wait" manner. Taking a calming breath, he tries to settle his mind.

Suddenly, the sound of electricity resounds from the container, along with violet white light shining from each opening at waist height. In unison, four skeleton-like droids emerge from the hatches, wielding meter-long stun batons. They stop two meters from the hatch and wait for those from the side to join them. Tobius watches in fascination and horror at the scene. Nineteen droids stand a meter apart. These droids stand two meters tall, but Tobius is curious about the odd number. He looks toward Phylox, about to mention the odd number, when the droids face toward the center as a three-and-a-half-meter tall droid emerges from the center.

A deep male monotone voice bellows from the huge droid. "Only those worthy of power shall claim the crystal." The droid draws two hilts and ignites the red blades. He gestures to the two humans. Without a spoken word, the droids rush in.

They both ignite their weapons, taking a defensive posture. Phylox says, "Remember that as long as we use their numbers against them, we should be fine."

Tobius looks at him, uncertain, but has no time to respond. The first droid brings its weapon down in an overhead strike, and Tobius absorbs the blow with the shields on the hilts. As soon as the first weapon makes contact with the shield, the droid jumps over his head. Tobius drops his left blade to absorb an incoming attack at knee level. The droid that jumped over head is now spinning his weapon around at his neck as a third one thrusts at his exposed ribs. He balances on his left leg and ducks under the attack from behind while kicking out at the third droid. His heel connects with the midsection of the third droid, but all it does is send a sharp pain through his right leg.

Tobius rolls to his left, trying to get some space between him and the droids. Getting back to his feet, he looks back at the three droids, only to back into a fourth. Tobius looks over his right shoulder right into the crimson eyes. The skull-shaped head looks at him lifelessly. He quickly thrusts both blades behind him. His sage and amber blades intersect the center of the droid in a shower of sparks. Tobius jumps forward as some of the slagged metal burns through his tunic onto his back. Tobius winces from the contact, spins, and severs the head from the droid.

Tobius has no reprieve as the other three droids again attack him. Taking a quick step forward, he starts to spin his sage blade. Two of the droids swing their weapons to try and get past the sage blade. The third droid steps to Tobius's left. Keeping the sage blade moving, holding two of the droids at bay, he focuses most of his attention on the third. Spinning the amber blade upright, he blocks a shoulder-high attack. He drops his left arm, blocking the next blow with the shield on the hilt. He steps back, making the droid on his left miss, and unbalances the other two. Taking a step to his right, he tries to finish one of the droids. Right when he flicks the sage blade into the opening at the droid's waist, a blast of electricity shoots through his back.

Stars explode in his vision, and the scar feels like it has erupted in flames. Tobius had not seen another droid step in to replace the one he destroyed, and his carelessness led to his agony. Before he can recover, the droid he was attempting to remove from the fight lands a blow on his right shoulder, and again stars fill his vision. Tobius frantically tries to clear his vision.

Tobius hears Phylox shout, "Stay down!" He is unsure why he said that, but Tobius stays down. The next instance, he feels a surge of power just over him, hurling the four droids a dozen meters. Tobius knows that he only has a few moments before the droids are back on top of him. Still seeing stars and his back feeling like it is on fire, he stands, readying himself. He focuses on what is at hand.

Kato wants me dead, Gamite and Melissa are in danger, and Sanguis is laughing at me, he thinks. He thinks of all the friends and family he has lost, and the rage starts to grow. He feels his eyes start to burn from tears of sadness and rage, and he wants to destroy the droids and seek revenge. Suddenly, he feels a cool presence touch his mind, and he tries to push it away. The heat from the rage is a comfort to him right now.

Suddenly, the deep bass voice from the Gatekeeper on Draken fills his mind. "I did not allow you to seek the Power of Justice to exact revenge or settle personal vendettas. You have the will to keep the Power of Justice pure, and you cannot do so with rage and vengeance. Sanguis tried to use rage as the power for justice, but it only brought destruction to any who crossed his path."

The realization of what he was trying to do hit Tobius like a supernova. Taking a deep breath, he slowly exhales. The heat from the rage dissipates and is replaced with the cool, steely strength of his resolve. He feels power rushing through him like nothing he has ever felt. Instantly, his vision is crystal clear, his body hurts no longer, and the will to protect his friends drives his first steps.

The droids stand six meters away when Tobius begins his assault. In two flow-fueled strides, he covers the distance. The sage blade sweeps in a searing arc from the floor to shoulder height, cleaving the arms off the first droid. Spinning the amber blade around his back, Tobius pierces the center of the damaged droid's head. Keeping the pace, he blocks the second droid's weapon on the back half on the sage blade's shield hilt. This deflects the stun weapon and rotates the sage blade around. Tobius snaps his wrist down, spinning the blades around and bisecting the torso of the droid. With a slight gesture, the second scrapped droid flies out of Tobius's next step.

The other two droids have now been able to face him on a double front, but Tobius does not back down. The droids try attacking from both sides, but Tobius summons the flow, dashing past and cleaving both droids at hip level. The speed of his cuts are quicker than the droids could process, and they try to turn and face him. Both droids' torsos fall to the floor and hit each other in the heads with their stun weapons. Taking a quick moment, Tobius surveys the surroundings. Phylox is holding his own against the four droids but is unable to gain an advantage.

The other ten smaller droids are standing where they stopped before the fight, and the huge droid still has his blades ignited. Sprinting toward the ten droids, he spins both blades facing back along his forearms as he challenges Sanguis. "You think you can best me with some metal puppets?" With that said, the ten small droids charge forward to meet Tobius. As the nearest droids approach him, he leaps, clearing the first four. He kicks out with his left leg, connecting with the head of the fifth droid, and smashes the right optical sensor out of the fourth droid with the butt of the amber hilt. Landing on his right leg, he rolls to place himself in the midst of the droids, but more importantly, it places him in front of the huge droid. As he comes to his feet, he taps the hilt of the sage blade on his leg, starting its counterclockwise rotation. As it rotates from the two o'clock to ten o'clock, three weapons are deflected. He simultaneously brings the amber blade perpendicular to the floor, intercepting another attack. He deflects the next attack from his left, getting the amber blade to rotate. This time, Tobius is not using this technique for defense but as deflection and attack. The ten droids now surround him, and he uses the rotation of his blade to deflect the stun weapons together. He slowly starts to disable or destroy the droids. He severs the hand off one droid and lops off the leg of another at the knee. He deflects a stun weapon in the torso of another droid. After two minutes, four droids are disabled enough to be out of the fight.

Tobius slips his amber blade past the stun weapon, removes the head and left arm of a droid, and catches a glimpse of Phylox. The older man has destroyed two of the four and just cut the third in half. Tobius blocks three weapons on the length of his sage blade, stopping its momentum. Summoning the flow, he rolls a disabled droid through the legs of two of the three droids, and the third droid gets tangled with the other two. Phylox just finished his final enemy with a stab through the chest, pulling it straight up and slicing the head in two. Without a second glance, he turns to help Tobius finish the other droids. Tobius takes a few steps back toward Phylox to present a unified front.

Apparently, the huge droid determined that he had seen enough of the smaller droids' failure, and it steps forward, cleaving four of the small droids in half with his blades. The massive machine bellows, "You both die here!" The droid takes one step forward. Phylox deftly extinguishes his blade and channels the flow.

Without looking at Tobius, he says, "This is your fight."

At first, Tobius is confused at the vague statement, but he realizes what was meant the instant Phylox unleashes a massive energy wave. Phylox times his attack just as the droid is starting its next step. The massive attack hits the left leg at the knee joint. It looks at first that it would hold, but a crisp metallic snap resounds through the cavern. The knee buckles sideways, and its other leg is in no position to stabilize itself. The droid falls forward, dropping both hands to keep it from slamming into the floor. Tobius locks his amber blade, flips it up, grabs the short end of the hilt, and flings it at the right arm of the droid. The blade slices through the arm just below the elbow joint. Tobius summons his weapon back to him as he charges toward the damaged droid. Three meters from the droid, he leaps, using the flow to amplify his height and speed. He flips 180 degrees and rotates so he is heading feet first, looking at the ground. The hilt of his amber blade slaps his left palm. He holds the blades' angles toward the ground, shoulder-width apart. The droid has just enough time to look up at the impending attack. Each blade pierces an optical sensor and continues to burn through the droid. Tobius's shins hit the lower back of the droid. He slides off the droid, swiftly pulling the blades the rest of the way through, and extinguishes his blades as the droid falls in a slagged heap of metal and circuits.

Tobius turns toward Phylox. "Well done," the older man says between breaths. "Just remember, next time you face large groups of enemies, you should find a good defensive posture and wear them down." Tobius's smile fades at the reprimand. "You were lucky that I was able to get a moment to help get them off you."

"But they were droids," Tobius replies, annoyed.

Phylox laughs. "Even droids have weaknesses."

Entering the center of the container, they see that Melissa and Gamite are still encased in their prisons. "What should we do?" Tobius looks at his mentor, but he only shrugs. Stepping toward the control panel, he tries to find a way to release his friends. The panel is a meter long and half a meter wide, but nothing is labeled. There are dozens of switches, levers, and buttons. He steps to either side of the console to see if there is a power cable, but he finds only that the console is centered in the opening with no cables coming from it that he can see. Stepping behind the console, he sees a small lever. This lever is no more than two centimeters tall, but it is directly below the culet of the diamond. Tobius reaches toward the lever but receives an unpleasant shock. He looks at Phylox.

"I think I found the power switch," he says, pointing to the lever.

Phylox looks at it for several long moments. "It may be a trap."

Tobius nods. "But I don't think we have much of a choice."

Phylox looks to his left at Melissa in a block of ever-growing ice, then his right to his old friend trapped in a stasis field. They spend some time looking over the console to find anything that indicates a trap, but they find no signs of trickery. Tobius reaches the lever, stopping just before the area he got shocked. Reaching out with the flow, he tries to move the lever right, then left, then back and forth, but it refuses to move. Opening his eyes, he steps back, only to see the lavender figure of Sanguis floating above the diamond.

Tobius instinctively takes a quick step back. He looks to where Phylox was standing before, but he is nowhere to be seen. Sanguis's menacing laugh fills the cavern as Tobius looks around. Against the wall behind him, he sees Phylox bound by cables at the wrists, ankles, waist, and neck. Tobius feel the rage flaring inside him.

Sanguis floats closer to the young man. "What chance do you think you have of escaping? I bested the foolish Keepers, and the Void-raiders have no idea that this is even here. Keepers want to share the power, but they have no idea what power is. The Void-raiders claim that the void will give them what they want, but it just brings ignorance. I am the only one who has true power. Power is simply held by the one who is unafraid to use it." The figure gestures to Tobius's friends. He points at Melissa. "She is subservient and will never be deserving of power." He gestures to Gamite. "This old man is only worried about his acquisition of wealth, and that will get him nothing in the end." The figure thrusts a finger at Phylox. "You," he bellows and floats through Tobius. "You are nothing. You say you are helping, but you do nothing but advance your own goals."

Sanguis glares at him for a few moments, then he turns, facing Tobius again. "I will let you leave this place, but you must make a choice." Tobius nods but stands defiantly. "You must choose one of your companions to die, and once you do, you can take the diamond."

Tobius stares into the phantom's eyes. "What if I just take the diamond, free my friends, and leave?"

Again, the figure laughs. "The diamond cannot be removed until someone dies. The diamond absorbs the power from them, and in doing so, I become stronger still."

Tobius finally understands how insane his foe is. "How many people have you devoured?"

Sanguis takes a moment to ponder the question. Tobius focuses his mind. Before the phantom answers his question, he draws, ignites, and throws his amber blade at Sanguis.

Sanguis is completely surprised by the sudden attack. Even though he is a phantom, he instinctively tries to block the attack. The amber blade cleaves the figure in half as it passes through. Tobius uses the second of confusion to reach to Melissa within the flow. With one thought, he crushes the ice surrounding her and summons her to him. Melissa stops by his side, and he wraps his right arm around her waist to keep her upright. Tobius sees Phylox grab the amber blade and start cutting himself free. Before he has a chance to free Gamite, the lavender shadow bellows in rage.

He quickly reaches to Melissa's mind and senses a strong life essence, and a sigh of relief escapes him. The hair on Tobius's neck stands on end and, reluctantly, lets Melissa fall to the floor, igniting his sage blade. He steps in front of the fallen woman in a defensive stance, his right foot half a meter behind his left at shoulder width, using the entirety of his blade to deflect and absorb a massive barrage of violet lightning. His sage blade sizzles as lightning dances across its entirety. Even the hilt's shield pops with each strike as he holds his blade in front of his chest with the tip a half meter above the ground, just in front of his left leg. Sanguis's eyes burn with a thousand years of hatred.

"You think you can defeat me?" Tobius says nothing. He just defiantly stands his ground against the relentless assault. He finally understands how he has been able to defeat so many people. He uses the droids to either defeat them or knock them out. Then they bring them in so Sanguis can absorb their power.

Tobius's arms burn from the exhaustion, but he refuses to give in. He feels his feet slipping as the barrage intensifies. Sanguis's eyes look as though they are made of pure flames.

"You think you are strong enough for the power of justice?" Tobius's feet slide back another centimeter, but he does not give a response. "I have grown my power for a thousand years!" the phantom bellows, shaking the entire cavern. Tobius feels yet another surge of power from Sanguis, and the lightning storm between them doubles. The light is so intense that Tobius is forced to close his eyes, but that only slightly blocks out the violet light. "I have destroyed my enemies, crushed those weaker than me, and eradicated any who stood against me!"

Phylox watches in stunned fascination at the event transpiring but is shaken from his fixation by a small stone that fell from above. He glances to Gamite, who is still in the stasis field. Without hesitation, he extends his left hand, summoning the flow to rip the stasis emitter from the wall. A shower of sparks erupts from the crater, and Gamite falls to one knee. The older man shakes his head and takes a few deep breaths. Phylox relaxes slightly as he sees his friend rise to his feet.

Sanguis is now barely a meter away, and the lightning seems to gain strength every second. Tobius's arms feel like lead, his legs tremble from exhaustion, and the smells of singed fabric and ozone are making him dizzy. Tobius's feet slip another centimeter, and he feels his right heel hit Melissa's unconscious form. That sudden contact made him realize the cost if he would give in to this monster.

Suddenly, he sticks his left hand out into the infinite forks of energy. The lighting dances across his arm, singeing the hair as he summons his amber blade from Phylox's grip. The hilt shoots through the chaos of lightning, handle hitting his open palm. He quickly ignites the amber blade and lets it spin clockwise. He stops the blade perpendicular to the sage blade tip down, blades crossing at waist level.

Rolling his shoulders, Tobius looks directly into the lavender figure's crimson eyes and takes a step forward. The distance is now less than half a meter, and the lightning looks like a ball of writhing tendrils of light to those observing the encounter.

"No matter how many people you drain of power, I will never lose to a monster like you." He senses the rage in the phantom, but he does not look away. "You think that power is your strength, but the more power you absorb, the weaker you become."

Tobius is now standing a mere ten centimeters away from the phantom's face, but he does not flinch in the unending crimson stare of rage from his opponent. He slides his right leg back slightly, and in one quick motion, he drops his right arm, spinning the sage blade around. He thrusts it through the lightning right through Sanguis's face. The tip of the blade pulls the violet lightning with it, and as it passes through the phantom, the lightning ceases, and the figure vanishes, a scream of agony echoing through the cavern.

Exhausted, Tobius lets his arms drop as the blades extinguish. He looks over to see Phylox and Gamite both standing in utter amazement. Tobius cannot help but laugh at the befuddled looks of his friends, and that thought surprises him slightly. *They are my friends*, he thinks. Suddenly, his body starts to give way as the adrenaline fades. He falls to one knee and tries to just take a moment to rest.

Gamite comes to him and smiles. "You did well, Tobius." The old man helps him sit on the floor. "Never in all my years have I seen someone so determined to stand their ground against something like that." They both laugh.

Seeing that Tobius is fine, Phylox moves to the console and looks at the obsidian diamond as it floats in the stasis field. Being a Master of Knowledge, he is amazed at the crystal and the workings of the console. He slowly walks to the front of the console. Carefully, he analyzes every lever and knob. His hands float over every centimeter, trying to figure out how it works. He sees one button in the top left portion of the control panel, and just like the rest, there is no label. Transfixed on the button, he moves his left hand to the two-centimeter-diameter brown object. This button, compared to anything else on the panel, is well used.

Tobius takes a few deep breaths to try and steady himself and pulls an emergency ration pack from a pouch on his belt. He opens one of the food bars and starts to enjoy the quick snack. In between bites, he explains to Gamite about what transpired while he was in stasis. Tobius is half listening to Gamite as he looks at Melissa, still unconscious at the base of the console. He takes another bite from the food bar. "Cost of making something like this must have been massive." Tobius hears the last of what the older man was rambling about and suddenly sees Phylox standing at the front of the console.

Jumping to feet, he yells, "Phylox! No!" He takes two quick strides. He draws and ignites both blades in a swift motion.

Phylox is so transfixed on the console that he is completely unaware of Tobius or anything else. He starts to press the button but is unable to see what happens. Suddenly, the sage and amber blades cleave the console into thirds. He jumps back in shock and anger at the sudden destruction of this possible treasure trove of knowledge.

"How dare you!" he snaps at the young man, rising from behind the console. He feels his rage boil as he sees Tobius grab the diamond and turn back to Gamite. Blinded by his anger from the destruction, he storms around the console to confront his apprentice. "What do you think you were doing?" he snarls at Tobius as he grabs his shoulder. Phylox was not prepared for the response.

"Why do you think that of all the different levers and buttons on there, the only button that was well used was the one you were about to touch?" Complete silence fills the gap between the two. Seconds pass as they both stare at each other.

The silence in the cavern rises to a deafening level, but neither man says a word nor breaks eye contact. Suddenly, the silence is shattered. "Are you having a staring contest?"

Tobius instantly breaks eye contact as he turns to the voice. "Melissa, are you okay?" he asks as he kneels besides her, helping her sit up and lean against the destroyed console.

She nods her head and smiles. Tobius is completely relieved just by her simple gesture. Tobius gives a food bar to each of his friends, and they sit together and rest.

Mirrors and Deception

Admiral Kato storms onto the bridge of Vorex's Might with Craven following close behind. "I want any ship trying to leave the planet brought on board and searched!"

A lieutenant approaches him. "Every ship, sir?"

In no mood to handle stupidity, he simply crushes the insubordinate officer's throat with a simple gesture. "Does anyone else not understand?" Kato leans back in his chair, relishing in the impact of his command.

* * *

Standing, Tobius stretches to help relieve his fatigued muscles. "So now I guess we have to find a way out of this place." He extends his left hand to help Melissa to her feet. She gets to her feet and gives Tobius a smile, squeezing his hand.

She looks to Gamite. "Which way should we go?"

The old man chuckles. "Well, I am not sure, but we should stay together. We don't want the lovebirds sneaking off." Phylox laughs, but Melissa and Tobius blush and look away.

They all leave the center of the trap with Phylox leading with hilt in hand. Phylox heads to his right toward the opposite side of the cavern from where they entered. The group moves at a slow pace, unsure if there will be a sudden end or another trap. After what seemed like forever, in the dim light, Phylox finds the wall at the other end. He takes a moment and places his left hand on the wall. Closing his eyes, he takes a deep breath and listens to the eddies within the flow. As he exhales, he sends a pulse through the wall. Tobius watches with interest. After several heartbeats, Phylox turns to him with a smile and nods. "This way."

They move to the left, following the wall for several dozen meters before a tunnel interrupts the solid wall. Phylox ignites his blade and keeps the blade pointed to the ground to prevent hindering his vision. Tobius and Melissa follow suit. The group moves through the tunnels quickly and quietly. Tobius is amazed at the pace that Phylox is moving. The group now moves at a light jog, continuing deeper into the tunnels. Ten minutes have passed…now twenty…now thirty-five.

Tobius whispers to Phylox, "Do you know where we are going?"

He slows his pace slightly and nods. "Yes. I used the eddies in the flow like sonar underwater." He looks back at the young man as he continues, "I was able to find the route out of the caverns, but it is difficult to know exactly how far it is. The eddies can flow great distances."

They take a quick break as Phylox checks the path to make sure they are still heading the right way. They continue onward, taking several rights and lefts before Phylox holds his hand up in a fist to stop everyone. They look ahead, and the tunnel intersects with clean-cut stone. As they move closer, they hear footsteps echo in the new hall.

"What is this?" Tobius asks quietly.

Phylox shrugs. Gamite laughs, walking to the front of the group. "This is the executive landing area for the academy." The other three stare at him, confused. "There are three bays here, and they are typically reserved for the academy leader and any high-ranking visitors."

Tobius looks at him, shocked. "The admiral is down here then!"

The old man chuckles. "I doubt it. Very few people know it even exists. And don't worry. I know the tech down here."

Phylox shakes his head in disbelief. "How do you know about this?"

The older man grins. "I pay about a million credits a year to keep my shuttle here."

Tobius's mouth drops open in shock. "How can you afford that?"

Gamite puts a hand on his shoulder. "That is nothing but a drop in the bucket. I am a Master of Wealth, after all."

Without another word, Gamite strides into the bay. The others follow and put away their weapons, except for Phylox, who keeps his hilt in hand. This bay is massive. It's over sixty meters tall and three hundred meters wide. There are three individual berths, with two on the left side about eighty meters wide. But the one on the right is big enough to hold three cruisers with room to spare.

Tobius is awestruck with the look of this bay. It's very well lit. The floors are polished to a mirrorlike surface, and a dozen droids stand against the wall, ready to assist anyone who arrives. There are also a dozen personal refreshers next to a small bar with luxurious chairs, stools, and couches. He is so amazed with the area that he trips over a maintenance droid carrying a tray of tools.

The droid whistles and beeps in aggravation at the sudden interruption. A two-and-a-half-meter tall man turns at the sound and yells, "What's your problem!"

Tobius gets to his feet while Melissa and Phylox help the droid. The man is moving at a slow jog when he gets to the scene and is about to backhand Tobius. Gamite steps up, grabbing his hand from behind. The big man spins. "Now, Phen, this was an accident."

The other man is shocked for a moment then laughs. "Gamite, my old friend." The two men shake hands.

Gamite gestures to Tobius. "Now pardon my young friend. He has never seen such an extravagant hangar."

Tobius nods and extends his right hand. "I'm sorry I knocked your droid over."

Phen grasps his hand, shakes it, and laughs. "No worries, my lad. Nothing is broke, so it's all fine."

Then Gamite introduces Phylox, and Phen bows with respect. "And this is my apprentice, Melissa."

The large man gently grabs her hand and kisses it, asking, "How did a beauty like yourself wind up with this old relic?" Gamite hits him on the back, laughing. "What can I do for you today?" Phen asks.

Gamite starts walking to the bar with Phen. "We need to leave quickly and quietly."

Phen nods and hurries away to prep the shuttle. Gamite turns to the bar and grabs four glasses, a bottle of brandy, milk, and a tray of snack cakes and fruit. Returning to his friends, he pours three fingers' worth of brandy for Phylox and himself and hands the milk and glasses to Melissa and Tobius. They both object.

"Why can't we have some?"

Phylox almost spits out his brandy as he laughs at their response. Gamite simply raises his glass. "It's simple. You are too young."

Tobius and Melissa could not help but laugh at the response. For the next hour, they sit at the bar, waiting on Phen to finish prepping the shuttle. No one really relaxes because they have no idea on what is happening elsewhere in the academy.

*　*　*

Admiral Kato sits on the bridge of Vorex's Might. "Ensign, please send an escort down to bring Master Krystelle and her acolyte to me."

The officer responds, "Yes, sir," as he relays the orders.

Kato stands and says, "Lieutenant, please summon all ship commanders to the war room." He strides from the bridge. The war room is like a conference room in many aspects, but Kato had this room modified in many ways after he assumed command. Craven is waiting outside the bridge as he strides out. Kato is surprised to see him there. Craven stands there, still in his armor, and Kato swears that he sleeps with it on. Craven has his helmet under his left arm, and his armor appears to be freshly polished. Craven's eyes are like black holes, and his short blond hair is barely a centimeter long, but the interesting feature is a comet tattoo through his hair and down the left side of his face, making his hair look like it is on fire. This catches Kato off guard because he never saw Craven with the helmet off before.

"What's going on, Kato?" Craven asks, falling into step with him.

The admiral says nothing as they move through the hall. They take the lift down two levels to where the war room and his personal quarters are. Leaving the lift, he heads to his quarters with Craven in his wake. Arriving, Kato enters a lengthy code into the panel then rests his palm on the scanner. A green light and soft chime come from the panel as the doors part. The two enter the room, and Kato turns back to the door, enters another code, and punches the enter key. Suddenly, the door closes, and a meter-long clasp peels from the left half and turns to join with the right.

"Wow, I am impressed," Craven says with a nod. "I need that on my ship."

Kato is too busy securing the room to even register the compliment. The quarters are thirty meters wide and eighteen meters deep with luscious furniture, a personal bar, refreshers, large bed, and even its own small entertainment subnet suite. However, Kato is at his desk, entering another command on the console. A half dozen orbs, three centimeters in diameter, rise from the desk and proceed to different sections of the room. After several seconds, each orb pulses green. Kato finally relaxes slightly.

"What is going on?" Craven asks again, concerned. "In all my years with you, I have never seen you paranoid."

Kato slowly stands from the chair, both his hands on his desk. "Craven, you are the only person I can trust right now." Craven freezes at the statement. "The Void-raiders have become complacent with the way things are. It is time to get away from the ranks of Void-raiders like it has become."

Craven asks, confused, "I don't understand."

Kato steps from behind the desk and over to the bar. "Would you care for a drink?" Craven nods as he sits on one of the chairs. "What do you know of Void-raiders history?"

Craven accepts the drink, answering, "Nothing much really, except that they follow the void, whatever that means."

A genuine laugh escapes from Kato. "A modest answer but an honest one." Sitting in another chair, he continues, "The Void-raiders go through cycles. Void-raiders come from the verge of extinction then band together to form an army to try and control the galaxy. After some time, the Void-raiders either crumble from within or become satisfied with coexisting." Kato takes a drink.

Craven takes a moment to think about what was said. "What does this have to do with now?"

The admiral finishes his drink then explains, "The cycle must end. I must stop this and bring about the true form of the Void-raiders."

Craven nods. "How will you do that?"

Kato leans forward, placing his elbows on his knees, and steeples his fingers together. "I have summoned all the commanders to the war room and called a meeting for the entire academy." Confused, Craven just nods. "I have also selected one to become my new apprentice."

"But why gather them all in two spots? Aren't they, combined, stronger than you?"

Kato stands, laughing. "Some would be, but I have a plan to end this in one swift stroke."

* * *

Phen comes up to Gamite, smiling. "Mirror's Edge is ready to go."

Gamite stands and shakes his hand. "Thanks, Phen." He turns to the others. "Let's go."

Just as they head toward the shuttle, an announcement echoes through the massive bay. "Everyone in the academy, please report to the training yard for a special assembly."

Phylox closes his eyes, rubbing his temples. "What's wrong?" Tobius asks.

"Something big is about to happen here. We must go." They rush to the shuttle, and Gamite grabs Phen's arm, pulling him with them.

They head up the ramp into the luxurious shuttle, and Tobius looks around, amazed. Phylox pushes him out of the way as he moves to the shuttle's cockpit. "Gamite, what is above us?" he shouts as he starts up the engines. Phen, Melissa, and Tobius strap themselves into the passenger chairs, and Gamite heads to join Phylox.

"The training grounds." The old man straps himself in the captain's chair and engages the thrusters.

* * *

A chime comes over the desk transceiver. Kato hits the acknowledge button. "Yes."

The lieutenant says, "The commanders are in the war room, the academy has gathered on the training grounds, and Master Krystelle and her acolyte are landing in bay 3."

Standing, he replies, "Understood." Rolling his shoulders to relieve the tension, he does a quick breathing technique. "Craven, it is time to change the Void-raiders."

Craven stands, donning his helmet to become the faceless monster so many feared. The admiral recalls the orbs, unbars the door, and they make their way to the bridge.

The bridge doors part with a soft hiss. Kato and Craven stride onto the bridge. The admiral steps to the center of the bridge while Craven stands just right of the door. "Does anyone here challenge my command?" Several silent seconds pass without even a whisper. "Lieutenant, secure the war room. Tactical, target the training grounds." The bridge instantly becomes a blur of motion as they jump to their tasks. Thirty seconds later, an almost simultaneous response comes from the lieutenant and tactical officer. "Life support, vent all air from the war room. Weapons fire." Kato hits the transceiver for the fighter bay. "Squadrons Alpha through Charlie, search for fleeing vessels. Delta and Echo squads, hit the training grounds and eliminate any survivors."

All twelve portside pulsar cannons unleash their crimson wrath. Five dozen fighters erupt from the belly of Vorex's Might, heading in every direction. Kato sits in the command chair. "Communications, open a channel to the fleet."

"Aye, sir," the ensign quickly replies. Five seconds later, "Channel open, Admiral."

Kato rises to his feet and steps forward, clasping his hands behind his back. "Attention all ships of the Vorex's Might. This is Admiral Kato. The Void-raiders, as you know it, are no more. I have eradicated the pompous fools and their ridiculous methods. I killed all your commanders, and your first officers are now in command. If any ship tries to retaliate against me, let me remind you that I have override codes for every ship. I will kill the entire crew if a ship tries to revolt." He looks to his own bridge crew as he continues, "Capture any outbound vessel. Ground troops, disembark to the surface and search the academy. Eliminate any survivors and collect all possession within." He nods to the communications officer, who ends the transition. He returns to his chair. "Navigation, let me know if any ship steps out of line."

* * *

Gamite gives the thrusters a moment to take the weight of the ship before he retracts the landing gear. He gives Phylox an uneasy look. "Something is wrong."

Phylox nods and powers up the shields. "How long does it take to get out of here?" he asks.

The old man answers as Phylox feeds power to the engines, "About ten minutes normally."

Phylox looks at him, worried, and inquires, "Why does it take that long?"

The old man guides the shuttle from the bay and turns to the hangar doors. "There is a two-kilometer tunnel underground that lets out in the desert to hide this access." The massive doors begin opening when suddenly, debris cascades from the ceiling. First, it is just some dirt and small stones, but after thirty seconds, one of the massive lights crashes onto the Mirror's Edge, knocking the ship into the deck. Gamite hears a scream of surprise from the passenger cabin, and he increases power to the thrusters and increases the throttle to two-thirds. Mirror's Edge scrapes the deck for a dozen meters before the thrusters get it completely off the ground.

"Phylox, put the shields to double front. We are going to ram the door."

Phylox does what he is told, even though he is unsure of his friend's intended course, but Gamite knows what his ship can handle. As the Mirror's Edge gains speed, Phylox yells back to the passengers' cabin, "You better strap in. It's about to get bumpy!"

As soon as Phylox finishes his statement, a thunderous crack emanates through the hangar, and a massive fifteen-meter-wide chuck of durasteel plating falls from the ceiling, embedding itself three meters into the hangar deck. Gamite's eyes widen at the sudden obstacle. He slams the yolk to the left, trying to kick the right side of ship up and out the way. The plate catches the stubby five-meter-long wing. An eerie shriek of strained metal echoes through the ship as the Mirror's Edge is spun almost ninety degrees, and alarms blare through the cockpit as half the right wing is sheared off. Phylox silences the alarm as Gamite fights to get the shuttle back on course.

The Mirror's Edge continues toward the bay doors as its captain attempts to correct its vector. Fifteen meters from the door, the nose of the ship is still thirty degrees off course, and the opening in the door is five meters too small for the ship to fit through. Sweat is beading on Gamite's forehead as he fights to control his ship. Another thunderous explosion echoes through the hangar, and the lights go out. Emergency lights flicker then fail. Phylox hits the lights and braces for impact. The Mirror's Edge collides with the doors.

Phylox shouts, "Shields to thirty-four percent!"

Gamite shoves the throttle to full and says through gritted teeth, "All reserve power to front shields." The extra power to the shields bends the edges of the hangar doors enough to get the ship through.

Gamite breathes a sigh of relief as the ship squeezes from the hangar. Phen climbs up to the cockpit. "You better push it. There is three hundred thousand liters of fuel back in that hangar, and I don't think the blast doors will close when it blows."

Phylox looks at the control panel. "Gamite, the right wing is in bad shape, and shields are at thirteen percent."

Gamite nods. "Okay, put the shields on the back."

Phylox nods as he complies, and just as he gets the shields adjusted, a massive shock wave slams into the back of Mirror's Edge. Phen gets thrown from the cockpit, his right shoulder slamming against the bulkhead, and crashes to the ground, sliding past Tobius and Melissa. Tobius quickly unhooks his restraints drives, grabbing Phen's leg with his left hand and holding the restraints with his right.

Mirror's Edge bucks from the massive energy wave, and alarms blare in protest. Phylox silences the alarms then grabs the yolk to help Gamite control the battered vessel. He glances at Gamite and says with a strained voice, "How much farther?"

The older man takes a moment to glance at the console then replies, "About seven hundred meters."

The engines on the vessel are straining to keep it from tumbling out of control, and in this tight space, it would destroy the ship. Gamite looks ahead but sees nothing but dark tunnel.

"Phylox, take control!" he yells through the increasing chaos. He leans to his right and enters the code to open the door but gets no response. He slaps the console and reenters the code and sees a mechanical failure alert. He curses under his breath and grabs a tablet from the side of his chair. Two warnings flash on both consoles: engines critical and proximity warning. "Three hundred meters to the end of the tunnel," Gamite says. "But the doors haven't opened."

Phylox looks at him, concerned. Gamite scrolls through the tablet on emergency procedures. He quickly tries a few different codes, but the doors still remain sealed. An automated voice says, "Two hundred meters until impact."

Gamite keeps scrolling and tries a few more codes. "One hundred twenty-five meters until impact." He finally finds the code and hopes it will work. Override all code, ADIF965PB3, and he quickly enters the ten-digit code. In the distance, he sees eight distinct explosions around the rim of the access. With just over fifty meters before the ship runs out of room, the doors fall flat to the tunnel floor, and the Mirror's Edge shoots out on a jet of flames and debris.

Gamite brings the ship around to see what is happening at the academy and cannot fathom the scene unfolding. A massive barrage of crimson lances pound the entire training ground. Both of them are stunned at the sight of destruction and are yanked back to reality as Tobius enters the cockpit.

"What's going on?" he asks.

Phylox glances back and sees complete shock on his friend's face. Clearing his throat, he begins to say, "We have no idea, but—"

Gamite cuts him off as he points ahead. "Two squadrons of fighters inbound." Gamite uses his left arm and gestures to the small console behind him in the corner. "Tobius, you need to man the defense turret there."

Without question, Tobius straps into the seat. "Okay."

"Put the helmet on and lower the visor."

He grabs the helmet from the hook above the console, dons it, and secures the chin strap. He lowers the visor, and a microphone slides out from the left side of the helmet, stopping just in front of his mouth. "Now what?"

Gamite enters a quick code into the console in front of him. "Now say the code, and it will power up for you."

Tobius reads the code on the visor. "Code red, Firestorm." The code flashes green. The visor goes black for three seconds and then flashes back on, but instead of seeing the console in front of him, he sees the top of Mirror's Edge. A joystick come out from each arm of the chair and flip up into the palms of his hands.

Gamite's voice comes through the helmet. "Tobius, this is a very unique system. Use your head to rotate the turret. The weapons are targeted with your eyes. You look at the target you want to shoot." Tobius is listening to his instructions and turns his head left. He sees the world shift to the portside of the ship. "The control sticks," Gamite continues, "control the right and left pulse cannon respectively, and you have six concussion missiles. These you fire by saying, 'Fire missile.' Any questions?"

Tobius thinks for a few seconds before responding, "No, I think I have it, but what am I shooting at?"

Phylox answers, "Hopefully nothing, but just keep an eye on our tail."

Tobius nods but gets a slight vertigo sensation as the turret view responds to the sudden action. Queasy, he responds, "Yeah, I got it."

Gamite laughs. "You nodded, didn't you?" Tobius could only laugh.

Tobius can see through the turret as the Mirror's Edge turns 180 degrees and heads away from the academy. He sees the last of the barrage impact the training yard. Several seconds later, as the smoke clears, he sees a wave of fighters executing strafing runs on the remnants of the yard. Tobius feels rage and sorrow gather inside him, and he closes his eyes, taking a deep breath. He hears Phylox through his helmet.

"It is okay to feel angry for what has happened. But remember, as a seeker of justice, you must keep your actions free of personal vengeance."

Taking in another deep breath, he responds, "I understand, but how can I not want some personal vengeance for this? No one there deserved that."

"Tobius, that is why true seekers of justice are so rare, and we are very careful on who we let follow that path," Phylox calmly says.

Through the turret view, he sees the ship accelerate and drop closer to the ground. This sudden action shakes him from his quandary, and he starts looking around. Gamite is flying the ship through the desert, staying mere meters above the dunes.

Apprentice

Admiral Kato watches the execution of his order with pleasure and even revels in the sensation of the eradication of the Void-raiders perversion the academy had become.

The communications officer turns to him. "Admiral, Master Krystelle and her acolyte are on board and headed to your study."

Kato nods, rising from his chair and stepping forward. "You have all done well in this time of change, and you all have helped start the new Void-raiders Empire." He turns, striding from the bridge. He can feel the loyalty and pride of his bridge officers.

Craven is following close, and once the door closes, he says, matching Kato stride for stride, "Nice move, but what's next?"

The admiral smiles. "Now I shall select my apprentice then retrieve the key of power." As they near the study, Kato senses Krystelle and her acolyte approaching. "Craven, unless someone directly attacks you, just stay back."

Craven simply slows his pace until he is three meters behind Kato. The admiral enters the code, opening the study doors, and they both enter, leaving the doors open. Kato leans against the front of his desk as Craven moves to the corner to Kato's left and quickly checks his pulsar pistol and gauntlet hold out pistol. No sooner did he steady himself to watch than Master Krystelle stormed into the room, eyes burning with rage.

"What do you think you are doing?" she bellowed as she stopped a hand's breath from Kato. "The Counsel of Masters will not allow you to get away with this."

Kato is a little surprised that her weapon is still attached to her belt, and he guesses that either she is curious about his intentions or knows she cannot defeat him. Keeping his expressions impassive, he lets her finish her rant about the actions he took.

She points her finger into the center of his chest, asking, "Tell me why you did this."

Kato smiles, gesturing to one of the chairs. "Please, Master Krystelle, take a seat and I shall explain." For several heartbeats, she does not move. "Krystelle, who is your acolyte?" This question catches her off guard as she takes an involuntary step back.

"Admiral Kato, may I introduce my acolyte, Morrin." The young man steps forward with a slight bow. "It is an honor to meet you, Admiral Kato."

The admiral gives a slight nod. Turning around, Kato moves to sit behind his desk while his visitors each take a seat. "I have summoned you both because you are the only people I trust. The rest of the Void-raiders have been destroyed. Their perversion of the Void-raiders is revolting." He leans forward, resting his forearms on his desk. "We must work together to ensure Void-raiders' survival. No longer will we allow just anyone who has some talent to earn the title of Void-raiders. The Void-raiders are strongest when we punish the weak." Kato smiles to himself, seeing as they are drinking in every word. "We eliminate any enemy. We must control everything with the void." Taking a moment, he looks at both of his possible apprentices as he stands. "Now there is only one problem that must be solved before bringing the galaxy under Void-raiders' control." Striding around the desk, he says, "Please follow me."

* * *

Mirror's Edge moves through the desert dunes, trying to move quickly and unnoticed. Tobius asks, "Why don't we just head to space?"

Gamite responds, "My ship was designed to be almost invisible on sensors, but with the right wing damaged as bad as it is, we would be like a flare at night."

"We can't just keep flying through the desert," Phylox states.

Gamite begins to explain, "I am heading to the terminator and—"

Suddenly, a voice comes across the speakers. "Mirror's Edge, decrease speed and turn to heading One Eight Zero."

Gamite mutes the transceiver, looking at Phylox. "What's the shields status?"

Phylox looks at him grimly. "Front shields are down, and rear are at twenty-six percent."

Gamite reluctantly pulls back the throttle to one-third and banks to the directed heading. "Tobius, shut down the turret." Gamite keys the transceiver, "Mirror's Edge complies. May I inquire as to our destination?"

The reply is simple. "Vorex's Might."

Gamite freezes at the mention of the ship. Phylox chimes in to prevent curiosity from the fighter pilot, "Thank you. Mirror's Edge out."

Tobius turns around, seeing Gamite's expression in the crysteel reflection. "Gamite, what's wrong?"

The older man makes eye contact through the reflection. "That is Admiral Kato's ship." A look of absolute shock and disbelief forms on the younger man's face.

Gamite unbuckles from the pilot's chair and heads back to the passenger cabin, gesturing for Tobius to follow him. As he enters, Melissa looks at them both. "Where are we going?"

Gamite heads toward the refresher but stops short of the refresher. The older man kneels, and a one-hundred-square-centimeter panel flips up from the floor. He deftly enters a code, and a chime emits from the hidden pad. The old man stands up as he closes the panel. Melissa unstraps the crash harness and joins them. They both wait for several moments, waiting for an action from Gamite. Suddenly, a faint sound of a latch is heard, and a safe lowers from the ceiling.

Tobius looks on with fascination. "Gamite, how much did you spend modifying this ship?"

Gamite laughs as he turns to face them. "I really do not know. As a seeker of wealth, I do not keep track of what I have spent, but I track the total value of things." The safe is a meter wide and long and half a meter tall. Gamite leans forward, entering another code on the top of the safe, and the top of the safe pops up a centimeter with a metallic clack. He holds his left hand out. "Hand me your blades. I will store them in here so they are not taken."

Melissa and Tobius look at each other, a little worried, but they hand their weapons to the old man.

Gamite hands them both two hilts in return. "Take these so you are not unarmed, and it will provide a better story to anyone."

* * *

Kato leads them from his study through a labyrinth of turns to a training room in the belly of the ship. "Now there will be a test to see who will earn the chance to become a true Void-raider." Stopping at a door, he turns to look at Krystelle and Morrin. "You now must choose. If you enter the room beyond, you must prove yourself worthy, but if you choose to walk away now, you will forever be branded as cowards." Kato turns, heading down the hall to a small lift set in the wall. "I will be in the observation chamber above, and you have ninety seconds to decide." Kato hits the control, and the lift rises fifteen meters.

Krystelle looks at Morrin and smiles, but it is nothing like the smiles he had seen before. This smile is full of rage and lust for power. "Morrin, you know how special you are to me, but I need to become more powerful." Her expression changes to one of devotion. "I am very proud of you, and if you choose to enter this room too, I will respect that."

Morrin stands there, pondering what just transpired. After a moment, he straightens and looks into his lover's eyes. "I will enter." With that, he pulls her in for a quick kiss. They both remove their cloaks and step into the room.

The room beyond the doorway is pitch-black except for two meter-wide illuminated circles three meters inside. Kato's voice echoes throughout the room. "Please step into one of the rings." They both step forward into their respective circle. A fifteen-centimeter-diameter cylinder rises from the floor. "Please put your hilts on the pedestal." Again, without hesitation, they both comply." A small shield appears around both hilts, and the cylinders vanish into the floor with a hiss. An image flickers to life before them.

"This is your target. A humanoid-looking creature two meters tall, with a scarred face and black eyes." Kato explains. "The one who kills it shall join me." Kato's face replaces the image. "You must find your weapon then defeat the target." Without another word, the image vanishes. Krystelle looks at Morrin one more time as the disks rise and move off in opposite directions.

Morrin is caught off guard from the sudden movement and uses the void to anchor himself to the disk. Ten seconds pass, and Morrin can see nothing but the slight illumination from the disk. After several turns, he feels it slow then lower him to the floor. Morrin takes a moment to look around, but still there is no light. Standing still, he listens and hears nothing. He reaches into the void to get a sense of his surroundings but senses nothing. He takes a few deep breaths and feels a tingle on the back of his neck. He lowers to a crouch and waits, but the tingling does not stop. Standing, he steps from the disk, and when his right foot makes contact off the disk, massive flood lamps snap on. Morrin closes his eyes from the sudden bright light and rolls to his left, but no attack comes. Standing, he shields his eyes to let them adjust to the light. The surroundings are not what he expected. There are plants of all sorts with thick humid air. He still cannot shake the strange feeling.

Morrin notices that he must be in the back right corner of the training room and moves right along a stone ledge. After several dozen steps, he comes across a small stream and waits to see if any animals are nearby. A minute later, he steps down to the stream and takes a drink. The water is crisp and clear with a hint of mint, and it is some of the best water he has ever tasted. Quickly, he takes a few more mouthfuls before moving on. Standing, he extends his awareness but senses nothing. So instead of trying to find anything, he focuses on locating his weapon. Morrin can feel his mind growing cloudy and curses himself for drinking from the stream. After thirty seconds, he finally senses his hilt and moves toward it.

Krystelle steps from the disk and moves quietly in the dark. She tries to sense her weapon. After moving several dozen meters, the panels snap on, illuminating the room, and she closes her eyes. Sensing no imminent danger, she slowly opens her eyes. As her eyes adjust to the light, she sees something shining a dozen meters away, on top of a ten-meter-tall cliff. The path to the item is relatively straight, but she finds the item is nothing more than a scrap piece of metal. The cliff gives her a good view of the training room, and she sees a tree with her hilt about thirty meters up on a limb. Extending her hand, she summons the void to pull the hilt to her, but it remains unmoving on the limb. Frustrated, she jogs to the base of the tree, but as she moves closer to the tree, her sense of the void grows more distant.

Kato watches as the two make their way through the area below. This training room is one of Kato's favorite spots on the ship. One hundred meters wide, one hundred fifty meters long, and fifty meters tall, this room has the ability to mimic almost any environment. Right now, it is set to Kato's favorite configuration—a combination of rocky and jungle terrain with a humid atmosphere. He always brings his apprentices down here to teach them about how the void is not the only thing a Void-raider needs to survive. He watches as they both struggle to find their weapons. This room is designed to disrupt one's connection with the void, and he uses this room often to remind him that he is not invincible. He had the room designed for everything to look real, but the plants are all synthetic. The only real thing in the room is the water, but the main purpose is to fill the room with ambient noise. Kato taps a control on the console in front of him, and another puff of mist emits from the top of the trees.

Craven looks on with extreme interest. "The plants are air vents then?"

Kato nods as he hits another control. "The tops are special canisters of different toxins and hallucinogens, and depending on the challenge, they are very helpful in providing the desired atmosphere."

Craven nods as he replies, "I may have to try it sometime to see how effective my suit's air purifiers are."

Morrin moves through the brush, finding a small crevasse. He moves to it and looks inside, catching a glint of light off something metal. He reaches his hand in to retrieve the object. His finger brushes against the smooth metal, and he knows it is his hilt. He pushes his hand farther in to get a grip on the weapon. Morrin winces in pain as something stabs into the back of his hand. He grits his teeth, and he finally grabs the end of the hilt, pulling it free. He looks at the back of his hand, finding a small puncture wound as if he just received a shot. Quickly, Morrin checks his weapon to ensure that it was not physically damaged and thumbs the activation switch. The blade hums to life, and Morrin give it a few spins. Satisfied that it is undamaged, he extinguishes the blade. "Now to eliminate the target."

Krystelle looks at the tree, enraged, after several attempts to summons the hilt to her. Reluctantly, she begins to climb up the large trunk to retrieve her weapon. There are nubs all over the tree to act as decent hand and foot holds. Twelve meters off the ground, she rests and checks on the hilt, still resting on a limb another twenty meters up. Growling in frustration, she resumes her ascent to reclaim her weapon. She pulls herself onto the half-meter-wide limb two meters below the branch holding the hilt. Rising to her feet, she slowly makes her way out to the hilt. Krystelle reaches up for the branch but is unable to grab it. Moving a meter back toward the trunk, she jumps, grabbing the three-centimeter-thick branch. Surprised at the stability of the branch, she shuffles toward her weapon. Just before she can reach the hilt, her left hand comes down on a patch of half-centimeter-tall thorns. Grimacing, Krystelle curses the tree, and she snatches the weapon as she drops to the limb below.

She lands on the limb and shakes her hand. Quickly, she ignites her blade and is pleased with the snap hiss of the blade. She makes her way back to the trunk, turns, and sprints the distance of the limb and jumps. As she propels herself away from the tree, she feels the power of void course through her. She smiles as she flips once as she free falls twenty meters. She rights herself as she summons the void, slowing her descent, and she lands like a feather.

* * *

The transceiver crackles to life with a crisp male voice. "Mirror's Edge, this is Vorex's Might. Please proceed to portside bay three and prepare to disembark."

Phylox calmly keys the transceiver. "Vorex's Might, this is Mirror's Edge. We understand, but why are we being directed here?"

The voice responds, irritated, "You will be informed once you dock."

The transceiver shuts off with a soft pop, and Phylox yells over his shoulder, "Gamite, get up here!"

The old man quickly seals the safe, returning it to its hiding place. Tobius and Melissa take their seats and strap in as Gamite climbs back into the cockpit. "Where are we going, Phylox?"

"We are to land in portside bay three and get out," Phylox says.

They both look out the view port at the ship looming in front of them. "What is the status of the shields?" Gamite asks.

Phylox looks up and enters some commands and then responds grimly, "We would have better luck standing outside with our blades."

Gamite straps his harness and reduces speed to one-third as they near the bay. The two men look at each other as the bay doors open. Phylox feeds power to the thrusters as the Mirror's Edge enters the bay. Ahead of them, they see a bay worker with two red glow rods, signaling where to land. The bay is empty except for a fancy shuttle.

"This must be the executive bay," Gamite says, impressed. They are directed to land on the opposite side of the bay from the shuttle. Reaching to the console, Gamite keys a couple commands. Suddenly, the view screen shows a full view around the ship.

Phylox lets out a whistle at this fancy option. "So you can watch every side of the ship at once, but you cannot afford good shields?"

The older man laughs. "If you could fly, we wouldn't have had an issue."

Tobius and Melissa look at each other nervously, but their tension eases when they hear their friends laughing from the cockpit. Gamite climbs from the cockpit and looks at the three in the passengers' cabin. "Phen, how long do you think it would take you to fix her up?"

The mechanic thinks about it for a moment. "Well, I won't know for sure until I see the damage, but I think I can get a quick fix in an hour."

Gamite nods then continues, "I did not see any guards, so they may not realize who we are. So we will just play it cool, and we might get out of here unnoticed." Gamite steps past them to the back of the cabin and pulls a fancy robe from the closet. The robe is as black as midnight and has gold thread at the hems. It is perfectly designed to fit Gamite. The bottom of the robe rests half a centimeter off the ground. He raises the hood and turns to his friends. Melissa lets out a quiet gasp at the look of her master. The hood rests over his head and casts a shadow over his face, but his eyes seem to triple in intensity. "This is the robe I use when meeting other masters or to intimidate someone."

Tobius nervously says, "Yeah, it works."

* * *

Kato watches from the observation deck as the two work their way through the room. Craven takes a step closer to look out the view port. "How many times have you used this room for these types of challenges?"

Kato leans back in his chair. "Me? This is only the second time, but my master had one similar to this that I had to face many times." A vengeful scowl forms on his face. "I actually killed my master in his own room." Leaning forward again, he taps the controls, and more of the chemicals are introduced into the room. Suddenly, the transceiver on the arm of his chair chimes. Kato ignores the transceiver as he watches his two candidates. Again, the transceiver beckons for his attention, and again he mutes it. He looks at his console and sees that they are now forty meters apart and enters another command. A mist begins to fill the lower two meters of the room. Again, the transceiver chimes, and he angrily hits the transceiver. "What?"

The communications officer responds in a shaky voice, "We have the Mirror's Edge in bay three."

The rage wells in Kato as he responds, "You interrupted me to let me know you have brought in a ship!"

"Ye…yes, sir" came the reply.

"Did the ship come willingly, or did they resist?"

"They came willingly, but their ship is damaged."

Enraged, Kato rises from his chair, summoning the void. He hears through the transceiver as the officer is flung from his chair across the bridge. He slaps the transceiver and bellows, "Lieutenant, send a crew to aid the ship and let them leave."

"Yes, Admiral."

"There had better be a competent communications officer when I get back to the bridge, and I am not to be disturbed." Without waiting for a response, he shuts off the transceiver.

* * *

Gamite hits the control, lowering the boarding ramp. As the ramp quietly lowers to the deck, he strides out, followed by the others on board. Fifteen meters from the stern of the ship stands a single officer. The officer approaches and gives a slight bow. "Admiral Kato sends his regards and apologizes for the inconvenience." Gamite gives a slight nod. "He also would like to assist you in repairs to your ship before you head on your way." The officer continues, "If you and your friends would like to rest in the lounge, it is right over there."

Gamite can see a very nice set of chairs and couches with a refresher and subnet station. He waves his hand. "Thank you, and my mechanic will just need some tools and supplies."

The officer gestures to the wall. "There is a rack of tools and a supply room beside the lounge."

Gamite nods as he heads to the lounge. "Thank you. That is all." With that, the officer bows again and retreats. Once the officer left the deck, he turns around. "Phen, take Tobius and Melissa and do what you can to repair the ship. Phylox, join me please." Tobius looks at Melissa and shrugs as they follow Phen.

* * *

Morrin moves carefully through the mist. He is unsure exactly where he will find his target, but he can sense something getting closer. Stopping, he listens for any movement, but the only thing he can hear is the water flowing through the room. He reaches out his awareness to try and sense the creature, but the atmosphere in the room makes it difficult to sense more than a few meters. Cautiously, he moves forward and finds a three-meter-tall boulder. He clips his weapon to his belt and climbs up. Crouching on the rock, he peers at his surroundings, trying to find a sign that his target is near.

Kato leans forward and pulls a small lever down, and the lights in the room beyond dim to one-third the illumination. Craven is about to ask about them seeing, but the view port shimmers as it automatically adjusts to the decreased light. Kato smiles as he watches both with extreme interest.

"Craven, who do you think will survive?"

He takes a step closer to the view port, pondering the question for several moments, then turns as he replies, "She has the knowledge and experience, but he has the hunger for power."

Kato nods in agreement. "I think Morrin will make a good apprentice."

Crouching, Morrin looks around as the light in the room diminishes. Even without the mist, he can only see a few meters. He keeps focus on finding the target. A dozen heartbeats pass when he spots a ripple through the mist. Securing his grip on the hilt, he focuses in the direction of the ripple, and he senses a somewhat familiar presence. Confused, he looks around, unsure if his senses are being clouded by the atmosphere. Lowering his left hand, he grabs a small rock. He waits until he sees another ripple in the mist and throws it into the mist. Several heartbeats pass, and nothing happens. Morrin thinks the ripples must just be due to the humid air when suddenly, the hairs on the back of his neck stand on end.

Quickly leaning left, he extends his left arm to support himself, but in the dim light, he fails to notice the dark moss covering the rock. As his palm hits the moss, it fails to hold his weight, and Morrin falls awkwardly onto the stone. He grunts in pain and surprise as the wind is knocked from him, but before he can get back to his feet, he slides from the top of the stone. Trying to stop his fall, he reaches with his right hand, but with hilt in hand, he is unable to. He falls a meter, and his back slams into a ten-centimeter outcropping, again expelling what little breath he has, popping his back and several ribs. As he continues his uncontrolled fall, his right thigh slams into the rock, and a yell of pain escapes him. The impact causes his nerves to erupt with the residual pain of the maroon blade that pierced his leg.

Krystelle keeps her senses alert for anything as she moves through the mist, and the sound of the stream grows to a deafening roar in the eerie silence. Moving quietly, she makes her way to a small bush and waits. Reaching out into the void, she tries to find her target. She shakes her head, trying to clear the haze from her mind. Suddenly, she hears more than senses an incoming attack. Rolling backward, she comes to a crouch and sees a rock bounce off the ground right where she was. Instead of using the void to attack the unknown assailant, she simply steps forward and grabs the palm-sized stone, throwing it back the way it came. A few heartbeats later, she hears a grunt and the noise of a falling creature.

Without a second thought, she springs forward, summoning the void to cover the twelve meters in three strides. Stopping at the base of a three-meter-tall stone, she looks all around, finding nothing. Suddenly, a scream emanates from the opposite side of the stone. Krystelle draws her hilt and readies herself as she moves clockwise around the stone.

Morrin hits the ground flat on his back, and his vision explodes with stars. Blind and out of breath, he forces himself to sit upright. Taking in a breath, he winces at the agony of his ribs, and he rapidly blinks his eyes to clear his vision. Before he can clear his vision fully, he sees a figure standing no more than three meters away. Rage and humiliation fills Morrin with power, and he jumps to his feet. His right hand moves to his belt for his hilt, but it is not there. Cursing himself, he scans the area for his weapon. The hilt lays a meter to his left, but his opponent is now two meters ahead. Unsure on what the other will do, he slowly steps towards his hilt.

Krystelle sees her target rise from the ground and, remembering what Kato had said, waits to see what it will do. Her senses clear as the adrenaline spikes with the imminent fight, and she sees the glint of a hilt on the ground. Her crimson blade springs to light, casting the surroundings into a bloodred hue. Her blade has three two-centimeter-thick shafts, each emanating one centimeter from the center of the emitter. The shafts merge to a point ninety centimeters from the hilt. The target lunges for the hilt when she ignites her blade.

Morrin jumps to his hilt, rolling to his feet and igniting his blade in return. He brings his blade around in a large arc as he turns toward his enemy. Almost as if he stepped on a switch, a drop of water hits his blade...then another...and another, as if the drops were counting down to begin the fight. Morrin charges forward to meet his foe, and as the two blades collide, a steady rain falls from above. Both stay locked with the blades touching a third from the tips, and both try to judge their adversary. Three heartbeats pass, and, as if choreographed, both spin to their right, separating to just over two meters distance.

Kato watches with extreme interest and pleasure as the two begin to duel. Craven laughs. "Did you start the rain?"

The admiral shakes his head. "No, I have the weather settings set to change randomly." Leaning forward, he continues, "But it does seem like even the room is craving the impending bloodshed." Craven nods his agreement as they watch.

The steady rain creates a constant hissing from both blades, with the dim light being accented by the blades, and the only thing they can see of their opponents is the eyes. Morrin spins his blade, bringing the hilt to shoulder height five centimeters from his chest blade pointing straight up. He takes in a breath, letting his rage build, then exhales. Charging forward, he hopes to catch his opponent off guard, but a half meter from his enemy, he gets knocked from his feet from an unexpected void blast. His vison blurs from the force of the attack, and his back and ribs suffer another beating as he slams onto the ground. He quickly rises to his feet. "You'll pay for that," he spat, walking toward his opponent and spinning his blade in frustration.

Krystelle can tell that her opponent is the better swordsman, but she is not planning it to be a battle of blades. Ever since Krystelle was a little girl, living on her own, she has used her abilities to make it where she is today. She would use her powers to distract street merchants and steal food. Also, when slavers would try and capture her, she would defend herself, even though she did not understand her powers. She heard rumors of the Void-raiders and snuck onto a ship heading to Vorex. She smiles at how far she has come in her life, reassuring herself that there is more to come. Seeing her opponent rise to his feet, she readies for another attack. She keeps her blade in her right hand at waist level, with the tip even with her left shoulder she waits.

Morrin slowly covers the distance, developing a strategy. He knows that he is no match for his enemy if it comes down to just abilities. Suddenly, he feels a third presence in the room. This presence is so strong that it pierces the haze like a blinding light. Suddenly, everything around him stops, even the rain. And for the first time since he entered the room, there is complete silence. He looks around, perplexed and awestruck. His sees a raindrop floating a centimeter above his blade. Stepping closer, he slowly raises his blade and watches as the drop sizzles into vapor.

"This is but a fraction of the power you could possess," a deep voice says behind him. Morrin spins, blade held to fend off an attack, but none comes. Before him, a half meter off the ground, floats a lavender figure. "I can teach you how to become so powerful that no one could stand against you." The figure lowers to the ground as it continues, "You would be able to control everything." The figure begins to circle counterclockwise around him. "Even Tobius could not defeat you."

Morrin's mind latches on to the mention of his nemesis. "How do I get this power?"

The figure stops in front of Morrin. "First, you must prove yourself by winning here." Morrin feels fear creep into his mind. The figure's eyes burn. "If you are afraid, then I shall destroy you now."

He takes an involuntary step back at the sudden statement. Realizing the error, he strikes at the phantom with his blade.

When the blade makes contact with the edge of the figure, it vanishes, and the rain falls again. Morrin looks around, confused, and sees nothing but the mist and his enemy. He hears the voice as if it is standing behind him. "Do not fail."

Rolling his shoulders, he lets his anger fill him, and he tries to think of how to remove the advantage from his enemy. Standing eight meters from his foe, he starts moving forward, blade held at his waist angled forty-five degrees from his body. He reaches out toward his opponent to try and sense what they will do, but he senses nothing. Five meters away, the rain begins to fall harder, and he feels the ground becoming saturated. An idea pops in Morrin's mind, and he grins. Reaching out, he uses the void to summon water from the stream and move it to the ground around his enemy. Keeping track of his enemy and moving dozens of liters of water is harder than he thought.

Krystelle watches as her opponent moves slowly forward, blade ready as if to deflect ranged attacks, but then stops three meters away. She reaches out toward them to try and glean a plan. Suddenly, the hairs on her neck stand on end. Panic flashes across her face as the ground beneath her instantly loses its rigidity. A heartbeat later, she finds herself up to her knees in quicksand.

Morrin feels the ground liquefy, and he charges forward, covering the distance in one leap. He raises his blade over his head to bring it down in a massive strike. His enemy is so shocked by the tactic that they are barely able to get their blade up to deflect his strike, but the power and precision of the strike did find its mark. His enemy lifts their blade in their right hand, blade pointing left, but it only redirects the blade down, grazing the entire upper left arm. His blade turns the cloth on their arm to ash and left an eighteen-centimeter-long, four-centimeter-wide burn starting at the shoulder. Even through the injury, his enemy raises their left arm and grabs him around the chest through the void. Morrin is lifted five meters off the ground and can feel the invisible vise tightening around him.

Quickly, he tries to release himself but cannot overcome the overwhelming strength of his enemy. The attack starts sending intense pain through his already battered ribs. Morrin hears and feels more ribs pop from the strain, and two of his left ribs break with a wet crack. He lets out a scream of pain as the fragmented bones pierce his lung. The pain adds more fuel to the fire of his rage. He bellows in rage as the grip on his chest tightens even more. He raises his right arm over his head and hurls his weapon at his enemy.

The blade makes two quick rotations as it covers the distance between Morrin and his foe in less than a second. The tip of the blade pierces the center of his enemy's chest with such force that they are knocked back onto the ground. The grip vanishes the instant his enemy's back hits the ground, and he falls. Unable to land gracefully, he grimaces as the broken ribs wreak more havoc within as another rib breaks. After a few labored breaths, he sits up and looks to his right and still sees his opponent pinned to the ground by his blade. As if the pinning of the body was a switch, the rain and mist begin to fade.

* * *

Phen, Tobius, and Melissa head to the lounge area where Phylox and Gamite sit, enjoying brandy and fancy pastries. Phen wipes his hands off on a rag and tosses it on the bar. "I want some."

Gamite hands him a glass and fills it with three fingers of the amber liquid, asking, "So how's the Mirror?"

Phen downs the drink in one gulp and gestures for a refill, replying, "I was able to patch the wing and replaced some of the fried circuits for the shields." Taking a pastry, he stuffs it in his mouth as he continues, "We even managed to find you a new shield modulator."

Gamite looks pleased as he fills some glasses with milk for Tobius and Melissa. Phylox passes some pastries to Tobius and asks, "How soon can we leave?"

Phen looks at him and smiles. "Just getting her fueled up, and we can leave in a half hour."

* * *

Morrin rises to his feet and makes his way to his enemy to retrieve his weapon but falls to his knees a meter away. There lying pinned to the ground is not the enemy Kato had shown him but Krystelle. Smoke rises from the hole in her chest with the scent of charred flesh. He summons his weapon. She does not move, and her face is frozen in shock from his tactics. His hands drop to his side as emotions roil inside him like a tempest.

"Well done, my new apprentice," Admiral Kato says, walking up behind him. Morrin finds himself in a blind rage. In one swift motion, he springs to his feet, ignites his blade, and charges at Kato.

"You lied to me!" Morrin strikes with reckless abandon, and even the pain from his broken ribs only fuels his rage. Kato simply summons the power of the void to stop the attacks. "You said I was to kill a creature, but I killed her." Morrin swings his blade from his left to cleave Kato from hip to shoulder, but the admiral just ducks under the attack. He spins the blade overhead and brings it down in a doublehanded strike, and again he strikes nothing but air.

"Yes, I lied," Kato replies. "Only one of you could become my apprentice."

Growling, Morrin thrusts at Kato's heart, but the attack gets deflected over the admiral's left shoulder. Kato steps forward and punches him in the stomach. Morrin's breath explodes from his lungs, along with some blood and bile. The force of the punch lifts him half a meter off his feet, and Kato lets him fall to the ground in a heap. "You become my apprentice here and now, or I shall pin you to her corpse and jettison you both."

Morrin takes a breath and rises to one knee. "Yes, Master."

Admiral Kato smiles. "Wise decision, apprentice. Follow me." Kato turns and is flanked by Craven.

Morrin uneasily rises and follows his master. Morrin, still enraged about the death of Krystelle and dizzy from the pain, hears the phantom's voice in his head. *Very well done. I am Sanguis, and just play along with Kato for now. I will help you get your justice for the death of Krystelle.* Morrin nods. *Tobius is in hangar bay three,* Sanguis says. *Detain him and get his possessions. There is something that will help you acquire the power you crave.*

Morrin falls in beside his new master and says, "Master, Tobius is on the ship."

Kato looks to his right at him and says, "Are you sure? I was not advised of any unwanted arrivals."

Morrin nods, saying, "He is in docking bay three."

Kato quickly keys the mic on his lapel. "Is that ship still docked in bay three?"

"Yes, Admiral. They are fueling and prepping for departure," the communication officer replies.

"Send Bravo Squad to bay three. Do not let them board their ship." Kato kills the transceiver and starts sprinting down the hall. Craven and Morrin follow suit.

Escape

Tobius grabs two pastries and hands the plate to Melissa. Relaxing on the luxurious couch, he takes a bite of the pastry. Leaning forward, he picks up his glass for a drink. On the wall on the back of the lounge, Sanguis appears. "You shall not find the seat of my power, nor shall you find the true power of justice."

Tobius stands to confront Sanguis, but the phantom vanishes through the wall. Everyone is now looking at Tobius as though he has gone mad, but he does not see that. Slowly, he makes his way to the wall and finds the symbol of Sanguis melted into the bulkhead.

Melissa walks up to him and places her right hand on his shoulder. "Tobius, what is it?"

Tobius turns to her and then looks at the others. "We have to leave!"

Phylox looks at him then the wall. "That is similar to the glyph of justice, but it is not right."

Tobius looks at him then Melissa. "Sanguis is the last seeker of justice that the Keepers have seen before me, and he nearly eradicated everyone." Taking Melissa's hand, he starts toward the Mirror's Edge. "He is the figure that we faced in the cavern, but he is here too."

Gamite stands and grabs a bottle of brandy and heads towards the ship.

Before they even leave the lounge, red lights start flashing as alarms start sounding, three half-second claxons and a second between sets. Keeping ahold of Melissa's hand, Tobius starts running toward the Mirror's Edge. Halfway to the ship, soldiers come sprinting up the access to the bay. The soldiers have on pulse-resistant armor covering their torsos, upper arms, and thighs. They also have helmets with full face visors, and the entire suit is equipped with a small life support system that lasts for fifteen minutes. The soldiers charge toward the ship, and over a dozen orbs are thrown from the squad.

Phylox yells, "Get back!"

An instant later, the orbs explode, sending dozens of gel-like balls covering the ground just in front of them, but Phen is unable to stop, and three hit him. Phen yelps in pain as the stun gels send enough energy through him to send him sprawled, twitching on the deck. The soldiers stop in a double rank formation, twelve in each rank, just on the edge of the stun gels.

One says through the helmet's speaker, "The admiral demands to speak with you."

Gamite steps forward. "What is this about?"

None of the soldiers move, but the voice replies, "The admiral demands to speak with you, and we have permission to use lethal force should you resist."

Gamite stands defiantly. "You have no right to demand anything from a Master of the Void!" Raising his left hand, his gauntlet glows as the stun gels fly back toward the soldiers.

As the orbs head toward the squads, several soldiers shout, "Shields!" The ones in front drop their left hands from the weapons grabbing a bar from their belt. They thumb the activation button, and the bar splits horizontally in half, and the two halves extend to just under a meter wide and two meters tall. The area between the bars fill with a blue silver shield, but some of stun gels make it through, and five soldiers drop.

One of the soldiers yells, "Open fire! Do not let them board the ship!"

In an instant, Gamite and Phylox ignite their blades, stepping in front of Tobius, Melissa, and Phen. They stand even with a half meter between their shoulders, allowing enough room to move. Both of them spin and slash their blades in a defensive web to prevent any shot from making it past them.

Phylox says, without turning, "Tobius, Melissa, get Phen on board and prep for takeoff."

Tobius and Melissa each grab one of Phen's arms and pull him upright with one arm over their shoulders. Tobius, being closer to the soldiers, grabs Phen's left arm with his right and draws the hilt Gamite gave him. He wishes that he has his blades. This one was poorly made, and the hilt is unbalanced. He ignites the blade as an extra precaution against the pulse fire.

To Tobius, that last dozen meters to the Mirror's Edge took forever to cross. But once they did, Melissa takes Phen in and straps him in one of the passenger chairs. She returns to the boarding ramp to see Tobius has joined Gamite and Phylox. The three stand, deflecting the bolts mostly into the floor or ceiling, but they manage to wound another five soldiers. Just as she is about to ignite her blade and join them, she sees the lift doors open by the lounge.

She yells, "Tobius, we have to go now! More are coming from the lift. Look!" Without waiting for a response, she spins and heads to the cockpit.

Tobius looks left and sees three people emerge from the lift, and he says to Phylox, "It's Morrin."

Without disrupting his rhythm, Gamite pats Phylox on the shoulder. "Go. I got this."

Phylox simply nods and looks at Tobius. "Let's go."

Kato steps from the lift to find three men standing their ground against the soldiers. Rage boils inside him at his quick dismissal of the information about their arrival. Taking off toward the three, he summons his hilt, and the black blade screams to life. Kato has always been proud of his unique blade. He had found three crystal shards—blue, green, and amber—and fused them into one crystal. Another aspect he liked about his blade is when anything makes contact with it, it arcs with a silver hue. Craven draws his pulsar pistols, shooting as he moves right from the lift toward the lounge chairs. Morrin, numb from the broken ribs, draws his blade, following his new master.

Phylox grabs Tobius's shoulder and pushes him toward the ramp. Without complaint, Tobius looks at Gamite, nods, and heads into the ship. Phylox knows that with the soldiers there, Gamite will not stand much of a chance, and he uses the flow to grab the fuel line connected to the Mirror's Edge. Carefully, he removes the line and turns it from the ship; with fuel still flowing sprays the soldiers. All the soldiers cease fire, knowing that any shot will ignite the fuel. Satisfied that his friend does not have to worry about the soldiers, he runs up the ramp, slapping the control panel and sealing the ship.

Tobius gives him a look of complete shock. "We can't just leave him!"

Phylox disregards the outburst as he heads to the cockpit. "Come on, Tobius. Man the turret." Understanding the situation, he sits. Melissa is sitting in the copilot seat, running the checklist.

"Checklist complete. We are ready to go," she says as they enter.

Phylox takes the captain's chair and hits the thrusters, and Tobius straps into the turret chair. As he dons the helmet, he looks at Melissa. "How did you know what to do?"

She gives him a quick smile. "I am a Keeper of Knowledge."

Kato's rage fuels his body as he sees how Phylox removes his soldiers from the fight. Five meters from Gamite, he yells, "I will not let them leave!"

Gamite spins his blade between his hands as he slips from the cloak. "You shall not catch them, nor my ship." The two men collide as the red and black blades cross with a thunderous crack that echoes throughout the bay. Gamite shoves Kato back a step, and he drop the tip of his blade to the right and slashes at Kato's left thigh. The tip of the black blade catches his and carries it in a loop. Gamite brings the blade back around, moving it across his body tip toward the ground, deflecting a thrust. He is mesmerized by the unique attributes that Kato's blade possesses.

Morrin held back at the start of the fight, unsure on whether he should help his new master. Seeing the old man hold off Kato like he was, Morrin gives him a little more respect. He watches as Kato parries and thrusts to try and defeat his enemy quickly, knowing that every second he fails to finish the fight, the farther the ship gets. Again, Gamite blocks another attack and spins away from his master. Morrin looks up just in time to see the Mirror's Edge engage the thrusters and shoot from the hangar. Gamite takes a heartbeat to look as his friends leave him, and Morrin takes that moment to charge.

He closes the distance in three steps. Bringing his blade around, he angles it toward the base of the old man's neck.

Gamite smiles as his friends escape. He knows that staying means certain death, but he knew that they could not make it if he did not stay. Sensing the attack from Morrin, he could not help but let out a laugh. Lowering his right arm, he hits a hidden lever on the hilt. Suddenly, a small cable shoots from the end of the hilt and connects to Morrin's belt. Just before the blade severs his head from his shoulders, he snaps his right arm up and across his body, pulling Morrin off-balance and sprawling to the deck. To finish him, Gamite thumbs the switch again, sending power through the cable, knocking him unconscious and incinerating the cable, freeing the hilt.

Kato speaks into his lapel mic "Scramble all fighters and stop that ship!"

Phylox shoves the throttle to full as they exit the hangar and head straight toward the system's edge. "Melissa, find us a quick jump." She nods and leans forward, entering information into the navigation computer. "Tobius, keep an eye on our six, and let me know if you see anything heading our way."

Tobius forgot that he had the turret helmet as he nods. "Got it." Cursing himself, he fights to get rid of the vertigo. The Mirror's Edge moves toward the edge of the system, trying to look as casual as possible.

* * *

Gamite turns to face Kato, and he is completely blindsided as a pulsar bolt catches him just under his left shoulder blade. Staggering to his right, he tries to find out where the shot came from and sees someone in armor walking from the lounge, pistols in hand. He moves his left hand up his back and feels blood. Closing his eyes, he focuses on his friends for a moment and feels them moving farther from the ship. Opening his eyes, he squares his shoulders and sets himself for his final fight.

* * *

Tobius shouts, "Fighters inbound, and lots of them!"

Phylox reaches forward and feeds power to the shields. "Melissa, do we have a slip point?"

Her fingers dance on the console. "Not yet. I'm trying to find a safe place to head to." Phylox growls as he keeps heading out of the system, willing the ship to go faster.

* * *

Kato strides forward with his black blade angled down and away from him. "Now, you old fool, you will die, and I will catch your friends."

Gamite laughs. "You will never catch my ship. That I promise." Gamite knows that his life essence is fading fast, but he will not allow Kato time to find his friends. He feels the rumble of the deck as Vorex's Might starts pursuit. Raising his blade, he points it right at the admiral. "You think you can beat me?" Gamite sees the rage in Kato's eyes flare at the rebuke, and smiles.

The admiral brings his blade up in a quick strike, and Gamite catches the attack in the center of his blade. The ferocity of the attack knocks him back a step, and he feels his left leg almost give way. Pushing off with his right leg, he shoves the black blade to his right. Foregoing any fancy moves, he simply drops the tip of his blade and thrusts it straight toward Kato's nose.

Kato did not expect the old man to lunge straight at him. He was in no position to deflect this attack. He jerks his left shoulder back, rotating his head counterclockwise, trying to avoid the blade. The tip of the red blade sears the skin on the bridge of his nose, but his left eye is not as fortunate. Kato screams in pain as the tip of Gamite's blade is the last thing that he will ever see from that eye. His left hand comes up to cover his eye, but he kicks out his right leg, making contact with his foe's left thigh.

Gamite's left leg bends awkwardly from the kick as Kato spins away, trying to recover from his injury. Before Gamite can attack again, another bolt hits his right shoulder. His right arm instantly goes numb, and his hilt falls from his hand. The tip of the blade scores the deck before the dead man switch extinguishes the blade. As he falls to the deck, he reaches out to his friends.

He touches Phylox's mind. *The ship is yours.* He then focuses on Tobius. *Take care of Melissa, and the code for the safe is 86914.* Finally, he moves his awareness to Melissa. *Melissa, continue to learn and grow. Also, keep an eye on Tobius. He is a good man. Farewell'* With that, he lets his awareness return to his body.

Kato uses the void to turn the pain from his injury into rage to direct at the old man now lying flat on his back. He strides up to the dying man "Where are they going?" Gamite smiles as blood slowly flows from underneath him on the deck. Kato lowers the tip of his blade, stopping the tip a centimeter from the older man's nose. "Tell me now!"

The old man laughs. "What good is threating a dying man?"

The admiral stares down at him, knowing he is right. His enemy lying on the deck in a pool of his own blood still managed to best him. He gives the old man one last look and, with a flick of his wrist, ends his life.

* * *

Tobius, Melissa, and Phylox all feel the flow ripple as Gamite falls, and they all freeze for a moment.

Tobius's emotions violently begin to battle within him. *I must go back and destroy the man who killed him, but what good would that do?* he thinks. *There is no point in trying to fight for justice. One man cannot make a difference. There is no way that I can change anything. Gamite gave his life, but why would he do that? I am no one.* Every heartbeat, he spins further and further into the black hole of despair. *Maybe that is why no one really tries to be a seeker of justice, because it is a dead end of loss and sorrow.* He lowers his head, closing his eyes as the tempest of rage and self-doubt starts eroding the foundation of his resolve.

Tobius is jarred from his thoughts as Melissa sits in his lap, wrapping her arms around his neck, crying. He is so caught off guard by her reaction that he does not know how to react. Her head is resting on his right shoulder, and he can feel her trembling. He slowly embraces her as she mourns the loss of their friend. After a few seconds, she stops crying and lifts her head from his shoulder. Using the back of her right hand, she wipes away the tears. She places her right hand gently on his left cheek and looks at him, her hazel eyes full of understanding, compassion, and resolve.

She whispers, "Tobius, do not doubt yourself. You and I cannot afford the crippling effect of doubt. I need you to be strong, because I need your strength to keep me strong." Tears begin to well up in her eyes again as she looks at him, "Promise me that you will be strong."

Tobius looks into her eyes full of life and takes a breath. "I don't…"

Melissa shakes her head. "Tobius, promise me."

Tobius swallows and looks at her. "Melissa, I promise to try and be strong."

Again, she shakes her head. "I need to know you will be." Tears begin to move down her checks as she closes her eyes.

Suddenly, regret hits him in the gut like a meteor. He lifts his hands, caressing her face and wiping her tears away with his thumbs. "I promise to be strong," he says, looking into her eyes. "For you."

Her eyes glow even brighter as he finishes his sentence, and she leans forward, kissing him lightly on the cheek, whispering, "Thank you."

Tobius's head spins like a top as her lips touch his cheek, but he is quickly ripped from the peace of their moment as a blast strikes the shield, rocking the ship. She stands to get back in the copilot's chair when Tobius grabs her left hand with his, giving it a slight squeeze. She looks at him and smiles.

Tobius smiles back, saying, "Thank you, Melissa." Letting her hand go, he grabs the controls for the turret. He looks at the visor as the view of space around the ship fills his vision. "We have a dozen Spit-Fires on us."

The Spit-Fire fighters are ten meters long with a wingspan of seven and a half meters. This ship has a flat base that curves up at the front, with crescent-shaped wings attached a meter from the ships nose. Each wing extends three meters from the main fuselage. The back tip of each wing is equipped with a standard ion engine, and one ion engine centered on the main fuselage a half meter from the bottom. There are four pulsar cannons, two on each side, mounted on the wings at points half meter and one meter from the fuselage. These cannons extend out seventeen and a half centimeters to a flash enhancer that is two and a half centimeters long, each in a pivot socket with a thirty-degree movement in all directions. The cockpit is just over a meter wide and two meters long located two meters from the nose of the fighter. The main fuselage angles back from the nose to three meters tall at the back of the ship, and the center of the top of the fuselage curves from the center to the edge where it angles down to the wings. The top of the fuselage is a meter wide, and the bottom is a meter and a half.

These fighters earned the name Spit-Fire for three reasons. First, they have an extremely rapid rate of fire—twenty shots from one cannon in six seconds. Another reason for its name is due to its design. The nose of the ship is designed to pierce any atmosphere with little resistance. And when these ships enter atmosphere, they look like meteorites. The final reason for this ship's name is the flash enhancers that not only reflect the light from the shot but also visually alter the laser's color to orange. These ships do not have shields but instead use a reflective coating on the hull, and they rely more on speed and agility than defense. This ship also requires two people to operate effectively. One person pilots the ship while another handles the weapons. The Spit-Fire also has a retractable concussion missile launch that lowers from below the cockpit, and there is also a rear defensive turret. The seats are back to back. The pilot sits facing forward, and the weapons tech sits facing back with two panels both a half meter wide. The top one, thirty centimeters tall, is the front facing array for the laser cannons, and twenty-centimeter-tall screen for the rear turret and concussion missile launcher.

Phylox shoves the yoke left, trying to keep the Spit-Fire's rapid rate of fire from eating through the rear shield. "Melissa, get us a jump out of here!" Frantically, her fingers dance on the console to find a place.

Tobius tracks the closest fighter and squeezes the trigger. Red lances leap from the turret. An instant later, they connect with the nose of the fighter. Tobius watches as the blasts dissipate on the hull as the ship continues on unharmed. Tobius fires again but misses as the ship jukes down and right. Tracking his target, he fires, and again he misses. He keeps track of the ship, adjusting aim and shooting again and again and again. Phylox keeps trying to move the ship evasively, but it is hard to outmaneuver the agile pursuers.

"Come on, Melissa!" Phylox says as more incoming fire finds its mark on the aft shields.

Tobius has sweat beading on his forehead as he tries to relieve the pressure from the Spit-Fires. He lines up on another fighter as it streaks in from the left, squeezing the trigger and firing a quartet of shots at the incoming vessel. His shots stitch their way up the nose onto the cockpit view port. The final shots pierce the crysteel, and the cockpit bursts into flames as it flies past. The beleaguered vessel flies out of control and clips the turret of the Mirror's Edge. The words *Turret failure* start flashing on Tobius's visor. He shoves up the visor and says over his left shoulder, "The turret is out of commission."

Phylox growls in frustration. "Melissa, do you have a jump yet?"

She slaps her right hand on the console. "Yes, I need thirty more seconds for the slip generator."

Phylox looks at her and begins to say, "Goo—" Suddenly, an alert flashes on the consoles as an alarm blares. Annoyed, Phylox silences the alarm and looks at the console.

Phen comes climbing into the cockpit. "What in the galactic core is going on?"

Phylox slams his left fist down on the arm of the captain's chair. Reaching to reduce throttle, he says, "The Sons of Vorex have us caught in their tractor beam!"

Melissa looks at him then Tobius. "Now what?"

Slumping into his chair, Phylox shrugs. "I have no idea."

Phen thinks for a second. "Do we still have concussion missiles?"

Tobius nods and says, "The turret was clipped by a ship."

Phen steps toward the console. "Let me see."

Tobius stands, handing the helmet to him. He sits down, and the mechanic's fingers furiously trample across the keyboard. "How long until we are in the ship?"

Phylox leans forward and does a quick calculation. "About fifteen seconds."

"Okay, give me eight seconds, then punch it." New life shoots through everyone as they get set for the count. Phen stands and hands the helmet back to Tobius. "Sit and fire the missile when I tell you." He quickly dons the helmet and sits. "Four…three…two…now!" shouts Phen, and Tobius fires the missile.

The orb leaps from the launcher and heads toward their captor. Concussion missiles already have an impressive speed, but being fired directly into a tractor beam increases its speed. A heartbeat after Tobius fires the missile, the beam disappears, and Phylox shoves the throttle to full.

"Melissa, now would be nice." She engages the slipstream drive and shoots off into slip space.

Flow Realm

Tobius removes the helmet and looks at Phen. "What did you do?"

He leans against the wall, smiling as he crosses his arms across his chest. "I primed all but one missile then ejected them from the launcher. And when you fired the last missile, it was targeted at the other missiles and not the ship."

Tobius thinks about what was said. "But why did you target the missiles?"

Laughing, Phen replies, "Those ships have sensors that track missile engines and target lock, but since I did not target them, they could not see them. Plus, using the beam against them prevented them from being able to react."

Phylox rises from the chair, stretching his back. Twisting left then right, he looks at Melissa. "So where are we going?"

She looks at everyone. "Well, we couldn't go to Nicht Ka or Bosthirda or even Rhelg since the fleet travels to those planets often. Thule was also out of the question with the storms. So we are heading to Corbos."

Tobius looks at her. "Why there?"

She smiles. "Well, it's a remote mining planet."

Phylox looks at them both. "We won't be staying. Melissa, please have another jump ready for when we get there."

She looks at him, annoyed. "What? Why?"

Phylox looks at her. "Well, for starters, there aren't that many systems out this way. So it will be easy for Kato to send some ships out to find us." He starts to make his way from the cockpit. "Also, the more we move, the less chance he can stumble onto us. Now I say we all take a break and see what food is on board."

Phen follows Phylox back toward the passenger cabin. Tobius places the helmet on its hook and stands slowly. Clenching his fist, he stares at the deck. "Is this why seekers of justice are so rare and feared?"

Melissa looks at him concerned but says nothing as she leaves the cockpit. Tobius stands for another heartbeat before he slumps down in the copilot's seat, and he props his legs on the edge of the console. Closing his eyes, he leans back and drifts off to sleep.

Melissa leaves the cockpit, joining Phylox and Phen. Both had a cup of java and some crackers. Both men eat their snacks in silence. She looks through the available food and grabs a glass of water. Instead of sitting on the luxurious chairs, she sits cross-legged on the floor. Taking a sip from the water, she places it in front of her on the deck. Closing her eyes, she lets her mind run free. For several heartbeats, her presence just lets the emotional turmoil of what transpired flow its course. Sorrow crashes through her being as the realization of the loss of her friend and mentor hits her like a wave crashes over stone. Tears fall from her checks as she lets the power of these emotions fill her. Being a Master of Knowledge, she knows that it is best to let these emotions cleanse her. She waits until the flow around her settles to look like a crystal lake. The lake glows red and boils as the anger and rage from today's events flow to the surface. All around her, flames of rage burn white-hot. The scorching wind of anger blows from all directions, turning the area into a blast furnace. Melissa's face tenses as the torrent of these emotions try and burn her from within. Taking a deep breath, she shields herself from the raging inferno.

Several heartbeats pass, and the storm still rages. Taking in a few long slow breaths, the storm begins to ebb. The cool and refreshing breeze of peace calms the surface. She smiles as she pushes her awareness beyond herself. Sensing Phylox, she sees his essence as a cool blue figure with a red-hot core. Taking extra caution to not disturb him, she moves on and sees Phen, a storm of all emotions, but most is the elation of being alive. Pushing her awareness out even more, she finds Tobius, as cold as a black hole. She contemplates whether she should touch him but chooses to let him be. She starts to pull her awareness back to herself when she senses a disturbance to her right.

She focuses on the disturbance. It is a massive amount of power in sphere about half a meter across. Reaching out, she touches the edge of the sphere, and nothing happens. After a few moments, she sends a pulse at the sphere. Instantly, it flashes red then goes black. Several seconds pass with no change to the sphere. Deciding to leave it alone, she begins to return to herself. Suddenly, an oily black tendril shoots from a crack in the sphere, wrapping itself around her. She tries to break free but is getting pulled toward the sphere. Lashing out, she tries to sever the tendril, but her attacks pass harmlessly through it. As the tendril pulls her to the sphere, she can feel thousands of different presences within. Massive waves of agony and hopelessness pour from the crack like an acid trying to dissolve her defenses. Quickly, she wraps herself in a cocoon of energy to keep the devouring forces at bay.

The tendril pulls her inside the sphere, and she hears a deep bass voice laughing. She looks around, trying to find out where the voice is coming from. As she descends into the depths of the sphere, the only thing she can see in front of her is a set of crimson eyes burning with ageless rage. Again, she tries to shield herself from the black abyss inside the sphere, but the tendril prevents her from being able to completely block out the toxic atmosphere.

"You shall not escape," the voice says, and another tendril shoots out from between the eyes. Melissa can see that this tendril is not grabbing her essence but piercing it. She has been tiring as she fights to release the grip of the tendril, but she still has enough energy to deflect the incoming spike of despair. "You have more fight in you than I thought," she hears. "You might be a suitable vessel for me." Emotions of panic, shock, and confusion course through her as she stops fighting the darkness. "Wise choice, my dear. You will be treated with great care as my pawn." The tendril that she had just deflected has circled around and is again heading straight toward her. Resigning herself to this fate, she reaches for Tobius one last time.

The black tendril's path is straight and true, and Melissa does nothing to try and stop it. Suddenly, a luminescent silver lance shoots into the sphere, eradicating the tendril's tip just before finding its mark. Melissa is shocked about the sudden intervention and has no idea where it came from.

A familiar voice bellows from the entrance of the sphere. "SANGUIS! Release her!"

She looks over her right shoulder and sees Tobius's essence burning bright and pure like the morning sunrise, and she cannot help but smile. In an instant, Tobius covers what seems like kilometers, placing himself between her and the phantom eyes.

The phantom howls with rage at the intervention and unleashes dozens of tendrils at them both. Melissa looks on, awestruck as Tobius forms a broad shield and sword from his presence. Raising the shield on his left arm, he blocks six tendrils. Spinning to his left, he knocks the tendrils away, cleaving two with his sword. Three tendrils are heading toward Melissa, still caught by the massive tendril. Almost instantaneously, Tobius severs the limbs and blocks four more. A half dozen shoot toward him from his right, and a dozen head toward Melissa in every direction. Melissa watches and is sure that this is her end, when Tobius blocks the tendrils on his shield and fires a dozen silver lances from the tip of his sword. These lances intercept and destroy every tendril.

"You will not win, Sanguis," Tobius says, slicing through another wave. Moving almost as fast as lightning, Tobius continues to block, deflect, and cleave through the endless waves of tendrils.

"I will devour you both, and then no one will be able to stop me!" Sanguis growls as his eyes flare.

Tobius blocks another pair of tendrils heading toward Melissa's left, then he brings his sword down on the tendril still holding her. The silver blade makes it one-third of the way through the tendril as it blisters from the contact. Tobius brings the bottom of his shield down on the tendril, releasing his blade. Tobius slam on shield down again, cracking the remainder of the tendril. He stabs his blade down, twisting clockwise, severing the tendril. The phantom howls, and a violet lightning storm forms behind the crimson eyes.

A moment later, a massive meter-wide bolt erupts from between the eyes at them. He braces himself for this attack. His shield expands to a radius of a meter and a half, smoothing out into a dome. He lowers his left shoulder and shifts his right leg back, leaning into his shield as the massive energy impacts the front of the shield. The sheer force of the attack pushes Tobius back a meter.

Five seconds pass, and the attack does not wane, then ten, then fifteen seconds. After twenty seconds of this massive torrent of violet energy, the edges of his shield start fracturing. Twenty-five seconds and a third of a meter on all sides of the shield has chipped away. Thirty seconds pass, and the shaft of lightning begins to increase its intensity. His shield has been battered down to a mere seventy-three centimeters, and Tobius's essence is all but touching Melissa's. Looking around, he sees that the black abyss is fueling the shaft of lightning. Every heartbeat that passes, Tobius feels his power ebb. Suddenly, he senses familiar presences, and he looks behind Melissa.

Standing behind her is his mother and father, grandparents, Hermi, the Gatekeeper, and others that he knew, but many are unknown to him. Tobius realizes that these are all the people who had died due to Sanguis. He stares in disbelief as he sees everyone. "Mom...Dad?"

Kalob looks at Julianne, and she smiles. "Yes, Tobius." He recognizes the voice, and he can feel tears stream from his eyes.

"Son," Kalob says. "You are a stronger man than I was. You can save her." He gestures to Melissa. "You can save everyone." Tobius nods, his resolve strengthened.

Hermi says, "I told you that your family was proud of you, and so am I."

The Gatekeeper steps forward. "I have not seen any seek justice in my life, but you are the perfect example of true justice. Before you is the one who has corrupted our view of power, and you are the one who shall end his millennium of torment."

His strength grows. He sets his shoulders and looks over the shield at the red eyes beyond. Aiming the blade parallel to the shaft of violet energy, he places the tip against the inside center of the shield. He looks at Melissa, then up to where everyone else had just been.

Clearing his mind, he focuses all his essence on justice. In a swift motion, he shoves the tip of his blade through his shield. As the blade pierces the shield, it dissolves, but the lightning does not advance. He straightens, shoving the blade straight toward the center of the eyes. A centimeter-wide beam shoots from the tip of the blade, straight through the meter-wide shaft of violet lightning. A second later, the beam is two centimeters wide. Five seconds pass, and Tobius's beam begins to increase its diameter exponentially. Eight seconds, and the beam is sixty-four centimeters thick, and Melissa cannot believe what is happening. When he pierced the shield, it became clear and inverted, and it is now redirecting the energy into the sword's guard. As the energy flows through the blade, it gets amplified with Tobius's own essence, and the malevolent intents are discarded. Between the red eyes, a silver sphere starts to grow, and the area surrounding them begins to tremble. Tobius lifts his right arm, raising the blade to shoulder level as it transforms into a spear.

"I told you that no one will bow to a ghost." He steps forward, letting his right arm roll back forty-five degrees and brings his arm down, releasing the spear. The spear rotates clockwise as it travels down the beam, absorbing the lightning. The phantom howls in rage and disbelief, and as the spear enters the silver sphere, Tobius and Melissa look away as the black abyss is dissolved in an explosion of silver light.

Melissa opens her eyes, face covered in sweat, and falls to the deck, exhausted. A moment later, she looks up and sees Phen kneeling beside her, concerned. Her head is spinning from what had just transpired. She sees Phen's mouth moving but hears nothing. Phen extends his hand to help her up, and she weakly grabs his hand, allowing him to pull her from the deck. He loops her arm over his shoulder and helps her to one of the chairs. Her vision has cleared, and she can hear everything again. Phen offers her a glass of milk and a small plate of pastries. She quickly downs the milk and grabs one of the pastries.

"Are you okay?" the mechanic asks, concerned.

She slowly nods as she takes a bite of the pastry. "What happened?" she asks with a dry voice.

"Well, we looked over when we heard you gasp, and you were as stiff as a board. Your face was twisted in agony…"

Phylox calls from the cockpit, "Phen, come help me!"

He sets the plate down to her left and hurries toward the cockpit. Phylox lowers Tobius down to Phen, and at first glance, Melissa thinks he is dead. She begins to panic, then she sees the steady rise and fall of his chest. Phen keeps the young man from hitting the steps as Phylox hops from the cockpit. Quickly, Phen and Phylox carry him to the small med bay and strap him in.

Phen works on attaching the leads for the different sensors and places a breathing mask on him. Phylox turns and sits down on Melissa's right. He places his elbows on his lower thighs and places his head in his hands. "Melissa, can you tell me what happened?"

She takes a bite of pastries to try and get her mind wrapped around what happened. She takes a deep breath and says, "Sanguis."

Phylox rolls his head onto his left palm to look at her. "Are you sure?"

She leans back in the chair, closes her eyes, and lets the events run through her mind again. A few moments later, she nods. "Yes. Tobius yelled the name."

He lets his head fall back to both hands. "How? He died almost a millennia ago."

Exhausted, she shrugs. "I have no clue, but I think Tobius does."

He lifts his head. "Well, hopefully, Tobius can shed some light on the situation when he wakes." Melissa nods as she falls asleep in the chair.

* * *

Kato stares down at the corpse of the old man. Without looking, he shouts, "Soldiers, dump this body in the trash!" He looks toward Craven, then toward his apprentice. Consciousness returns to Morrin as he hears some boots approaching on the deck. "You must be more aware, my apprentice," the admiral says, approaching.

Accepting the outstretched hand, he slowly gets to his feet. Grunting, he twists and tries to relieve the tension from that old man's trick.

"Sir," one of the soldiers say. "What should we do with his weapon?"

"I don't care. I just don't want to see it again," Kato says, heading toward the lift with Morrin. He turns as he enters the lift and keys his transceiver. "Do we know where they went?"

Three heartbeats of silence pass before the officer responds, "Not yet. We are still calculating destinations from their last known trajectory."

"Very well. Advise me the moment you have any location," he says, ending the conversation.

Morrin stands beside his new master. "What do we do now, Master?"

Kato looks to his left toward his new apprentice. "We have to find that relic so we can acquire the power to conquer the galaxy." Morrin nods and keeps his thoughts to himself.

The trio leaves the lift, making their way to Kato's study. "Craven, do not let anyone disturb us."

Again. the only response is an almost imperceptible nod. As they enter the study, Craven turns just on the hall side of the threshold back toward the study.

He hits the door controls as they enter. The door closes behind Kato. "Now we will assume the mantle of the Void Masters." Moving to just in front of his desk, he raises his arms as he turns around. The glow panels in the ceiling shut off and four meter-tall panels in the corners come on, illuminating the area in a red orange hue. Kato's eyes burn red as he speaks, "Power is for the strong." Morrin recognizes the Void-raiders code. "The strong command the void." Morrin kneels before his master as they finish the code. "The void devours the weak. Embrace the void, and all shall be yours."

Everything in the room that is not secured down is floating around them both. Taking a deep breath, Kato revels in the sensation of being immersed completely within the void. A small violet and crimson sphere of light forms a meter off the deck between them both. A set of pitch-black eyes form on the top of the sphere. An animalistic growl fills the room, and the eyes drift toward Kato. For several heartbeats, Kato and the sphere lock gazes.

He closes his eyes, lifts his head, and a takes a deep breath. "I am Master Nexis! Master of the Void-raiders." The black eyes drift and look at Morrin. "Well done, Morrin."

Grinning, Morrin looks at the sphere, then at Kato, and back to the sphere. "Thank you, Master. So you gave him his new name?"

Chuckling, Sanguis replies, "Yes, he is very close-minded, but he still has a purpose."

He nods his agreement. "What shall I call myself?"

"The changing of one's name is something you do yourself."

Sanguis says, "I always knew I was strong but did not have any training. Until I was noticed by a group known as Keepers of Power." Glancing at Nexis, Morrin nods. "These people feel that power is neither good nor evil but a balance of both. They pursue knowledge, wealth, or justice and feel that it must be shared. A millennia ago, I was a seeker of justice. At first, I strived to keep justice, but then my wife was murdered over a handful of credits." Morrin could sense Sanguis's rage flare in remembrance of his late wife. "All of them told me that I cannot seek out the ones who killed my beloved Serina, but how could justice not be sought?" Lightning started to arc from the sphere. "I was set to leave the Keepers and seek them out, but they confronted me." Morrin looked at Nexis, but he was frozen like Krystelle was. "It was then that I realized that power cannot be shared. I destroyed every last one of the Keepers on Feridus and tortured the Master of Knowledge to get the location of another village. I traveled from planet to planet in the cluster to find the next village. It was on Detritus Prime when my plan failed. I approached the clan, giving the same story I had to all the others. However, the Master of Knowledge from Vorex made their way to Detritus Prime to warn them." His rage arcs out in violet lances of power, shattering crystal goblets, data pads, and any other item floating around. "The Gatekeeper stood at the entrance with the same blade that Tobius used to slay Kato's old apprentice. They managed to defeat me, but I had found a way to preserve my power."

Morrin looks at him, amazed at his ability to last for centuries. "So have you always been known as Sanguis?"

The lightning dies down as he laughs. "No." Morrin takes a moment to think. He sets his shoulder and looks from the sphere. "From this day forth, I shall be known as Mendax." A deep laugh echoes through the study.

"Very well done, Mendax. Your enemy is headed toward Corbos." With that, the sphere vanishes as the glow panels return the room to normal light.

"Master Nexis," he says, bowing. "I feel that our enemies have fled to Corbos."

"Very well. Take our cruiser, Rage of Vorex, equipped with two squadrons of Spit-Fires, and pursue them."

Backing away, he responds, "Yes, Master." With a wave of his left hand, he opens the doors. Turning, he strides out.

Craven turns as the doors open and sees the apprentice leave with a purpose. He enters the study. "Now what, Kato?"

He laughs as rounds the desk and responds, "I am now Void Master Nexis."

He looks at the man sitting and thinks, *All that trouble to change his name? He has lost his mind.*

Nexis hits the transceiver on the desk. "Lieutenant, my apprentice will take my ship to the Rage of Vorex. Advise them that they will be under his command."

"Yes, Admiral," replies the officer.

Craven stands, waiting on him. Several moments pass with nothing but silence. Standing, Nexis walks to grab a goblet for some brandy, but all four of them lay shattered on the counter. "Craven, I have a mission for you," he says as he reaches under the counter for a glass. "I want you to follow my apprentice and observe how he handles his mission. They are heading to Corbos."

Craven straightens. "What? Now I just have to go watch some kid chase after some people who escaped you?"

Nexis spins to his left, raising his right arm. Craven flies to the far wall, crushing a picture frame. "You will do as I command! You and I have an agreement. I pay you ten thousand credits per week, and you do what I ask. Do you have a problem with that?"

He feels the back of his armor beginning to buckle under the pressure. "N…no," he manages to reply. Suddenly, he falls to the counter, smashing a vase and small statue.

Nexis takes a drink of his brandy and walks toward Craven. "I need you to plant one of your tracking beacons on their ship. Just in case they manage to escape." Nodding Craven starts to rise.

Nexis ignites his blade, with the tip a centimeter from his faceplate. "Doubt me again and I will end our agreement. Do you understand?"

He snarls through his helmet, "Yeah, I got it." Craven rises to his feet and leaves the study. "I swear, I'll find a way to kill him," he mutters to himself.

The Chase

Tobius lies on the medical gurney unconscious as the sensors monitor his condition. To anyone else, he would seem to be at peace, but inside, his mind is a storm of cataclysmic proportions. The events of his latest fight cycle through his head, and each time he feels the exhaustion of the fight. The momentary meeting with his family and friends renews his strength and purpose, and he wishes he could see them again.

Melissa is jarred from sleep as she hears alarms sounding from the medical gurney. Quickly, she blinks her eyes against the lights as she peers toward Tobius. "What's going on, Phen," Phylox asks as the mechanic's fingers dance over the control panel. After a few moments, he checks the connections on the monitor probes, and the alarms cease.

"Good job," Phylox says, patting him on the back. "We have about an hour before we get to Corbos, and we need to figure out the next jump." Both men start heading toward the cockpit, and she smiles as they pass.

Once the two men sit in the cockpit, she makes her way to the medical gurney. The gurney is three meters long to accommodate almost any species, with biometric and neurologic sensor feeds. A retractable breather lowers from ceiling, and an adjustable intravenous cuff extends from the front. The neurological sensors are attached all around Tobius's head, and the biometric sensors are attached to his neck, chest, and right wrist. The intravenous cuff is secured on his right arm, just above the elbow. Relaxing slightly, she sees the steady rise and fall of his breathing. She hits a button on the console, and a small stool slides from under the gurney. She slides it toward the head of the gurney. She places her left hand on his shoulder. "Thank you."

Tobius's body lies motionless on the gurney, but his presence is restless. Scenes from the mental fight flash all around him. Dozens of red eyes surround him, and he can see the tendrils writhing just behind each set of eyes. All he can do is look on as the eyes continue to multiply. Every time the eyes split, the air thickens with rage and malice, and his strength to keep the toxic cloud at bay wanes. The sounds of laughter begin to echo from all around, and Tobius drops to his knees.

"What do you hope to gain by destroying me?" he asks, gasping for breath. The only response he gets is increased laughter. Struggling, he looks and sees hundreds of eyes stacked on top of each other, with millions of tendrils squirming around, in, and through all eyes, except for two. So he focuses in on those eyes. "Sanguis, what is your plan?"

His entire essence shakes as the phantom booms, "You are not able to comprehend my plans. I have been working for centuries, and I finally have a vessel to achieve it." The tendrils writhe around, and one leaps forward, but Tobius rolls left out of the way. Again, the laughter increases in volume. The tendril that tried to sucker punch him explode, sending acid of hate everywhere. A meter-long glob of acid falls onto his back, instantly searing his essence, and he screams in pain.

Melissa jumps as a scream of pure agony rings through the breather. She looks at him and sees smoke seep up from his back, and alarms blare from the gurney. A moment later, Phylox leaps from the cockpit. "What happened?"

She takes a step back, shaking her head. He disconnects the intravenous cuff, rolling the young man on his left side. A half-meter-long section on the back of his tunic is charred, and the skin is red and blistered. Phen arrives and grabs the burn salve, spraying it on the wound. Then, pulling out a meter square pad, he lays it on the gurney. Carefully, they roll him onto his back. A three-bell chime sounds from the cockpit, and Phylox looks at Melissa. "Stay with him. We are almost to Corbos." Again, she nods as they leave.

Tobius stands up even through the pain. "You will not break my will! You shall never be able to find true power." He braces himself against the imminent attack, but instead of rolling to dodge it, he spins counterclockwise. Snapping his right arm out, he catches the tendril, and it arcs back. Bringing his left hand up, he slices through the tendril.

"You really think you can beat me?" he says through clenched teeth as the acid burns his hand. "You are nothing but a coward!" Suddenly, all the eyes merge into one set, one hundred meters wide, thirty meters tall, and the tendrils form the phantasmal form Sanguis prefers. Tobius continues, "I know that you think you have a worthy vessel, but no matter who you choose, you will fail. Someone who thrives off pain and suffering can never comprehend the true meaning of power." He stares into the burning eyes, undeterred. "The Keepers have it right. Life itself is something that cannot be kept. No matter what species or what system you go to, power flows through everything." With every breath, his resolve grows. "No matter what you seek—knowledge, wealth, or justice—you cannot keep the power to yourself.

"Sanguis!" Tobius shouts, thrusting his finger at him. "You try and keep all this power, and the more power you absorb, the weaker you become." He rolls his shoulders, and his essence begins to glow brighter. "The power we seek is something we borrow, and we use it how we feel is best."

Suddenly, the Gatekeeper appears to his left with the other fallen seekers. "If you try and keep the power to yourself, it becomes putrid, but if you help it grow, then you have truly found its meaning."

His family appears to his right, with the hermit at his shoulder, whispering, "Feridus is where you must finish this."

Breaking his eye contact with Sanguis, he looks left, and the Gatekeeper nods, then he looks right where his family stands. He looks back into the eyes of his enemy. "I will meet you on Feridus, and that is where your millennium of torture ends."

He opens his eyes, squints against the light from the medical gurney, and tries to sit up. Melissa hops from the stool and quickly removes the sensors. "Are you okay?"

He can see in her eyes that she is genuinely concerned. "Yeah, I'm..." He grunts in pain as he tries to sit up.

Melissa grabs his shoulder and helps him sit up. "What happened?" He looks at her, really confused. "Here, have some water," she says. With the mention of water, his body screams from thirst, and he quickly empties the glass.

"I know where we have to go." He pushes off the gurney, takes a step, then collapses to the deck. Melissa enters a code into the medical gurney, and an adrenaline stim slides from the console. Grabbing it, she turns and injects it into Tobius's right shoulder. Grunting, he pushes off the deck as Melissa helps him to his feet. She lifts his right arm across her shoulders, and they head toward the cockpit.

"Phen, cut the slip drive on my mark," Phylox says, holding his right hand up with a countdown. Five...four...three...two...one. He points to the mechanic at zero. The violet surrounding of slip space gives way to normal space, and Corbos floats in the center of the view port. "Where do you think we should go next?"

Phen starts running different destinations through the navigation computer. He puts his left hand on the back of the captain's chair. "I know where—" Tobius starts, but proximity alarms sound. Looking at the console, two hundred meters above the Mirror's Edge, a Void-raiders cruiser exits slip space.

The nose of the cruiser casts its shadow over the cockpit, and Phylox pushes the throttle to full, angling toward the bottom of the cruiser. The collision alarms start sounding, and Phen silences them. Tobius grips the back of the chair tighter as the bottom of the cruiser grows larger. Looking at his friend, he starts to wonder if he intends to ram the ship, but at ten meters, the Mirror's Edge angles to match course with the cruiser. Pulling back on the throttle, Phylox leans back. "Okay, Tobius, where do we need to go?"

Tobius looks at Melissa then quickly explains what happened while he was unconscious.

* * *

KEEPERS OF POWER

Mendax stands in the middle of the Rage of Vorex's bridge. "Navigations, are there any ships in this system?"

The officer responds, "No, sir," still scanning the system.

"Deploy the fighters and have them sweep the system." He smiles as the officers jump to complete his order.

Less than a minute later, an ensign says, "Fighters outbound to sweep the system." Returning to the command chair, he thinks about all that has transpired and lets his mind wander.

Craven exits slip space thirty seconds behind the cruiser. He guides the Phantom's Blade up to get a good view of the entire system. Once the ship is one kilometer above and two kilometers behind the stern of Rage of Vorex, he turns on his scanners. The small monitor flashes as readings begin scrolling across. Craven has always liked using his scanners before entering an area when he is following someone. Infrared, communication, and emission readings pan across the screen. Looking out through the view port, he sees the two squadrons of Spit-Fires stream from the cruiser, one squadron from each side. The scanner chimes. Craven looks at the monitor. Again, it chimes, and he sees that there is a spike in emissions. Tapping some commands on the navigation console, he tries to find the source of the spikes. Reaching forward, he flips a switch, changing the view of his view port to see infrared. The cruiser burns like a star with twenty-four dots dispersing from it. He watches with extreme concentration to see if he can spot the anomaly. After thirty seconds, he flips the switch. And right as the view port starts to revert, he sees a small flare from below the cruiser.

Knowing that he is supposed to just observe, he slaps a button on the left side of the cockpit. A small compartment opens just behind the cockpit, followed by three thumps. Three black cylindrical cones, a half meter long and thirty-five centimeters in diameter, glide past the view port. He enters a command on the keypad. In sequence, the cones open three two-centimeter hatches 120 degrees apart, and a six-centimeter tall fin extends out each hatch. The first eight centimeters of the cone split in quarters and slide back to uncover a half spherical droid eye. Craven sees three green triangles light up on the console. After he enters their destination coordinates, the three set off. He shuts off his scanners, and the monitor shows the views of the three drones. He watches through the view port, knowing that it will take a few seconds for the drones to get close to where he sent them.

* * *

Tobius takes a deep breath as he finishes explaining the struggle that he endured while on the gurney. Stroking his chin with his left hand, Phylox leans back. "So you are certain that Feridus is where we can end the traitor of the Keepers?" Leaning forward, he checks the console to see if they have spotted them hiding under the cruiser yet, and when he sees the fighters still on a search pattern, he looks back to Tobius.

"Yes. After he was beat on Draken, he fled to Feridus, where his physical body died, but he discovered a way to preserve his life essence."

* * *

Three chimes come from the console, alerting Craven that the drones are within five hundred meters of their destination. He taps on each drone's icon, and their view fills the monitor. Drone 1 shows nothing but open space with a few visible glows from the fighters. The second one shows nothing but a field of stars, but the third one shows the stern of the cruiser. The view fades to white and static for a moment as the drone passes one of the cruiser's engines. The stars scroll down as the drone levels out with the bottom of the ship, and one hundred meters in front of the drone sits the Mirror's Edge.

Laughing, he says to nobody, "Void-raiders. They think they are so powerful and better than anyone, but they are dumber than a pile of dung." He enters a command, and the drone closes the distance. When it gets half a meter away, it retracts its fins and engages two electromagnets to secure it to the hull. A moment later, a quick double chime comes from the monitor, signaling that the drone is anchored, and Craven recalls the other two drones. As the drones are returning, he enters the calculations for the jump back to Vorex. And once the drones are secure, he engages the slipstream drive.

* * *

Mendax relives times when he was waiting to see if he would be accepted into the Void-raiders academy and how quickly he became the strongest. His memory replays the first time he met Tobius and Melissa, and his rage immediately boils. Next, he recalls when Phylox made him look like a fool and Gamite belittled him. Suddenly, Krystelle's face comes to his memory, and a pang of regret hits him like a brick. She had always favored him ever since he entered the academy, and he misses her presence. She was the one constant he had in his life until Nexis made him kill her. At that memory, he clinched his hands into fists. Screaming from the bridge crew made him open his eyes.

In his reminiscing, he had not realized how much he was letting his emotions flow. Two officers had been smashed against the view port. Another officer was injured when his console suddenly exploded, and the bridge lieutenant is floating a meter and a half off the deck, grabbing at his throat to free himself from the invisible noose. Quickly, he scolds himself at his lack of control and takes a deep breath. As he exhales, the lieutenant drops to the floor, gasping for breath. The officer collapses on the deck, trying to recover. All the other officers freeze as he stands up, except for the officer writhing in pain from the shrapnel of the console.

"Have they been found yet?" he says, ignoring the chaos he caused.

The lieutenant coughs hard and rises to one knee. "The fighters," he wheezed, "have swept all forward quadrants." He tries to take in another breath, but he starts coughing and spits up blood. After eight seconds, he continues, "Squadron Alpha is sweeping around the planet, and Bravo is heading to scan the surface."

Mendax glares down at the man and kicks him in the left shoulder, dislocating it. It sends the man tumbling across the deck, slamming into wall. The ensign at the navigation console watches as the lieutenant slams against the wall. He shouts as he stands from his station, "What right do you have to treat him like that?" Raising his right hand, he points at him. "You are the one who did all this damage, not him or any of us." He snaps his hand away from his body, and a small holdout pistol ejects from his sleeve. Mendax glares at this major insubordination. An instant later, the ensign squeezes the trigger, and the red lance leaps from the pistol.

The sound of the shot barely fades from the bridge, and it looks as though nothing has happened. Even the wounded officer is silent. There are no marks anywhere near Mendax.

"Would anyone else care to express how they feel now?" he says calmly. Three heartbeats pass with no response. Suddenly, the ensign, arm still outstretched, collapses to the floor in a heap.

The communications officer speaks up. "Sir, what…how?"

Chuckling, he says, "I merely deflected his own shot back at him."

Again, the officer says, "You didn't even move!"

Mendax bursts into a full laugh now. "Oh, don't worry, I did, and I would be happy to show you," he says, igniting his blade.

* * *

The hairs on the back of Tobius's neck start to stand on end, and he looks up really quick. "What's wrong?" Melissa asks, grabbing his right forearm.

Without looking down, he says, "Phen, are we ready to jump?"

The mechanic shakes his head. "Another minute to get everything set."

* * *

He extinguishes his blade, sits in his chair, and looks at the deck. He can feel Sanguis attached to him like a leech, and he both enjoys and hates the sensation. He feels a ripple through the void from below. Focusing on the ripple, he clears his mind and reaches toward the source. Three heartbeats later, his blood boils as he senses his archenemy.

"Get the fighters back here! Our target is below us." Rising, he strides to the center of the bridge. "Navigations." No response comes from any officer. "Navigations!"

The replacement communications officer shakily responds, "Sir, he was the officer that tried to shoot you."

Growling, Mendax turns and heads toward the hall. "Catch that ship." As the door closes behind him, he grabs his transceiver. "Ready my ship."

* * *

Phylox grabs the controls and shoves the throttle forward. The Mirror's Edge jumps forward, and an instant later, it shoots from underneath the cruiser's nose. Once the ship clears the front of the cruiser, Phylox pulls back on the yolk, bringing it around 180 degrees, heading back along the right side of the cruiser. Tobius holds onto the back of the captain's chair, watching as Phylox does his best to get them some space to jump. The cruiser flies by just fifty meters away, and Tobius can see the pulse turrets turning to try and target them. He guides the ship over the right edge of the cruiser but has to suddenly bank up. "Phen, are we ready?"

The mechanic enters a few more things on the keypad and then nods. "Go for it."

He hits the slipstream drive, and the Mirror's Edge leaps from the system.

* * *

As Mendax pilots the ship from the hangar, collision alarms sound. He slams the alarms silence then hits the transceiver. "Where are they going?"

Five seconds of silence pass, and a shaky voice replies, "They went to slip space."

He slams his fist against the arm of the chair. "Recall all fighters and return to the fleet." He ends the communication and begins to enter in calculations to jump back to Vorex.

"Where are you going?" Sanguis asks as his lavender phantom body appears before him. Mendax ignores his leech of a master as he completes entering in the information. "Ah, so you are heading back to your master like a good little apprentice." The phantom waves its left arm, and the navigation data changes from Vorex to Feridus.

He looks at the new destination and tries to understand what could be there.

Sanguis responds to the unasked question. "They are heading there to destroy your chance to become stronger than every other being in the galaxy." Without a second thought, he engages the slipstream drive, chasing after them.

* * *

The Phantom's Blade exits slip space and heads right toward Vorex's Might. Before he gets a chance to open a channel, his transceiver pops to life. "Where is my apprentice, Craven?"

Rolling his eyes, he quickly relays what transpired at Corbos. "I have one of my drones attached to their ship."

A heartbeat of silence passes. "Meet me in hangar two, and we shall find out where they go." Moving along the left side of the ship, he enters the bay and sees Nexis striding from the lift.

Nexis is dressed in all black. His midcalf high boots are polished to a high sheen, pants bloused into the top of the boots. His pressed tunic is tucked into the pants with a hide utility belt secured around his waist. With each stride, his silver hilt glistens in the hangar bay lights. His hair is cut to Void-raiders fleet standards, a half centimeter on the sides and a centimeter on top, and his pitch-black cloak bellows out behind him. Craven could not help but admit that Nexis can present a rather intimidating aura when he wants. Increasing the power to the thrusters, he spins the Phantom's Blade around its vertical axis, lowering the boarding ramp in the process. Nexis is able to step onto the ramp without breaking stride. Craven increases throttle, leaving the hangar as Nexis enters the cockpit, sitting in one of the two passenger chairs.

"Once they emerge from slipstream, we will have their location."

The First Keeper

The Mirror's Edge heads toward Feridus. Tobius leaves the cockpit, followed by the others. Kneeling on the deck, he touches the corner of a panel. Underneath is the same panel that Gamite used to secure their weapons. The memory of his lost friend makes his eyes go misty. Blinking a few times to clear away tears, he reaches out and solemnly enter the code: 86914. He takes a deep breath as he enters the code. A moment later, the same chime echoes through the cabin. The safe lowers to the deck, descending from its hiding spot above. The instant the safe makes contact with the deck, the top opens. No one in the cabin says anything. Tobius reaches in and extracts both his and Melissa's hilts and replaces them with the one he has. He turns to Melissa and sees tears rolling down her cheeks.

He extends his right hand, takes her left, and gives it a soft squeeze. "I promise, Melissa, that he did not die for nothing." Releasing her hand, he grabs her weapon and holds it up for her to accept. Shakily, she takes it in her right hand while returning the other with her left.

Placing the other hilt in the safe, he closes it and closes the panel. The safe rises to its place above. Standing, he clips his hilts to his belt, reassured by the comfortable weight. "I know Feridus is where this will end, but I have no idea what to expect there."

She wipes her eyes with the back of her left hand and smiles. "What would you like to know?" A confused look forms on Tobius's face. "Why the surprised look?" Looking at Phylox, she laughs. "I am a seeker of knowledge." She looks at Tobius. "Feridus is where the Keepers were founded. The Keepers have been around almost ten millennia. Bren Yarden had a natural instinct using the flow. The village elder noticed his unique skills when he was four. When he turned fifteen, he wanted to learn more about his power and bargained his way onto a cargo hauler. Agreeing to work on the crew for almost nothing, he was able to travel all over the galaxy. Over the next decades, he managed to gather knowledge on his skills. On Vorex, a man confronted him about his abilities. This man claimed to be a Void-raider, and stronger than any other person. Bren Yarden refused his statement, and a moment later, the man drew his weapon. The Void-raider held a blue bladed weapon and tried to scare him into joining the Void-raiders.

Bren looks at the hilt. There's a moment of confusion before the realization hits him. It was the weapon of his village elder from his youth. Guilt, rage, and pain hit his gut like a metric ton. He looks at the Void-raider standing in front of him.

The Void-raider smiles. "Yes, my friend, I killed him, and if you refuse to join me, I will kill you!"

Bren charges the murderer, bellowing in rage. His reckless action caught the Void-raider off guard, and his right shoulder slams into the Void-raider's chest. Planting his left foot, he spins counterclockwise, pushing the Void-raider into the wall of the alley. Adrenaline and emotions are in complete control. As soon as the Void-raider's back smacks into the wall, Bren Yarden glares at him and shoves his hands forward. The Void-raider doubles over as a massive blast knocks him through the wall. Stepping through the three-meter-wide opening, the Void-raider lays on the floor, barely breathing. Extending his left hand, he summons the hilt to his hand. Looking down, he ignites the blue blade. "You killed my friend and mentor then threaten me to join you? You do not deserve to live."

Raising the blade above his head, he stares into the man's eyes. One second passes, then two, then three, but neither man moves. A light female voice breaks the stalemate of the two. "You are no murderer."

A blue-skinned crytan female is standing next to the hole in the wall. Confused, he lowers his arm to his side and turns to his right, keeping the blade pointed at the Void-raider.

She continues in her musical voice, "I have been following you for the last few days, and I know that you are no murderer. Your essence is noble and pure, and the selfish act of vengeance is one that you cannot perform."

The only sound that can be heard is the sizzle of the blade and the labored breathing of the injured man. The energy from his rage has ebbed, and now he feels only exhaustion. "If you ever try to force me to join you again, I promise that I will end you." Extinguishing the blade, he turns away from the man and starts to leave.

"Mercy is for the weak!" yells the Void-raider. Rising from the ground, he pulls out two daggers and begins to charge. However, before he is able to get a second step in, he falls to the floor. Bren looks at the man, stunned, and he sees a simple throwing dagger buried to the hilt in the man's chest.

Bren looks at the crytan then at the dead man. An instant later, he is bracing himself against the edge of hole while his body reacts to the gruesome act he just witnessed. He had traveled dozens of planets but has never seen someone killed. This new experience did not agree with him as he violently vomited from this scene. After ninety seconds, he grabs his canteen from his belt and washes the vile taste from his mouth.

"Why?" he asks, pointing and having to fight off puking again.

She simply turns away without looking back. "Come. We should talk."

For several heartbeats, he stands there frozen. Then as if struck by lightning, he races after her.

He follows her for thirty minutes and tries to figure out where she is going but gets nothing. After almost an hour of twists and turns, they come to a small rundown three-meter-tall shack. The crytan enters and holds the door open.

Several seconds pass, and Bren hesitantly enters the shack. "Why should I trust you?"

She laughs. "Oh, so me saving you is not enough?"

His cheeks flush at how ridiculous he just sounded, and he steps into the shack.

KEEPERS OF POWER

Once he passes the threshold, she shuts and bars the door. "I am very glad that you decided to follow me. There is so much I would like to talk to you about." The room beyond looks more like a library at a major spaceport than a shack. Scrolls and data pads litter the four tables along the back wall. "I am Maya-Lina, and I, like you, have a strong connection with the flow, but I do not agree with other views on this power." She hurries and dumps the data pads off a stool and offers him a seat. He sits on the stool as she continues, "The flow is more than just a dark or light. Do you agree?" Caught off guard from the sudden question, he just nods. "I have traveled to many different planets to learn more, but everywhere I have gone, the views were tainted with each location's beliefs." She keeps explaining as she rummages through everything on the tables. "I sensed you about six months ago or so, but I was not able to meet you before your ship left." Tripping over another stool, she mutters something under her breath and continues, "I think I have found a place which has been untainted by either side, and I need your help to get there."

He gives her a perplexed look. "Why me?"

She laughs as she moves to the final table, still looking for something. Suddenly, she turns, flinging her right arm up. "Here it is. Feridus is the planet that I need to get to, and I feel that it would be a benefit to you as well."

He stands up from the stool, holding his arms out. "Now wait a second, Maya...a—"

"Maya-Lina," she replies, aggravated.

"I have no idea why you need me. I work on a cargo freighter, and that is—"

Before he has a chance to finish, she rushes up to him and thrusts her left index finger into his nose. "Look, you are the only person I have met in my travels that has the same views as me. I have had Void-raiders trying to get me to join them, but I am not a Void-raider nor any of the other groups on other worlds."

Bren begins to argue with himself. *Why should I help her? You know she is right though. The power we feel is not light or dark. It just is.* He takes half a step back and looks her in the eyes. "You are correct, Maya-Lina. I know there has to be a pure source to this power everyone talks about."

She smiles and lowers her hand. "Good. When can we leave?"

* * *

A chime comes from the cockpit, and Phylox stands to check it. Tobius looks at Melissa, both fascinated and confused. "So what do Bren Yarden and Maya-Lina have to do with the Keepers?"

Melissa laughs as Phylox returns from the cockpit. "We will be to Korriz in ten minutes, then just a quick jump to Feridus."

Melissa nods as she continues to reveal the founding of the Keepers.

* * *

Bren spoke with his partner, and they take the ship and head to Feridus. Once they arrive, they fly over the planet and find a field in the northern hemisphere. This field is over twenty thousand square kilometers and meets up with a forest with a four-hundred-meter-wide river flowing through it. They land the ship in the field. Bren and Maya-Lina leave the ship, wading out into the waist-high grass. The grass is smooth as silk, and each blade is five centimeters across. The tip of each blade flares out into a clover formation, with each of the three cloves a different color. They both stand amazed as the wind makes the grass dance, and the light reflects all colors from every direction.

* * *

"They headed into the forest following the river," Melissa continues as Phen and Phylox move to the cockpit to prepare for the next leg of the trip. "Once they found the river's source, they began to study the power of the flow. The more they learned, they realized that the groups were all right on some aspects but not completely correct. Some groups would use this power for peace and harmony, and others, like the Void-raiders, tried to rule through pain and anger. After a week, they returned to Vorex and managed to buy a ship so they could travel the galaxy. For the next ten years, they discovered the runic language of the Keepers and developed dozens of Keeper villages around the galaxy."

The Mirror's Edge drops from slip space just on the edge of Korriz's gravitational field. Phen starts entering the information into the navigation computer for Feridus, and Phylox pilots the ship toward the Feridus side of Korriz. Thirty seconds later, the console pings as another ship exits slip space behind them.

"We have company, Phen."

The mechanic keeps working on getting the destination set and snaps, "What do you want me to do about it? Get out and push?"

Phylox opens his mouth to respond, but after a moment, he closes it. Thirty seconds pass, and the computer accepts the destination. "Here we go," Phylox says, engaging the slipstream drive.

They exit the cockpit and look at Tobius and Melissa. "Someone followed us," Phen says.

Looking at Melissa then Phylox, Tobius says, "It felt like Morrin and Sanguis, but I'm not sure. Their essences seem to have merged."

Phen slips past the trio and gets a drink. "There is also a tracking device on the back of the ship." Turning around, he sees the three of them looking at him as if he was a ghost. "What?? Tracking devices give off a very distinctive transceiver burst that most people never notice."

Tobius looks at him. "Could it be a Void-raider's tracker?"

Phen laughs, shaking his head as he heads back to the cockpit. Phylox gives him a scolding look. "Tobius, you should really be more mindful. The Void-raiders fleet would never rely on something like that." He closes his eyes for a moment. "It must be the bounty hunter that was with Kato."

Tobius falls back into his chair and slumps his shoulders. "Sanguis said that it would end where it started. I guess he wasn't joking." They all agree to get some rest before they arrive at Feridus.

Chimes sound as the glow panels increase illumination, waking them as they are almost to Feridus. Each one takes turns getting some food and using the refresher to prepare for the impending confrontation. Once they are all ready, they gather in the cockpit. Phylox shuts down the slipstream drive, and the Mirror's Edge slows to sub light speed, and Feridus snaps into existence. They are coming in opposite of the two suns. Phylox keeps the throttle to full as he tries to give them as much time as possible before their unwanted guests arrive.

* * *

Mendax exits slip space and sees Feridus ahead. He also sees the engines of the Mirror's Edge just two kilometers from the atmosphere. A malicious grin spreads across his face. "I will personally end every single one of them, and after that, I will end Nexis."

As if summoned by the mention of his name, the console pings as another ship exits slip space one hundred thousand kilometers to starboard. The name flashes over the icon: Phantom's Blade. His grin morphs into a scowl as the transceiver opens. "Apprentice, why are you here? and where is my cruiser?"

He takes a quick breath and keys the mic. "The cruiser is heading to Vorex. The crew is completely inadequate at completing the simplest of—"

"No, my apprentice!" Nexis growls. "It was you who failed at completing the simple task of catching the fugitives." He takes another deep breath and decides to let his master continue. "I now have to finish what you could not. You may follow us and learn how to be a true Void-raider."

The communication is terminated from the other end, and he feels his rage build. Again, the phantom shows its crimson eyes. "Yes, you will find that it is he that will not survive this."

Field Fight

Phylox brings the Mirror's Edge into the atmosphere at the steepest possible safe angle. "Melissa, look at the charts and tell us where we need to land."

She nods and steps up next to Phen as he brings up the chart of the planet. Relying on the information from the Keepers' history, along with the current planet layout, she finally finds the possible spot where Bren and Maya-Lina landed several millennium ago. Phen enters the destination in, and an icon pops onto Phylox's console. He nods, looking at Phen. "You have a choice now. You can either come with us when we land, or you can take the ship and head to the other side of the planet."

The mechanic takes several seconds to ponder the choices before him.

Five hundred meters from their destination, the navigation console chimes. Phen looks at the sensors and see two ships entering the atmosphere behind them. "Well, I guess I will stay with you guys. The ship is out of weapons, and the shields are shot. So I would probably get blasted if I tried to leave." He stands and leaves the cockpit as Phylox brings the ship to land. He returns with a rifle, pistol, and a survival pack. "Who's ready for a hike?" They all could not help but laugh because the mechanic looks like he's going on a hunting expedition.

The Mirror's Edge sets down as the boarding ramp lowers. The dawn still has yet to break on the field. They all depart from the ship, cautiously looking around. They are one hundred meters from the field's edge. The field has yet to wake from its night slumber as the blanket of dew gently covers all in sight. The starlight shines through the wispy clouds, reflecting off the dew as though the night is seen through a kaleidoscope. The amazing view the four sees is broken as the sound of inbound ships echo overhead. Pointing to the left, Melissa says, "The river is this way."

* * *

Mendax follows the Phantom's Blade in a large loop around the field where the Mirror's Edge came to rest. He can see four people emerge from the ship and head toward the tree line.

He opens the transceiver channel. "Master, they are heading for the trees."

Five seconds of silence pass. "Land, my apprentice. We will follow them."

The Phantom's Blade settles to land three hundred meters from the Mirror's Edge, but he cannot stand the thought of letting them try and escape into the trees. Pushing forward on the yoke, he aims the shuttle at them and prepares to finish them off quickly. Lining up his targeting reticle, he arms the lasers on the shuttle.

* * *

Tobius looks up to his right and sees the ship coming right for them. He knows that there is nothing he can do to dodge an attack from the ship. As if the planet itself is there to defend them, the suns crest the horizon, casting its cleansing rays of light across the field. The dew on the grass adds its own aid to help defend them as it refracts the morning's first rays. The combined light casts a golden hue on the sky with thousands of rainbows shining and spinning on any surface it can land on. Though this view lasts for but a heartbeat, it is enough to cause the shuttle to fly harmlessly overhead. With unspoken agreement, they all sprint toward the trees.

* * *

Still blinded from the sudden light show, Mendax curses as he banks around toward his master. Landing the shuttle fifty meters port of the Phantom's Blade, he powers down the shuttle. He takes a brief moment to collect some emergency items, secures them to his belt, and lowers the boarding ramp. Before he can make it halfway down the ramp, Nexis bellows, "What was that? I want them alive!"

Rolling his eyes, he continues down the ramp without answering. Once he gets to the bottom of the ramp, Nexis stands twenty meters from the ship. "Maybe I was wrong in choosing you as my apprentice."

Mendax glares at him and remembers how he was tricked into killing Krystelle.

Sanguis's phantom figure appears behind Nexis, and only Mendax can hear him. "End this imposter now, and I shall show you true power." Nodding, he lets his robe fall from his shoulders to the moist ground. Extending his right arm, he summons his hilt to his hand, and as soon as the metal hits his palm, the crimson blade leaps forth, screaming for blood.

"Nexis, you are a deceiver, a cheat, and a coward. You are nothing more than a scared child." Silence falls over the field, and Craven steps from the ramp. Seeing the standoff, he quickly turns, heading back into his ship.

Nexis stares at his apprentice and his weapon. "You really think you can defeat me?" He slips his robe off and tosses it behind him. "I will give you one chance to reconsider this course of action." He starts walking to his left to get away from the two vessels. "If you cross blades with me, then only one will walk away from this." After fifty meters, he stops, freeing his hilt from his belt.

Mendax keeps pace as Nexis moves toward the open field, keeping his blade pointed at his foe. Undeterred from his course, he stops, feet shoulder width apart, left foot ten centimeters behind his right. Rolling his shoulders, he takes a deep breath, letting his emotions fill him and to ease the anxiety. "The only nexus you will ever be is for my attacks and the tip of my blade!" He can sense the building rage in the man standing twenty meters away and knows that his course is set. He drops the tip of his blade in a counterclockwise loop, sizzling through some blades of grass, stopping in a doublehanded grip with the hilt at waist level, blade forty-five degrees from his chest.

Nexis cannot believe the situation at hand and ignites his blade to end this arrogance. Adjusting his feet, he adopts a fencing stance, left leg almost a meter behind him with most of his weight on his right leg. With a deft flip of his wrist, the blade spins a quick figure eight around him and stops the blade just below his shoulder level parallel with the ground.

Sanguis's voice booms inside Mendax's mind. *Let me in and I will help you defeat him.*

Quickly, he cuts him off from his mind. *Like I will let you fight my fights.* He starts forward cautiously. Ten meters from Nexis, the grass starts to fold over at him, as if it were bowing. Realizing that it is a void pulse, Mendax dives to his right, rolling back to his feet. He quickly spins his blade back between him and Nexis just as a silver lance of energy shoots toward him. Catching the energy on the top third of his blade, he manages to deflect it into the ground five meters behind to his right. Even though he manages to avoid the attack, his right hand instantly goes numb from the force of the attack. Still over ten meters from Nexis, he growls in frustration. "If I can't get close, then he will finish me without a scratch."

Nexis watches as Mendax rolls to avoid his pulse and tracks him with his arm, unleashing the silver lance. He smiles, but it fades as he sees it miss its mark. Rising to his full height, he looks at his enemy and lifts his right arm once again.

Mendax charges at Nexis, hoping to catch him off guard to no avail. He gets knocked back almost two meters as he has to block another lance of energy. Now seven meters away, he takes three quick strides then summons the void, leaping four meters in the air. He sees Nexis raise his arm, pointing straight at him, and he braces for another attack. Instead of the lance of energy, he gets hit in his legs with a void pulse, sending him spinning out of control. Landing in the tall grass, he rolls uncontrollably for a few meters, sliding to a stop.

Enraged, he summons the void, wiping the grass from under his enemy's feet. Surging to his feet, he covers the gap in three quick strides and brings his blade down in an overhead strike. Again, his attack misses his target as Nexis rolls forward under his attack. Landing in a crouch, he flips his blade over his head, deflecting the thrust from behind. He shifts his weight to his right leg and arm, blade sizzling in the grass and dirt. Quickly, he sweeps his left leg back at his opponent's leg. Catching his left heel on the outer calf, he forces Nexis to spin away from him, and Mendax pushes off with his right leg, cartwheeling away and leaving two meters between them.

Spinning from the kick, Nexis glares at the nuisance before him. He stomps his left leg to try and stop the throbbing. "You have done well. Now I will give you one last chance to submit and be my apprentice." Thirty seconds pass with nothing but the sound of the wind through the grass and the hiss of the two blades. "Very well. Have it your way," he says, stepping forward.

Striding forward toward his enemy, Mendax spins his blade, sizzling through a dozen blades of grass, then angles it toward Nexis's waist. His opponent expertly blocks the blade with no effort. He has to lean his left shoulder back to avoid the quick thrust of the counterattack. Snapping his left arm up, he forces the attacking weapon up and out of position. He shoves his blade at the stomach of his enemy, but already being off-balance, he stumbles, barely scorching the tunic. Moving with the momentum, he plants his left arm and rotates, coming to his feet and keeping his blade still between the two.

Before Mendax has a chance to try and attack again, the older man charges him with earnest. Instinctively, he grabs his weapon with both hands, blocking slashes and thrusts with only centimeters to spare. He is forced back farther into the grass, and his boots begin to get caught up in the tall grass. Staggering from the attacks, he is unable to find a way to separate himself from his enemy.

A minute passes with no break in the massive assault. Mendax steps back, left boot snagging on the grass, but instead of stepping where the ground should be, his foot drops half a meter. He gasps in surprise as he falls to his left. This sudden change catches them both off guard as Nexis brings his blade around in a slash that would have cleaved his right arm off had he been there. In a desperate attempt, he lashes out with his blade and manages to contact Nexis's right thigh. His enemy instinctively reacts to the sudden pain, giving him a brief moment to recover.

* * *

Melissa leads the way into the forest. "We need to follow the river." Heading single file, they follow the massive flow of water toward its source.

Tobius follows two meters behind Melissa. Phen and Phylox take up the rear of their group. The trees tower overhead more than one hundred meters tall with trunks almost ten meters across. The bark appears to be crystalline in nature and consist of colors from brown to blue to green and any mix between. The canopy is wide enough to cover most of the four-hundred-meter-wide river. The leaves are clover shaped like the tips of the grass in the field. These translucent leaves are of all different colors, and the darker the trunk, the lighter the color of the leaves. The entire forest floor is cast into a mesmerizing prism of colors, which shift as the wind dances through the leaves.

Melissa leads them, trying to stay within a couple meters of the riverbank. The underbrush around the river makes the path difficult to follow, and there are several points they have to cut a path. After five kilometers, Melissa stops, and the others quietly join her. About a dozen meters ahead, one of the massive trees had fallen, but that is not what made her stop.

"Why…" Tobius starts to ask as he joins her. Just on the other side of the massive trunk, dozens of oily violet tendrils writhe. A massive stone of despair lands in Tobius's stomach as he sees what lies ahead. "This will make it difficult," he says as Phylox joins them. Melissa and Tobius could not help but laugh at Phylox's expression as he looks at the tendrils.

* * *

Mendax gets to his feet and makes three quick jumps back to get extra space between him and Nexis. He looks around at the tall grass, summoning the void. He moves his left palm down, releasing a pulse and flattening the grass fifteen meters in every direction. He can see Nexis steady himself and leap toward the clearing. Charging forward, he plans on attacking the instant Nexis lands. Suddenly, the hairs on his neck stand on end, and he dives to his left. As soon as his right foot leaves the ground, a silver lance impacts where he was, and he completes the roll, rising to a crouch. Rising to his feet, he glances around but cannot find his opponent. Again, his hairs stand on end. Jumping back, he does a one-handed backflip, but the silver lance scorches the inside of his right calf. He lands on both feet and grunts in pain.

Looking up, he sees Nexis floating with the aid of the void several meters in the air. Glaring at his enemy, he tries to find a way to finish him, but all he can do right now is avoid the silver energy lances being fired every few seconds. After a dozen consecutive attacks and several near misses on his left shoulder, waist, and losing part of his right ear, perspiration streams down Mendax's face as he barely dodges another lance of energy.

Two can play this game, he thinks as he sets his feet. Sensing where the next attack will be, he swings his right leg back behind him, twisting his torso clockwise. As adrenaline courses through his veins, time appears to slow.

The emitter around Nexis's hilt glows silver, and once a centimeter-wide ring forms, it then leaps forward. The silver energy dances down the length of the black blade, momentarily collecting at the tip. The lance then explodes from the blade at light speed toward him. Having already adjusted his body, he wraps his left hand just below his right on the hilt. He swings his blade in an arc from his right hip to left shoulder. His blade connects with the tip of the lance fifteen centimeters from the hilt. The force of the collision instantly numbs both his arms from the elbow down, but he grits his teeth. Focusing all his energy on the impact, he summons the void to redirect the silver bolt back the way it came. A crack of thunder sounds as the energy leaves his blade, and a small spark of energy hits him in the chest.

At the same instant, both combatants fall toward the ground, smoke wisping from their chests. Mendax struggles to breathe and lies on the ground like he just got hit by a fighter. After a few raspy coughs, he takes in a full breath. Rolling over, he pushes himself to his knees, seeing stars as he rises. Forgoing waiting on clear sight, he forces himself to rise. Once on his feet, a familiar weight is missing from his hands. Panic now takes complete control, and his eyes dart, trying to locate his void blade.

Three seconds pass, and still no hilt can be seen, but he senses danger. Diving forward, he tries to summersault but slams his left shoulder into the ground. It tosses him onto his back. Looking up, he sees Nexis staggering toward him. The older man has a singed hole just under his left collar. A look of pure rage is plastered on his face, and any finesse he had is now gone. Mendax rolls to his right as the black blade scorches its length in the ground. Stopping chest down, he forces himself to push off the ground as the blade sweeps just off the ground at him. Mendax rolls a meter away and gets to his feet. Still without his weapon, he charges, driving his right shoulder square into Nexis's sternum with a bone-jarring thud. He takes three more strides then dives, taking his adversary straight to the ground. Using the momentum, he rolls off his enemy, flipping to his feet a meter and a half away.

Exhaustion and injuries immediately catch up with him as his legs tremble and hands shake. Taking in a deep breath, he summons the void to fuel his body enough to finish the fight. Turning, he sees light glint off something eight meters away, and he instantly knows what it is. He extends his right hand and summons his hilt. The cool metal relieves the trembling of his hand, and the blade springs to life eager for vengeance.

Stepping forward, he spins his blade, letting it sizzle through the grass. Nexis, slowly rising, stares at him. No words need spoken by the two men as their blades hiss through the air, colliding in a static scream. Mendax uses the simplest of attacks, trying to save his energy to outlast the man a half meter in front of him. Flipping the blade with his wrist, he attacks Nexis's injured shoulder. His opponent still manages to deflect his attack. But with his left arm injured beyond use, it is only a matter of time. He brings his blade around and slashes at the left elbow, but the experience of his enemy allows him to block attack after attack.

The liquid lead of exhaustion starts pouring into his limbs, and he finds himself struggling to maintain the steady flow of attacks. Breathing becomes short and haggard as Mendax now must use both hands to control his weapon. Sweat has found its way into his right eye, stinging and blurring his vision. Another attack, and he swings at his enemy but gets deflected left. Suddenly, his eyes go wide as a wicked grin forms on his enemy's face. He reangles the blade and tries to aim it at Nexis's waist. But instead of getting the blade to move, a fist slams into the right side of his chin.

Stars explode in his vision, and his jaw pops from the impact of the blow. Spinning counterclockwise, he rotates completely, arms outstretched like a marionette doll. The stars clear as he finishes the spin. He hears his blade sizzle into the grass then deactivate. Nexis now holds his weapon with both hands at his right shoulder with an arrogant grin spread across his face. "You thought you had the power to defeat the Void Master?" The black blade arcs straight for his neck, and he finds himself unable to react.

* * *

"This is a first for me," Phen says. They all are standing behind a trunk as they contemplate the newest obstacle. Slinging his pack from his back, Phen rummages around and withdraws out a pulse charge. Before anyone can say anything, he thumbs the activator and tosses it. Three seconds later, the crack of the detonation echoes through the trees. They all look around the tree, but the tendrils appear completely unharmed. The only visible sign of the explosion is the charred tree trunk. They take cover and all look at each other.

Melissa thinks for a moment. "Maybe we could try and find a path around in the woods."

Phylox shakes his head as he ponders the situation. Tobius leans back against the trunk, and something hard gets shoved into his side. "Ouch!" he says, jumping. He takes off his pack, opens the top, and flips it over, emptying its contents on the ground. Three emergency rations packs, two liter-and-a-half canteens, emergency med kit, and three glow rods litter the ground. Tobius gathers the gear and begins to repack, and the only thing still on the ground is a small cloth-wrapped object. Hesitantly, he picks it up. He holds it in both hands and slowly unwraps it.

The obsidian diamond is released from the folds of the cloth and is bathed in the light of the forest. He looks at the diamond as if he had never seen it before. He picks it up, holding it just above the culet with his left hand. A violet light emanates from the glyphs. The gem appears as though it is absorbing the surrounding light to fuel its own intensity.

Tobius steps around the tree, holding the gem in his left hand and the hilt of his weapon in his right. As he approaches, the tendrils sense a powerful essence and extend up ten meters in the air, each half a meter thick. Stopping twelve meters from the down tree, Tobius waits to see what the tendrils will do. Cautiously, he steps forward, and three tendrils from the middle lazily arc toward him. Taking another step, he adjusts his grip on the hilt but holds off on igniting his blade. The center of the three tendrils extends forward, meeting Tobius just over nine meters from the tree. Five heartbeats pass, and nothing happens. Tobius slowly extends his left arm. The first half meter of the tendril splits into eight individual limbs, extending toward the diamond. As the limbs get five centimeters from the gem, they split even further into hundreds of hair thin threads. The violet light from within the obsidian stone starts pulsing as if communicating.

* * *

Mendax stares into the abyss as the blade nears him. His breath catches in his throat. Without warning, a scream shatters the ambiance of the situation. He cannot understand the sight before him.

Nexis is frozen stiff with his blade still ignited. He walks to his hilt, never losing sight of his enemy. Reaching to grab his hilt, he sees a half meter thick black tendril extending from the ground three meters behind Nexis. He walks up to the tendril and touches it with his left hand. Instantly, his hand begins to burn. He yanks his hand back. Some of the dark violet oil remains, burning into his fingers. Shaking his hand to free himself from the gel, he shouts, "Sanguis! What did you do!?" Like a genie summoned from a lamp, the lavender phantom floats from the tendril where he touched it.

"Our time is running out. Our enemies are nearing my source of power, and if they reach it unopposed, then we both will die. I… we cannot afford to lose this power." Nexis's hilt falls to the ground, burning the grass as it is dropped for the last time to never again be lifted by its creator. "I am using his power to stall them so we can prepare for their arrival and end them all."

Growling, Mendax walks forward, igniting his blade. In one crisp motion, he cleaves the man's head from his shoulders, giving him an honorable death. The phantom's eyes flare as the body falls lifelessly to the ground. "Let's go." A black blob leaks from the ground and forms a sky bike. "Get on," Sanguis says as he and the tendril disappear into the ground. Timidly, he touches the vehicle, and it is cold and solid. Clipping his hilt to his belt, he climbs onto it, and as soon as his weight settles, it speeds off, shooting above the trees.

* * *

Craven sees Mendax fly off on some vessel, and he cautiously exits his ship. He draws his pulsar pistol as he leaves the boarding ramp, and he quietly makes his way through the field. Twenty meters ahead, he sees the flattened spot where the fight finished. Crouching, he moves forward, both hands on his pistol grip, ready to shoot at any sign of trouble. At five meters, he stops scanning the area ahead with his infrared sensors, but nothing shows. Slowly, he stands as he keeps scanning the ground ahead. He enters the area where the fight concluded. He sees Nexis facedown on the edge of the flattened grass. He kneels beside the body and rolls it over, finding the head is no longer attached. Smiling, he stands and looks around. A meter into the tall grass is a scorched line. Stepping forward, he picks up the hilt of the dead man's weapon. He thumbs the activation stud, and the black blade leaps to life once more. Carefully, he swings it a few directions and then extinguishes the blade. He turns back toward his ship. He attaches the hilt to his belt, boards his ship, and leaves the planet. Removing his helmet, he sets a random course to see what new adventures await.

* * *

Tobius slowly pulls the diamond away from the tendril, returning to his friends. "I think we can get past as long as we have this. So we all need to move as close together as possible."

They get their packs back on and start around the tree. Tobius first, then Melissa, Phen, and Phylox taking the rear. He leaves his weapons clipped to his belt and takes Melissa's hand with his left.

He meets her hazel gaze, and the universe vanishes, time appears to stand still, and everything becomes pure. For the briefest of moments, there is nothing but two people. The majestic change of prismatic color dances over her face, and the light breeze flows through her hair. He realizes why he is pursuing justice. He is not doing this for his family and friends that he lost. Yes, he misses all those he has lost, but just doing this for those gone is a path straight to a black hole. The true purpose of why he is here to stop this evil is right before him. Without any hesitation, he gives Melissa's arm a slight tug. She takes half a step forward, and Tobius releases her hand and embraces her with both arms. A breeze carries some loose hairs across her face. A heartbeat later, he passionately kisses her, and her hands slide up and around his neck. She kisses him back with equal emotions. Tobius could not tell how long this kiss was, nor did he care.

Melissa is the first one to end the kiss. She looks at him with tears streaming down her face. "Promise me you will come back alive." He does not answer, quickly knowing the trouble that they face. "Tobius," she says with an unsteady voice. "If you don't come back, then I will never leave this planet."

He wipes away the tears with his right index finger. "I don't know what will happen, but I will forever love you."

She lays her head on his shoulder and hugs him one last time. "I love you too, Tobius, and I will stand by you no matter what happens." Tobius feels his resolve strengthen with her support.

The rest of the universe snaps back into view around them, and they look at Phen and Phylox. "Do we need to leave you little lovebirds alone for a while?" Phen asks, laughing. Tobius and Melissa blush and start laughing.

* * *

Mendax rides the black bike for several kilometers over the canopy of the forest. A small opening in the canopy, no more than fifty meters across, comes into view, and the bike descends into the opening. The bike settles just off the ground. It lowers until his feet hit the ground then dissolves completely. Sanguis appears, like a mist, and floats past the young man.

"This is where the Keepers were founded." A perplexed look forms on Mendax's face, but he just waits. "The Keepers were a void-sensitive people who used power to pursue different ideals, and they do not follow the one-sided view of the Void-raiders." He follows as the phantom continues, "They were short-sighted and naive. They believed power is to be used to share with everyone, and for that, I destroyed them. However, before I could complete the purge, the Keepers stalled my plans." The phantom waved an arm, and a panel slid back from the ground, revealing a secret path underground. "I had come back here, knowing that no one would find it. This ensured that my power would not be disturbed." Mendax draws a small glow rod from a belt pouch and follows. "It was here that I found out how I can preserve my essence and gain power until I can destroy those who stopped my path of justice."

* * *

Grabbing the diamond, Tobius extends his hand and starts toward the tendrils again. This time, all the tendrils bend forward, forming steps over the fallen tree. The four quickly step over the tree and hurry past the tendrils. After fifteen meters, Tobius looks back. He stops and points back, "They're gone."

The others look back and see nothing but the fallen tree with the scorch marks from the pulse charge. Without wasting any more time, they ready their weapons and continue following the river.

* * *

Mendax continues to follow the ghost around the spiraling staircase for what seems like hours. Finally, the stairs end, and a vast chamber lies ahead.

"This cavern was hollowed out by the river, and I redirected the water to allow me to hide here." An arc of lightning shoots from Sanguis's hand, hitting a torch to his left. He continues around the one-hundred-meter-wide room. "The area above us is where the Gatekeepers from each enclave would bring their successors. They would test them, and if they pass, they take them back to the enclave as the new Gatekeeper."

The area had smooth walls from years of water flowing through it, and Sanguis had used the void to create a small living area to the right of the entrance.

He stops at the stone chairs, gestures for Mendax to sit, and continues, "It was in this cavern where I found the secret to preserve my essence. I had set up clues near the enclaves that I visited. Those strong enough would be able to find them, and I would challenge them. If they failed, I would absorb their power into my own."

* * *

They have been following along the edge of the river for more than thirty minutes since the interaction with the tendrils. Still moving quietly, they stop every few dozen meters. They take a quick break by river, eat a quick snack, and refill their canteens from the river.

"How much farther?" Tobius asks.

Melissa takes a quick drink from her refreshed canteen then says, "I'm not sure. I don't see it being much farther." That said, they all continue up the river.

* * *

Mendax looks around the room and then at the phantom. "So what's your plan now? You say that if I help you, I will have the power to defeat all my enemies. And so far, I have not seen much."

The eyes of the phantom burn with rage for a moment then cool. "If you are that eager to get this power, please follow me."

He stands and follows the phantom across the entire length of the room to a very dark outcropping almost directly opposite from the entrance. Stopping just on the edge of the shadowed entrance, the phantom gestures with its left arm for him to enter. He looks warily at the phantom and then squints at the darkness, trying to see what may lie beyond. Normally, he would grab one of his emergency glow rods. Instead, he ignites his blade as he unclips it from his belt. Slowly, he steps forward into the darkness.

The floor and walls are uneven with what feel like loose stones under his feet. The light from his blade does little to combat the unnatural darkness. Mendax continues into the darkness but feels like he is slowly being devoured by it. A twinge of fear shoots through his spine, and the hair on his neck stand on end. Bumps form on his forearms as the darkness closes around him. His eyes dart in every direction as the twinge of fear has become a raging waterfall of fear and panic. He decides that whatever this power is, he wants nothing to do with it, and he turns around. But as he turns back the way he came, there is no light to be seen.

He instinctively raises his weapon into a defensive position. He keeps looking around to find a way out. A massive bass laugh echoes through the darkness, sounding as though the darkness is hundreds of kilometers wide.

"You really think I spent a millennium gathering power for a puppet like you to use it?"

Mendax goes into a full-fledged panic, lashing out at the darkness and trying to keep it from swallowing him entirely. Looking down, he sees the darkness surround his boots and slowly rise up his legs as if he is sinking in a tar pit. He lashes at it with his blade, but nothing happens to the darkness. As the darkness progresses up his legs, he tries to summon the void but finds his concentration very sporadic.

"I brought you here for one reason. I need your body to be my vessel so I can exact justice on the galaxy and eradicate the Keepers." As if two stars going supernova, Sanguis's red eyes flare in front of Mendax.

Four tendrils shoot from the darkness. Two secure both of his wrists while the third wraps around Mendax's neck. A slight gasp escapes his lips as the tendril cinches around his neck with a meter of the tendril hanging down his chest.

"I will now give you the power needed to destroy your enemies." A malicious laugh echoes as Sanguis raises the tip of the fourth tendril. Mendax' eyes widen as he sees the tendril's tip spilt into five parts.

Sanguis slowly moves the tendril toward his helpless victim, reveling in the torture of extracting every single moment of fear and panic possible. The tendril tips touch the young man's face and move over the skin like a group of worms. He laughs as his prey screams in horror. Sensing the approach of his real enemies, he moves the tendrils into position. The tendril tips insert themselves into the ears, nose, and mouth. In a moment, Sanguis forces his power and essence into this body.

Mendax tries to defend himself from the massive attack, but he is not prepared to protect himself from the acidic presence. In a heartbeat, Sanguis erodes his defenses and begins to absorb his enemy into himself. His presence flows like a flood crashing into a city, destroying any barrier in his path. Nothing is hidden from him. He sifts through the young man's memories, slowly extracting those with deep emotional roots. Sanguis relishes in the moment as this is the first time he has ever been able to extract someone's power through direct contact.

Face of Evil

They can see the clearing a dozen meters ahead. Quickly, they run to a tree on the edge of the clearing and look around. Nothing looks out of place. It looks as though no one has been here in years. Suddenly, Phen yells in agony, grabbing his head and falling to his knees. Before anyone else can react, a massive toxic ripple pulses through the flow. Tobius and Melissa grab their heads and stagger from the pure rancid pulse that hit them. Melissa drops to her hands and knees, face white from the toxic energy. Tobius leans forward and places his left hand on his knee and right on the tree trunk. He doubles over as he vomits. Phylox, being two meters farther away from clearing, had enough time to fortify himself against the mysterious new presence.

Phylox kneels next to Phen and rests his left hand on the chest and right on the forehead of the mechanic. Closing his eyes and taking in a deep breath, he simply says, "Rest."

The mechanic's facial features relax, and his head tilts to his left. He is sound asleep. Standing, Phylox staggers slightly as the putrid energy has begun to seep into everything. The leaves closest to the center of the clearing have started to curl and become opaque with a black and violet hue.

Tobius keeps his right hand on the trunk as he straightens. He takes his canteen with his left hand, rinsing his mouth out with some water. He spits it out at the base of the trunk. "It has to be Sanguis." He takes a large drag from his canteen and puts the cap back on, wiping his chin with his right hand.

Phylox looks at him, concerned, as he steps over to help Melissa. Tobius secures his canteen back to his belt and removes both of his hilts. "Stay here. I am the only one who can finish this." He steps up to Phylox and extends his right hand.

Phylox stands, grasping his friend's hand with his own. "May your justice be swift and true."

Tobius nods. "May your knowledge keep you safe." Without another word, he looks at Melissa, smiles, and heads toward the clearing.

Moving cautiously, Tobius focuses all of his senses ahead of him. After two minutes of a slow and steady pace, he sees a set of footprints, as if someone rose from the ground to walk away. He follows the steps for several meters when just as suddenly as they appeared, they are gone.

Squatting down, he examines the area to see if he can figure out where the person went. Three quarters of a meter to the left of the footprints, Tobius senses a familiar sensation. He shrugs the pack from his shoulders and withdraws the cloth-wrapped stone. Carefully, he uncovers the gem, but instead of the obsidian diamond lies a diamond-shaped sandstone. For several heartbeats, he tries to fathom what could have changed this to an ordinary stone.

Tobius is startled from his pondering as a crimson blade erupts from the ground a half meter in front of him. Falling back, he drops the stone and catches himself on his elbows. He pushes off with his legs and summersaults backward, getting himself clear of the crimson shaft, rising to his feet. He stops with his left foot a half meter in front of his right, both long ends of the hilts along his forearms, left arm slightly higher than his right.

The crimson blade vanishes back into the ground, and a stream of black smoke rises from the hole. The small pillar of smoke widens as it rises, and Tobius cannot believe the amount of smoke rolling from the ground. Ten seconds pass, and the smoke shows no sign of dissipating. Fifteen seconds, and the smoke is now over fifty meters above him. Looking up, he sees that the smoke is now forming a cloud, rotating clockwise as it expands. Forty-five seconds have passed since the face-to-face encounter with the red blade, and the smoke has now expanded to cover the clearing.

KEEPERS OF POWER

Taking three steps back, Tobius looks around. The trees on the edge of the clearing are turning black, as if the cloud is pure poison. Suddenly, a boom erupts five meters ahead, just in front of where he was kneeling only a minute before. A two-meter-long and meter-wide section of the ground explodes up and out in all directions. The smoke still rolls from the opening in a massive plume. The hairs on Tobius's neck stand on end, and he ignites his blades, rotating his amber blade 180 degrees, tip at knee level a half meter in front of his right leg.

Five heartbeats pass, and still it just looks as though the underground is a raging inferno. The cloud has now accelerated its advance through the trees, as if it is feeding off the trees' energy. Tobius feels a few drops of water and looks up as the clouds start a steady rain. He looks over his right shoulder and sees Phylox standing by the tree, watching. He extinguishes his sage blade and quickly hangs it from his belt and retrieves an emergency glow rod. In a swift motion, he activates it and tosses it at the base of the plume. It lands half a meter from the black column and rolls into the base. Tobius listens and hears it roll down a few steps before it stops.

A bass laugh echoes from within the smoke, and Tobius quickly retrieves his sage hilt. Thumbing the activation stud, he flicks both wrists, spinning both blades in three quick rotations as he takes two steps back. Stopping seven meters from the smoke, Tobius stands knees bent with both blades along his forearms, his left wrist ten centimeters above his left knee while his right hand is even with his waist.

The clearing has darkened like it would be at midnight on a moonless night. The rain continues to fall at a steady pace, and Tobius's tunic is almost at saturation. His blades sizzle like an angry hive. The sage and amber blades barely provide enough light to see the pillar of smoke ahead. Ten meters to his right, a violet and silver lightning bolt flashes, but no thunderclap follows. Two seconds later, fifteen meters at his ten o'clock is another bolt, but again, nothing but the drizzle of the rain. The laughter begins again as another bolt flashes behind Tobius, but this bolt burns half a meter over his head straight toward the base of the smoke. A second later, another bolt leaps toward the smoke pillar, but it came from the ground.

A figure steps out from the base of the smoke. "So you really think you can stop me now?" Tobius stares through the darkness at the figure. Unsure on who he is facing, he simply remains quiet. "Yes, I can understand your confusion." The figure grunts in pain as his left foot catches the lip of the top step, sending him sprawling to the ground. Tobius smiles and stifles a laugh at what just happened. Five meters away, the person's head snaps up, and he can see the burning eyes of Sanguis. "So let me guess. You are confused on how I have a physical body now."

Tobius shakes his head. "All I care about is that now you have a body, and that can be destroyed."

Another bolt jumps from the ground, but instead of ending at the smoke, it strikes Sanguis in the back. Tobius's eyes widen as he sees his enemy stand without even a burn from where the energy struck him. Closing his eyes, he tries to sense where the next bolt will come from. Energy ripples from every direction, and it is as though the flow is being sucked into a black hole. The smoke is nothing like what it appears. It is nothing more than the spread of the putrid power that Sanguis has been storing for centuries. Directly behind him, he senses a buildup of energy. He dives forward and to his right, barely avoiding the shaft of energy. The energy leaps straight toward Sanguis's chest, and he absorbs the energy.

Sanguis looks at Tobius and smiles. "Now, once I exact my justice upon you, no one will be able to stop me from cleansing the galaxy."

The nervous feeling vanishes from Tobius's spine when he hears what will happen should he fail. Rising to his full height, he squares his shoulders and thrusts his right arm at Sanguis, allowing the sage blade to rotate to point at him. "I will not allow you to ever leave this planet."

Sanguis smiles a wicked grin. "How do you intend to stop me?"

For several seconds, they both stand there, neither one willing to give in. Sanguis stands, arms at his side with a hilt hanging from his belt. Tobius's right arm is extended with the blade sizzling straight forward, with the amber blade angled behind his back. As if needing an official start to their impending clash, a lightning bolt arcs from the smoke above to the ground at equal distance between the two. The thunder rattles through both of them, and Sanguis draws his hilt with his left hand. Even through the constant sizzle of the rain on the sage and amber blades, the crimson blade's call for blood resounds with a screaming sizzle.

Driving with his left leg, Tobius charges the eight meters to start the winner-takes-all battle. After four steps, he lets the momentum start the spinning of his blades. Two meters from his enemy, Tobius plants his right foot and spins counterclockwise, simultaneously swinging his right arm over his shoulder level. He rotates twice, covering the remaining distance. Flowing through the attack, he drives his right arm down, with the sage blade extending from his forearm. He lands on his left foot and continues the spin, which would have cleaved his opponent in half from head to toe.

At the last second, the crimson blade screams, stopping the attack half a meter above his head. Tobius looks at him, surprised with the ease in which his attack was neutralized. At this close range, he notices in the sage crimson light who he faces. Standing before him is the body of Morrin, but the face has been twisted by the massive amount of putrid power forced inside. The skin on his face is gray and appears to be decaying every second. Sanguis smiles, and razor-sharp teeth shine behind the lips.

Breaking contact, Tobius takes a step back, and the hairs on his neck stand on end. Looking over his left shoulder, he sees something moving in the darkness. With that slight distraction, he loses focus. Sanguis brings his left arm across his chest and swings at Tobius like he will backhand him across the face. The blade sizzles through the falling rain, and Tobius can barely get his hilts in position to absorb the blow. The shields on the hilts hold the blade from slicing through the hilts, but the attack is so powerful that it lifts him off the ground. Sanguis completes the arc, his arm even with his ear, blade pointing up at a thirty-degree angle.

The force of the attack lifts Tobius two and a half meters off the ground, and before he even has a chance to recover, Sanguis steps forward, grabbing his enemy's left ankle with his right arm. Sanguis slides his left foot back half a meter and shifts his weight onto his left leg. Pivoting on his foot, he swings his opponent over his head. Realizing what will happen, Tobius quickly extinguishes his blades. Sanguis snaps his arm down, slamming the young man flat on his back. Stars explode in his vision as everything from his hips to his shoulders connects with the ground simultaneously, violently expelling the air from his lungs. Without releasing the ankle, Sanguis shifts his weight to his right leg. Then, spinning counterclockwise, he throws Tobius like a rag doll.

Tobius has no time to recover when Sanguis starts to drag him in an arc, lifting him from the ground and releasing his ankle at shoulder height. He struggles to regain his breath and clear the stars from his eyes as he soars fifteen meters before slamming into the ground on his left shoulder. He grunts in pain as all his weight lands on his left shoulder. The momentum makes him roll, knocking the wind from him again. For another five meters, he rolls uncontrollably. Clearing the pain from his mind, he summons the flow to stabilize his roll. Getting a foothold, he pushes up, changing the angle of his roll. He drives both his feet into the ground, furrowing five centimeters deep. Tobius ignites both his blades and drives them both into the ground ten centimeters out from his shoulders. After three meters, he comes to a stop.

His left leg bends under his torso, with his right leg at full extension, facedown toward the ground, and both blades buried to three centimeters from the emitters. Tobius feels his rage boil in his veins and every fiber of his being calling for the blood of the man before him. He takes a deep breath and slowly exhales, letting the rage and bloodlust fade. Without moving, he thinks about his family and friends that have been lost due to this evil. Another breath, and he feels his resolve strengthen.

The Gatekeeper's voice echoes through his mind. *Tobius, you are a true seeker of justice. Even when we fought on Draken, I knew that your vision was pure. Justice itself must dance the razor's edge. A misstep one way, and it is lost and becomes corrupt. You have proven that you have the steady hand to be a seeker of justice. And now, even in the face of pure evil, you have shown that you are a Master of Justice. Now rise and face this monster with your head high. Do not waver, and you will not fail!*

Taking in another deep breath, Tobius rises to his feet. Stepping forward confidently, he begins to cover the twenty meters between him and Sanguis. The violet arcs of power are leaping from the ground almost every second. He sees Sanguis raise his right arm, palm facing him. A three-centimeter-wide lance of energy shoots from the palm at Tobius. Without breaking stride, he flips his left wrist, spinning the amber blade clockwise, deflecting the energy over his left shoulder. Another blast of energy and Tobius starts to spin his sage blade, deflecting the blast harmlessly past his right leg.

Twelve meters from Sanguis, Tobius has both blades spinning, forming an amber and sage shield, effortlessly deflecting the energy attacks. Eight meters away and Tobius begins to quicken his pace, rolling the spinning blades as he readies himself. Three meters away, Sanguis charges at him with the crimson blade. The red blade arcs in at Tobius's shoulders, but he deftly uses the sage blade to block and spin it away. Rolling with the motion, Sanguis brings the blade around in a thrust. Tobius catches the blade on the shield of his left hilt with the blade pointing down. He brings the sage blade around and sears a ten-centimeter-long gash in his enemy's left thigh.

Sanguis howls in rage. A violet arc of energy leaps from the ground right to the wound. A heartbeat later, the energy is gone, and so is the wound. Tobius glares at the monster before him. The crimson blade thrusts toward his heart. Both the sage and amber blades intersect, stopping the crimson blade eight centimeters from his heart. The two men glare at each other through the rain for a second. Tobius shoves the sage blade to his left, spinning and angling his amber blade at the waist of his enemy. Sanguis jumps to avoid the attack, backflipping over the blade, landing on the balls of his feet. Sanguis lunges, not giving Tobius time to recover.

Tobius deflects the blade off the shield on his amber blade, but the tip of the blade briefly touches his shoulder. Tobius growls in pain and kicks out with his left leg, catching Sanguis in the side. Pushing the crimson blade away, he pushes off the ground with his right leg, bringing it around and kicking his enemy's chin. Sanguis flips from the attack, sprawling to the ground as Tobius drops to a three-point stance.

Phylox stands by the tree, watching the battle unfold while Melissa kneels, half watching the fight and half fearing the worst. The cloud has now extended to over a kilometer from the center of the clearing, and the only thing that can be seen are the three blades dancing in the darkness. Even the steady rain drowns out anything except for the clash of the blades. Melissa looks up at him. "Do you think he can do it?"

Phylox looks down at her and shrugs. "He is the only one who can."

Tobius charges forward and raises both arms with the blades along his arms. Leaping, he hopes to land and pin his enemy to the ground. But before he can land the attack, Sanguis jumps to his feet, hitting him in the stomach with his right elbow. A mix of spit and bile fly from his mouth as he doubles over the arm. Sanguis quickly pulls his arm away and spins, connecting his left heel with Tobius's temple.

Again, stars explode in Tobius's vision as he falls to the ground. He is unable to focus or clear his vision; his entire existence revolves around his pain. Sanguis laughs. "You have failed to defeat me like all the other Keepers." With his right foot, he pushes on Tobius's shoulder, rolling him onto his back. "If you would have joined me, I would have given you everything you desired, but now I will slowly kill you." He moves the crimson blade and drags the tip across the young man's chest, vaporizing the tunic and burning the skin beneath.

Melissa's head snaps around as she feels Tobius's agony ripple through the flow. She stands and grabs Phylox's left arm. "He needs our help." After several seconds of silence, she ignites her blade and tries to race into the fight, but Phylox grabs her shoulder.

"Melissa, patience. Tobius will be fine." Tears well in her eyes as she looks at him, and she extinguishes her blade.

Even through the chaos of the fight and pain, Tobius feels a faint ripple. He feels Melissa's fear and sorrow, and he can sense her tears rolling down her cheeks. Tobius reaches out to her to reassure her.

He sweeps his legs around, knocking Sanguis back, and he springs to his feet.

"No, I have not failed, nor shall I!" Tobius thrusts with his sage blade and renews his assault. The crimson blade knocks it upward, and he flips his wrist to continue the rotation. He then arcs the amber blade at Sanguis's knees. And as it gets blocked away, he drives the sage blade into his enemy's foot.

Sanguis howls in rage, but he is quickly quieted as the hilt of the sage blade catches him under the chin, snapping his jaw shut. He staggers back and rubs his jaw as violet energy leaps forward, healing his foot. Raising his blade, he blocks a slash from the amber blade and has to jump to avoid a slash at his knees. He takes another step back and has to block yet another slash from the torrent of color spinning before him. Another glancing blow sears his right shoulder, then his left thigh. And as soon as an injury occurs, energy leaps forward to heal the wound.

Tobius keep pressing the attack, keeping the blades spinning, throwing in kicks where he can, but it is as futile as trying to dam a river one pebble at a time. Sweat and rain stream down his face, unwilling to give his enemy a chance to recover. It has been half an hour since the two started their battle, and the fatigue is wearing him down. He brings the sage blade down, and his foot slips. He stumbles and rises to one knee. He looks at his enemy. Sanguis stands unfazed by the battle, tunic and pants in tatters, the only sign that he has managed to land any blows.

Tobius rises to his feet, looking at his enemy three meters away. Sanguis's body has aged decades over the course of the fight. The skin has begun to sag from the bone, and the hands have started to look like a skeleton wrapped in leather. Even the eye sockets sank into the skull, further resembling the phantom eyes that he was used to seeing. Raising his left hand, Tobius sends a pulse at his enemy, but Sanguis blocks it with ease.

Tobius rolls his shoulders and his neck to relieve the exhaustion that plagues his body. Foregoing his typical attacks, he simply holds the blades along his forearms as he faces his foe for the final time. Closing to a little over a meter, he waits for the attack. Sanguis glares at him and swings his crimson blade, doublehanded at his right shoulder. Tobius blocks the attack on the sage shield, stepping forward inside his guard. Bringing the amber hilt across between them, he smashes it into the unprotected elbow with a wet crack. Tobius draws back with his left arm, driving the ten centimeters of the back of the hilt into the chest of Sanguis, forcing two ribs apart. Again, he draws back, driving the metal post into his enemy's hip with a loud pop. He swings his right arm in a wide arc to force the crimson blade away. He drives the back of the hilt into the armpit, dislocating the left arm.

Tobius knows that these attacks will do little to permanently disable his enemy, but it may reveal a weakness. Bringing his right arm up, he punches him in the jaw, left to the stomach, right to the ribs, left to jaw. Tobius hits him in the chest with both hilts, sending Sanguis back falling to the ground. Staggering, Tobius looks on. Dozens of violet tendrils jump from the ground and dance over the fallen man, and a deep bass laugh fills the air. "You think you have won, but you have not. I have found a way to live forever."

The battered form before him begins to rise. Stepping forward, Tobius spins the sage blade around and severs the left arm just above the wrist. Still rising, Sanguis swings his right arm, and Tobius catches it on the shield, bringing the sage blade around and severing the limb at the elbow.

He staggers left as his enemy hits him across the face with the severed stump of its left arm. Spinning around, he steps back, flipping the sage blade to be an extension of his arm and drives it to the hilt through the chest of his opponent. This attack does nothing to the form standing before him as he again is hit in the face. He looks at the form, and there is no longer a face on his attacker. It has become as dark as a black hole. Tobius gets kicked in his left knee from his puppet attacker. The bass laughter continues to grow as he starts getting beat like a drum. The puppet is using anything it has at its disposal. It kicks, punches, and even headbutts. Tobius feels the swelling of his left knee from the constant kicks. His right eye has become blurry from the multiple headbutts and punches.

A knee to the stomach lifts Tobius half a meter off the ground, and he staggers away from the puppet. He drops his amber blade and grabs the sage blade with both hands. He swings with all his might, screaming in frustration as he does. The blade slices through the left shoulder and continues through exiting the right hip. The puppet falls in two pieces as the laughing stops, and Tobius takes a few steps farther, falling to the ground. He rolls onto his back and lets the rain fall, rinsing his face for a few heartbeats.

The laughing starts again, and the phantom eyes form in the clouds above him. "I told you that you failed."

Tobius sits up in fear as the laughing grows. He looks around, trying to find his enemy, but the body remains in pieces two meters away. Ten meters to his right, he sees a steady stream of violet light. The rain slows, and the smoke flows back into the underground cavern. Against the protest of his battered body, he gets to his feet and starts limping toward the light. Eight meters away, he sees a lump on the ground. At five meters, he sees the sand stone diamond. Doing his best, he hobbles his way toward the flurry of energy. Two meters away, something grabs his left leg, trapping him. Looking over his shoulder, he sees a slimy tendril wrapped around his calf. He ignites his sage blade and rolls over, tip scorching the ground in a large arc as he hacks at the tendril, cleaving it in half.

He kicks and moves another half meter toward the stone. He looks back toward the energy and sees it beginning to resume the look of the obsidian diamond. The stone stands on end with all the glyphs pulsing with white light. The culet has become black once more, and the energy is leaping from the ground, flowing through the glyph on the top. As the energy flows into the crystal, the stone steadily becomes black.

The laughter continues and grows as the stone transforms. "I told you that you would fail." The stone is a third of the way transformed back into the diamond, and Tobius can see the outline of the phantom. "No matter what you do, I will not die. The Keepers could not stop me over a millennia ago, and you will not stop me now. I will outlast you or anyone else who opposes me!"

Tobius crawls on his hands and knees the remaining meter and a half, fighting off tendrils that sprout from the ground to stop him. Seventy centimeters from the stone, and some of the energy diverts from the stone. Raising his blade, he catches the arcs of energy on the shield on the hilt. Ozone fills the air from the mix of the shield and energy, and Tobius's stomach lurches at the new scent.

The cloud is now back to the edge of the clearing with all the leaves it touched black and withered. A tendril shoots from the ground half a meter from Tobius's left. The tip spears through his left calf and winds its way around his knee and up his thigh. Tobius screams in pain as the tendril writhes in the wound, burning him. He drives his right leg into the ground for one last step. Now thirty-five centimeters from the stone, he kneels, his body on the verge of collapse. Another tendril shoots from the ground a meter behind him. The hairs on the back of his neck stand, and he shifts to his right. The tendril slices through his back, slipping between two ribs and continuing through his body, piercing his left lung. It erupts through his chest.

Melissa and Phylox are watching from the edge of the clearing. Phen shakes his head as he sits up. "What happened?" he asks, looking around. Looking over his shoulder, he sees Tobius in the middle of the clearing. They see a tendril rise from the ground and lance through the young man's chest.

Melissa takes off from the brush and runs toward Tobius. Phylox chases after her. Phen grabs his pack, throwing some items carelessly on the ground. He grabs a tablet and enters the slave control command for the Mirror's Edge. Leaving the discarded items on the ground, he slings the pack on and follows the others.

A howl of agony rips from Tobius's lips, and his left leg goes numb. Tobius falls left, catching himself with his left arm. Blood streams from the tip of the tendril in his chest, and his vision begins to blur. He pushes off the ground and looks at the phantom floating in front of him.

"Sanguis," he says between labored breaths. "You only think you will last forever." With his sage blade in hand, he lifts his arm straight up with the blade pointing at the ground. "Now as a Master of Justice, I execute your sentence." With that said, he drives his right arm down, plunging the blade in the center of the diamond's table.

A bellow of rage erupts as if from the stone itself. A viscous black liquid spurts from the edges of the glyph as Tobius continues to drive his blade farther into the stone. Sanguis's phantom figure explodes as the eyes burn brighter than any sun. Dozens of tendrils spring from the ground, continuously stabbing Tobius in a desperate act of self-defense. Lifting his left hand, he places it on top of the hilt.

"Sanguis, you shall not harm another being ever again." He pushes down with all his remaining strength and drives the sage blade through the stone up to the emitter. Black liquid squirts up from the stone as the top of the stone begins to glow red. The tendrils stand straight from the ground and wave like tentacles of a dying beast.

The entire crown of the stone glows red hot, and Tobius keeps the pressure on the hilt. His breaths are short and labored from the dozens of wounds over his body. Sanguis's eyes still burn in front of him, and Tobius looks back into the burning inferno. With one last effort, he drives the hilt through the stone, fracturing across several facets. A heartbeat later, one final scream fills the clearing, and the stone erupts in hundreds of fragments. Tobius looks up into the clear blue sky and then collapses to the ground, his hilt buried three centimeters into the ground. He lands on his right side and just lays on the ground, black ooze and blood flowing from his wounds. He closes his eyes and feels peace rush through his body.

Melissa, ten meters away, watches as Tobius looks up then collapses with his back toward her. "Tobius!" she yells as tears begin to stream down her face. Two meters from him, she drops to her knees and slides on the wet ground to him. She grabs his left shoulder and his neck and rolls him onto her lap. "Tobius," she says, rubbing his cheek. "Say something." Tears again start to roll from her eyes as she holds his head.

Phylox steps around to Tobius's right. Kneeling, he presses two fingers on the inside of the young man's wrist. "His pulse is very weak."

Phen drops his pack on the ground and pulls out an emergency med kit. He grabs a set of scissors and tosses them to Phylox, who starts cutting off the tattered tunic. He sets the kit on the ground, opens it up, and grabs a painkiller and adrenaline stim. He injects them into the thigh.

The sound of the Mirror's Edge breaks the silence. Phen grabs the tablet and enters the commands. It lands and opens the boarding ramp. He hands Phylox some sterile bandages and opens a palm-size canister. He pours about a shot of water into the canister, removing a metal rod from the side. He quickly whisks the water around. Phylox tries to clean the wounds on his friend's chest. After a minute, Phen begins to apply a blue paste onto the wounds. Phen uses all the paste, managing to cover almost three quarters of the wounds, leaving the smallest open. Quickly, he drops the empty canister, rises, and runs up into the Mirror's Edge thirty meters away.

Phylox uses the remaining cloth and begins to tear them into small pieces to cover the wounds, starting with those that Phen did not cover.

Melissa asks through the tears, "What is that stuff?"

Without looking up from Tobius, he explains, "It is an algae-based protein. I have no idea where he gets the stuff, but it really works. He says that it helps coagulate the blood, and it helps prevent any serious infections. It is similar to med gel, but he won't say how he gets it."

Phen comes from within the ship with the medical gurney floating on thrusters. Stopping parallel with Tobius, he hits the thruster control, lowering it to ten centimeters from the ground. Phen steps around the gurney and grabs his feet while Melissa keeps his head steady and Phylox helps lift him onto the gurney. Stepping to the head of the gurney, Phylox raises it up to just over a meter as Phen starts attaching some sensors. After the breathing mask and heart rate sensors are attached, Phylox spins the gurney and pushes it back into the ship.

Once inside the ship, Phen heads to the cockpit to prepare for departure while Phylox locks in the gurney. Melissa holds onto Tobius's right hand and pulls out the stool. After hooking up the intravenous equipment, Phylox checks the readout and then places his hand on Melissa's shoulder, giving a light squeeze. Then he heads to the cockpit. "Phen, set course for Detritus Prime."

Home

Six months have passed since the events on Feridus, and Melissa walks with her left arm looped through Phylox's right. "I wish Tobius was here," she says as they stroll through the Coltin spaceport. He smiles, looks down at her, and nods. For the next kilometer, they both just look at the different vendors lining the street. They come to the intersection of the main vendors and the main entrance to the spaceport and stop in front of a three-story corner building.

They stop by the building's entrance and wait for several minutes. Phylox glances at his chrono and looks around, then at Melissa, confused. "This is where Phen said to meet him, right?"

She pulls out her tablet and scrolls through the message. Putting the tablet back in her purse, she looks at the building. "Yeah, this should be it."

They move to the bench next to the door and look through the crowd, waiting for the mechanic to get here. Phylox grabs his transceiver and tries to contact Phen, but he gets no response. "He must have it shut off." Another fifteen minutes pass, and still he is nowhere to be seen. Phylox stands and strolls over to one of the fruit vendors. He returns and hands Melissa one of the exotic fruits. They both sit on the bench, watching the bustle of the spaceport, waiting on the mechanic to arrive. The sun slides smoothly across the partly cloudy sky as they both just enjoy the laziness of the day.

The sun is nearing the far horizon when Phen jogs up to them both. Phylox stands, smoothing his trousers. "Well, at least his repairs are always on time." Phylox laughs as he extends his hand.

Shaking his hand, Phen replies, "Hey, blame the magistrate's office." He gives a half bow to Melissa then turns, gesturing for them to follow. They look at each other, and Melissa laughs when Phylox shrugs. They follow him from the middle of the spaceport to the speeders. Phen hops into a four-person luxury speeder and hits one of the controls, lowering a small ramp. Phylox steps to the side and, with a slight bow, gestures for Melissa to board first. She gives him a slight curtsey and walks up the ramp. Once they are seated, Phen powers up the thrusters and heads from the city.

They have never been outside the city, and they both are in awe with the countryside. The orange red hue bathes everything, giving it a surreal glow. Ten minutes from the spaceport, Phen slows the speeder and banks right into a hidden path between the trees. Keeping the speeder slow, he follows the scenic path through the trees. A minute later, the trees end, opening the area before a massive home.

The home is almost one hundred meters across the front, three stories, with two grand marble staircases leading to the front door with a fifteen-meter diameter, eight-meter-tall fountain between them. Granted, the house has been vacant for nearly twenty years, and the forest has begun to take over the area. Phen stops the speeder just before the fountain and lowers the ramp, letting them off.

Melissa slowly rises, looking at the house. "Why would someone just leave such a beautiful home?"

Phen smiles as he starts up the stairs. "The owner stated in his will that it must remain vacant until the heir claims it, or fifty years pass, whichever comes first." She begins to object to what he said, but Phen waves his left hand, dismissing her next thought as he continues, "That is what took so long at the magistrate's office." Deciding to let it be, she follows him up the steps toward the home.

Phen begins to describe the home. The main floor has a dining room enough for three dozen and a full communication suite with subnet projectors, kitchen, study, and family room. The top floor is where the sleeping quarters are—two master suites at opposite ends with private refreshers and six additional rooms with a public refresher. The bottom floor is the main garage with enough room for at least twenty speeders. There is also a firing range and flight simulator.

They arrive at the front door, and Phen pulls an archaic skeleton key from his pocket. He inserts it in the slot just below the handle and jiggles it for a few seconds. Then with a metallic click, Phen turns the knob, opening the door. A musty wave of stale air flows from the house. Phen pulls out three glow rods and hands one to Melissa then Phylox. "Stay up here, and I will go see if I can get the power on."

Melissa looks around and sees handcrafted doorframes, polished stone floors, and a crystal chandelier hanging overhead. A pair of spiral staircases ascends on both sides of the entryway, just past the chandelier. Melissa hears a loud clatter coming from farther in the house, followed by Phen cursing as he trips over something.

Moving to the left, she enters what she assumes to be the family room. She spots an old painting on the wall and slowly makes her way through the room. She holds the glow rod up and sees a family of two men standing behind two women sitting in chairs, the younger one holding a little baby. Something looks familiar about the baby, but she cannot seem to place why.

Suddenly, a loud pop comes from the back of the house, and the hum of energy sounds through the house. Glow panels begin to slowly repel the darkness. Lowering the glow rod, she looks closer at the picture when suddenly, the sound of a ship rips through the silence. Startled, she looks at the window and sees a massive ship approaching outside.

Melissa turns to head outside, slamming her shin into the end table next to her. She bends down and rubs her shin then makes her way toward the entrance, where she meets up with Phen. They both step outside, meeting Phylox standing by the railing. A freighter is descending into the opening in front of the house, but they can all see that the ship is in bad shape. The sides of the ship are riddled with rust and corrosion, and the thrusters are struggling to keep the vessel level. A breeze rushes through the trees, buffeting the ship, and the pilot struggles to keep the ship level. Twenty meters from the ground, a large snap comes from the portside of the ship. Sparks fly from underneath the vessel, followed by smoke as the left side drops eight meters, pulling the ship sideways. Another snap resounds through the clearing as the thrusters kick in again. It is now twelve meters from the ground. The pilot lowers the landing gear, and once the landing gear is fully extended, another loud crack thunders from the ship.

Without warning, the ship drops to the ground, and the force crushes the front landing gear. The ship slides forward, shearing the remaining landing gears from the ship. It slides forward, flipping the speeder, and it crushes the fountain. The starboard hatch of the ship flies off as the person inside engages the emergency release. A figure dives from the cockpit, escaping from the rancid smell of smoke and melting electronics.

They all rush down the stairs to their right to aid the pilot. Halfway down the stairs, the figure rises. He removes the cloak, turns, and looks at them. Melissa's eyes widen.

"Tobius!" she yells.

Tobius smiles and starts up the stairs to meet her. A meter and a half apart, Melissa jumps at him. He extends his arms and catches her, bringing her in for a kiss. After several heartbeats, she pushes away from him and slaps him across the face.

"Ouch!" Tobius exclaims. "What was that for?"

Tears stream down her face as she looks at him. "Last thing I knew, you were in a coma on Detritus Prime, and then you show up here with a wrecked ship!"

He throws his hands up. "Hey, this was their idea," Tobius says, pointing. She turns and glares over her shoulder at the two men laughing. She looks back at Tobius and starts laughing as well. She punches him in the chest then slides up to him, enjoying the feel of him next to her again. She grabs his tunic and cries softly into his chest.

Tobius holds her close to him and looks at Phen with a wry grin. "So I found it, but do you think you can fix it?" They both laugh. "It was mothballed on Marina."

Phen steps forward and pats him on the back. "Yeah, we will get her running again like new. Here is your key, and you owe me for the fight I had to deal with to get it for you."

Tobius takes the key. "Thanks, Phen." He kisses her again and then leads her back up the stairs. "Melissa, what do you think about helping me rebuild my grandfather's business?"

She looks back into his eyes, and she never looked more amazing to him. She smiles at him, tears renewing themselves in her eyes as she nods. He kisses her passionately then caresses her face.

"I will never leave you, Melissa." Without another word, they all turn and watch as the sunset fades over the forest.

About the Author

Joshua Undem is excited to share *Keepers of Power*, his first novel, with the world. He was able to get this far with the love and support of his wonderful wife, Anne; his parents, Tim and Laura; and his two beautiful children. He enjoys spending time with his family in his hometown of Anderson, Indiana.

As a young man, Joshua was in the Boy Scouts, where he earned the rank of Eagle Scout. He enlisted in the US Air Force in 2008 and was medically discharged in 2012. During his service, he received the Army Achievement Medal while deployed in Afghanistan.

In his spare time, when he is not working on the sequel to *Keepers of Power*, Joshua enjoys drawing, gaming, and reading sci-fi novels, which helped him in his writing.

CPSIA information can be obtained
at www.ICGtesting.com
Printed in the USA
BVHW082128280922
648041BV00001B/4